BY CAROLINE KEPNES

*You*

*Hidden Bodies*

# PROVIDENCE

# PROVIDENCE

A NOVEL

## Caroline Kepnes

NEW YORK

Published in the United States by Lenny, an imprint of Random House, a division of Penguin Random House LLC, New York.

LENNY and colophon are trademarks of Penguin Random House LLC.

LIBRARY OF CONGRESS CATALOGING-IN-PUBLICATION DATA
Names: Kepnes, Caroline, author.
Title: Providence : a novel / Caroline Kepnes.
Description: First edition. | New York : Lenny, [2018]
Identifiers: LCCN 2017051943 | ISBN 9780399591433 (hardcover) |
ISBN 9780399591440 (ebook)
Subjects: LCSH: Paranormal romance stories. | BISAC: FICTION / Thrillers. |
FICTION / Coming of Age. | FICTION / Romance / Paranormal. | GSAFD: Romantic
suspense fiction. | Love stories.
Classification: LCC PS3611.E697 P76 2018 | DDC 813/.6—dc23
LC record available at https://lccn.loc.gov/2017051943

Printed in the United States of America on acid-free paper

randomhousebooks.com

2 4 6 8 9 7 5 3 1

First Edition

*Book design by Susan Turner*

It is true, we shall be monsters, cut off from all the world;
but on that account we shall be more attached to one another.

—MARY WOLLSTONECRAFT SHELLEY, *Frankenstein*

# PROVIDENCE

# NASHUA

# JON

I brung Pedro home for Thanksgiving break and tomorrow I have to bring him back to school. You're not supposed to say brung. You're supposed to say brought. But I like the way brung sounds, like you're cold and ringing a bell. *Brrrrunggggg.* Nobody can kick your ass for what you think in your mind, not even your mom. Mine is stirring spaghetti sauce on the stove and shaking her head at me.

"Get that rat outta my kitchen," she says.

"Pedro's not a rat," I say. "He's a hamster."

My mom doesn't budge. "Whatever he is, he's not staying in my kitchen. I'm not gonna keep repeating myself, Jon. Take that thing outside. Now."

She always calls it *my* kitchen, same way my dad calls the TV *my TV* and the puffy chair *my chair.* My only territory is my bedroom. I guess my shed too, but that's in the woods and technically it belongs to Mrs. Curry. Everything else, in the house, indoors, belongs to my parents.

I take Pedro outside to the swing set even though I'm too old for it. He shivers.

"Come on, little guy," I say. "You're from New Hampshire. You can handle it."

The truth is, I don't know if Pedro was born here. Maybe he was born in Bermuda and got shipped here. This is my home, where I started. I was born at Derry Hospital outside of Nashua. Three days before Carrig Birkus. Sometimes, when he's kicking my ass, I think about how we were in the hospital at the same time. I picture us as newborns in nearby cribs. I see our dads waving at us. We were equals in a way. Back then you probably couldn't tell us apart. But now we're opposite. Carrig is a jock. One of those guys with *buddies*. His life is keg parties and girls. He cracks a joke and everyone laughs, and he knows how to speak to people, how to get to them. Last month his picture was in the window at Rolling Jack's, the sports store in the mall. He was ATHLETE OF THE MONTH.

I'm not anything of the month. Chloe laughed when I said that to her.

"That's a good thing," she said. "The worst thing you can do is peak in middle school."

She always says the right thing, the nice thing. I can picture her photo and her name up at another store, PERSON OF THE MONTH. I'd never say that though. I know that much.

Tomorrow we go back to school, which means seeing her again, Chloe Smells Like Cookies. That's what I call her in my head. Every time my mom makes cookies, no matter what they are, oatmeal raisin or chocolate chip or caramel, they smell like Chloe. Chloe Smells Like Cookies doesn't make fun of me. She sits with me at lunch even though the other girls laugh at her and the other guys tell her she is wasting her time on a *faggot*.

Chloe hates that word. She says after high school she's gonna live in New York City where nobody uses that word. She thinks the people in our school have small brains and small hearts. She says New

York is like *Sesame Street* for grown-ups, everyone has big hearts and you can be anything you want to be. She was there for Thanksgiving this week. Her parents took her to see the parade. She saw all the floats when they were shriveled and flat on the ground.

We've been texting a lot all week. She says I'd love New York.

**It's so much bigger than New Hampshire even though it's smaller, you know?**

**I get it, Chloe. I wish I was there.**

**Of course you do. You always get it!**

My mom yells: "Dinner!"

I write back fast: *See you tomorrow.*

She sends me a smiley face. That's code for *Me too, Jon.*

The house smells like spaghetti and broccoli, and my mom asks if I left Pedro outside and I tell her I did even though he's in my pocket. My dad picks up the broccoli and puts it in the microwave.

"What are you doing?" my mom asks. "It's cooked just fine."

"I can't stand that smell," he says.

"It's good for you, that smell."

My dad grunts. He's a burly guy who does drywall and plays pool. A lot of the guys around here think he's weird because he has a Scottish accent.

I sneak bits of spaghetti into my pocket. I almost get away with it but Pedro nips at my finger and I yelp and my mom slams her fork down.

"These damn schools. What the hell is there to be learned from taking a *rat* home at your age? Aren't you a little old for this nonsense?"

"We're mentoring a class at the elementary school," I tell her. "None of the kids in third grade could take him so I volunteered."

My parents look sad, like all this time they thought Pedro was here because he *had* to be here, not because I wanted him.

"A lot of people have pets," I say. "Carrig Birkus has a dog."

I shouldn't have said his name. They know I'm not friends with Carrig Birkus anymore. The last time he invited me to a birthday party was in fourth grade, when people still had parties with invitations, when your mom made you invite every kid. It was a Batman invitation so I showed up in my Spider-Man outfit but everybody else was in normal clothes. Sometimes I feel bad for my parents, like they'd do better with one of the other babies from that day, the kind who plays sports and wears the right clothes to a stupid party.

I look at my mom, right at her, like you do when you want something. "He's a clean animal," I say. "I promise he will stay in my room."

My mom cuts her spaghetti. She doesn't roll it around her fork like people in New York do on TV. Her name is Penny and she's from New Hampshire, so she talks the way people here talk and she grew up on a farm where the animals stay *outside*.

"It's your room," she says. "You want to live in a disgusting pig sty and let animals poop about your things, that's your business. Just don't go coming to me to clean up."

On the way upstairs I sneak a box of Oreos out of the cupboard. My dad is talking to my mom about the Patriots and the Super Bowl and my mom is talking about Giselle and how beautiful she is. They speak the same language only different. What comes out of my mom's mouth never affects what comes out of my dad's mouth. I think Chloe and I are better at talking. What Chloe says always affects what I say.

Upstairs, I put Pedro on my bed and bring an Oreo up to my nose and inhale, but Chloe smells like homemade cookies. I take out today's Nashua *Telegraph* and reread Pedro the headlines from this morning. Today is Sunday, the biggest paper of the week. I can't read the whole thing to Pedro, but I do my best. We make it to Section C, Lifestyles, and I think he likes it.

I love news. It reminds you that there's a whole world out there, a world of people who've never even heard of Carrig Birkus. Every day is new, every paper, every story. In a book or a movie you only get one story. But in a newspaper, you get happy stories, sad stories, stories that you can't understand about mortgages, scary stories about robberies, meth heads, that kid who got kidnapped in Dover.

Last Christmas my parents got me a subscription to the *Telegraph*. It was all I wanted. I was nervous they weren't gonna get it for me and I opened my last present, a sweater box. I was bummed. But I tore away the tissue paper and found a receipt for a subscription. I cheered and my mother laughed. I love it when she laughs, and it doesn't happen a lot. She said she will never understand me.

"I hate newspapers," she said. "Who wants to know about all the terrible things people are doing?"

"I want to know about everything," I told her.

"But it has absolutely nothing to do with you whatsoever, Jon," she said, befuddled. "Nothing in there is your business at all."

My dad was tearing the tag off his Patriots jersey. "Well," I said, "those Patriots don't have anything to do with Dad."

I never heard my mom laugh so hard. She hit the couch, and my dad flew into a light rage, telling me it's not *those Patriots*. It's *The* Patriots. We had ham and cake and peppermint ice cream and the only thing wrong about that day was that there was no newspaper. They don't publish on Christmas. Then again, it only added to the joy of the next day, when I woke up early to get the paper out of the special box my dad had installed next to our mailbox. It was good to see that the world was back on again.

When it's time to go to bed, I make a special place for Pedro. I use advertising flyers to build him a cozy bed. My mom is crazy. There's nothing dirty about him. If and when he poops, it won't even get on my sheets. "Good night, Pedro," I say. I close my eyes and I like the sound of him breathing, like it's a hard thing to do.

The next morning my mom hits my door once. "School!"

It's what she says every morning. Pedro pooped in his advertising bed and I crumple it up and bring it downstairs and throw it in the trash in the kitchen. My mom points at the trash with a spatula. "Is there poop in there?"

"Yes," I say.

"Then bring it outside."

"But it snowed."

"And since when are you allergic to snowflakes?"

I take Pedro and his bed outside and look at the trees at the edge of our yard. My mom and dad don't know that it takes double the time for me to get to school every day because I have to go the back way, through Mrs. Curry's yard, with the thorns that branch out, then alongside her fence and through the mud clearing near the Dumpsters and then back through the Shawnee family's yard, by their swing set, and then finally down their driveway and onto Carnaby Street where my school is. It would be so much faster to walk out the front door of our house and turn left and walk down Birch all the way to Carnaby. That's what everyone on my street does. But I can't. Carrig and Penguin and those other guys, they come after me if I go the short way, they pound on me. They take my newspaper and smack me with it or they throw snowballs at me, black and brown and icy, the kind that hurt. When it's hot out, they jump me or knock my bag onto the ground.

Chloe Smells Like Cookies takes the bus. She knows about my back way bramble route to avoid Carrig Birkus. She knows everything, more than my mom or my dad or the teachers. She's the only person who knows about my shed, our shed.

I go there every single day after school and I bring Fluffernutters. Some days I hear her coming and my heart beats fast and then she comes in, throws her backpack down and starts complaining. Other days she doesn't come and it starts to get dark and I go online and see that she's busy with her other friends. But those days she does come, when I hear her in the woods, charging toward me, those are the ones that count.

Chloe always says we get along because we're both *only children*.

She hates that phrase. "It's bad any way you cut it," she said once. "It's either like, 'Oh you, what do you matter? You're only a kid.' Or it's like you're just not enough because there's only one of you." And then she licked her lips and looked away. "We're not only anything," she said. "We're *great*." See, I have that going for me, being an only child. Carrig Birkus, he has four brothers and a couple sisters. Imagine living with all those kids. I can't, not really. Me and Chloe, we have more in common.

My mom opens the slider. She yells, "Breakfast!"

Inside, she made burnt eggs and bacon and my dad is reading the paper. He gets to have it first and he gives it to me section by section. I put the pages back together so that it feels new, like nobody has looked through it. The good thing is that most days he only reads the sports section.

"So, at the end of the year somebody gets to keep Pedro," I say.

My mom looks at my dad and my dad puffs out his cheeks and my mom groans and my dad looks at me. "You keep him out of your mother's kitchen, yes?"

"Yes!" I say, and I can't wait to get to school and tell Mrs. McMurphy that I want to keep Pedro. I can't wait to tell Chloe Smells Like Cookies. I think you can invite a girl over without weirding her out if you have a pet. I think that's why Carrig Birkus has a dog.

I can't get to school fast enough. I tear through the brambles and I'm out of breath as if I'm running from bad guys. I run too fast and a thorn snags me. My cheek bleeds. I stop. I take off my glove and put my hand on my face. There is bright red blood. Pedro is in my pocket, shifting. I take him out and now there is blood on him. I apologize.

I hear something in the bushes though there is never anyone else here. I turn around and my whole life doesn't flash before my eyes, just the past few hours, the headline on the cover of today's paper—CYBER MONDAY: IS IT WORTH IT?—and the smell of last night's broccoli against the morning eggs, Pedro's heavy breathing, the snow, my blood on Pedro's Ovaltine-colored fur.

But it isn't one of the kids from school coming at me. It's a sub we had last year or the year before. *Mr. Blair.* Nobody liked him. He wore his phone on his belt and he was losing his hair on the top of his head and people laughed at him all the time. But I didn't. I didn't.

He's coming at me fast and it turns out I am not the kind of kid who springs into action when it's time to fight. I freeze. I choke. Same way I do on the baseball field at recess.

The blow comes from high above and something hits my head. *Brrrrungggg.* Pedro runs when I hit the ground. He can't send help. He's an animal, and like my mom says, he belongs out here. I don't.

# CHLOE

They can't find Jon. When he wasn't here, they called his mom and she said he wasn't home sick. She came to school, his dad too, and the whole school started to buzz. In that sick way, like when Kitty Miller got leukemia. People get excited about horrible things happening when they're not happening to them. I'm no better, I remember staring at Kitty, wondering what it was like to be her, as if she was a painting and you were allowed to gawk at it.

Kitty was loved, people made cards for her. With this situation, people are acting like it's news, like it's exciting, *that Jon kid might be missing.* The day is halfway over and he's not at school. He's not at home. He's not at the movies and he's not at the mall, but did they look in all the right places? Most kids who run away would go to a packie and rip off beers, get messed up and then go to Rolling Jack's and try out new hockey sticks. But Jon would never do that.

I told them to start in the woods, I told them how he takes a weird way to school. I didn't mention why. It's a hard thing, wanting to find him but also not wanting to look at a cop and be like, *Jon had to take the long way through the woods because he was getting picked on at the bus stop.* I think the cops get it anyway though. They're searching, but they still haven't found him. I wish the school day would end because when it does I'm going to the shed.

I don't like the way everyone assumes the news is gonna be bad, they act like he's already dead. Like if he's not at the movies and he's not at the mall and he's not in the woods, then where could he be? You can feel what it would be like if someone else disappeared. Someone like me or Carrig. Someone people love. Jon Bronson was not loved when he was here and so he's not loved when he is gone. It's nobody's fault. It just is.

At free period, Noelle and Marlene and I meet up at our round table in the library. It feels wrong, acting like Jon isn't missing. He says things to me, things that don't count when they come from your mom, your dad. He thinks I'm special. I sent him a filtered picture of the floats in New York last week and he was so impressed. I laughed it off. *It's not me, it's the filter.* He was so serious. *No, it is you. You used the right filter, framed them just right.* Jon is my champion. That person who sees more than what's there. I sent the same picture to Marlene and Noelle and they just sent back heart emojis. And you need that too, people who don't put you on a pedestal. Everything between Jon and me is a secret. He wouldn't leave without telling me.

When I say this, Marlene and Noelle look at their phones.

"He's fine," Noelle says. "You need to chill."

Marlene says it's weird he didn't text me. "Is he mad at you about that thing with the frog picture?"

Noelle snaps at her. "Leave it alone."

The frog picture. The thing I've tried so hard not to think about all day. A few days before the Thanksgiving break, Jon brought this old stuffed animal to the shed, this frog, this soft green thing he loved as a baby. There was something painfully vulnerable about the whole moment.

"There," he said. "Shed sweet shed."

The frog was up there like taxidermy, as if this was a home, Jon's way of pushing us together. My heart was pounding. He was reading this book about Marshmallow Fluff and talking about the history of fluff, the machines, the secrecy surrounding the recipe. I couldn't process his words. I couldn't take my eyes off that frog. *Is this what I want?* We've never hooked up. Not even a kiss. Jon was reading a passage from his fluff book out loud and I was taking pictures of that frog. I put one up online. I knew what I was doing. It was a dog whistle to Carrig.

Within a few minutes Carrig was at the shed, pounding on the door. *Chloe, lose that faggot and come hang with us.*

Carrig was with Penguin, saying terrible things about Jon. And then Carrig's BB gun went off. A single pop. No one was hurt. Nothing was hit. It didn't matter though.

"You gotta go," Jon said. "Don't worry about me, they just want you."

Now he's missing and this is the world without him.

Noelle shakes her head. "And what were you supposed to do?" she says. "Sit there with him until Carrig tore the walls down? Chloe, that whole thing has *nothing* to do with this."

I nod. Noelle is naturally authoritative. She says things and you believe them even if you don't. "I know," I say. "I just hope Jon didn't run away."

Marlene shakes her head. "He didn't," she says. "I mean, that kid would never leave you, right?"

On we go, a dark version of a normal day. Noelle digs up terrible facts, the odds of Jon being dead. She chews on her Dartmouth pen. Everything, everyone, reminds me of Jon. I look at Noelle, I remember telling Jon she hates *The Middle*. He said a sense of humor is like a sense of smell. Some people don't have one. See, that's why I miss him, why he's the best. He's funny. He gets it. What other kid, what other *boy*, would like *The Middle*? He says it's great because all the

Hecks are smart and stupid at the same time. He says most other shows make you be one or the other.

"Shit," Marlene says. Her laces are tangled. That's Marlene in a nutshell. She cares about what's happening in front of her face, the laces on her shoes, the tennis balls on the court. It would be insane of me to expect her to be the kind of friend who cries with you. And the same is true of Noelle, Noelle and her Dartmouth pen and her class rank. They're both very intense. Jon is more like me, his heart spreads out in the stupidest ways. He cares about things easily, things that don't matter to anyone else, the history of the Marshmallow Fluff in his sandwiches, the class hamster.

"Listen to what Penguin just put on Snapchat," Noelle says.

Ugh. *Penguin.* Again I'm thinking of that night, the green frog beating in my mind like a slimy heart, the white and black of Penguin's trademark Bruins jersey, Carrig's scent, gunpowder, sweat.

Noelle drones on and what if Jon is here, in the library, crouched in the stacks and listening? What if he can see this, us being normal? Talking about Penguin, who is just a loser, he'd never move to New York like Jon and I will. *Jon.*

I remember in fifth grade, I told him how Noelle said I was *pretty but not slutty pretty* and he said I'm *pretty pretty.* But then he never said it again. And that's when things felt settled or something, like we were just friends. And I was young, I was fine with it. Noelle and Marlene and I were all young for our age, hunched over our bagged lunches, no idea how to talk to boys, and here we are years later, still no idea, the way Noelle gushes about Penguin. I squeeze my milk carton. I miss Jon. And he is *missing.* Is this real? Noelle winks at me *calm down* and Marlene pushes my milk carton with her ruler. They're not bad people, they just don't get it.

"Sorry," I say, shaky. "I'm just in shock."

Noelle sighs. "You can't act like this is *your* thing, C. You guys are buddies but you scribble *Chloe Birkus* all over your diary and I know you hang with those guys at Forty Steps."

My cheeks turn red. It's true. I hate that it's true. I hate that she can be mean and cold and right all at once. "Anyway," I say. "What did Penguin say?"

"Well," she says, all gossipy. "Penguin's dad's a cop and he told Penguin's mom that Jon's parents told the cops that Jon was *sleeping in bed* with the hamster." Marlene shakes her head. "I'm gonna pee."

When she's gone, it's just me and Noelle, like it was when we were little, before Marlene moved here and made us into three best friends instead of two. Noelle clicks her pen. "Chloe," she says. "Does Jon really sleep with the hamster?"

It's not a fair question. Jon loves Pedro. Carrig's family has a golden retriever. Nobody makes fun of him. You can love a dog, you can't love a hamster. I shrug. "No idea," I say. "Why?"

All day I am more aware of how close Jon and I are. He has nobody but me. Nobody knows him like I do and there's this pressure building every hour that he doesn't show up. The bell rings. Noelle pops her pen. "Hey," she says. "You know I'm only giving you a hard time because I know everything is gonna be okay. For the most part, everything is always okay. Your little friend is probably at Tenley's having a frappe."

I think of the red and white stripes on the Tenley's straws, the awnings. Jon likes it there. A lot of kids think it's for babies and old ladies. Every time you go, you hear "You Got It All" by The Jets at least twice. My mom always looks around. *Didn't they just play this?* Jon loves that song, the video too, it's all frappes and puffy clouds, sweet things, Jon things. When Marlene comes rushing back to grab her books, late, same as always, when we're walking down the hall, talking about nothing, it feels like Noelle is right, like everything will be okay.

After school I take the bus and get off at the stop closest to Mrs. Curry's. I sneak through the woods and I run. I want him to be in the shed, he *has* to be in the shed.

I knock on the door. "Jon?"

He doesn't answer, but then he knows I never knock. I remember this morning, the policeman asking me who else he could talk to about Jon, other kids.

"No one," I said. "Just me."

I open the door, but Jon's not there.

# CHLOE

For weeks I harassed my mother about these bright white boots I found online. Jon knew about them. I showed him a picture.

*And what will happen after you get these magic boots?*

*I'll wear them and I'll be happy.*

*And then what?*

We were on the floor of the shed. It was a few days before Thanksgiving break. We were watching *The Middle* and talking about nothing. The question haunted me. *And then what?* I didn't have an answer then. I don't have an answer now.

The day before he disappeared, he sent me an article from the *Telegraph*, a meteorologist predicting less snow this winter. *Show your mom and she'll get you the boots,* he said. My mom broke down last night when she overheard me crying. So now the boots have arrived.

"This is a mistake," she says. "These boots will help for a minute and then they will only hurt you. They'll only remind you of this mess."

"You think he's gone, don't you?"

She doesn't answer me. We're both picturing the same thing, Jon dead.

She breaks the silence. "You better hurry."

We're going on a search party. It's Day Five and Jon is out there, who knows where. I feel the reflexive spike of adrenaline as I tear into the brown box, the scent of new shoes, the pleasing pink tissue paper, the shiny sticker, how easily it gives. The boots are as pictured, impractical, but I wanted them, and when your best friend disappears, you get what you want in other ways, lesser ways.

We haven't even started walking yet and I'm pretty sure I have a blister. The police are here, some people from town I don't know, some kids. The Girl Scouts made little sustenance brown bags, cookies and nuts and bottles of water so small you can down them in one gulp. Rolling Jack's donated hand warmers. I heard a kid from my algebra class say he only came for the free stuff. But people often say things like that to deal with their own fear. At least, I hope that's true.

Noelle glares at the boots as soon as she sees me. "Jesus," she says. "Are those the ones you showed me online?"

I wish I hadn't shown them to her. I wish the cop who heard her say that knew that I showed them to her *before* Jon disappeared. "Yes," I say. "Is Marlene here yet?"

Noelle rubs her hands together. "No," she says. "But there's a van from Channel 5."

The cop is young and he touches his holster a lot. His cheeks are red from the cold, from being young. "You're the friend, right?"

Noelle locks her arm through mine, proving that she wants in on the drama, any drama, all drama. "We're the friends, Officer. I'm her best friend and Jon was like . . . well, we're the best friends."

He nods. "Are you expecting more people?" he asks.

And then they both look at me, Noelle and the cop. And other people too, Jon's parents, his crying, chain-smoking mom, his sad, drinking dad, the lonely girl from my gym class, the foster kid who shows up at school before the doors open, a couple other parents— they must know Jon's parents. It's a horrifyingly small group and I look down at my white boots.

My mother steps forward, I forgot she was here. "Officer," she says. "I can hold down the fort and follow with all the latecomers."


In the movies, when you see people searching for the missing kid, there's a wall of people. Their voices overlap and you get this sense that even if it's not today, someday they will find the kid. We are the opposite of that. We're a thin crowd, uneven. Jon's mom is crying and she fights with the cops a lot. *I swore there was something up that tree, the birch tree back there. You didn't see the guy in that house? The split-level? The peeling paint? You don't think he was a weirdo? Who sees this happening and closes their blinds? Can't you send someone over to talk to him?* There are so few of us that you can't have a private conversation. There's no din where it's okay for me and Noelle to talk about random things. But we're just big enough and spread out to the point where we can't have one conversation as a group.

Officer Young Gun leads the way with his flashlight and his megaphone. Jon's dad is full-on drunk and he sings. *Counting the cars on the New Jersey Turnpike, they've all come to look for America.* The more we walk, the more he drinks, the less sense it makes, the more it feels like this is a dead end.

At some point I don't fight the tears. Noelle squeezes my arm. "It's okay, birdie," she says. She hasn't called me that since we were little kids, and it isn't okay and I'm not *birdie* and I'm crying because we can't find Jon, because my ankles are bleeding, because the blood is going to soak through the white leather, because the brain is a horrible thing, how much it can hold. My mother was right. The boots were a mistake.

When we get back to the shed, my mom is sitting there with her Kindle. She shoves it into her bag and fixes her hair like a married woman who was caught making out with the real estate agent.

"No one else showed up," she says. "Did you have any luck?"

The news team is still there. Only one van stayed. My mom says they want to talk to me, and they have a camera with a bright light. The guy has the whitest teeth I've ever seen, whiter than my boots. He asks me about our search and I open my mouth to answer but he winces. *Can you step three feet to the right? We need to fake a crowd. It's just better that way.*

At home I bury my boots in the back of my closet near my old dance recital costumes. I soak my feet in the bathtub and think about all those stupid things I said to the TV man. They asked me to talk to Jon in case he can hear me and I looked into the camera and smiled.

"Jon," I said. "One thing you don't have to worry about is the *Telegraph*. I'm saving them all for you, even the circulars and the coupons. And of *course* I have the comics."

I smiled. As if I was so afraid for people to know how sad I am. As if crying is something I can only do here, in the bathtub over my poor bloody ankles. When I get out and go back to my room, I can tell my mother was there. There's a brand-new box of Band-Aids on my bed. She's folded over the sheets like she did when I was little.

There are no more tears left in me right now, and I pick up my phone but I don't have many pictures of Jon. He hated having his picture taken.

*Hates.*

I sneak down the hall to my mother's office and steal one of her yellow legal pads. Back in my room, I lock my door. I hide under the covers with a flashlight. I try to draw his face. To re-create it right here, to make it as close to the real thing as possible, the same size, a head only slightly bigger than my own. I can see him in my mind, the feeling in his eyes. But I can't make it, I'm not good enough with a pencil, a pen. My bloody ankles don't hold a candle to this frustration, the boiling rage inside of me when I review my pathetic scratches on the tear-soaked yellow paper. My drawings don't match the inside of my mind, my heart.

The next day there's a brand-new callus on my finger. I stroke it with my thumb. It's soothing and I want it to deepen. I don't get out of bed to get ready for school. I pick up the legal pad and start drawing again.

# CHLOE

I get up extra early every morning to draw Jon's initials on my neck or my collarbone or my wrist and then I go outside, I pick up the *Telegraph* and pull it out of the plastic sleeve and smooth it out before I add it to the stack in my room. My parents don't like any of it, the papers, the fake tattoo. I wish I could get a real one. I want a permanent mark on my body. I hate the way people are already forgetting that he was here.

I want people to know that I miss him, that I love him, that it's wrong to carry on. They didn't shed a tear for Jon—*shed*—and every day I try to make them all squirm. I chopped my hair into jagged, uneven strips. I stopped shaving my legs, my armpits. I wear chunky black eyeliner and these stiff, bell-bottom fireproof jeans. The day those jeans arrived, my mom pulled at her hair. *None of this will bring him back.*

I hate when people say that. Obviously I know this won't bring him back. I realize that cutting my hair won't alter the course of the universe. But I do these things because if and when he *does* come back, he's going to see how much I miss him. It's all proof. He will gasp, *Chloe, is that you?* I want to look like a different person because I am a different person. And when we hug, I'll be that person that feels like home again, that person I was with him, that person I can't seem to be without him. I bought the fluff book. I can't get into it, it's not the same without his take on it, all fired up.

Noelle and Marlene want to help me feel better but all I want to do is feel worse, to shrivel up, to be the girl who went off the deep end when her best friend disappeared.

Noelle stares at my big fake tattoo. "So," she says. "Can you go in the water with that thing?"

"In what water?"

Marlene sighs. "Water Wizz," she says. "Class trip."

"Oh," I say. "Yeah. I can go in the water."

Noelle bites her lip. "I was kidding," she says. "You gotta lighten up at least a little."

Marlene picks up her tray. "I'm sorry," she says. "I have practice."

She's sick of this fight, sick of Noelle lecturing me to smile, wash my hair, go to the mall—*there's a sale at Rolling Jack's, we're gonna get new bathing suits*—and I'm sick of being on the other side of this. Sick of saying that I don't want to smile, don't want to wash my hair, I don't want to go to the fucking *mall* and try on bathing suits. I want to be sad and miserable because my best friend is *gone*.

Noelle picks up her tray. "For the record," she says. "The tattoo on your neck looks stupid and Jon would be the first one to say it. And if he's even *half* the person you say he is, he would say you really suck like this, Chloe."

In art class it's easier. People don't know me, they don't care, they like the fact that I'm trying so hard to look fucked up because most of them are doing the same thing.

Rosie Ganesh plucks a hair out of her cheek with her fingers. "Got it," she says. "Look at that little fucker."

Rosie Ganesh is a freak. She moved here last year and it's just her and her dad and a bunch of chickens. She has piercings and she's obsessed with Ian Ziering and wears T-shirts with his face plastered all over them. None of her quirks makes any sense, none of it goes together.

"Would you ever get a real tattoo?" she asks.

"Of course I would," I say. "But they won't let you if you're not old enough."

She grins. She's missing one of her bottom teeth. "My aunt's coming this weekend," she says. "With her boyfriend."

I stare at her. "So?"

"So her boyfriend is a tattoo artist," she says. "He travels with a kit. Do you want a tattoo for real?"


At dinner, my mom can tell I have something on my mind.

My dad is so different now, so afraid of me. He picks up his plate. "In case you girls want some alone time."

"Dad, no," I say. "You can stay."

He looks at my mom and she nods. They treat me like I just got home from a mental institution and might start breaking all the lamps in our house at any moment. They don't like my new clothes or the way I never smile.

"Well," I say. "My friend Rosie asked me to sleep over this week-end."

My dad chokes on his Coke. "Wow, well that's great. Who's Rosie?"

My mom is tepid. "This weekend?" she says. "But you have Water Wizz."

"I'm not gonna go."

My mom's heart practically falls onto the table. Thump. "Oh," she says. "Well, isn't this a class trip? Didn't I sign a permission slip?"

"Yes," I say. "But it's obviously not a requirement."

"But everyone goes."

"Not everyone," I say, and it's a lie. Everyone goes. Even the kids in art class. It's a big thing in the school, a rite of passage.

My mom shakes her head. "You know what I'm going to say."

"You don't have to say it."

"Chloe, honey, it does you no good to protest things in your life that bring you joy."

"It's a stupid water park with piss in the water. Dad, you know that's true."

He nods. "Nobody's saying you gotta go in the water, kiddo. But your mother's got a point."

Here it comes, another lecture on participation. I've heard it all before, my mom's testimony that the best parties are the ones you *force yourself* to go to and my dad's proclamation that the bus ride alone would be good for me, *get outta Dodge, get you outta your head.*

I pick up my plate and throw it at the wall. I've never done anything like that before. It doesn't break. There was no red sauce, there is no physical mess, only a measly little blob of mashed potatoes. I want my parents to hurt like I do. I want them to miss him. I can't stand how alone I am and I wish they cried more, I wish they were nicer to his parents and I wish his parents were nicer to me and I wish I'd been nicer to him. I might be going crazy. But the missing is too much, it's like a tetanus shot that never ends, this needle in my arm, this ringing in my ears, *Where is he how he is why?* My mom puts her hand up.

"Okay," she says. "Okay."


Rosie Ganesh's house is on a scab of land way far away from the center of town.

My mom puts the car in park. "Are you sure you feel safe?"

I groan and say what she needs to hear. "Mom, I'm *fine.*"

It's a long walk up the driveway and my eyes are watering. The whole way here I was on my phone looking at all the videos from Water Wizz. I feel stupid for being here. Phony.

Rosie grins. "Are you getting cold feet?"

"No," I say. "Why? Did your uncle forget the needles or something?"

She laughs, waves me into her house. "He's not my uncle. He's my aunt's boyfriend."

None of them are what I expected. I was thinking bikers but they're more like hippies, cooking *quinoa* and talking GMOs and thrift shops. The tattoo artist boyfriend is Devin, and he has long hair and a smile that eats his whole face; it starts on his forehead and spreads over his skin, pulling it tight. His girlfriend—the aunt—her name's Anita and she has a lot of tattoos and hair almost as long as Devin's. Rosie's dad is a farmer in overalls, he's a giant, especially next to skin-and-bones Devin and Anita. He has a really red face but it's not from drinking. It's from sun and laughing. They're all so goddamn *happy* and Rosie's always with her gloom-and-doom stories. She's a liar. She's a phony. But then what am I? I've gone to the bathroom twice already just to see Water Wizz updates.

We sit down around a table outside like a normal family and the aunt's boyfriend catches my eye. "I'm sorry about your friend," he says.

I look at Rosie and she shrugs. "I mean it's illegal for you to get a tattoo," she says. "I had to tell him what's up."

We eat our veggie burgers and our quinoa and we talk about Jon, about other sad stories of kids disappearing, kids kidnapped, the black market, heroin, all the dark things in the world, all the possibilities of where he could be, why. Rosie says she was really moved by my art, *That's how we became such good friends.* I look down at my empty plate and I am queasy. All I can think is, *I am not your friend. I am no one's friend.*

Devin stands. "Okay," he says. "Rosie, I think you should wait here. You ready, Chloe?"

I can't believe what I am doing. I can't believe what I am, who I am, following Devin the tattoo artist around this house I don't know. Devin set his things up in Rosie's art studio. He says he won't say stupid things like *relax* and *breathe*. He says this is my chance to ask him anything, anything I want.

I blurt out my question. "Do you think Jon is dead?"

He sits in a chair. I can't tell if he's twenty-five or forty-five. Beards are weird that way.

"The thing is," I start, "if he's *not* dead, and I mean I really don't think he's dead, I don't want it to look like it was RIP, you know?"

"True," he says. "But a tattoo is really just for you, we can put it someplace small, someplace out of the way. It's nobody's business but yours."

I blush a little. I feel young. Stupid. I never thought of my tattoo as a thing for me.

Devin closes his book of fonts. He says it's okay to back out, that we'll tell Rosie that this was his decision.

"Thank you," I say. "You're a nice person."

He laughs and hugs me and says that I shouldn't believe anyone who tells me it's gonna get better. "Ride the wave," he says. "Don't wait for it. Don't fear it. Just ride it."

Rosie's no dummy. She knows I wimped out.

"If God himself walked in here and said you could trade me for Jon, would you do it?"

"Rosie, that's stupid."

My non-answer was an answer, and I'm not surprised when she doesn't sit by me in art class the next day. She doesn't ice me out or anything. She says hi and we crack jokes about everyone wearing their stupid Water Wizz shirts but we both know we aren't friends anymore. It's a thing you can feel, a thing I know well by now, when I see Marlene and Noelle in the hallway, how they've adjusted to being two best friends instead of three.

At night it occurs to me that I officially have no friends. No friends except Jon. And Jon always had one friend, he always had me. I pick up the book he was reading when he evaporated, the book about Marshmallow Fluff, but I fall asleep and dream about Carrig Birkus. In my dream, I have long hair and smooth legs, I wrap around him, tight.

My therapist says it's natural for girls to separate lust and love, to rely on Jon for intimate connection and *lust* after Carrig. She says life is a process, a journey, not a destination, that fantasizing about Carrig doesn't mean that I don't miss Jon.

"Now," she says. "Tell me about your class trip. I know this was going to be a challenge for you, I know it's hard, but tell me about Water Wizz. Did you have fun?"

I gulp. "Great," I say, because my whole life is a lie, even the part where you spill your guts. "I'm really happy I went."

# CHLOE

My heart isn't broken, but it's cracked.

I had been so loyal, saving every *Telegraph,* drawing him every night. My mother is happy about that; *art is a positive coping mechanism.* I would carry the number of days in the front of my head. But things have popped up, distractions. I got an A in art and they let me move up to a junior seminar. I got the flu. I fell behind in my classes and I forgot to save the *Telegraphs.* And suddenly I don't know how many days Jon has been gone; I lost track at some point. All these life events that Jon missed made me feel less close to him, like this wound was healing and there was nothing I could do about it.

My phone rings. I still hope it's Jon. I always hope it's Jon.

But it's not him. It's never him.

It's Marlene's mom, wondering why I didn't RSVP to Marlene's birthday party. I feel my insides heat up in the bad way. I didn't respond because I wasn't invited. I've drifted away from Noelle and Marlene, fading into a haze on the floor of my bedroom with my sketch pads. I never said yay for Marlene making #1 singles on the tennis team, never helped Noelle hang posters for student council. They must feel stung. I take a breath. This is what my mom would call an *achievable goal*. I promise to go to Marlene's party and my mom hugs me so hard that night. "It's spring," she says. "I want to see you have some fun."

At the party, I rejoin the land of the living. Me and Noelle and Marlene stay up all night talking. Marlene is gooey, *we missed you,* just like her mom. Noelle is wary. She points her Dartmouth pen at me. "I think *you* should sneak downstairs and get us a bottle of Fireball."

I tiptoe down the stairs, I open the cabinet. I think of our sunflowers in the backyard, how they lean toward the sun. I think that's what this is. And I like being drunk. Noelle says my boobs got bigger. I forgot that I'm a girl, that I'm pretty. I'm not like Jon. I think of Jon's eyes, how hard they were to get into, the opposite of Marlene's family's liquor cabinet. I hold the bottle of Fireball and close the cabinet. I hesitate before I go upstairs. This could be my life from now on, sleepovers and shots. Jon is probably dead. It doesn't matter that I miss him. It didn't bring him back. Time is passing and I can't stop that from happening with my sketch pads.

The next day, I wake up with a hangover. I feel older. I go home and reach under the bed for the box of *Telegraph*s. I carry them outside into the blinding sun and dump them into our trash bin. I catch my breath. I stand there waiting for him to come back, because isn't that how life works? The second you give up, you get what you want.

He doesn't reappear. The trash truck comes and the papers are really gone. My mom doesn't say anything to me about throwing away the papers, but when I get home from school I notice that she vacuumed under my bed, her way of saying thank you.


I kiss a boy at Noelle's cousin's party in Manchester. I don't know his name. His tongue is enormous and alive. I don't know Jon's tongue. Probably never will.

Noelle kicks my leg at lunch. The Monday After My First Kiss Since Jon Disappeared.

"What?" I ask. I assume I did something wrong.

"Nothing," she says. "It's just good that you're like, here."

She's bossy, Jon always said. But bossy can be good. I think she'll run the world, be president or something. She taps her Dartmouth pen on the table. "We should hang out at my pool," she says.

Sometimes I picture the crack in my heart. It flares up when something reminds me of Jon. He always said pools are full of germs, even the clean ones, especially Noelle's pool because of the old tiles. Everything is connected to Jon, and Jon didn't know how to swim underwater. What babies we were. Everything is Jon.

I snap at Noelle. "Your pool is gross. Indoor."

"A pool is a pool," she argues. "And I'm the only person who has one. So we should be the pool people. And we should make sure everyone knows. Boys love pools."

Marlene shrugs. "I'm there if I can do laps."

The last time Noelle tried to make her pool happen we were in fifth grade. I got an infection in my toe and I told her Jon said it was from her pool. She said *he* was the infection. She knows I'm thinking about him, siding with him. If I fight her indoor pool, I'm not gonna see her at all this summer. So of course I tell her that I'm in too.


Noelle's parents retiled the area around the pool and Carrig started following me on Instagram and liking the pictures I put up of the pool, and suddenly this is our life.

My mom is happy I'm having a *real summer.* I like being in a pool. Once you're in the water, you have to stay afloat. It's simple. It's comforting to be somewhere I've never been with Jon, and maybe the water is sealing up the cracks in my heart. Marlene and Noelle are the best in here, childish in the nice way.

One night we go to the movies with our wet heads and we run into them, the boys, *the* boys, Carrig and Penguin, and Eddie Fick. Noelle does all the talking. They are sick of the pond and they want to go in her pool. It's a miracle, the way they want to be part naked with us. After we hang out with the boys, I go home. And now I can't sleep. I imagine my toes in the water, brushing against Carrig's. It doesn't matter that he's a jerk. He'll be in shorts. No shirt.

I should hate him because of how he picked on Jon. Because of the picture he posted of himself, crouched over a dead deer. He was smiling like a new dad, like a football hero. *#ByeBambi*. He defended himself in the comments, *Hunting is legal look it up dickwad*.

He oversimplifies things. As a person he is oversimplified, it all goes together, his attitude, his rifles and his six-packs and his sweatpants. But in that picture of life and death, he was life. There was something forgivable about his smile. He's not a monstrous old dentist extinguishing the life of an endangered species in another country. He's just a kid. A dumb kid. A happy kid. A hunter born in a place where people like to go hunting. You can practically hear his heart beating.

Saturday, I wear a red-and-white two-piece and my mom says I seem different. I blush. "There might be boys today."

She smiles. "Good."

They arrive. No shirts. I'm too shy to look at Care so I flirt with Eddie, a jock with tiny eyes, soft brains, a giant baby of a boy who could kill you if he wanted to, which he never would, being a giant baby. I always know where Care is though, and I sense him watching me. Noelle gets first pick and she goes for Penguin; she's a winner that way, choosing the one who's guaranteed to say *Hell yeah, kid, come up on me right here*. Marlene and Eddie pair off and then it's just me and Carrig, treading water, hesitating, stupidest small talk in the world, *How's your summer; good how's yours good*. But it feels real. Lump in the throat kind of heavy, the sound of another world opening up. There is a string pulling us together.

I love Jon. I want Care. My heart must be bigger than normal. Or maybe that's just this pool, this summer, the summer we got boys, the summer Jon became like an eyelash that gets stuck beneath the lid, that makes me blind and tearful, but eventually falls away.

FOUR YEARS LATER

# JON

Chloe and I talked about death once. I told her I thought you just die, that's it, and she said she thinks you transform into something, *maybe not a bunny, but something*. We were both wrong. Death is monotony. A walk in the woods. There is no way to know how long I've been doing this. Mr. Blair lags behind me and it's always Monday morning in late November, the gray cold, the dead leaves on the ground, shimmying in the sky on their way down. I don't know where we're going, and though we never stop walking, we never get anywhere.

And I miss her. I *miss* her.

But I can't cry. There's no crying in these woods. There's no food because there's no hunger. There is no yawning, no sleep, there are no leg cramps or sunsets or Fluffernutter frappes. There's no world in our world, it's just me and him. He goads me when I slow down, when he knows I'm thinking about her, when I'm slipping. *Come on, Jon, steady as she goes.*

I can't speak. I have no voice. He does though, muttering about leaves, life. I start to wish I would die so I wouldn't have to miss her but I'm already dead. And this is hell because the leaves have teeth and sometimes they nick me and there is no blood, only pain.

You screwed up, Jon. You had your chance and you missed it.

I look up at the blank canvas of sky, the threat of snow, the crackling hiss that never bottoms out. I wish snow would fall in lumps, making me deaf.

You wouldn't be here if you'd told her how you feel, Jon. You know it, you do.

I try to turn my head, I try to talk, but the leaves on the ground flare up, they glow bright green and the electricity seeps through veins in the leaves into me, my veins.

Don't turn around, Jon. I told you there is no going back. You should know by now.

But then, everything stops. The leaves hang in the air, as if someone hit pause on the screen of our world. My legs don't move. There is no walking, no talking. I'm choking. My ribs are crushing, cracking. I can't breathe. My throat is full. Marshmallow Fluff. I drop to the floor of the dead forest and my windpipe is closing and the sky is hardening, turning to concrete, whitening and stiffening. I didn't want this world but now I'm losing it, the whiteout inside of me, outside.

And then there is nothing.


And then I see red. A deep red in my mind that thwarts everything else, darker than blood, pain.

I don't know where I am or what happened. But I must be alive because this is the worst pain I've ever known, the searing, pulsing red of my throat. Slowly the rest of the world comes into focus. The twisted sheets in my hand. The hospital bed beneath my body.

But I'm not in a hospital. I am in a narrow room. The ceiling and walls are concrete, windowless slabs. A halogen lightbulb sizzles near my head and there are dozens of houseplants, ferns like you see at Kmart.

I don't know what this place is, this musty underground, but it feels like a basement. I start to think about the last day I remember, the last thing I remember. The woods. Pedro shivering. And then the sub. Roger Blair. He took me.

He took me and here I am. My body on this bed. The pain in my throat. And I realize. A breathing tube. He put a breathing tube in me.

But why? How?

I tear the top sheet off and to my shock I am in normal clothes, jock things, track pants and a hoodie. But this isn't the body I know. This body is too big and this can't be right, this can't be me. My hands are a man's hands, not a boy's hands, Pedro would drown in them now. Pedro. My legs are long, too long for my body. My chest is wide, muscled. I don't fit in my skin and for a minute I'm not sure this is my skin. Maybe he extracted my soul and shoved it into a dead body. But I know I'm being stupid. I'm me. My left index finger curves like it's trying to get away from my hand. There is hair on my arms. I'm just more of a man now. A coughing man, a tall man, a Brawny paper towel man who could unscrew the lightbulb in the ceiling fan in our living room—my parents, where are they?—and I sit up in the bed.

I pull at the muscles—they're hard, they're not mine, they can't be mine—but they are mine, under my skin, attached to me, holding me, containing me. How is this possible? How long has it been? And then—

*Chloe.* The wanting is a scream deep inside of me.

I remember this thing about life, about feelings, that they are fleeting, they go away whether or not you want them to. I sit and I breathe and I let the shock ooze out of me. I need a clear head, a calm head. I need to get out of here.

There's a nightstand by the bed and it feels like he left things here for me, that sicko. There's a tall glass of water—*don't drink it, Jon*—but I sip the water because I'm still me, because my throat burns and I don't have the willpower to resist. There's a battered little book and I pick that up too. *The Dunwich Horror* by H. P. Lovecraft. Eerie green tentacles spread over the front of the book.

It's pretty beat-up. If you brought this back to our library at school, Mrs. Wyman would ream you for it. I open the book. It's tiny, less than a hundred pages. I stop on Mr. Blair's favorite parts, the things he underlined.

Wilber Whateley was born at 5 a.m. . . . deformed,
unattractive . . . dogs abhorred the boy . . . Yew grows . . . an' *that*
grows faster . . .

The most important words aren't in the story, they're on the other side of the front cover in a letter from Mr. Blair to me. I know his handwriting from school.

*Jon,*

*You were in a medically induced coma. You are fine. You are free. Free to do as you wish, but a few words of advice from your old teacher . . .*

*Time moves forward. You should too. You have power, power that will present itself to you slowly, so as not to overwhelm you. Take it in stride.*

*You're special, Jon. You always have been. But going forward, you'll find that being special is a good thing. We did good work down here, Jon, and it will be interesting to see the way things play out.*

*You're welcome, Jon.*
*R.B.*

The words blur before my eyes. *We did good work down here.* No we didn't. There is no *we*, you sicko. I don't know what he's talking about. I don't remember anything. How long have I been down here? I didn't like Mr. Blair then and I don't like him now. My head aches and my hands quiver, trying to build a bridge between the then and now of it.

Back then, he was a weirdo with a frizzy mullet. He was always eating yogurt and licking the lids in front of the whole class. He was always trying to be my friend, he'd look at me sometimes, in front of everyone, like I was a teacher, like I wasn't a kid. *Do you believe these idiots, Jon?* People laughed because nobody wants to be buddies with the sub. When Carrig superglued my hands to my desk, Mr. Blair said I could *run circles around that moron.* I remember thinking that he was making it all worse by standing up for me. There's nothing worse than the wrong person being on your side.

*You have power, power that will present itself to you slowly, so as not to overwhelm you.*

What the hell does that mean?

Back then, he was the weirdest sub, hands down. He called us *pussies, you care so much what other people think, you let your peers know that you care, waste your energy collecting approval from strangers.* The next time we had him, we were scared of him, he called us *delicate flowers, didn't your mothers teach you about the difference between sticks, stones, and words?* No matter what he did he always came back, even after the time he spit at Carrig. *You'll never be anything, you khaki little shit.* Nobody told the principal. You don't tattle on a sub; you just go to your next class. I never made fun of Mr. Blair. But here I am.

*We did good work down here, Jon.*

I throw *The Dunwich Horror* at the wall. I wish he didn't write anything in the book, I wish there was no letter, I wish it could be simpler, that some bully freak kidnapped me and locked me up, me against him. But the thing about the book, the letter, now he's made me a part of something. I can't leave the book here for someone else to find. It's mine now, like it or not, my fucking *Horror*.

I shove it in my back pocket. *You're welcome, Jon.*

There are brand-new sneakers by the door, Nikes, socks too. It's a shock, to be tying up laces, blinking and crouching. I am surprised that I can move, that I can run up the stairs. I must be over six feet tall and I take two steps at a time. I was never this strong, this big, and I spin a globe in my mind. I could be anywhere in the world. Siberia. Tennessee. I'm not even a little bit out of breath when I reach the top of the stairs and my throat is less sore now than it was before. I open the door and step into a black box of a room where the walls are covered in old calendars. There's something familiar about it, a scent that tells me I'm not in Siberia.

I open another door and it's brighter in here, this is an empty shop and the storefront windows are plastered with aging yellow *Telegraph*s. Home. I hear Muzak. There are stronger smells now. Mustard and cinnamon, things you put on pretzels. And then it hits me.

I am in the mall. *The mall.*

It's almost as bad as the book in my back pocket, the impossible lameness of it all, that I get kidnapped by a sub and shoved in the basement of the mall. *The mall.* I stare down at my large body. This whole time I was down here, however long it was—*We did good work down here, Jon*—this whole time while I was asleep, everyone I know was up here, on top of me, buying stuff on sale and returning it and stealing gum, trying out lacrosse sticks in the back room on that puke-green carpet at Rolling Jack's. They were going to Tenley's, to the movies, giving hickeys and getting hickeys. They were here. And I was here. The mall.

*The mall.*

I don't know why I expected to be far away, but I did. Something extraordinary has happened and it feels like the journey home should be more dramatic, like years have passed and people should be zooming around in jet packs.

The Dunkin' Donuts is still here, the same as ever, always with new items, this time they're pushing Snickerdoodle Croissant Donuts. An old man sits at a table with a glazed cruller and a *Telegraph*. When he finishes his doughnut and stands to go, he leaves the paper behind.

It's scary but I have to do it. I have to know what year it is, and I look at the top corner of the page and there it is. The number blinks out at me, unfathomable. Four years. *Four years.* I lost four years of my life. Roger Blair took them from me. He stole the one thing you can't get back. Time.

My hands shake as I turn the pages of the paper. I see coupons for restaurants I know, restaurants I don't know.

And then I'm on the move. For a while I just walk, the way old people do in malls. I have to get my head together before I go back to my life. I make decisions without meaning to make decisions.

I will tell them the truth. I woke up in the basement, I don't remember a single thing.

But I will never tell anyone about *The Dunwich Horror.*

I will never tell anyone about his letter.

I tuck the evil little book into the waistband of my pants and I go into the old Radio Shack. Now it's called Meditations. Wind chimes are tinkling and fountains are gurgling and a happy hippie greets me at the register. She says of course I can use the phone. I remember my mom's number and I'm dialing and my fingers are big, too big, and the woman squints.

"Wait a minute," she says. "Are you . . . are you . . . Jon Bronson?"

# CHLOE

Noelle pumps the squirt gun. "So did you guys do it yet?"

It's one of the grosser things about my friends, their curiosity. We're about to graduate and the summer is starting to feel like this painful stretch of highway we have to get through before college. I'm ready for a new world, one I can't fully imagine. One where people don't say *do it*.

Marlene intervenes. "Noelle, you know they didn't do it yet. Why do you even ask?"

"Unreal," Noelle says. "By now his balls must be dark blue. Or light blue. Sky blue?"

I'm the Virgin with a capital V in the horror-movie version of our lives even though Marlene's a virgin too. It's because I'm with Carrig, have been since the summer after Jon disappeared. Noelle's been annoyed ever since, that I would go from being Little Miss Goth Girl to Little Miss I Fuck Lacrosse Players. But technically, I don't, and this annoys her.

"Chloe," she says. "Don't take this the wrong way, but it feels like you're *clinging* to your drama. I mean what are you trying to prove by putting it off?"

I throw her a bone. "We'll probably end up doing it after prom."

It was the wrong thing to say and she rolls her eyes at Marlene, as if I'm blind. "Well played, Sayers. Way to make prom night all about *you*."

She's not wrong. There's something phony about me that I don't like, something that keeps me from sleeping normally, from sleeping with Carrig. I can't help but think that a true artist wouldn't be here sipping on spiked seltzers and waiting for her jock boyfriend to show up. A real artist would be in her studio, painting, pining, like a whaler's wife. You can't have it both ways. But you have to defend yourself, so I remind them that Care's going to BU and I'm going to NYU. "We're not even gonna be in the same city, so it's like why take it to the next level, you know?"

Noelle grunts. "Right. Because none of us are in the *exact same boat*. Jeez, Chloe, we're *all* going away."

And then it's back to talking about prom, about dresses and limos, the generic glory of being this close to the end.

Noelle squeals. *They're here. The boys.* And the butterflies do flutter inside of me. I love my boyfriend, gorgeous, patient, *we-can-wait* Care. I scramble to fluff my hair, adjust my bikini bottom. I tread water, full of want, unable and unwilling to scrape the smile off my face, grateful that it's there, that I'm here, waving to him as he yanks his shirt over his head, revealing his body, the lacrosse bruises, the way he winks at me as he dives in the water, inviting me to wrap my legs around him. *Hey, C.*

I love his voice. I love this pool. I love going to Rolling Jack's with him, being the girl to his boy. I go weeks without looking at a newspaper. I giggle whenever we sneak into his dad's back room where he hoards his guns. I chew gum and I don't know who's the secretary of state. I don't miss crying myself to sleep. Explaining to police officers that Jon and I were just friends. Care is here, always. When our legs touch, I feel alive. My whole life I've wished that he wouldn't go around shooting helpless animals and picking fights with younger kids, weaker kids. *Jon.* I've always thought you can't change people. But in the pool I feel powerful. I see how much he wants to be with me. How willing he is to make the first move. I imagine a world where he doesn't hunt, where he isn't a bully. A world where he's with me. We're good for each other, better together than we are apart. Sometimes I almost think Jon left so I could be here, in the water, fully.

Carrig's it now, moving toward me. Our toes touch and he smiles. "Marco," he says.

I know how the game works. I don't say Polo. I take a deep breath and disappear down into the water, silently inviting him to come find me, unlike Jon, who left nothing for me, not a note, not a clue, nothing. Instead, I hear a noise. The unmistakable sound of Noelle's mother opening the sliding door, invading our space. I reach the surface and everyone is staring at me. They know something that I don't know.

Noelle's mom is waving her phone. Pacing. "They found him," she says.

"They found who?" I ask.

"Jon," she says. Like he was my hamster. Mine. "Chloe, they found your friend."

We are treading water. We are supposed to go to the movies, to the woods. I am going to ruin everything by leaving. It won't work with an uneven number. Without me. Five are not six. I look at Carrig but he looks at the wall, leaving me before I can leave him. So I do it. I go. I get out of the pool. I dry off with a towel.

Everyone else stays. I shiver. I feel so naked, as if I have no bikini on.

"Hurry up, Chloe. Your mother's already on her way."

I don't know if I am going because I want to go or because I have to go. I just know that this feels like going to the dentist. *They found your friend.* Four years ago I was a different person. I would have given up everything for Jon.

I have things to give up now. Jon is taking them away. I'm a shittier person than I was back then. I want to be in the pool.

It doesn't matter. My mom is outside beeping.


I'm in the front seat of my mom's car, looking out the window, my hair soaking wet. My teeth chatter. Marco. Polo. Jon. Carrig.

"What's wrong?" my mom asks. "Besides the obvious. I know I'm in shock. Are you okay? Because nobody says we *have* to go over there."

"Mom, of course we do," I say. "I'm fine. I'm just cold."

She blasts the heat. I look out the window. My phone is ringing. Carrig. I put it on silent. And now a text comes through. *It's me, Chloe. Me!* I don't know what to write back to him. I am not the girl who saved the papers for him. I am the girl who threw them away. I can't think of anything to say and everything I come up with sounds trite or cold or just plain shallow. And now it's too late. We're here. I put my phone into my bag and feel my heart start to pump. It's real. There are trucks everywhere. TV crews.

My mom puts the car in park. "Do you want me to go in with you?"

If she wanted to stay, she would turn off the engine. It's as if we're in a time machine. She wants to know how long I'll be, which is not a question she asks when she brings me to Noelle's. And then she gasps. I look out the front window and I know why my mom is slamming the brakes.

It's my Jon, but it isn't. The man standing in the driveway, waving, is what they'd call a *hunk* in one of those old TV shows. My mother just about swoons. "My God, Chloe, that can't be him."

My heart bursts. "That's him," I say. "I'm sure."

I've been so worried about the ways I've changed that I forgot about him. How *he's* changed. All the times I imagined him at this age, every time I drew him, pushed him forward another year, lowered his brow, his eyelids, widened his jaw, all my machinations never resulted in anything like this.

When I step out of the car, he starts to jog toward me and I'm rushing toward him, crying. I am so close I can smell him, but then I lose my balance, my legs, my breath. I trip on my own feet. I feel blood drip from my nose and the TV trucks are swirling into a tornado up, up, and away, and the ground is sucking me in, pulling me under. I don't get to say hello. I don't get to kiss him. I disappear, out cold.

# JON

And just like that, everything is wrong again, everything is like it was back then, everything is off, askew. She was supposed to throw her arms around me and we were supposed to kiss and start this new chapter in our lives but instead she took one look at me and she passed out.

The doctors say it's normal. She went into shock, this sort of thing happens.

But it didn't feel normal. It made me hear Mr. Blair in my head again. *We did good work down here, Jon.* It made me want to read his letter.

My mom knocks on my door. I bury the book under my pillow. "Yeah?"

She comes in, beaming. I've never seen her this revved up, she's like a brand-new car, full of pep, jerky, laughing one minute, crying the next. "We're gonna need to get you a new bed, honey. Start thinking about what color sheets you might want, maybe we could paint? Maybe a nice bright blue?"

"Maybe," I say. I move closer to the pillow. I put my elbow on the pillow. She can't see that book. Ever. I feel like Gollum with the ring, I feel like the goddamn book is making me weird, undoing all the good she sees, *so handsome, so big!*

She doesn't realize I'm a mess. She's tearing the tags off shirts that someone brought over. All day our house has been a zoo with cops and doctors and reporters, friends bringing casseroles and clothes. The dog's barking again—they got a dog, *Kody Kardashian Bronson*—and she winces. My mom said it saved her life, to get a dog. "Are you sure you don't want him to come in here?"

"Mom, I just kind of want some space."

She nods. She fiddles with the book I was reading when he took me, the book about Marshmallow Fluff. "I wish I had better things to say," she says. "You know . . . wisdom."

"Mom, you say the right things."

She hugs the fluff book. "I just missed you so much. I'm sorry I'm such a basket case. I'm sorry that we took your Spider-Man wallpaper down. I'm sorry the bed's not big enough and I'm sorry about Chloe, and I'm sorry I keep falling apart on you."

I take the book out of her hands and hug her. I feel bad that I'm not crying, and I feel scared of my body, like I'm not holding her right, like I don't do anything right, the same way I felt when I was a kid. I think of Chloe falling onto the ground, the blood spilling out from her nose, her split knee, and suddenly my mom gasps.

"Whoa," she says. "Honey, I don't think you realize your own strength."

When we pull apart, there are two little streams of blood dribbling from her nose. I held her so hard that she's bleeding.

I hear him again, Roger Blair. *You're welcome, Jon.*

It was the same thing with my mom as it was with Chloe. The doctors say it's shock, *perfectly normal to have a physical reaction in a situation like this.*

But nothing feels *perfectly normal* to me. I've been home a couple days now and Chloe hasn't come back to see me. Her mother thinks she's sick, she thinks she caught a bug, so she's making her stay home. My dad passes out a lot. He drinks too much and he leaves his records on but it's another thing that feels off somehow, the way we'll be sitting there watching TV and one minute he's awake and then one minute he's not.

I lock my door. I read *The Dunwich Horror* three times in a row.

It's a hard book to get through, and I skip around to the parts that Mr. Blair underlined. It takes place in a small town in New England, and of course I picture our town, our streets, even though this book takes place a long time ago. The main guy is Wilbur Whateley and he's basically the town freak. He grows really fast. People are horrified by him. Dogs run away. He's a *giant*.

Wilbur is really smart and twisted and he's missing a couple pages from his *Necronomicon* book. He needs those pages in order to summon the bad guys, *the old ones*. But the librarians are onto him. They're afraid of what he's gonna do if he gets his hands on those pages. So they ice him out. He won't take no for an answer and he dies trying to get those pages. A dog eats him. There's no blood, no guts. He's only part human.

I hear Roger's voice again. *You're welcome, Jon.*

The main part of the book, the actual "horror," comes at the end. This invisible beast ravages the town; he leaves giant prints on the ground. I picture a dinosaur but I don't know if I'm right. I tell myself I will put it away and put it out of my head. I should focus on real things, figuring out about school, talking to reporters, police. But it's almost as if the tentacles on the book are holding me, as if they've grown out of the cover and onto my hands, snaking up my arms, into my ears.

Eating with my mom and dad always helps.

I feel more like me every time I eat her overcooked broccoli and hear about *Grey's Anatomy.* My dad and his red Solo cup of scotch, teasing her about the broccoli, about her shows. This is my life. This is my family.

But I always blow it somehow. I eat too fast. I ask my mom for her phone. She puts her fork down. "Why do you need the phone?"

"Cuz I was gonna text Chloe."

They say nothing.

"I won't be on it all night, I swear."

My mom sighs. "Jon," she says. "I think you need to cool your jets."

My dad won't look me in the eye. My mom scoops the dog up onto her lap.

"What do you mean?" I ask. I am already turning red. "We're just talking. She's just telling me about stuff, you know, stuff I missed, she's going to NYU, stuff about school, what's the big deal?"

My dad drinks his scotch. My mom kisses the dog. "Jon," she says. "Does she mention anything about her boyfriend?"

My heart starts to pound because I knew it. You always know it. You feel it and you push the hunch away, like the bad book, the bad letter. I knew she was too polite and I knew she was using too many exclamation points and I knew something was a little different about her. I told myself I was staying off Facebook and all the other social places because the shrink I saw the day I got back said it would be too overwhelming. But the truth is I didn't want to see it with my own eyes. I didn't want to know.

"It's Carrig, isn't it?"

My mom shakes her head no but the word comes out like a hiss. "Yes."

I can't sleep.

I did text Chloe again but I didn't tell her I know. She asked me more questions. *Do you even kind of remember anything? Were you dreaming? What did you do when you woke up? Do you remember that first moment? What's the very last thing you remember? Why do you think he took you? I mean were you ever scared of him? It's all anyone can talk about at school, how weird he was, how it's so scary to think of him out there, how it's such bad luck that it was you, it's not fair, Jon. Do they think they'll catch him? You remember when he wanted us to prick our fingers for some genetic test thing? When he wanted us to pull out our hair? It's literally insane that he was in our school. I think about it, I get so mad. You must get so mad, do you?*

I can't ask her my questions. Do you really like Carrig Birkus? How did it start? Why? Did he kiss you? Do you bring him into our shed? Did you ever want to kiss me the way you kiss him? Do you have sex with him? Do you talk like this with him? How can you be one way with me and another way with him? Did you miss me? Did you stop missing me? Do you really love him? Do you? How can you love him? How?

When Kody Kardashian scratches at the door, I decide to let him in for once. I pat the bed, *come on up.* He wags his tongue. I want to tell him he's wasting his time, that I'm a hamster person. But he's hell-bent on being my friend. He rolls over and yelps and snuggles into me, burrowing. He loves me. Chloe doesn't. I start crying again, and Kody doesn't turn away the way a lot of people would. He moves closer to me. I scoop him up. *Thanks, little guy.* And then before you know it, I'm sleeping. I'm dreaming of being with Chloe. We're in my house, which is the shed, and then the curtain falls the way it does when you leave a good dream, when it hurts to wake up, to realize that nothing is that simple right now.

As soon as I wake up I feel it. The hard form curled next to me, cold where there had been warmth. The silence where there had been panting breath.

I feel it in my bones and I start to cry before I see Kody's lifeless body. I know what happened. I know the smell of death. I think we all do.

I can't scream. I can't wake my parents. I can't believe what I see, this dead dog. He came into this room in perfect health. And now he's gone. *He saved your mother's life.* She can never know. I put on those new sneakers that I was excited about only a few hours ago. I pick up his little body. There's no other way around it.


My parents are still asleep when I get back home from burying Kody.

I am on high alert, as if I've had ten cups of coffee. I'm awake, jittery. My body hums like a city that never sleeps, green lights as far as the eye can see, lights that never turn red, the chaos, the noise in me. The zzzz.

My mother is up first, like always. She whistles, *Kody Boy. Come find Mama.* When she can't find him, when she doesn't hear him barking, she wakes up my dad. He startles and she snaps, *I told you that doggy door was a bad idea.* He groans and I learn the brief history of the doggy door. Kody goes out and he doesn't come home. Like a criminal, I realize that I'm gonna get away with this, as if I did something.

I didn't. Did I?

My dad opens the slider and I peer out of my window and watch him out there, clapping his hands, whistling. *Kody Boy, come on!* My mother's downstairs, puttering around, looking for a lighter, finding a lighter, making her way up the stairs and closing her bedroom door. She squeezes the doorknob so that I can't hear the button pop when she locks the door. She probably thinks I'm sleeping, has no idea that I'm pretending. She's a good mom. She doesn't want to wake me, doesn't want me to hear her crying. She did this when I was a kid, when she wanted to be sad about something, when she didn't want to be a mom for a minute or two. Soon, I can hear the familiar old sound of her choking on her tears as my dad screams, *Kody!*

I open *The Dunwich Horror*. Roger's words jump off the page: *You're welcome, Jon.*

I'm starting to get paranoid, starting to think something's wrong with me. Chloe fainting. My mom's bloody nose. My dad passing out. Kody is *dead*. And I spin out. I imagine myself the invisible monster, slaughtering them all.

*Cool your jets, Jon.*

That's a made-up story and it's possible it doesn't even have anything to do with me. Roger Blair is a weirdo and weirdos read weird things. He probably just needed a place to write his letter but then I'm spinning again because that's right. *The letter.* What did he mean, *interesting to see how things play out*? What did he mean about me being special, having power? What I would give to see him again, the painful irony of wanting it more than anything, more than a kiss from Chloe.

I hear my mom on the phone. "Hello," she says. "Is this the right number to report a missing dog?"

When she's downstairs, I go online and look at pictures of the new me, the articles about *Basement Boy, Miracle in Nashua.* I'm a feel-good story, standing between my parents. The before-me is puny and awkward and the now-me is strong, towering over my parents. I see the drawings Chloe made for the police. It all looks so good in here, like things worked out.

It's like the producer from *Ellen* told my mom, *We love your son because he's an inspiration.*

I Google Roger Blair and find every article I can about him. How he was a professor at Brown before he was fired. How he did experiments involving plants and bananas and the sun. None of it makes sense and soon my head is spinning. I turn off the lights and stare at the ceiling. I can't see in the dark and I can almost pretend that I'm back in the basement and Roger Blair is gonna come in and tell me what he did to me, what he did to me for real.

The next morning my mom is posting pictures of Kody on her Facebook page and my dad is scrubbing the front porch.

"Someone egged our house last night," she says. "What can I tell you, Jon? When it rains it pours."

# CHLOE

There's no good place to break someone's heart.

I choose the patio in front of Starbucks. Maybe it will be easier to end things because I'm wearing my uniform, because my break has a beginning, a middle, an end. And we do need to end it. It started fizzling the day Jon got back, the moment I climbed out of that pool. Carrig hasn't forgiven me for ditching him to go see Jon, he's been cold to me ever since, he doesn't trust me anymore. But he won't let me slip away either. Boys like Carrig, boys who play lacrosse and take abuse from coaches, they want everything to be official, winners and losers, goals and misses, so here he is, crunching on the last chunks of ice, refusing to let me drift away.

"Sorry I haven't been around much," I say. "I picked up some extra shifts. New York is just gonna be so expensive, you know? And I'm so behind in everything, I even had to get an extension for my art class."

He smiles at the concrete. A shitty smile. "Right," he says. "You're busy."

"Carrig, I don't know what you mean by that. I'm telling you the truth."

"I'm not stupid, Chloe."

"Who said you're stupid?"

He bites his lower lip. I've never seen him cry. I don't want to see him cry. I reach for his hand but he pulls it away. "Stop saying you're busy with work," he says. "Just fucking say it."

"Say what?"

It's easy to imagine his eyes exploding right here on the patio. "It's fucking Jon," he croaks. "Just say it."

"Nothing is happening between me and Jon."

He squeezes his empty cup. "Just say it, say you're fucking done with me."

I don't want to say it. I want Carrig to give up on *me*, to stomp off into the parking lot, delete my number, tell me to go fuck myself. His left leg shakes. His cheeks turn red. He will suffer and simmer but he won't be the one to go.

"Is this cuz I egged his fucking house?"

"You did what?"

He clenches his jaw. He thought I knew. Now he knows I didn't know. And now I have this image of him throwing raw eggs at Jon's house. I can see the yolks dripping on the windows. I rub my eyes.

"It was just a joke," he says.

"Care, egg whites are corrosive. You can really do damage."

"It's just egging a house."

"No," I say. "It's not."

"Yeah," he says. "Well you can do some pretty sick shit too, Chloe. Just saying."

There is no swearing or stomping. He just walks away.

I watch him charge into the parking lot, he doesn't look both ways and he almost gets run over by a truck. He flips off the driver and yanks his door open and I've never felt so mean in my life. So powerful and responsible, so bad. I did that, me. I try to write to Jon but I can't find the words. How can I tell him it's over when I hate having to admit it happened in the first place?

A few weeks later I show up at Noelle's with cake pops and Frappuccinos and she looks me up and down. "Who *are* you?" she asks.

"Noelle, come on. People get jobs."

She takes the Frappuccino. "So," she says. "How are things in Jon Land?"

That's what she calls it. She won't just say *How's Jon?*

"He's great," I say. "Same as ever. I sit down to talk to him and we never run out of things to talk about and sometimes we're texting *and* chatting and then we find a movie to watch and before you know it it's four A.M."

She stares at me. "So let me get this straight," she says. "You broke it off with Carrig and *still* it's just talking? Christ, I assumed by now there would be something going on."

"Noelle, come on. You know it's complicated."

"Do you even *go* to a movie ever?"

"He has PTSD."

"Wait," she says. "When is the last time you just plain even hung out with the kid?"

I don't answer the question because she knows the answer. She knows Jon won't *hang out* with me. She says she's not mad *at* me, she's mad *for* me. She rolls her eyes. "You're like a human security blanket. You even *look* different, Chloe. Are you painting at all? Or do you just like text 24/7?"

"Yes," I say, I snap. "I'm painting."

She shakes her head. She knows I'm lying. "Dude," she says. "He survived. I don't feel sorry for the kid. He didn't get molested by aliens."

"Noelle."

Her eyes bulge. "Did he?"

She does this every time. Her tone shifts and everything is a question, a doubt. She wants to know what we talk about. I tell her the truth. Last night we spent several hours comparing live versions of the Hippo Campus song "Way It Goes."

"No," she says. "What do you *talk about*?"

I know what she wants because I would want it too. She wants the goods, the things you tell your best friend, his nightmares, the things they don't put in the paper. But I don't know anything. It hurts to feel the words come out of my mouth, "We still don't talk about that stuff."

I avoid her eyes. I know it's odd that Jon doesn't talk to me about what happened. It's like he's always trying to prove that he's normal. We talk about me, about my art, about his conviction that nothing will ever top Hippo Campus at the Valley Bar in Phoenix, Arizona, on May 7, 2016. But he won't talk about himself, not really.

"It's fucked up," she says. "You dumped Carrig and you don't even *see* Jon. I don't understand this doormat syndrome."

The word stings. "I'm not a doormat."

"So why isn't Jon here right now? You don't think that's weird that you never see him?"

The worst times in life are when you do know and you don't know. Day after day I ask him to come over for a *Middle* marathon and he deflects, harps on me to read that *Dunwich Horror* book. I never ask him why he won't so much as go for a walk with me. Our connection has always been more about how we implicitly understand each other. I don't want to prod. I don't like talking about Jon with Noelle and I bite her head off with words I can't take back, "I think nothing is ever easy with your soulmate."

It was a mean thing to say, the kind of thing that makes her pick up her phone and twirl her hair. There's a silence now. I know I should apologize and tell her that she's right, that I *do* wish Jon would see me, that it's eating me alive. But the thing about things that break your heart, it's hard to validate them by saying them out loud.

I just keep thinking tomorrow he'll show up. Tomorrow I'll be telling Noelle about our first kiss and everything will be normal.

"So," she says, in that little girl voice you only hear at times like this. "Are you guys gonna go to prom?"

I shrug, *we'll see*. I drop hints about prom to Jon every day. He never says yes, but then he also hasn't said no.

She sighs. "I'll tell Penguin to tell Care that he can bring his soph*whore*."

I've known about Carrig and the new girl for a week. But still I gasp. "Wait," I say. "He has a girlfriend?"

Noelle needed to have something over me, me and my *soulmate*. I put on a show, playing the exasperated ex.

"Jon is bad for you," she says. "You might not realize it, but he's punishing you for being with Carrig. And you're letting him. Chloe. The thing is, you're allowed to be happy. If Jon loved you, he would want you to be happy. You look like a zombie." She is on her feet, emboldened. "I'm getting you some water."

When she's gone, I look over those last texts with Carrig. He texted me the very first night he met the soph*whore*. He was drunk, jealous. He was all over the place, *I love you I hate you*. I called him the next day to try and talk about it, but he didn't pick up. He just sent one last text. *Don't remember any of that. Senior moment. Delete.*


Later that night I'm tipsy on spiked seltzers.

I stare at the white space in the chat window, the absence of dots, he doesn't know what to say to me and I'm too drunk to say the right thing, so I say the crazy thing.

*I want to see you. Really see you.*

And then I see those little dots. Here he comes.

*I know*, he says. It's an infuriating response. Especially because of today. Defending him comes so naturally to me in the moment. But then to come home to him—to my computer—and realize nothing has changed. That today isn't tomorrow. Today is going to be more texting, more typing. He starts in about an article on the founder of Starbucks that he found online and that launches us into a big talk about discovery and invention and risk and ambition and knowing and not knowing and original thinking and it feels like a dirty trick of the universe.

We can talk about everything except us.

I tell him I want to see him and he says it again. *I know.*

What does he know? Does he know he's making me crazy? Does he know I go to sleep with makeup on in case he shows up? Does he know I drive by his house? I see him on the swing set in his backyard. I watch him as he lies to me about being busy. I try to tell myself that it's got nothing to do with me, that it's PTSD. But deep down I don't believe it. People do what they want to do. And if Jon wanted to see me, he would. You can't make someone love you. He never kissed me when we were kids. Why should it be any different now? I vow to end this thing. Block him. I open the email I keep in drafts, my literal *Dear Jon* letter where I tell him I can't do this anymore, can't set myself up for this daily rejection. The wording is strong, direct. I tell him I'm not a horny monster who's going to attack him. *I will always be here for you if you just want to be friends.* Of course, I don't send the letter.

He pops up in a chat window. *Chloe, are you home?* I should ignore him. Noelle says you have to train men like dogs. Marlene says to buck up and ask him to prom. But I'm afraid of what he might say, that he doesn't love me, that I come on too strong, too hungry. It's easier to slip into conversation, into Hippo Campus. As always, it gets late, really late, and he drifts away from the chat. It was the opposite with Carrig. With him, I was always first to go. I miss the power that comes with being the one who doesn't say goodbye, the one who just disappears.

# JON

I always log off first.

I know it's a shitty thing to do, to leave her hanging. But this thing in me, the thing that *might* be in me, the invisible poison, the thing I have no name for, the thing I call my jets, the thing that kills dogs and makes my dad pass out, this thing is scary. I don't know how it works. So far it only seems to work when I'm physically close to people, but Roger said I'm *growing*. And if he was talking about this thing, the *power*, then who's to say it's not strong enough to worm its way through the computer, into Chloe?

I think I'm paranoid. And maybe crazy.

Sometimes I think he only gave me this book and this letter to fuck with my head, that this is just the kind of thing an evil person does. I grab my jacket, I look in the mirror and I think, *Just do it, go to her house or show up where she works and kiss her already.*

But then I remember Kody's little body, the stillness.

I'm running out of time. Eventually she's gonna get sick of me.

She's gonna want more, she's gonna want less. Every day I expect her to say the terrible words, *We need to stop talking*. But she must feel it too, the connection, this thing between us, a vine.

My shrink Beverly says I'm not a parasite. She's older than my mom but younger than a grandma and we Skype like this once or twice a week. I'd never tell her about my *Dunwich* theory, but it's nice to pretend she knows it all, to think of her thinking she has the whole story.

"So," she says. "Did your mom get her test results?"

"Yeah," I say. "She doesn't have lupus, they don't think."

"Well, good," she says. "That's good news, Jon."

She's a little too cheery sometimes, or maybe she does that on purpose, to set me off. I start ranting at her about how it isn't that simple. *Good*. My mom is weak and sick and she passes out all the time, she has no balance, she gets bloody noses. My dad nods off. They're both sick and no doctors can figure out what the hell is going on.

Beverly says what she always says. "It's not your fault, Jon."

This is the hardest part of the session, when I want to tell her that she doesn't get it, that it might be me, that I might be making them sick. Literally. She talks about emotions and stress but she doesn't understand that this thing in me, it's not in her books. And if I told her, she'd probably make me go into a hospital where you do puzzles and take drugs.

And then she says the thing she says every week, the warning about so much in my life, *Our time is up*.

I still haven't found Roger, and the cops have no leads and in all the crime shows it's harder to find someone every day. After I talk to Beverly, I always call Detective Shakalis.

"Hi there," I say on his voicemail. "It's Jon Bronson. I was just calling to see if there are any leads on Roger Blair."

A few minutes later he sends me a lame-o email. *Take it easy, Jon. Be happy you're in such good health. Try to be happy, Jon. We'll let you know if anything comes up.*

But I can't be happy. I have too many questions for Roger. I've marked up every page of that stupid evil little book and I can't figure out what he meant by it. Lovecraft talks a lot about Wilbur being an albino, and I asked my parents if we have any albino blood in our family and they looked at me and laughed and my dad said, *Scottish is a euphemism for albino, son, what made you wonder about that?* I lied and said it was something for my GED class.

I pull the blankets over my head. I try to cut through four years of fog. I walk through the woods in my mind. Didn't I hear *something* in all that time? Didn't my eyes open once, commit one image to the back of my mind? Did Roger carry me or did he stuff me into a wheelbarrow? Did he have a friend waiting with a car or did he act alone? Did he mumble or was he silent? Did I struggle?

My mom knocks on the door. "Hungry?"

The comfort of her overcooked broccoli, my dad's scotch in red Solo cups, it isn't the same as it was when I first got home. I'm too old. I'm in the house too much. I don't fit here. We all know it and things are starting to get tense.

The only thing we can talk about with ease is Roger Blair. My mom is always game to rave about the fact that my school should have known he was fired from Brown University. *Shoulda been locked up then.* My dad's sick of seeing Blair's co-workers on TV, telling stories about how weird he was, *so why didn't they speak up back then?* My parents blame everyone for everything. They blame Roger for the kidnapping and they want to see him *fry.* They blame Harvard for educating him, Brown for employing him, my school for not running a stronger background check, the mall for letting him keep that lease when he never even opened a shop.

"You know," my mother says. "The *Ellen* show called and they still want to fly you out for the special. And the invitation's not gonna last forever. It's been a few months now, Jon. It's time to act."

My dad sighs. "Penny."

My mom puts her hands up. "They would settle for a Skype."

"Mom, I mean it. I don't want to be Basement Boy anymore, okay?"

When she drinks wine, she gets gloomy. She talks about justice. "They're not even looking for Blair anymore but if you put yourself out there, they'd have to."

"Penny," my dad says. "He doesn't want to go on TV."

"You mean he doesn't want to leave *Chloe*." She pounds her little fist on the table. "Jon, the girl won't even eat supper with us and you put your whole life on hold for her."

My dad butts in. "Pen, leave it alone."

"I won't leave it alone. The girl is sucking the life out of him, I'm not gonna stand by and watch it happen. Her texting and her emailing *all the time*."

"Mom, I told you, that's how we like to hang out. I just don't feel like going out and doing stuff."

My mom rubs her forehead. "I think this wine is bad."

My dad laughs. "You wanna switch to the hard stuff?"

But my mom is on a mission. "See, you boys don't understand. It's a civic duty. The man kidnapped you and for all we know he could be out there kidnapping someone else. You do everything you can to stop that, to hold him accountable, to keep your story in the news. You want to sit around here and go on and on about it and talk to your little friend Chloe at all hours, but this doesn't do anything. You need to talk out *there*."

My dad kicks me under the table. He winks. Once he told me that my mother is a cat, *you have to play with her, let her chase the string*. She gets going like this, you can't stop her. She says we all deserve a little sunshine, a free trip, she's sick of being here, sick of seeing me waste my time up in my room. My dad tries to lighten things up, makes a joke about how this is just Mom's ploy to go find Dr. McDreamy.

But she isn't laughing. "It's Mc*Steamy*," she says. "The one I like is Mc*Steamy*."

My dad looks at me. "Chime in here anytime, son."

But our house is sour and I can't fix it. My mom sighs. "You know, unlike you two, I live in reality. And the reality is that before you know it, some other kid's gonna get kidnapped. The *Ellen* people will be all over him. Nobody stays in the news forever, Jon. Just think about it. You'll feel better with some structure in your life. That's all I'm trying to do for you."

I see her trembling. I gulp. "I know, Mom."

When I speak, the whole atmosphere changes. It's hard to explain. It's my fault. It's their fault. We don't know how to have dinner together. They got used to me not being here. We all know this isn't fun for anyone, it's not what any of us expected. None of it is.

I don't ask if I can leave the table to go up to my room anymore. I just pick up my plate and put it in the dishwasher. They wait until I'm gone to talk about me, but I can always hear them as I reach the top of the stairs, *Well, what does the shrink say? It hasn't been that long, he'll get bored of that room eventually, right?*

I close my door and I see her green light. Relief.


Chloe


Jon


Hi


Hi


Chicken?


Salmon. My dad's going to McDonalds lol.


Ha. We had chicken. My mom's plotting to take down the Nashua Police Department.

Ah, Friday.

Ah, Family.

Jon.

Chloe.

Silence. This happens sometimes. And then I see those dots and relief washes over me.

Sorry. Getting stuff together for prom tomorrow . . .

Prom. Cool.

Do you want to see my dress?

Of course I want to see her dress. I want to stand next to her. I want to hold her hand and wrap flowers around her wrist. The wanting sets off my jets. The *Dunwich* sizzle. I close the computer. This might be me blowing my chance, again.

The next morning I have a Google alert about Roger Blair.

A woman who runs a shelter for battered women in Portland, Oregon, wrote an article about Roger Blair. She knew him as *Magnus Villars*. She met him while she was an undergrad at Harvard. He was doing research on solitary confinement. She was strapped for cash, so she signed up. She says she was in dozens of experiments. There were things going on with her family, she was *all over the place* and she didn't realize that the release forms weren't standard issue. He put her in a room and he turned off the lights. He released rats. She could hear them and she bloodied her hands trying to get out of there.

When he finally turned on the light, there were no rats. It was only a tape.

She didn't report him to the school. She just left.

I Google the name Magnus Villars and the first stuff that comes up is Chianti, but then I go to Twitter and there he is, @MagnusVillars. His profile picture is a hamster eating an Oreo, and the goosebumps are immediate, the chills. He hasn't tweeted in years, but when he was active, he was a vicious bitter nutcase, assaulting *Science* magazine, prizewinning professors, tagging Harvard and Brown, accusing them of being *closed-minded hacks*. He sounds like someone who really did lose his mind, as if his mind fell out of his skull and into a gutter. The relief is enormous. Nothing is as scary as it was. He's crazy. He fucks with people's minds but he can't really *do* anything. He got to me. But now I see him, all of him.

I grab *The Dunwich Horror* and read the letter he wrote me and it doesn't feel mysterious now. It sounds loony. I leaf through to one of the parts he underlined in the story, a part that I now think is important:

. . . the diary as a madman's raving . . .

I forgot that the world is messy. Girls faint. Small dogs die. Boys get kidnapped. It's not a symphony; it's just life. Meanwhile, I reactivate my Facebook account just so I can see her. I have to see her. Prom pictures are starting to show up. Chloe's dress is a two-piece and her hair is swooped up like you're not allowed to touch it. She looks sad. I did that when I blew her off. But it's still light out. I can fix this.

I open my door and scream, "Dad! Do you still have your tux?"

That got my mom's attention and it's the first time she's bouncing around since she lost Kody. *Maybe you'll be prom king, honey!* My dad rummages through his closet for his old tux and my mom claps the dust out of his dress shoes. It's like Shakalis and Beverly are always telling me, *PTSD is a monster, but one of these days*, boom, *you'll feel better.*

My dad pulls the suit out of the closet. "Jon," he says. "She's all yours."

It's true what they say about riding a bike, you really don't forget.

The wind whips at me and I'm pumping, I forgot how beautiful the world is when you're a part of it this way, when the sun is relenting and the moon is rising and the night is magic, it can change your life if you let it, if you pedal. I haven't even kissed her yet, and already I feel different.

I am nervous, but it's the good kind of nervous. Chloe's at Noelle's with the whole mess of friends for pictures, and I'm almost there, slowing down as I approach Noelle's street, as my heart expands, a balloon. I'm not used to exercise, not used to love. I see them all, exactly as they were online, the girls in bright dresses, the boys in tuxedos, lined up on the front lawn of Noelle's house, posing. I slow down the tiniest bit. I'm scared. I wish I was on a motorcycle instead of a bike. But then again, I'm kind of like a celebrity around here. None of them got invited to go on *Ellen*. And when they see how much Chloe loves me, the smile that will spread over her face, the way she'll run over to me, they'll be on board with it, me.

I start to ride again but they're piling into the limo, one by one. I'm way farther away than I realized and it's like a horror movie, the way they don't stop, the way they disappear into the car. I pump, I ride, but I'm not fast enough. The brake lights on the limo light up. Red. A plume of smoke shoots out of the exhaust pipe. It's no use. I slow down and jump off the bike. All the buttons on my shirt are popped. I look like a nutcase.

The limo rounds the corner. There's always more time until there isn't. And it reminds me of the most important text that Chloe sent about tonight: *The actual prom is lame but Noelle's pool parties are fun in this cheesy way. Do you remember playing Marco Polo as a kid? You should come.*

So now I will. The ride home is better. I ride shirtless. A couple of random girls whistle at me. I'm handsome. I'm free. I'm loved. I have to be. No girl would text you that much if she didn't love you. No girl would keep asking you to come over.

And this is a night when girls want big things to happen. I think it's gonna be good we waited to see each other. And I'm happy I don't have to be on a loud crowded dance floor pretending to like songs I don't know. I remember something Roger Blair tweeted. *There's always more time until there isn't. You are born dying. Science could fix this. But they won't. #ProgressRequiresPain.*

Maybe he's right. Maybe it's finally our time.

# CHLOE

I have to say, Noelle is right. I did look like a slut in that dress. I hate that word, but there are girls who can wear that dress and project confidence. There are girls who want to show it all off, *shake what your mama made*. I was only wearing it for the pictures, hoping to get under Jon's skin, break his heart a little. I wanted him to see me in that dress and fill up with regret. The dress was wearing me, and if he even bothered to look at pictures, he was probably revolted by the desperation of it all. I keep thinking this is it, *The End*. Next year I'll be in college painting and Noelle and Marlene will be these people I talk to once in a while. Next year I'll be myself. No more this, no more hanging out with people I don't even really like at Forty Steps, no more home. Part of me wants to leave now, pull an Irish goodbye and sneak out of the room, swim down to the drain and squeeze myself in there, out of my life, my life here that didn't work out, that stupid dress.

I really did think something would happen tonight. I thought Jon would feel something. Feel something and *do* something. I watched the door all fucking night, waiting for him to charge into the ballroom and profess his love in a John Hughes kind of way. But he didn't. And that's that. I think of Carrig flipping off that guy in the parking lot when I broke up with him. I get it.

I did dance with Care once. I tried to be nice. I wished him luck with his soph*whore* and he kept his hands on my waist, like an eighth grade boy.

"Can I say something?" he asked.

"Sure."

"Chloe," he said. "Just be careful."

"Be careful how?"

"If a dude likes you," he said, "he shows up. We're dudes. We're simple."

All at once I could hear what everyone had been whispering. *Poor Chloe throwing herself at Jon and he won't even see her and Carrig's new girl is actually hotter and he's happier and poor Chloe's at home on her computer it's so sad so sad.*

Now prom is over and half the senior class is at Noelle's. I jump into the pool in my dress, because the dress failed. I failed.

Noelle is barefoot on the deck. "Dude," she says to me. "One line."

She's been all over me to *experiment.* "Maybe in a bit," I say.

"You're an *artist,* Chloe. At least pop a molly."

I eat a pot brownie and this night is a nightmare. It's too crowded in the pool, too many bodies everywhere, people we're not even friends with, people I never want to see again, people who didn't show up to the vigils. I am unattracted to everyone on every level. I want Jon. I miss Jon. I was so brave about New York because I thought he'd be there with me. But now it's hitting me. He's not going. I'm going alone. I remember what Jon only just told me a few days ago, that a younger banana will suck the life out of an older banana. I painted those bananas. I sent him the picture. He wrote back. *I love this so much!* That's not *I love you so much!*

But how could he love me? I'm not a good person. Once he asked me why I was still friends with Marlene and Noelle. I tried to be cute. *They're assholes but they're my assholes, you know?* He LOLed but I bet he was horrified. That's a terrible thing to say about your friends. I tried to take it back, but he said my name. *Chloe.* And then I said his name. *Jon.* And then there was a beat of silence, the lull. I read so much into that silent bridge between our names. I thought that was love.

Marlene offers me a spiked seltzer. "You okay, Chlo?"

"I'm okay," I say, popping the can of caustic semi-booze I'll never drink again after this summer. "I think I had too much of that pot brownie."

Marlene reaches for my bottle. "Oh no," she says. "You don't want to mix. It's early."

We both hear it at the same time. Noelle, blowing her whistle. Someone shuts off the music and someone is here: It's him.

It's Jon.

The love must be written all over my face because Carrig glares at me. Carrig. I forgot he was here. I'm trying to swim closer but Marlene grabs my arm. "Whoa," she says. "You look like you're drowning."

And at the other end of the pool, on the patio, there they are, Noelle and Jon. She points her fingers at the door. "Out," she says. "Invite only."

Jon is so quiet it's hard to hear him. "I just want to say hi to Chloe," he says.

I try to yell but the damn brownie won't let me do much of anything. I can't lift myself out of the water, I can't make it to the stairs. Noelle's hands are on her hips, you can practically see the coke in her eyes. I ask Marlene to go up there but she looks at me like I'm

crazy and I get it. Noelle is scary. In third grade we did a dance routine. Noelle was the choreographer. It was terrifying, how she cut us
down when we couldn't get the steps right.

People have their phones out because Jon Bronson is scary too.
Basement Boy. The guy from TV. And again she orders him to leave.
But he won't. Like a soldier, she moves her squirt gun into firing position in one swift gesture and Jon cowers. He puts his hands up like
some kind of a criminal. People are laughing and I think my heart is
breaking. She hates him. Always did. "Take your shorts off," she says.
"Let's see what you got in there."

"Noelle, I'm sorry," he says. "I'll go."

She pumps her gun and he flinches, as if it isn't full of water,
harmless water. I don't even think he can see me and I feel like I
can't see me, can't feel me. This is how it was when we were kids
sometimes, when Carrig would do something cruel to him and I'd
freeze up.

And then Jon speaks. "I just wanted to say hi."

Noelle cackles. "'I just wanted to say hi.' Are you a fucking dog?
Are you a dog?"

"No," he says. *Oh Jon, don't. Don't.*

There is no stopping Noelle, Noelle and her mouth, her gun.
"Let me lay it down for you, Basement Boy. First you ruined her life
by *being* here, acting like she should save your life or some shit. Then
you ruin her life by *leaving.*"

"I was kidnapped," he says, trembling.

"And then you ruined it *again* by coming back."

She takes aim. This time he doesn't flinch. There is no laughter
left in the room. Phones are down. This is a horrible thing to see.

"Chloe doesn't love you, Jon. She feels *sorry* for you." She pumps
her gun again. And then just like that, her nose starts bleeding. Her
breath comes in a rasp and she drops to the floor. And then we're all
screaming, moving. Someone steps on my hand while I'm trying to
hoist myself out of the pool. I can't see through the people and finally

I get out. I'm running along the edge of the pool and there is shriek-ing. *Someone call 911!* I push my way through the crowd.

Jon is gone. The slider is open, he didn't bother to close it. In the middle of all this chaos, he hurts me again. I get it now. That's what Jon does. He disappears.

And Noelle never disappears. She's the most dogged person I've ever known. Her favorite movie was *Election* and she could do any-thing. When we did that dance routine, she withheld our yogurts until we mastered our moves. Even when she was weak, there was something strong about her where it was hard to believe that she was afraid of anything. Last week, in Forever 21 in the dressing room, she quivered, *What if I get to Dartmouth and everyone's way smarter and just . . . better?* I remember this one time at a spelling bee, this other girl made fun of her accent. I remember how Noelle looked her right in the eye. *My voice is my favorite thing about me because it makes it so easy to spot the pretentious snobs like you.*

She's my best friend, my first friend, my flawed friend, and now she's flat on her back on the pool deck. Dead.

# I AM PROVIDENCE

*Six Years Later*

# EGGS

L o has dozens of students. Every semester there are more of them, in and out of our house for dinner, for coffee. There are always a few favorites, and right now it's all about *Marko*. He's not a bad kid. It's just the little things, the way he tucks his hair behind his ears, repeats everything that comes out of Lo's mouth, as if he hasn't already won her over. Lo says I'm too hard on him, on everyone. *He's just trying to commit things to memory, Eggie. A lot of writers do that.*

I have kids too, sort of. Mine just don't come over the house for pasta. They don't cry on the sofa about their evil boyfriends and their impossible professors. My kids can't do any of that because my kids are dead.

Lo knocks on the wall downstairs. "Marko's coming over for dinner."

"I'll alert the media."

She sighs but she's not mad. Lo doesn't like to come up here to my unofficial home office. Once upon a time it was our boy Chuckie's room. But he doesn't live here anymore. And that isn't because he's away at college. He'll never go to college. He's eight years old, stricken. Some doctors call it autism, but it's not the kind you see on TV or at the park. Others tell us it's a mood disorder, a neurological affliction. The bottom line is that our boy has a mess inside of his mind, a mess no one can figure. He was violent when he was with us, trying to set himself on fire, pulling his own hair, the screaming, the wordless pain in his only language, the shrieking. We were no good for him, couldn't protect him from his pain. They told us we had no choice. We had to send him to a special residential facility at Bradley Hospital. And there he lives, there he sleeps. *It's not your fault, not anyone's fault,* but that's easier said than done with this, the kind of nightmare that makes your friends forget to call you back. There is a God because so few kids are sick this way, but there is no God, because this is my kid, our boy, on the other side of town with rubber walls around him.

And so, of course Lo has her kids. Of course I have my kids. You have to survive.

Back before Chuckie was born, we were excited. Lo wanted ducks everywhere in his room and we bought every duck thing we saw, soft, stuffed ducklings, ceramic ducklings we found at an art-for-art's-sake kind of store out in Newport. And then he was born. *Quiet.* I prayed for him to be loud, boisterous. It's too painful for Lo to be up here now, the walls still flush with ducks, ducks we stenciled when we were *expectant,* when she would come home high on a Hemingway lecture, giddy over *Make Way for Ducklings.* She had her favorite pages of that book framed, hung. It's duck soup in here, my lamp is a duck and the bureau meant for his knickers is home base for an army of dusty rubber duckies. Then there's my desk, a cargo ship in a duck pond. We got it a few years back at a tag sale in Cranston. We love this kind of furniture, the kind that makes you think of Cary Grant and cigarette smoke. Lo squeezed my hand. "You know where this could go."

"That back corner of the living room?"

She looked down into her purse. "Or maybe Chuckie's room."

So we put my desk up here. *Now you have somewhere to do your research, Eggie.* She rubbed my back.

I should have seen it coming. Lo was no fan of my "research." I was trying to figure out why our boy was the way he was. The doctors said you can't go there, but it's in my nature to solve the puzzle, to go with my gut. I had so many angles. I was investigating the bones of our house, was there something in the walls, something that got into Lo while Chuckie was gestating, some chemical in the insulation? I had calls out to the manufacturers of the milk we had at home, the milk they use at Dunkin' Donuts. I was online finding other parents. Did they go to Dunkin' Donuts?

Lo would see me on the floor with my boxes and papers spread out. One day she spotted a bottle of her perfume on the floor. *Angel.* She grabbed it. "What's this?" she sniped.

"Lo," I said. "I'm doing this for us, for everyone. If there's something in the perfume, well maybe there's a way to reverse it, help other people from being in this situation."

She walked away. She'd never yell at me. We'd been to hell together. Our Chuckie never laughed. You could hold him but he wouldn't hold you, he wouldn't rest his head on your shoulder, wouldn't lean into you. You scream less when you've been through that kind of thing. And a week after that incident with the perfume, I was up here with my desk.

We have our system worked out. I haven't even been to see Chuckie since we dropped him off, whereas Lo, she goes all the time. She isn't a martyr about it, but it's there, brimming, and once in a while she'll confront me. *You spend all that time up there with your boxes and maybe if you saw him, maybe you'd be able to relax and just be.*

My alarm goes off on my phone, which means my tea is ready. I drink Throat Coat, marshmallow root tea. Lo can't stand it, *too sweet and soothing.* But I love this stuff. It's tender. You have to steep it for fifteen minutes, covered. It's just like they say on the box, gives you this inner layer of protection. *Protection from what?* Lo always wants to know.

My phone rings, as it often does this time of night. I sit back in my chair and prepare for the deluge. "Maddie," I say. "How are you doing tonight, my dear?"

Maddie Goleb's son, Richie, died in his yard. He was only twenty-three, another coronary, one of the four unexplained that's happened in the past few years. His mother calls me every few months, she gets on a tear, thinks there's more to the story. Whenever Lo accuses me of being obsessive, I think of Maddie, living proof that time doesn't heal all wounds, not wholly. I never tell her to stop crying. I just wait.

She blows her nose. "Eggie," she says. "I had a dream last night."

My heart sinks for us both. There's nothing I can do with dreams. I listen as she describes the color of Richie's shirt, the vein bulging on his forehead. But I'm only humoring her. I'm like those Harvard mucky-mucks who tolerated me when I would go in there with Chuckie's file, tell them about my theories. The answer was always gonna be no. *Thanks for coming by, but your kid's on the lonely end of the spectrum.* And sometimes I wished they had told me to piss off. Sometimes I think I'll tell Maddie to piss off, maybe that would help her, but not tonight. I take copious notes. I follow up with questions. This time, she dreamed that Richie came home.

"Eggie," she says. "He didn't just come home this time. Normally I hug him, you know I hold him, but this time he was cold. He gave me an envelope."

"What was in it?"

"I tried to hug him but it was like he couldn't cross over."

"Did you take the envelope?"

"There he is, my one and only, and he won't come in and he wants me to open this envelope and I want him to come in and he says the man in the envelope broke his heart."

I make a note: *broke his heart.*

"He wasn't seeing anyone at the time, was he, Maddie?"

"No," she says. "He'd broken up with Brian, Brian who didn't even go to his funeral."

Then she's crying again. It's more of a spasm, as if there are earthquakes in her heart. And then she's fine again, back to her dream.

"When I opened the envelope, there was nothing in there."

I bring things back to the physical reality, I ask her if she's gotten any strange mail over the years, but she cuts me off. "Let me finish my dream," she says. "He stole my envelope."

I put down my pen. "Who did, honey?"

"The guy who broke his heart," she says. "The man in the dream, he got to the envelope before me. I saw him running out of my house with it."

It's a painful thing, to hear yourself in another person. Maddie finishes her story and she says what she always says, *A heart doesn't just break for no reason.* I turn the light off so I can't see anything but my computer screen, so I can't see the ducks on the wall. I pick up my tea. It's cold. And then a little while later the doorbell rings. *Marko.*


Lo is always animated when her kids are here. Especially Marko; I think he has a crush on her. When I said so the other night she laughed at me. *I'm almost old enough to be his mother.* But here he is on his iPod, finding music for her. Lo thinks I'm jealous of him because he's young, and maybe I am a little envious, his goddamn able body and me, I've got a new little ache every day, a pinch in my gut. Marko, he's just so damn blond, chiseled, his ski slope face, his unnecessarily blue eyes. Any man would be annoyed. He's so *alive* and my kids are so dead.

"So, I think I have a title," he says, wiping the corners of his mouth.

Lo grins. "For your thesis? Is it 'Darkness in Light'?"

"I improved on that," he says. That's why I don't like him. A better kid would say yes, let Lo have the win. He bites his lip, white man's overbite, and he says it like he's a magician, "'The Darkness at the End of the Tunnel.'"

Lo jumps overboard, *That's eloquent and compelling.* Marko says he was inspired by something she said in class. She freezes up. He's overstepping somehow and I look at him directly for the first time. "What was that, Marko?"

He looks at her for approval but she just swallows.

"She told us about your family," he says. "The naming through generations. The men all named Charles DeBenedictus. You're young, you go by Eggs, and you're Eggs until you have a son, and then you become Chuckie and your son is Eggs, but with your situation . . ." He tucks his hair behind his ears. "It broke my heart, the notion of you being Eggs forever, no end."

Marko puts down his iPod and Lo looks at me. "Eggie," she says. "It's my smallest class, you know all the kids."

I know Lo's teaching style. I have no grounds to be wounded. "Am I complaining?"

"No," she says. "Marko honey, did you want more bread?"

And this is where I kind of *do* like Marko. He apologizes for being *so blunt.* He means it. He's a good kid. The kind of kid I wanted Chuckie to be. And I can't be mad at Lo for talking about me and our son when I haven't seen him in two years. *Two years.* And still she lets me sit at this table. I wink at her. She nods. She knows. She and Marko start talking about a band that's playing downtown next week. I eat my pasta. This is what happens when your kid is sick, you wind up with someone else's offspring, sitting down as if he's yours. He picks up on my gloom, looks at me. "I have to ask," he says. "Do you ever have to break up any fights at Lupo's?"

Lo laughs. "Thank God, no," she says. "Eggie's a detective, it's mostly paperwork. Anyway, Marko, tell us more about your paper."

I twist my fork into the pasta. "Actually, I had an interesting call about a cold case tonight."

Marko's eyes light up. It's a given with Lo's kids that they're always mining you for stories. They love to hear about our chief, Stacey, this ultimate character, a woman with *five kids* running a police force. Lo reads me excerpts of their short stories, all the different versions of Stacey. In truth, she's not very interesting, not to me, anyway.

Lo's fork drops into her salad bowl. "A cold case?"

Marko perks up. "Is this about those kids with the heart attacks, Officer?"

I nod. Lo bites her lip. I will pay for this later.

"I heard from a mother of a victim tonight. Now this might be nothing, but police work is more about your gut instinct," I say, channeling my old man. "It's about *thinking*. Imagination. It's about looking away from the autopsy report and thinking about the body. Asking the right questions. Trusting your gut above all else because that's your own little Internet right there, that's your *gut*. And the way you pore over your writing, I pore over the facts."

Lo grabs on to that word. "Facts," she says, eyeing me.

"Anyhow," I say. "It turns out that one of these kids, well, there might have been a person of interest that we didn't know about until just now."

Marko nods, he's half listening, half observing, like all of Lo's kids. I can see him using me already, knows more than he should about me. Lo has opened up to him, *My husband and his boxes. You know those boxes have gotten him into trouble? He was on probation a couple years ago because he won't let go of this theory that these deaths are related and this is the sort of thing that could cost him his job, but there he is, night after night, up there with his boxes.*

"Anyhow," I say. "It's sensitive material and I have to leave it at that."

And then we're back to talking about Marko's life, his paper, his housemates, they made up a drinking game where you have to say Nancy Ann Cianci three times fast. The three of us sit here like ding-bats, croaking, *Nancy Ann Cianci, Nancy Ann Cianci, Nancy Ann Cianci.* I watch Lo. I wonder how much trouble I'm gonna be in after dinner.

After we finish and clear the plates, Marko unplugs his phone from the charger. He yawns, faking it. "I guess I should be hitting the road."

Lo grabs his arm. "You can't leave without dessert," she says, she's never ready for good night. "Do you like brownies, Marko?"

"Love 'em," he says, and that's my cue.

I pop the brownies in the microwave and listen to Lo and Marko discuss a documentary Lo has to see on Netflix. I watch the frostbite melt on the brownies. Marko laughs at something Lo said. She smiles because it feels good when you tell a kid a story and the kid reacts. I wish Marko were my son. I wish my son were Marko. The brownies go round and round and I wish Maddie had been calling about anything other than a goddamn dream.

"I'm not mad," Lo says. "Are you mad?"

"Of course not."

"I'm just looking out for you, Eggie. It's just not smart. It's one thing if I tell a vague story about us, about you, but you're on thin ice when you tell these kids about specific cases. You know, what if Marko goes home and writes about one of your cases? He writes about a heart attack and it gets back to a family and the family calls Stacey. Then you're out of a job."

"I know."

We settle into the bed and we try to get close to each other but we're tired and we're off. We put on a movie—*American Splendor*—and we sit there in the glow of the TV like kids staying up past their bedtime. We're both forty-nine. We're both from Rhode Island. We both fell in love with this house because it's weird and we like weird. We both feel a strong sense of civic duty and actively use the library and the post office to ensure that our neighborhood remains just that. We both cried when Buddy Cianci passed away, mayor, husband of *Nancy Ann Cianci*. We both rejoiced when we realized what we had found in each other, one night in a movie theater, when we went into the wrong show and nearly killed ourselves laughing, stifling our laughter, the way she squeezed my hand, that thing when there is no one else on earth whose laugh could fuel you, whose hand could hold you. We're both inherently grateful people. *A cop and a teacher,* Marko will probably write in a story one day, *servants with imagination, a more compatible couple you could not find.*

She's eyeing me. "You're so quiet, E."

"I'm just thinking."

She hits pause. I prepare for the lecture, *You and Your Boxes.* She sighs.

I stare at the TV, Harvey Pekar. He and his wife, they fell into a child, adopted a girl, a grown girl.

"Eggie, you know I don't want to lecture you."

"Lo, I know." And Lord do I know that the odds are against me. Every autopsy is conclusive. Aortic rupture. Their hearts broke the way some hearts do and it's bad luck that they should all go in my territory. Me with my overactive imagination. My gut and my boxes.

"But honey," she says. "Sometimes, it's just about one little step."

I look at her. I wait.

"We could get out of the bed and get in the car, we could drive to Bradley."

Chuckie. All this time she's been thinking about Chuckie.

"You don't even have to go in," she says. "We could just sit in the parking lot."

When she puts the movie back on, I send a text to Maddie. *I was thinking about your dream, might be worth having another look at his email account. The thing about these cases, you think you've looked at everything, but sometimes you go back, it all looks different to you.*

She writes back a couple minutes later: *Sorry Detective, and a big thank-you for being there for me in my crazy moments. I had a good visit with my sister and her kids, I'm calmer now. No more paranoid calls from me, I promise. I know you have real cases to solve. Sorry again.*

I put my phone away. I never feel calmer. I wonder what that's like.

# JON

This is where Yvonne Belziki died, right here, right on Dorrance Street.

I had only been here a couple days and I was walking around, circling a nightclub called Lupo's Heartbreak Hotel. That's what I did to Noelle. I broke her heart. I was sure of it. I was sweaty and overheated after she died, as if I had used my own hands to reach in there and twist her arteries, shredding them until my knuckles were raw, red. I hadn't meant to do it. I would never do that to anyone. But I had done it.

I'd been trying to understand what Noelle did that caused my body to flare up like that. But it wasn't fair to blame Noelle. I killed her. Me. I hated it when people blamed my mother's "loose parenting style" for what Roger Blair did to me. You can't blame the victim. You blame the kidnapper, the murderer.

And now I was the murderer, like it or not.

Noelle did not deserve to die.

And then, one day, right here on Dorrance Street, there she was, though I didn't know her name, *Yvonne Belziki*. I liked every part of her—her legs, her fingertips, all of her—and it wasn't a Chloe kind of love. She just looked full of goodness. She smiled at me, and it was contagious. I hadn't made eye contact with anyone since Noelle died. But I looked at Yvonne and thought, *Things can get better.* Her eyes latched onto mine and I should have run then, should have looked away, because my heart was pumping in a way it hadn't since Noelle died. I should have run. Instead I froze, a venomous deer in headlights. And for the first time I really listened, and I could hear the change in me, as if Roger had rewired my insides, added a circuit system between my emotions and these invisible bullets bursting out of me.

Yvonne went fast, maybe even faster than Noelle.

I tried to do a better job of keeping to myself. I only walk at night, no eye contact, no chance of anyone getting to me. Sometimes I get paranoid and swear someone is following me, and those nights I go straight home, where I'm safe, and so is everyone else.

I focus on my plan. I can't find Roger Blair, no one can, but I try. I do my research, I concentrate on the science of it, read about Blair, his other experiments, the guy he worked with at Brown, *Dr. Terence Meeney*. If I can figure out what he did and how he did it, maybe I can fix it. Science could blow your mind, chemistry, in particular, with the codes and the numbers and the potassium, the chloride.

And when I can't take the equations anymore, I step away from all the long, unwieldy words in the bio books and move over to the long, unwieldy words in the Lovecraft books. *Cthulhu. Necronomicon.* After all, there's no denying that I'm a monster. And maybe the key is learning how to tame these powers. (I hate that word.) I read about Lovecraft the writer, the letters he wrote to his friends, his stories, but everything is cycles, seasons, and sure enough, after a few days of *Dunwich* life, I get weary. I'm back online, in *Wired,* in *Science.*

Part of the problem is there's no name for what I am, what I do. I don't know why my mom and Chloe and my dad only fainted while Noelle and Yvonne died; the romantic part of me thinks it has something to do with love, but that feels indulgent, silly, nothing to do with science, with the heat of my jets as they take off, one heart attacking another.

Providence is the best place for me. A lot of quiet, open streets, I pace around the city the way Lovecraft did in his day. I walk and wonder, *Where is Roger Blair?* That's the only way I'm gonna figure it all out. Deep down I know it and it gets to me, the feeling that all my research, my reading, it's all a waste of time. I'll never find him, never fix it, and I can't live like this, the danger I put into the world just by walking down the street.

But then another month goes by, the college kids arrive and grow and I stay, in my same basement apartment, in my same job delivering papers for the *Providence Journal*. The thing I keep realizing is that there is no bottom of the heart, no darkest moment of your life, there is only darker, darker still. Noelle died because I was mad at her. Yvonne died because I smiled at her. Kody died because I was so upset about Carrig and Chloe. There's no end to the frustration, the curiosity, the horror that my feelings are poisonous. They have consequences for other people.

And it's maddening, it's stupid. As if the act of feeling is undesirable, as if highs and lows aren't the whole point of life, to be mad at Noelle, to be dizzy over a beautiful girl on a spring day, as if we all don't want to live at Lupo's Heartbreak Hotel.

I remember what Beverly once said about the cycle of abuse, that I shouldn't be surprised if I had thoughts about hurting someone, that it was *natural* for a victim to repeat that kind of behavior. I remember how hard I meant it when I told her that I had *no desire to hurt anyone ever*. And then the tears came, hard as the waves, harder.

My dad used to have crazy dreams. My mom would groan,

*Dreams are like exercise, no one wants to hear about it.* Now I have crazy dreams, I see all the people I killed, I try to save them but there are no clues in my useless goddamn dreams. Roger Blair's there, but he doesn't help me. He doesn't listen when I scream. He doesn't open up and explain what he did, how to stop it.

Five people and one dog. Dead. Because of me.

*Where the fuck are you, Roger Blair?*

He might be going by Magnus Villars. And I understand why he became Magnus. He had ideas that no one wanted to hear, things he could only do as another person. I'm the same way, which is why I gave up my life as Jon Bronson. I have two names now: Theo Ward and Peter Feder.

Theo Ward (a mash-up of Lovecraft's pen names: Lewis Theobald and Ward Phillips) is a normal dude, rents the basement apartment, delivers papers for the *Providence Journal*. I have an email account for Theo, but it's never that exciting.

I do all my science work under my other name, Peter Feder. Peter is for Peter Parker (*Spider-Man*) and Feder is for Lenny Feder (*Grown Ups 2*). I came up with the name on the first night of my paper route. I was so tired, so new to this place. I didn't even have a mattress. I turned on the TV, a leave-behind from the last guy who lived here. *Grown Ups 2* was on, I sat there on the floor and I laughed. I actually laughed. There were no tombstones, no Lovecraft, just these normal dudes joking around, drinking beers and jumping into quarries. There was no mystery, no unknown.

"Peter Feder" has a Facebook page where he runs a *victim advocacy group*. People think Peter is *an online bounty hunter who cannot reveal his physical identity for legal reasons*. I tell people I'm looking for Roger Blair on behalf of the Bronson boy's family (not an outright lie, I am the family, I am *Basement Boy*). And I hear from dozens of people who knew Roger, people who think they spotted him. I have pictures, war stories, former students ready to testify that he *made them feel uncomfortable.*

But I still can't *find* the motherfucker.

Roger Blair was a loner. But even people like that have to confide; everyone has someone. Roger never married, and as far as I can tell, his closest friend was the head of the biochemistry department at Brown, that Meeney guy. I actually saw him at the police station when I got out. He was a person of interest when they started looking for Mr. Blair but he was cleared right away. Shakalis said it was a no-brainer because Meeney *banned* Roger from the Brown campus. I remember him on the local news, outside of the station, almost smiling, *You allow adults to be near children with minimal vetting and you want to point at me?* I don't think he's in cahoots with Roger, but I know he has to know something. They were close until they weren't. People who know you, they know your places. Same way Chloe and I had the shed.

Roger and Meeney were research partners. They were on this Animal Planet show *The Machiavellian Life of Plants* a few times. They talked about biochemistry, this plant called the dodder vine, a parasitic weed that sucks energy—life, essentially—out of others to survive. They saw the potential for power in this and they were also interested in the photosynthetic potential in mankind. They had this idea that people could, one day, be more like plants, and sustain themselves on sunlight and soil, become a part of the ecosystem. Roger's reasoning was that with technology, we don't use our bodies as much, *we're down to eyes and fingertips.* This is where Meeney was the normal one who would audibly groan and correct his partner, *What he means is that there is more untapped energy in other parts of our bodies.*

They got a lot of grant money, but nothing ever panned out, as far as I can tell. Blair was notorious for dropping one project to start another, and the two squabbled about research ethics a lot. My dad would say they're a couple of Garfunkels with their high voices and curly hair, but Meeney's camera-ready. It's not surprising that he wound up with the job, the power. In the video with the most hits, Meeney calls Roger a *sadist* and warns the host that Roger will *hurt someone someday*. Roger Blair rolls his eyes.

People who live to know a sicko are very eager to tell you their story. There's a pride, a sense of having survived someone. I hear from people every day who knew Roger, and they all say the same thing: *You should find Meeney. He knew Roger better than anyone.*

And every day, I call. I pretend to be a student, a professor, a reporter, but it's always the same.

*Dr. Meeney suggests you visit during his office hours. Dr. Meeney is preoccupied with research at the moment. Dr. Meeney does not speak with reporters.*

If I wasn't poison, I could go to him during his office hours. Of course, I think about blowing my cover, *I am Jon Bronson, the guy who was kidnapped by Roger Blair and I think Dr. Meeney can help me.* But I don't trust him; look how he treated Roger, his best friend.

Look at him now, talking to a girl in front of the Dean Hotel, they were drinking, eating. The girl is not his wife, and who knows if he's *sleeping* with her, but his smile is for her, his hand is on her elbow. I follow him every day, trailing him on the way home, where he kisses his wife, his dog. He's so available, I could knock on his door, stop him when he's emerging from his biweekly squash games at the campus gym, tap him on the shoulder.

But I can't do that without the risk of killing him.

What I can do is what I do every night at this hour. I pick up my papers and start my shift. My favorite part is Hope Street. There's a girl who lives in this old Victorian. *Crane Comma Florie.* That's what I call her in my head, the way her name looks on her paper. Her car is plastered with bumper stickers: KEEP PROVIDENCE WEIRD, HUGS NOT HORNS. It's like she's trying to talk to the world with her little red sedan, hoping somebody beeps back.

I've never met her before, but last Christmas she gave me a pair of gloves with a special finger fabric that lets you text.

*So you can stay in touch while you help us stay in touch.*
*Merry Christmas, Theo*

I kept the card. It's on my fridge. Most people don't give you anything at all. So I do nice things for her. When it rains I double bag her paper. I use two twist ties.

When my shift ends, I park by the Brown chemistry building. I like watching it come to life. Meeney meanders down the street with his travel mug and I can't see him once he swipes his card and enters the building, but soon enough he appears in his window on the second floor, at his standing desk, where he stretches his arms above his head and starts his day, which always includes ignoring me. Still, I try.

His assistant, Patty, answers. She's new this month, but we already have a rapport. When I say hello she sighs, exaggerated for my benefit. "Peter, you know what I'm going to tell you."

"But I have a good feeling, Patty. I just need two minutes."

She puts me on hold and I watch as she goes to Meeney, as he waves her out of the room.

"He's in a meeting," she says, and then she lowers her voice, asks me when I get back from Stockholm. I forgot that I told her I'm on *a semester abroad*. It was my explanation for why I can't visit him in person. The sun is getting stronger and the streets around me swell with students.

"Patty," I say, pleading. "I'm not a reporter, I'm just a psych student and a victim advocate. We just want to ask him a few simple questions."

"I know," she says. "And I'm telling you, Meeney *would* help you if you walked into this room. He doesn't speak publicly about Roger Blair but we all know how he feels and I *know* he would come through." She sighs. "Peter," she says. "He's that type, you just have to see him face-to-face, you know?"

When I get home there's a box waiting for me out front. I climb down the stairs into my hovel and tear into the package. It's a hat I ordered. I forgot all about it, a baseball cap with three words sewn onto it: *I am Providence*. That's what it says on Lovecraft's tombstone.

I put on my new hat and I put on *The Middle*.

The wanting overwhelms me, the way it does sometimes. I hit the mute button and I feel my heartbeat quicken as I dial her number. I know I shouldn't. I know she's moved on. She's in New York. I could kill her if I walked up to her, if I saw her, if she saw me. I have to stay away from her until I'm fixed, I have to stay away from everyone. But sometimes you need someone. Sometimes it's enough to call my parents, I only stay on for a minute—it's too hard to hear their voices—but the last time I called, my mom said *we haven't heard from her in ages*. Time changes people.

She picks up.

"Jon," Chloe says. "Is that you? Please talk to me. You don't have to tell me where you are. It's me. I'm alone."

I lose my body to my distorted heart, the thing that keeps me alone, alive. It's like my dream, where her paint runs through my veins, her breath is in my lungs. I'm lost in her voice, so lost that I don't realize it when I unmute the sound on my TV. And TV is louder during commercials, especially this one, an earworm jingle for a furniture store downtown. *Alex Interiors will come to your home. Shopping is tough. Alex Interiors, you're never alone.*

# CHLOE

I Googled Alex Interiors while we were still on the phone.

It's a chain of furniture stores in Rhode Island. There are four of them in the Providence area. And now I know for a fact that Jon is in Providence, that he didn't want me to know. He hung up when he knew I could hear.

And now I can't sit still. I'm pacing around my apartment, pulling at the curtains, looking out the windows. He does this every once in a while. Tonight, I picked up on the first ring.

"Jon," I said. "Is that you? Please talk to me. You don't have to tell me where you are. It's me." I held the phone like a seashell. "I'm alone."

I'm never far from my phone because every time might be the time he finally talks to me, the time he tells me why he ran, where he went. I've made my life an open book for him. My address, my phone numbers, my website giving advance notice of every move I make, every show. I think of that word. *Feed.* I've tried so hard to feed him; everything is an invitation, *Come home, Jon, come back.*

And now I'm reading about Providence. There's a Tenley's in that city. My heart beats.

This is why I've never had a boyfriend, because of these nights wondering, hunting. I've put myself out there, I've had my flings, my flirtations, but I've never been able to make things stick with any other guy. They feel me drifting and they never want to stay the night. I always kiss them goodbye, whimpering, *I'm married to my art.* They don't come back. Which is fine.

They know I'm not available, it's a thing you can feel. I'm buoyed to this process, the search, the wonder.

My freshman roommate in college thought I was nuts. She said so to my face. *You can fry your brain if you keep the phone on your pillow.* When that didn't work, she sent me articles about how phone chargers and bedsheets can lead to house fires. I lived alone the following year. And then in my senior year, that reporter from *The New Yorker* called about a *where-are-they-now* story on missing kids. I told him I didn't know where Jon was. They wanted to put one of my paintings on the cover. I said yes. And then my life became what it is now.

I'm an artist. I really am. I'm not a struggling painter and I'm not a paralegal who takes sculpture classes in her spare time. I make money doing what I love, and it's a wonderful thing, an obnoxious thing, always waiting for the knock on the door, *There's been a mistake, this isn't your life.* And then there's the reality of how I got where I am. Because of him. Because I missed him. I missed him and I drew him and it could very well be that my art wouldn't have hit without my story, our story, the one I told to so many reporters.

I could call his mother and tell her about Alex Interiors, but she hates me. She's called me a vampire and a parasite, an exploitative hack. *You made a profit off my son's tragedy.* My cheeks burn. My heart races. All the memories. How hard I tried to help. How many flyers

I posted all over town, online. The pictures I drew of him. I still draw him on his birthday. I've sent a portrait to his parents every year since he vanished. I took a goddamn class on police sketches so that I could better imagine him now, older, how a nose changes, how skin sags. Last year when I paid to run an ad in the *Globe,* she huffed, *Well, you must be doing well with your art, having that kind of cash to throw around.* It stings. And she's not the only one to make that accusation, but she never liked me and I know there's a little truth in there. I hesitated over the years, I worried that there was something inherently corrupt about my whole life. But that's true of everyone, everywhere.

There's Jon's father. I could call him. But I know it's a waste. He never recovered from the first time around. When I think of him, I still see him in the woods, drunk, singing his old songs, preparing for his son to be gone because it's easier than hoping he's coming home.

I could call Alexandra, my assistant, the person I pay to groan at me, *Chloe, don't read the comments. Chloe, you gotta put your phone down. Chloe, you need to get out.* She's cool. Literally. Her hands are always cold. Not an obsessive bone in her body. I can't call her right now, I don't want to wake her up. I also don't want a rational, cool girl telling me that it was probably a wrong number.

It was him. I know it.

I lie down on my bed. *Providence.* Sometimes I think it's my fault. I say too much when he calls. I feel too much, it's like I'm being pulled underwater and I cringe when I hear myself say his name, my voice turning like milk in the fridge. He was missing when we were kids, but this is different. This time he left. I'm the missing person. That's what I do all night, all day. I miss him. He's in my skin, my sleep, the unfinished feeling, the wonder.

But now I have a clue. *Alex Interiors will come to your home. Shopping is tough. Alex Interiors, you're never alone.*

I pour a shot of tequila. I mark his call in the notepad on my phone.

The first time he called was the month after Noelle died. I was still reeling, staring at her Dartmouth pen every day, feeling the bite marks. The two people I knew best were gone, ripped away. I wondered if I was cursed, indulged in this dark fantasy of me, the poisonous one. And then my phone rang, as if he was reading my mind, as if he knew I needed him. It was 2:45 A.M.

"Jon," I said. "I know it's you."

He hung up right away. There's no pattern, no way to make sense of his calls. The timing isn't romantic. He's doesn't call on my birthday, on Christmas. This is how you drive a hamster nuts in an experiment. You give it treats for no reason. At random. You don't let it learn how the system of rewards works. I look at the painting I was working on, the painting I can't even look at right now, the painting I can't finish because now my mind's on Jon.

# JON

shouldn't be calling her. And it's stupid that part of me expected her to show up in Providence, stupid that I wanted to go to Alex Interiors and wait for her. But I looked the place up online and there are four showrooms in the city and there's only one of me and beyond that, above it all, I know what could happen if I were to see her, hold her.

I'm supposed to be finding Blair, learning about what he did to me, how it can be undone. This isn't one of those stories where she and I fix things together. I was kidnapped, not her. I am poisonous, not her. I have to do this, not her.

I put on my new hat. *I am Providence.*

It would be easier to stop calling Chloe if I didn't know so much about her. I've seen her on Facebook, pictures of her, videos. I've watched her go to college, to New York. I saw her on the *Today* show after the world went crazy over her *New Yorker* cover and she became this overnight adult, this artist. And her hair got even shinier and her art was for sale. She's let me into her whole life, her apartment, the pictures she posts of random things in her kitchen. I know what her coffeemaker looks like and I know what my eyes look like from her perspective. She tells people I'm the reason she's an artist: she was drawing pictures of me for the police, trying to keep me alive with her paintbrush, her pencils. You could even say that my going away was the best thing that ever happened to her. People do say that kind of stuff in the comments of the articles about her, but other people stand up for her. *You're forgetting the fact that she clearly LOVED the guy and was drawing him because she missed him so much. It's not like she put him in the basement. Duh.* Sometimes the other people are me; I make up a fake name, I get in there.

She's not married. She doesn't have a boyfriend. She keeps all of her pages open to the whole world and sometimes it feels like that's a magic trick, that every time she looks into a camera with those searching eyes, she's looking at me, for me, wanting me to know she misses me.

After I called her, she posted a blurry photo of the moon with no caption.

I'm pretty sure that was for me. I pick up my coat. I gotta eat something that doesn't come out of my freezer. And it's finally late enough for me to be out in the world. One thing I've noticed about my power, if that's what you want to call it, it's nothing without my feelings. If I don't get worked up, agitated or excited, if I'm chill, then I can do things like get a snack, go for a walk. People in the middle of the night are mostly mellower, they're tired, they keep to themselves, they don't look at you if you don't look at them. And if one of them *does* look at me, if I do start to feel something, anything, then I know by now what I have to do.

I have to run. Fast.

I forgot about Thirsty Thursday. College kids get wasted at the bars and the parties and then they want falafel. They're all so together, in heaps. I remember thinking I'd go to college and be in a heap of people, and it's weird to see the heaps, the madras shorts, the BROWN CREW windbreakers, and know that Roger or no Roger, this never would have been my life.

I walk slowly. I keep my head down in a crowd and pretend to be doing things in my phone, like some random guy would. In the note-pad part of the phone, I write to Chloe as I walk inside.

*What's up nothing just waiting for falafel I couldn't help it you know when you gotta have it you gotta have it haha how are you?*

Because my head is down I don't see the guy. I bump into him or he bumps into me, I don't know how it begins, whose fault it is. I only know that he drops his falafel, *splunk,* and the sauce spatters. He screams. *Fuck.* His shorts are plaid and his legs are long and his eyes are wide and he smells like beer spilled on a floor and then attacked by a mop. I bend over to pick up the falafel but he kicks it like a soccer ball. "The fuck is your problem, you pussy? You walk around with your head in your phone walking into people, the fuck is wrong with you?"

My heart is starting to tick in the bad way and his friends are gathering and there are too many people, so many people.

"Sorry," I mumble and put my phone in my pocket. Burger King has a drive-through. I can go there. I should go there. I will go there. I start to walk but he pushes me.

"The fuck do you think you're doing, phone boy? You just walk in walk out."

"I'm sorry."

He mocks me. *"I'm sorry."*

Some of his friends laugh and some have their phones out and a girl slings her arms over a guy's back. I have to leave. My heart is involved and I know what will happen if I don't leave now. I say I'm sorry again and I start to walk but he grabs my shoulder. *No.* His hand is too big and strong and he won't let me go and his friends want him to calm down. They say his name, he has so many names, *Krish* and *Potter* and *Swain* and *Krish-P* and *Krish-P Kreme,* and he is spitting at me, swearing at me. I try so hard to calm down, I say my sorrys and every time I go for the door he stops me. His hand. His big hand. There is a wall of madras and spandex and shiny windbreaker material and I can't get through it and my heart is on fire.

The first blow is to the back of my head and I hit the ground hard. There is screaming and giggling, all the nervous sounds, scared sounds, some people want this and cheer and others are afraid. The falafel guy at the counter, he's calling the police and I can't move, I hear my ribs *crink* and my face *splooch.* I smell my own blood as he turns me over. Punches me in new places now, my cheek, my chest. Telling me this is real life *not your phone you piece of shit.* I try to stop my heart before it can stop his. His friends try and pull him off me and they can't. I can't. They can't. Oh no. *No.*

Alarms sound all over my body and my heart churns, oh no. I think of Krish as a kid, a kid I would have wanted to be friends with, even as he punches me in the ribs, *crink.* I think of him as an old man deep into the future. But my heart beats faster and blood leaks from my cheeks, split open. He knees my groin.

By now I know what it feels like when my heart takes over. The earthquake inside when the jets fly out of me and they zoom into him and he can't punch me anymore. His nose bleeds, his eyes freeze up, and only I am close enough to hear the death rattle, the breath caught in his throat as he stops breathing, stops living, sinks onto my body, *thunk.* He is dead. I know it and nobody else knows it yet and I am stronger by the second, I can hear my ribs reconnecting, feel my skin resealing, a fast-forward video of a scab, healing. *You have power. You're welcome, Jon.*

There is screaming now as people try to figure out what happened, as if I stabbed him, as if I did something.

I tried to leave. I did.

The heaps of people come to save him because he is the friend and I am the alone guy, the random guy that nobody knows, scrambling to my feet. I am healing up so fast, the fastest rewind you can do and I have to get out before the madras people realize what I did, what seems impossible, what should be impossible. To kill someone without a knife, without a weapon, without a fist even, to kill someone with your insides, your *heart*. This is mean magic; my body took his energy and used it to pull my skin back together, to line up my ribs.

I back away from the heaps of people, the screaming and the crying and the swarm of plaid, the love, the squeak of their jackets and the shrieking, and there is a girl and she's gonna ask me if I'm okay. I can feel it, feel her eyes, her wonder.

I have to go. Now. I grab my phone, my hat. *I am Providence.*

It doesn't matter what I meant to do. It only matters what I did.

# EGGS

It's almost three when I hear Lo up and puttering. It sends my whole body into high alert.

I don't know how anyone gets through life alone. If she died, I'd be dead straightaway. We'll be those people you read about where one goes, the other goes within seventy-two hours. She'd be okay without me though. If I croaked, she'd keep teaching, keep going to events, keep buying coffee. I think that might even be why we're such a good fit. Someone's gotta be the iceberg and someone's gotta be the sun. She's walking up those stairs, not charging, this won't be a fight.

She yawns in the doorway, beautiful. "Your phone's ringing, Eggie," she says, handing it to me.

If I was forty instead of pushing fifty, I might silence the phone and make a move, stop her on her way back downstairs. But sometimes when you're fifty, it's enough to know what you'd do to the woman in your life. You don't necessarily have to do it.

With a sigh, I answer the call. "DeBenedictus," I say into the phone.

It's Joann, the night dispatcher. There's an incident on Thayer Street. A call to arms. I always feel guilty leaving Lo, but she will nestle into the sofa, she has her kids, her papers.

Downstairs, her eyes follow me to the unnecessarily wide entrance to our home, the kind of hallway that requires a response from people because they immediately feel thrown off by the expansiveness. *Imagine living there, imagine they thought they'd have all these kids, ugh, next time they're coming to our place, not so depressing.*

"Now where are you off to?"

"A frat boy dropped dead on Thayer Street."

"Brown kid?"

"Yeah, apparently there was a whole to-do."

"Sounds like drugs," she concludes. I pick up my gun off the table, my piece that would be locked up if we had a kid.

I feel a little guilty about being so excited to leave. Ever since the business with Chuckie, it feels like the job description changed. I used to get a call and think, *God no* a dead body, an awful thing, some tragedy, something bad. It's a funny thing, what changes when your life changes. The split second of gratitude that someone *else* got fucked over, knowing that this time around I just might be able to make a damn difference, find some goddamn justice, make sense of things, get the goods, answers, peace, *righteousness*.

"Be careful, Officer." She winks at me, a little jab at Marko.

In the car on the way to Thayer Street, I'm at ease, humming even, thinking about what it would be like to be on my way to Bradley. And the mere thought is enough to throw me. I run a stop sign. Someone beeps. *Fucking asshole.* Yep.


You always want a witness like Romy O'Nan. Pragmatic, in the scene but outside of it—she's the coxswain on the crew team, which means she's about a foot shorter than everyone else, inherently ostracized, observant. And she had a crush on the deceased, so she was watching him like a hawk. She doesn't say it, doesn't have to. I can see it in her eyes every time she looks over at the body, back at me. Romy wanted a chance with Krishna Pawan, senior, rower, God, and now she's not going to get it. You forget about death, how it kills other people's dreams. As she said when I got here, *Me and Krish talked a lot tonight, more than we ever had, I still can't believe this, like that this happened now, on this night of all nights. It's not fair. I know how stupid that sounds. And I know I'm in shock. But I mean . . .*

People are human and humans are selfish. We have to be. Little Romy, she just meant that she thought she was gonna get this guy in the sack tonight. Not that he'd stay, she's smart, a squeaky thing, freckled, lonesome, but she thought she was gonna have a night. It's easy to imagine her older, with someone more like her, forever longing for *that night with Krish*.

"A heart attack?" she asks. Again. The other kids are bawling and hugging each other, but Romy sticks by me, makes her feel closer to the vic, like she's his person. Other kids, they got what they wanted out of him and they can wail, moan, they can mourn. Romy wants more.

"Romy," I say. "If it's any consolation, this is a horrible, freakish thing that happens. You know, I've seen four kids like Krish, maybe not *quite* as young, but young, twenty-two, twenty-four, seen them all die suddenly for no reason."

She shakes her little head. "No, but Krish is an *athlete*."

I nod. I know the script. "He probably had a heart condition."

"He didn't," she says. "He was ridiculously healthy."

"Nobody's immune."

"No," she says. "This is insane. This is not happening."

"I know how it feels," I tell her. "But this is the problem with the human body. It lets you down, one way or another. My dad always said the only guarantees in life are death and taxes."

"Did you *look* at him?" she asks. "He was in *perfect* health."

The same way they describe some people as being larger than life, Romy is smaller than life, drowning in an oversized windbreaker. The way mothers call their daughters their *mini-me*s. That's what I'd call Romy, a mini-me, there's gotta be a bigger version out there, life-size. She keeps on that Krish was special. He was gonna be in the Olympics. Gently I ask if there is any chance he'd taken anything harder than a shot of Fireball tonight. She gets teary. "We literally just bonded over how we've both never done coke," she says. And then she starts crying.

The last few heart attacks were different, smaller crowds, quieter streets, the dead people, they weren't in college, they weren't gonna be in the Olympics. The other heart attacks I've seen in the past few years, the young ones, the people weren't *special*.

Well, Yvonne Belziki, but I can't go thinking about her again.

All of the heart attacks, they were fine, like anyone, all of us plopped onto this planet with crummy hearts, hearts that break in the end no matter what you do. Romy's just not old enough to realize that. Until tonight she thought death was for *grandparents and gold-fish*. She blows her nose. I tell her she can take all the time she needs. My job is like any quest in life. You get the best story from the person who wants to talk, not the one who *has* to talk.

And now she's ready, all business. "Okay," she says. "The first thing you should know, tonight only happened because of *Ellen*."

Romy explains that Ellen is an *art fuck* who goes to RISD. She and Krish were dating, seriously. Earlier today Krish found out Ellen was cheating on him with *another art fuck, also from RISD*. Romy says Krish was a wreck. "We got together to party and take his mind off it," she says. "And it was working. We got a keg and we played Beirut, he was okay. But then this hipster dick, you know, the type with a *beard* and a hoodie and a hat, ugh, he walks in, totally oblivi-ous, barges into Krish."

"Did you know this guy with . . . the beard?"

The words click with me right away, *the beard*. I write them in my pad for no reason other than that thing in your gut, that voice that says *the beard*.

Romy says nobody knew the hipster. I ask if Ellen might have known the Beard and she rolls her eyes. "The guy she's been cheating with is the other kind of RISD art fuck, the *bald skinny guy*. This guy was huge."

I write it down: *huge*.

"And then Krish snapped," she says. "He just started beating the guy."

"The guy fight back, the Beard?"

She shakes her head.

"Did the bearded man provoke him in any way, verbally, at any point?"

"No," she says. "Which is actually weird, because the guy *was* big. Not Krish big but you know . . . he just took it. Like a lump." She starts to cry again and I lie to her again, *It's okay honey, it's okay*. It isn't. It isn't. She wipes her eyes. "Look," she says. "Ellen literally broke Krish's heart. That's the only way I can believe that he had a *heart attack*."

She cries harder, she wasn't in his heart, not the way she wanted to be, his heart that isn't beating anymore. "Honey," I say. "You've been wonderful and we can get you home now."

"Wait," she says. "The hipster guy, is it possible he like, stabbed Krish or poisoned him? Like some James Bond thing, some pen weapon."

I pat her on the back. This is also par for the course. Everyone wants to play *Let's pretend someone is to blame, someone besides God or Mother Nature*. "No," I say. "Romy, the EMTs are certain that this was heart failure." I say the words I've had so much trouble believing myself.

"But it was so sudden."

"As it is sometimes."

A *clang* over by the coroner. "Jesus," Romy says. She's never seen any of this, never seen a person become a body. I promise her this is normal. The waves, the tears. You don't accept a death all at once. "It's an awful thing, hon. You take it as it comes."

She thanks me and I'm helping her. Sometimes I think I would have been a good father. I offer her a lozenge.

"Thank you," she says. She pops it in her mouth. "Oh!" She wrestles the lozenge with her tongue. "One more thing about the guy." She holds up a finger. "I am Providence."

"Who is Providence?"

"That's what it said on his hat," she says. "'I am Providence.' Can you think of anything more narcissistic to put on a hat? I mean screw you, guy, you're not *Providence*. You're walking around in a haze with your head in your phone. Krish. *He* was Providence."

Her voice trails off, and then more tears. I scribble the words in my notepad: *I am Providence.*

"Where did this guy go? Did they get him in a bus to a hospital?"

She shakes her head. "I have no idea. He just disappeared."


There is no case. This was a heart attack. We get the security footage and Romy described it to a T. The Beard is lost in his phone, oblivious. He bumps into Krish. Krish goes berserk. He pounds on the Beard. Until Krish clearly goes into arrest. People swarm, and the Beard slinks away, for the most part his hat blocks his face. But who wouldn't get outta there? All that madras, all that noise. The Beard probably figured he caught a break, slinked off to one of the local hospitals to get his wounds licked.

But then I call the local hospitals. I call all of them. The campus infirmaries. I call every CVS, every pharmacy. Nothing. No Beard.

I watch the video again, but there is nothing there either. No clue about the Beard.

I go to Stacey, Stacey, who's seven months pregnant, tearing the lid off a yogurt. I tell her about the video, the kid Krish beat up, how he's nowhere to be found. She eats her yogurt with that stupid plastic spoon they stick at the top. She has a metal spoon right there on her desk.

"Krish had a heart attack," she says. *Declares.* That's the word.

"While beating the hell out of this kid. Gave the kid a cracked rib, at the very least, a broken nose."

She licks the lid of her yogurt, as if it's so delectable, as if it isn't just yogurt. "Eggie," she says. "Krish was an Ivy League Olympic contender. A *good* kid. This kid you can't find, hanging around Thayer Street. He's probably a dealer. A *bad* kid."

I make a mental note: *a dealer.*

She glares at me. "But he's not our problem and he didn't throw a punch." She glares harder, a mother, a *mom.* "Krish is a good kid, Eggie. We're not gonna go making him bad, trying to look for a connection that isn't there."

An hour later I still want to know what happened. I get like this. It's the cop in me, the true detective. Stacey is in this to protect and serve but I am a bloodhound. Like Lo tearing through one of her books, wanting to get to the end, I am the same way. I have to know what happened.

*I am Providence.* It sounds like the kind of thing some shit-for-brains politician would say if he was trying to get elected. I write down all my young kids, the ones whose hearts gave out on them. I wonder, did they know the Beard? And that's when it's time to go home, when I need to go upstairs to my office, when I start to wonder.

# JON

I didn't have a nightmare last night. I don't even remember dreaming. Not having the nightmare is worse than all the nightmares combined. It means I'm getting used to this.

I tear the sheets off the bed and shove them in the washing machine. Then I go online to punish myself with all the stories about Krishna. It's a relief that it hurts my soul, that I'm crying, that the pain is a dagger, the guilt. He was a *good* fucking guy. He was the oldest of three kids, Seat Four on the Brown University crew team. He loved Harry Potter. His friends called him *Krish Potter, Krish-P.* He was Harry Potter every Halloween, this giant guy in these little glasses and this cape that's not big enough.

The *New York Times* talks about him being a minority on the water and the *Pro Jo* praises him, he was *good for our city.* His parents are said to be *broken* and he's never alone in any of the pictures unless it's part of a joke, like he's standing by a statue of a bear, posing. He was gonna win us some Olympic medals. In this fucked up way that I can't even wrap my head around I didn't just kill a person, I killed America.

I check my Peter Feder mail and there's a form letter response from Lynn Woo, a Lovecraft expert I found online.

*Hi Peter,*

*I wish I could respond to all inquiries personally, but I'm on the road right now. As you might suspect, I'm sharpening my talons for NecronomiCon in Providence, where I'd be happy to answer your questions. Tickets are on sale now.*

*Cthulhu you there,*
*Lynn*

I throw my sheets in the dryer. How can I go to the convention? There are so many people. I can't control my powers. And unlike Wilbur, I blend in. Lovecraft went on and on about how *weird* Wilbur was, chinless and pale, growing too fast. And that's fair. The townspeople were right to be suspicious, wary. The playing field is leveled when you can identify your enemy, when you can protect yourself. Everyone could look at Wilbur and sense that something was dangerous about him, off. But I look like a hipster who eats bacon and has a girlfriend and a bunch of plaid shirts and plans on Friday night. I could have a Twitter profile with retweets, a hangover from cheap beer, and tickets to a sweaty concert where I'd bounce so close with all the other sweaty people. You look at me, you assume I have ex-girlfriends and pictures of me doing stuff with these girls, picking apples out near Johnston, going to the old movie theater on Thayer Street, pushing our way through all the people to the bar at Paragon to get drinks and talk about the movie and laugh and then go for falafel because we're drunk and we need to eat before we have sex.

*Sex.*

My dryer buzzes. I take my hot sheets and wrap them all around me. I think this is how sex would feel. The other body would be hot and it would be like a blanket touching you in all different places. The warmth of another thing.

I call Chloe and I get her voicemail. It's just as well. I don't deserve the sound of her voice, not today.

Sometimes you can't win, but the second I get better, I'll tell her everything. I'll apologize for being such a douchebag, my mixed messages, for disappearing. I'll be the person I am, the person I was before he took me, a good person. And I'll never be that person if I don't do everything I can to try to find a cure.

It's the sick truth of what Magnus said, *We did good work down here, Jon.*

I may not like the work, what he did, but he worked hard, he did it. He made me this way. And now it's my turn.

*Ya gotta try.*

It isn't safe to go to Lovecraft, but it wasn't safe to cut through the woods all those years ago. You don't win without risk.

# CHLOE

There's a crack in the ceiling and an old couple bickering about a pillow-top mattress. It's my third Alex Interiors in one day and it's the smallest yet, there's no chance he's here. There's no clearance section, no walk-in closet where fabrics hang like skirts.

Another salesman approaches. "How are you today, miss? You dreaming? You browsing?"

I tell him it's a little of both and he says he can help me. "But I'm not a helicopter," he says. "You want my help with something, I'm right back there in the chair."

He can't help me. No one can. But I do the same thing in this store that I do in the others. I test sofas. I pretend to be shopping, to be interested in the foam cushions, the available fabrics, the delivery time. I might be having an actual nervous breakdown as I sink into a clunky leather sectional. I didn't feel so crazy when I decided to come here, when I was in Penn Station running like a girl in a movie, exasperated, shoving my credit card into the machine, buying a one-way ticket to Providence.

I knew it was only a commercial. I knew there were four furniture stores. But then it hit me. *He knows I know.* So it made sense that he might be waiting at one of these stores, that it was on me to come here. Sure, I've been leaving a trail of breadcrumbs since he disappeared so many years ago. He could come find me if he wanted.

The salesman comes back with a transparent pillow. "This will give an idea of just how much you're abusing yourself with that old mattress of yours."

I sit up and nod along as he lectures me about dust mites and coils, as the old couple shake hands with the woman helping them— *I knew you kids would come together one of these days!* I wonder what it's like to be old, with your person. I have never felt so lonely in my life.

"So," the salesman says, offering his transparent pillow. "Do you wanna give this a push, see for yourself?"

An hour later I'm walking along the riverfront. They have something here called WaterFire where there are lanterns on boats. There's excitement for this, families around, college kids on mushrooms. I didn't make a plan. I didn't bring a suitcase. I don't know if I'm staying overnight. I don't know if there are hotel rooms available. I don't know what I'm eating for dinner.

The only thing I know is that Jon didn't send me on a scavenger hunt. I'm here alone.

I should have gone to a real restaurant, but it's hard to resist a Tenley's.

The waitress brings me my dinner, a jalapeño burger and a Fluffernutter frappe. "I hope you enjoy this, honey. You get to be my age, this stuff sticks to your bones."

"Thank you," I say.

"You Got It All" by The Jets comes on, the way it always does in Tenley's. It doesn't change in here. It doesn't age the way we do. The music is always the same, the burger has the same sauce, the peppers have the crunch they did all those years ago.

"Can I get you anything else?" the waitress wants to know.

I take my phone out and pull out a painting of Jon. "Actually," I say. "This is so random, but can you tell me if this guy has been in here? He would be a little older now."

She puts on her readers and squints, holds the phone away, then up close. "He's a looker," she says. "An old beau?"

I shrug, which is a weird thing to do for such a yes or no question. *An old beau.* Technically, no. She slides into the booth. Jon and I used to think this was spontaneous, that the waitresses were really caring, friendly. I remember his mom laughing at us one day, *When you go through job training there, that's on page one of the rules. They're not being friendly. That's just part of the shtick.* Jon and I decided that his mother was wrong, that the waitresses may be obligated to do this, but that they chose to work there because they *wanted* to be nice to people. My mother thinks the whole chain reeks of *sexism and heart disease.*

The waitress studies the picture. Her name tag reads PAULA. "You know," she says. "Before this I was a paralegal."

"Oh."

"Thirty-one *years*," she says. "A firm not far from here. Bigwigs. Heavy-duty stuff."

"That's amazing."

"Do you know why I quit?"

I shake my head. "No."

She reaches across the table for my hand. "Because I wanted to be happy," she says. "I wanted my days to smell like cheeseburgers and Marshmallow Fluff. I wanted to hear music and wear something comfortable and worry about *nothing.*"

I gulp. "That's really cool. To make that kind of leap."

She takes off her readers. "Honey," she says. "This is the thing about men. If they're right, then they come looking for *you*."

She pats my hand twice and slides out of the booth. I look around the restaurant. There are waitresses in all the booths, saying comforting things to people like me, gushing over kids, doling out advice to moms. I don't want his mother to be right. I don't want Tenley's to be emotionally fraudulent. When "Make It Real" comes on, I look at the door, and I expect Jon to show up. Instead, a group of guys tumble in, four of them, loud and self-conscious, amped up, full-grown man-boys high on sugar. They're completely lost in each other, in black T-shirts and hats that say *I am Providence*. And then I see more people like these guys, a man on his own, blissing out with a stack of books, all of them by the same author, *Lovecraft*. Toward the back of the room, a couple sharing a stack of pancakes, they wear matching shirts that say LOVECRAFT.

And then it hits me. *Lovecraft*.

That's what Jon was trying to get me to read when he came home, when he was so different, and now I'm searching through our old chats, all the Hippo Campus, and yes, all the Lovecraft.

*Did you read it yet, Chloe?* He meant *The Dunwich Horror*.

Usually I changed the subject. I didn't want to be in a horror book club with him. I did try to read it but I could never get into it. My feelings were hurt, and then I would feel like a stereotypical girl for *having* hurt feelings. The book wasn't my style. It was horrible and scary and dense and it wasn't a love poem. There was no parable of us in there and I was always embarrassed that I wanted there to be something like that, a me and a him, some context for what we were. My face is red, the memory is too sharp, the combination of him talking to me about Lovecraft and refusing to see me in person, how it needled me, broke me. It was sexless. It was like these boys at this booth ordering onion rings. The furthest thing from their mind is girls.

Jon would send me passages of *The Dunwich Horror* and ask me what I thought. It was like I was being tested, like he was trying to tell me something about us, that *we* were different, that I was supposed to read the right thing into the story and then, *then,* maybe he would see me. I wanted him to just come out and say what it was he wanted from me. But he never did.

Lovecraft was his thing. And if it's still his thing, then that would make these people his people. My heart races and the waitress comes back with my check. "Excuse me," I say. "Why are there all these Lovecraft fans here?"

She follows my gaze around the restaurant and she cackles softly. "It's the big convention," she says. "The Lovecraft people, we get a lot of them this time of year. And my God, let me tell you, they don't have eyes for anything but *Lovecraft*. Which is pretty ironic, if you ask me."

I give her my credit card. "Where is it?" I ask. "Where is the Lovecraft convention?"

# EGGS

The bulb in the duck lamp blew, so there's barely any light in here. It's a good omen, the universe's way of warning me, *If you're gonna do this, Eggie, if you're gonna go on another wild-goose chase, you best do it in the dark.*

I pick up Yvonne Belziki's file and I can smell her perfume. I got in trouble over her. This is where it all began, I couldn't accept that this girl was gone, she was the picture of health. Stacey cut in, *You mean youth, Eggie.* And yes, Yvonne had a look, but it was more the vitality, the sparkle. You could tell, *this is a nice person, this is a kind person.* It felt like her sparkle, the very thing that should have added something to her life, was the thing that killed her.

I had to find out if something went wrong that day. What if there was a secret boyfriend who let her down? Something we missed. It's all still here in my boxes, the files, the security camera footage on my zip drive. There she is in her summer clothes, Yvonne Belziki. She doesn't look put-upon. She looks nervous, but this is because she was going to interview for a job. She walks at a good clip and she looks over her shoulder. It's grainy, but you know lust when you see it, heat. I pause and zoom in the way I did so many times back then. The guy she's looking at is offscreen. I nearly got myself fired trying to find this guy. Was he a stranger? A boyfriend? Was he older? Younger?

Because it bumps me to this day. When she drops, the man off-screen, he doesn't barge into the frame. He doesn't come running to rescue her. He didn't stick around to be interviewed.

*Maybe you need a break, Eggie.* That was Stacey's response when I told her about my hunch that this guy might have something to do with Yvonne's "heart attack." She said to leave it alone. Instead, I started sniffing around, using my badge in the way you just can't. Stacey came into my office. This time around there was no more *maybe* in her speech. She sent me home, *a little leave, a breather.* And when I got back to work, everything was upside down. People knew that I'd been sent home. They giggled, teased me. I was the resident conspiracy theorist whack job.

It's not the kind of stigma that goes away. I know the way people look at me. But I also know that my gut won't let up. Nausea that washes over me when I think about Yvonne's feline smile, Krishna's fist, pounding. These things feel connected to me and it's my duty to honor that instinct. Good police work is math. It's also speculation. Constellations exist because someone saw them, pointed, and someone else said, *Yes, I see it too.*

I pop a cup of water in the microwave and dig into my boxes. The first one after Yvonne was Maddie's son, Richie Goleb. He was a hot-head chef, dropped out of Johnson and Wales. Maddie was in denial about the drugs, called it *recreational self-medication, all chefs have to keep on their toes.* Richie died at night, in his yard with a leaf blower in his hand. Last time I heard from Maddie, she thought he had been poisoned, *like they do in Russia.*

The next kid to go was Derry Sears. A real prize. He and his wife were regulars in the system, beating the hell out of each other, con-

stantly losing custody of their four kids. He died when he was drag-
ging the wife into the front yard. The two of them lived hard. I
remember her jagged teeth, her bloody face. I asked her if there were
any witnesses. *Hell if I know,* she said. I remember the light breaking
through the leaves. I remember thinking it's a miracle that these
trees could thrive in this hell. Needles everywhere. Diapers too.
These people die and people sigh, *Good riddance.* The end.

And Rita Bolt? She was only twenty-four. Textbook junkie on her
way into Dunkin' Donuts, she leaves her kid in a hot car. She saved
the kid's life when she died. They got off on that in the papers, but
there's no mystery. Heroin is hard on the heart.

Lo gets home, calls up to me, *You okay?* It's the scary thing about
marriage. Already she knows. She can smell it when I'm on a trail.
*Yep!*

I could stop. I should stop. I should delete the files. Instead, I
type:

POSSIBLE THEORIES FOR EARLY "CORONARY" DEATH
- Could be an illness we don't understand. A virus that goes unde-
  tected. You know the movie with Gwyneth Paltrow that disturbed
  the wife? *Contagion.* Could be something like that.
- Could be something in the water.
- Could be a drug cut with something that causes cardiac arrest.
- Could be an over-the-counter that reacts with alcohol.
- Could be laced steroids?

Lo calls. *Dinner!*

I go down there but I don't tell Lo what I'm doing. Same way I
won't tell Stacey I have a *feeling* about anything. Never tell anyone
you have a *feeling*. You can tell them about a *hunch* or an *instinct* but
you can't go around talking about your *feelings*. That was the one
question Lo asked when it was time to put Chuckie away. *Will his
feelings be hurt? Will he know?*

Their answer, the phrase they used. *We can't know.*

"Hey, Lo-Lo. You ever heard the phrase 'I am Providence'?"

She smiles. "What are you doing reading Lovecraft?"

I shrug. "Just saw it somewhere."

Lo, love of my life, Lo who *loves* Lovecraft, me. This is the part of me that gets in trouble, the part that thinks, *That has to mean something.*

"Hey," I say, all normal, like I'm Stacey, like I'm not already mapping it out in my head, making the connections. The Beard's hat said *I am Providence.* The Beard loves Lovecraft. He's real to me now, real as Krish, as Yvonne. I smack my lips. "Are we waiting on Marko or anyone or should we dig in?"

"Dig in," she says. "It's just us."


After dinner, off we go to our bedroom, where she claws at me, a different person. Screwing Lo saves me every time. It gets me out of my head. It erases everything in the world. It's a power she holds over me, with her thick thighs. She always starts by nuzzling me in the kitchen, my little animal. Then she undresses. Long ago she said she had no patience for me and my *untrained fingers* with regard to her complicated blouses, her numerous buttons, she likes buttons, won't wear any shirt unless it's covered in buttons. *Your hands only know what they're doing when they're on my body* was what she said to me that first day this plan was made. Was anything so wonderful ever said to a man, naked?

I'm down to my boxers, slipping out of my socks. I watch her on the other side of our bed, unbuttoning one shiny pink button and then another, another, imagine how Marko and the other young bucks in her class must go home and get their rocks off just thinking about what they'd do, how they'd tear those shirts of hers off, buttons flying all around. She's near the end and her breasts are out at me, her ever-softening breasts, *sagging* is what she calls it, but that's a woman for you, finding the negative. She sighs at one of the buttons, stubborn. It flashes through my mind, *What's gonna happen when she's older and arthritic?* How soon that is, what a horrible thing your body is, the way it's doomed from day one, your fate is death no matter what you do. Like Yvonne, that kid.

She whistles, nods at me below the waist. "What's down?"

I redden. "Nothing," I say. "Just thinking."

She folds her arms over her breasts. "Not about me I hope."

"God no," I say. "Hey, you know how I asked you about the phrase 'I am Providence'?"

She flops on the bed, on her side, breasts out again. She pats the bed. "Office hours are Tuesdays and Thursdays, Eggie. Three to five."

I sit down. "It was on this kid's hat."

She unzips her pants, *slacks* she calls them. "You can sign up for a fifteen-minute block on the whiteboard outside of my office or you can do it online."

"Lo," I say.

She stops messing with her slacks. She knows when to give up on me, when to ride me. I'm on thin ice, flaccid, distracted. "What is this really about?"

I can't lie to her. I stare down at my feet. I wish I kept my socks on.

"Damn it, Eggie, you can't go obsessing again."

"I'm not obsessing."

"Oh you're not obsessing? You mean to tell me you're just suddenly jacked up on *Lovecraft?* That you'd rather sit here and talk about books than get into this bed with me?"

"Lo."

"I know your face, Eggie."

"I'm sorry."

"For the last time, dear husband, people die. You're gonna die. I'm gonna die. Young people have heart attacks. It happens. Is it odd that it happens? That you would see it this much? Sure it's odd. But you know what, Eggie? Everything in life doesn't have an *answer* or a meaning. This is true in *fiction* where someone's orchestrating things. But it isn't life."

"I know that," I snap. And I do. She's right. Stacey's right. When they tell me, it makes so much sense. I can turn around and make the same argument to Romy. But when I get alone . . .

Lo lifts her head. Her brown eyes. "Are you with me?"

"Always," I say. "Yes."

I could have been having sex with her all this time. By now we'd be done, we'd be turning on a movie, maybe *A Perfect Murder*. We like that one on nights like this, sex nights. But I can't drop it.

"Lo," I say, like some college boy with a big idea. "I was just, you know, it was a tough one. And there was this kid with this hat that said 'I am Providence.' Just got in my head. That's all. This isn't me digging around trying to get to the bottom of any unsolvable problems." I should stop now. But I don't. "I swear to you, this isn't that."

But he who doth protest too much never wins, and she is on her feet, calling me out on my *stinky bullshit,* hammering at me for being unable to let go, unable to accept things as they are, looking for answers that don't exist, because sometimes *things just are what they are and you have to accept them.* She is yelling at me, yelling at herself. I forget sometimes that he was inside of her, Chuckie, that all those times I was asleep and she was awake with heartburn and rubbery feet, swollen, she had all that time with him, all that alone time. I forget that he came from us, but he came through her. He was never in me. Her pain is something I like to think of as buried, but there it is, *you fucking idiot, Eggie. You crude bastard.*

Those pathetic words spill out of me. "I'm sorry, Lo."

"There is no case." She puts on her no-sex clothes, pajama bottoms and a moth-eaten old Haven Bros. T-shirt. I follow her lead. I get into my no-sex clothes too.

"I know, Lo. You're absolutely right on every count."

"So let it go," she barks.

"I am."

She gives me a look. "You think I don't know you're up there squirreled away watching that video over and over? Rewinding over that kid in the hat?"

"Lo."

"No," she states, not giving. "We *need* your income, Eggie. So never mind what's possible for a minute here. Let us please live in the reality that we are not able to manage our expenses on my teaching."

"I know that."

She glares at me. "Good." She's pulling at her duvet. "May your penitence be your guide." She's searching for her glasses, scooting under the covers, shielded. We're not gonna have sex or watch *A Perfect Murder*. She's turning on a light, opening her book, *Seinfeldia*. She's not mad. She's sad. I messed up and because of me her mind has drifted to Chuckie, to the expenses. She's softening, which is why she is the love of my life, asking me if I want her pillow because of my back, *No thank you honey, you keep it*. She turns the pages of her book and she's not reading, not taking in the words. I can feel her mind, full of me, full of worry, she probably thinks things like, *Let your husband have his little obsessions. He doesn't get to have his son. It's the least you can do.*

She looks at me. "Well now you've got me thinking about Lovecraft."

"Is this a good thing?" I ask.

She chuckles. "This is a wonderful thing."

She's in her groove now, lecturing me about Lovecraft, *I am Providence*. That was Satan's line when he went to see Saint Anthony. "I am God and I am Providence," she booms in her teacher voice. She explains the link between the Bible and H. P. Lovecraft, who wrote the words *I am Providence* in a letter to James F. Morton. "See, listen." She tucks her hair back. "I teach Lovecraft's stories, but you can't delve into his work without reading his letters. He spent most of his life writing letters, so many letters, and he was all these different things, a recluse, a bigot, a man of letters, a creative person, a depressed person, a political person but then also, Eggie, he knew so much about the boundaries and specifics of our government, our law, the man *knew* so much, he was an adviser about so much, to so many. And he writes these letters and then he writes these stories, these wild stories, almost as if the more he knew of this world, the more driven he was to make other worlds, worlds that must have been born out of some unknowable depth of confusion. His peace with that mystery—turbulent peace, if you can imagine such a thing."

I see Chuckie, in a room, alone. I see Lo, in this room, not looking at me, looking at the floor, this is how she survives: she thinks about other things.

She clears her throat. "You know," she continues, "when he was married, he and his wife were in New York and she had to go away for work and he left her. He came back here. Back to good old Providence." She chuckles. "Lovecraft was *interested* in the world. People like him, they knew all of it, they could talk about anything and they *did* talk about everything." She runs her hand over the book in her lap. "The Seinfeldian minutiae of a trip to the store, the meaning of life, the existence or lack of a God, this is where they had us beat, you know?"

She's pointing her finger at me, I'm hard as a rock, but I keep it concealed. She needs this, this is her fire, her case.

"Sean Anders." She nods. "This kid last year, tells me he thinks reading fiction is a waste because when you read nonfiction you learn about something real and when you read fiction you learn about something someone made up."

She cackles. I want to bend her over the side of the bed, pull those damn pants off. I wish I could listen to her and be with her at once. I wish the two desires weren't two equal beasts, jaws of life, clamped.

"And Lovecraft, oh, I wish he was here. I wish he could explain to Sean Anders that from the facts come the imagined. From the imagined comes the real. Because that's what happens when you read Lovecraft's letters, letters rooted in what is, nonfiction, and then an hour later you read his fiction, wild things, things you can hardly comprehend, you think, this is *horror*. The worst that's possible, worse than what we can imagine. This one monster, *Cthulhu*, the idea is that none of us pronounce his name correctly because his name is ultimately not meant for humans, we *can't* pronounce it correctly."

*Can't.*

"And you read fiction because it reminds you, someone like Lovecraft . . ." She runs her hands through her hair. One of her nipples is hard. "Well," she says. "It reminds you that there just might be more to the world than you realize. Maybe. I mean you see a kid in a Lovecraft hat. You know why? Because the man is dead and he's still pulling us together. Like at the Biltmore this weekend, every year, there's a whole conference, people flooding here to talk about H. P. Lovecraft as if he's some kind of rock star." She laughs. Both of her nipples are hard now, bottle caps beneath the cotton. She untwists her legs and slips down, deeper into the bed, under the covers. "I guess the shorter answer would be, the kid wearing the 'I am Providence' hat, he might be at that convention. He's wearing that hat, I hope, because he gets it, or he wants to get it, that you are fate, *you* are Providence, and fate is you, but then also, so what? What the hell is *providence*? What good does that do ya? 'I am Providence' is a question disguised as a statement. It's like any faith, it's blind."

She smiles at me, the mind alive and calming smile, sideways, half-open mouth, shimmering teeth, the smile that says *come here, baby*. So I do.

# EGGS

Every time that damn door opens my whole back seizes up on me. This has to be a four-star hotel and you'd think they'd fix a door like that on a day like this, knowing there are gonna be so many people in and out, in and out.

I could stop a waiter and ask if someone from maintenance could take care of it, but I'm trying to be invisible here, blend in, and it's bad enough, the way I stand out. I can't figure out why, exactly. It's not like everyone is so young. For the most part, sure, the people here are on the younger side, but you have your fair share of over-forties too. A lot of them wear T-shirts to show their love of H. P. Lovecraft, and they mill around pointing at each other's chests, *Cool shirt, dude.* I've seen three hats that scream I AM PROVIDENCE.

But zero hats attached to a face that is bearded or bruised or both.

Which is why my neck tingles when that door opens again, *waank.* But it's just a girl, a girl with long black hair and a big fat smile. Her smile. That's what it is. It's the happiness that gets me. Sure, I've been in happy rooms. But this is different from a wedding or a retirement party. This is a bunch of people sharing happiness, feeding off each other, as if they're a bunch of vampires biting each other's necks. *Mmm, delicious!*

The door *waanks* again and I spin around. Nope.

This room, these people, are here because of *books,* and if Lo were here she'd smack me. *Of course they are, Eggie. I've told you, books save lives.*

And the plain truth about me being in here, I stand out because I'm *un*happy. I get a chill through my achy backside, as if I saw myself in a mirror, a cold mirror. I don't like it. I don't like knowing that nothing in my life makes me this happy, nothing except Lo. You're supposed to have more than a woman. You're supposed to have interests, things that make your eyes pop out of your head like this geek here, taking a picture of the placards above the coffee––OUTER GOD COLD BREW, DARKNESS DARK ROAST, UNDEAD (FRENCH ROAST)–– everything here is renamed to honor their hero, their Lovecraft.

The door again. All the hope in me zings through my veins, like some kid waiting on Santa. Two guys come in. Both too skinny and old to be the Beard, who would probably be alone, we have that much in common. But that's all, insofar as I can figure.

I know what to expect. I know his height, his weight. I know his hat. *I am Providence.* I know he'll have facial lacerations. There will be bruising. Possibly a broken nose, a black eye, maybe even two. Damn hat, damn grainy footage. But the kid will be jammed up. Maybe he'll be limping. Even if he didn't go to a clinic, he'd have to do something about his ribs. If he wrapped himself up, he'll be bulky, wearing a loose shirt.

The door again. *Come on, buddy.* I got that feeling in my gut. This is it. I smell him. A large hand. A strong leg. But then the top half, red hair, eyeglasses, another big fat smile. I sink. Nope.

The Beard might be Army. Or he might have done time. He might have been pro ball. Might have known Krish from a gym. This morn-ing I told Lo that it might be a love triangle, or he might be a dealer. Could be a situation where the Beard might know *all* my heart attacks.

"Eggie," she said. "Now you're just making up stories. Is it time for us to trade jobs?"

The door again. *Yeaan.* But even from here I can see fingertips painted, long and pointy. It's a girl. *Damn it.* She holds the door and the hope swims up in me. But then it's a chubby kid, can't be more than five-two, couldn't grow whiskers let alone a beard. *Damn it.* I wrangle a tea bag from my pocket. I plop it into a cup of hot water and slam a saucer on top and set my timer.

The woman next to me is humming, pouring coffee. "That's a lot of work for a little cup of tea."

She's smiling too, she laughs when she spills hot coffee on her hands. The guy next to her, he's offering ice, just because he's a nice guy, not even trying to get into her pants. The magic of people who want to be together, who are together, getting what they want. This must be what it's like inside a working brain. She beams at me, lifts her cup. "Here's to dancing sober."

"Excuse me?"

"Oh come on," she says. She scrolls through her phone. "Well the exact words, 'Almost nobody dances sober, unless they happen to be insane.'"

I blush. I look at the door. Nothing. It's becoming possible that I was wrong, that I misdirected my focus, that the hat is a dead end, that he doesn't even know who said *I am Providence.* That he only bought it because he liked it. The happy little woman gives up on me, moves on to another festivalgoer, *Did you see the bathrooms where instead of Girls it says Kassogtha?* The two of them drift off together and I am alone, *dancing sober.* I did not see the bathrooms and I do not see the Beard. The lights flicker. They're gonna start. Another fan comes up, little guy.

"Random," he says. "What's your favorite book? Go."

If Chuckie were okay, this is what I'd want for him, this kind of joy.

But I don't answer the question. The door opens again, slowly this time, someone who must have been out there hearing what I hear, that *yeean* screech that grinds on your nerve endings. There is a hand. A big hand. This guy is hesitant, delicate. *Yes.* I see it all at once and one piece at a time, *I am Providence* on the hat, pulled low, so low that the bill almost reaches the beard, the full beard, *my beard.* He must have two black eyes because he's wearing sunglasses, just like Romy said, *textbook hipster.*

This is why you hang around by the coffee, why you abide your gut. It's true what they say about those hipsters. They like their coffee. The Beard, he makes a beeline for the station, walking hard, tall. Ex-cop? Maybe. Drug dealer? Maybe again. I take the saucer off of my cup. I dig out the bag with my fingers. The tea is gonna be thin, not steeped all the way, but the Beard is here. He's pouring coffee into one of those reusable cups the hipsters enjoy.

I smile, the way all the happy people do. "You see those bathrooms?"

He shakes his head. Hiding behind those sunglasses. Hiding from who?

"You should see 'em," I say. "You know, they covered up MEN and WOMEN with Lovecraft words."

He pours cream. "I'll check 'em out."

Nothing in his voice. Ice cold.

"You hit any traffic on the way here?" I ask.

He shrugs. "Not really."

Evasive. Alone. The Beard. Looking around the room. I move closer to him, he moves away from me. But I'm close enough to see what he's hiding, the bruising around his left eye, blue indents, scratches. This is him. This is it.

"You remember last year?" I say, in my shooting-the-shit voice. "Last year this room was *bulging* with people. This year not so bad."

"This is my first time," he says.

"Oh yeah?"

He nods.

"You from here?"

He shakes his head. Still keeps moving away from me, ever so slightly, or maybe I'm moving in too strong. "Nope," he says.

"I'm a lifer," I say. "Born and raised."

He nods. "I moved here a little over five years ago."

The timeline fits. Just in time to poison people with some untraceable drug that doesn't show up in an autopsy, in your blood. He's cold. I can imagine him selling powder to people. I bet Krish scored some when the girl cheated on him, when he wanted a breather. Yvonne, she probably thought it was something fun, something like molly, one of the dancing drugs. Fuck this Beard. Fuck him and his poison.

I raise my cup. "Here's to dancing sober."

He doesn't look at me. "Yeah."

I catch his eye. "You look like you're looking for someone."

His eyes skate around. "Just figuring out where to sit."

"You meeting anyone here?"

He shrugs. "Just looking for a chair."

"You working?" I ask.

He looks at me. Now he gets it. Now he knows that I'm working, that I want him to know I'm working.

"Yes," I say. "Yes, I'm a cop."

He backs away, tiniest bit. "Cool."

"Is it?"

His hand is shaking. Up front there's a woman walking up to the podium. People are on their feet, hooting, clapping. The door opens and I don't hear that noise. The Beard is sweating. This is easier than I thought it would be. I put down my cup—tea's not steeped enough anyway, no loss there—and gently take the back of his arm—he's jacked, he could have fought back—and lead him to the door. Nobody notices because all eyes are on the front. All eyes except my eyes. My eyes are on him. The Beard. I tap his head. He jerks.

"Calm yourself, son. I'm just here to ask about that hat of yours. That's one hell of a hat."

You can see his heart beating like in the old Bugs Bunny cartoons. He gulps. "Thanks. I should get a seat."

But he doesn't move, he knows he can't, feels it, me.

"Sure," I say. "You remember where you got that hat? I didn't see 'em downstairs. Maybe you could show me. There's so much down there, you know, hard to know what's what."

He nods. No words left. And we're walking out the door and I ask him about his black eye. *Rollerblading,* he says.

I hit the button for the elevator. "My son rollerblades. What kind of skates you got?"

He hangs his head, silenced. We wait for the elevator. He can't answer because he's lying. I caught him. I hear the muted roar of applause inside that ballroom and a wave of nausea crushes me. It's no fun getting old, when your whole body is turning against you, I get like this a lot lately. The twinge in my gut, the feeling I might faint. Fall over.

The kid eyes me. "This is harassment," he says. "You have no grounds to be doing this."

Little shit. Cold-blooded. But of course he is. The elevator dings. I turn it on now, the big dip, the big switch. "I suggest you shut your mouth so you don't get another shiner to match the one you already got."

He didn't fight back with Krishna, and he doesn't fight back with me.

# EGGS

I was able to make the lineup happen because it's Saturday. Stacey's at a birthday party and I'm senior enough that nobody's watching me, not on the weekend. Amazing, how even in a police station you can feel it, the weekend, the desire to work a little less harder, to skate by.

I got six guys in the lineup and this could never be admissible in court. But this isn't about court. The Beard shut down on me in the car, when I cuffed him. Wouldn't tell me where he gets his shit, wouldn't say a word when I drove him by Brown, down onto Thayer, where you can't even get into the falafel place because of all the flowers.

"Any of this ring a bell?" I asked him.

Nothing. I tried again. "Did you wanna tell me how you knew Krish?"

More nothing.

"Is that what the poison is called? 'I am Providence.' Is that why you wear the hat? Or were you there because you were selling to someone? Where's your stash? Did you rip off Krishna? Do you move hard on the RISD kids? I imagine they enjoy their drugs. Goes well with their art."

Every question got more nothing. The hat. The silence. The guilt. And now it's time for something.

"Bring 'em in," I say, commencing the lineup.

The Beard walks out along with five other scuzzos I pulled in, all of them with their mangy hairy faces, all in those heavy-billed hats, the hoodies, the loose jeans. And my witness leans forward, my Romy, ever the good citizen.

"Well," she says.

"Nah nah," I say. "I want you to be quiet for a few minutes. I want you to *look*. Not react. Not yet. You just *look*."

What I've learned so far today is that Romy is a philosophy major (God help me) with an *Addy* prescription and a paper due. She talks a lot. She was dying to come in here because she loves *real life* and she's *like a lost kitten* since Krish died. See how people do that? How they make someone into something? Romy forgets that I know it all, how close they were, how close they weren't. But when she got here, she was wearing a men's crew sweatshirt, drowning in it, as if it was hers to wear, as if he was hers to mourn.

She wants so badly to be the hero, the bereaved savior who overcomes her red eyes to bring justice to Krishna. She wants it so bad she can't put that fever aside and *think*. She's posturing, an actress waiting to make her entrance. She told me she read a lot about the justice system and she's hesitant to rely on her own eyes, subject, as they are, to her *sentimentalizing the incidents at hand*. I told her to put her faith into herself as well as the system.

She talked over me, about the nature of observation and perception, her hesitance to *assume a participatory role in justice without comprehending the extent of my contribution*. I promised her that this is way too early for consequences.

"Romy," I say, lowering my voice. "You are one witness and this is all very preliminary and your identifying this man isn't enough. So don't worry. What you're doing here today is helping me out. You don't have the power to put anyone away. Now . . . which one is he?"

She sucks in her cheeks. "Well," she says. She holds that air in, kills me, puffs it out. "Well, he's not here."

"Romy, take a minute."

"I would know him if I saw him. I would *know*."

"As you yourself said earlier, your memories are colored by your emotions."

"Right," she says. "But that has nothing to do with the fact that he's . . . not . . . here. He was bigger than these guys and he looked sad, lonely somehow."

"That's likely you projecting your own feelings onto him."

"No," she snaps. Confident. Excruciating. "Believe me, I got a good look at him. A long look."

"Were you on Addy then?" Her cheeks burn. *Watch it, Eggie.* "Sorry," I say. "I just want you to take time, I know you've got your paper due, your stress, losing Krish. This is a situation in your life where you can relax. You can take all the time you need. You know, I can talk to your professor, get you more time if you need it on that paper."

She looks into the room, where my beards are all lined up, as I told them to be, but something strange is happening. My beards are filing out of the room. One by one. I run to the door and Stacey's right outside.

"Eggie," she says. "How's your weekend going? You having some fun?"

"Stacey." How much did she hear? How much does she know?

"How about you come down to my office and tell me about all the fun you're having? Because that's much more important to me than Sonny's baseball game."

*T-ball.* "Sure thing, Cap."

She spins around and I can't face Romy. The room where all the beards were, all the hope. Can't even follow my own train of thought right now. What am I going to say? How am I even possibly going to defend myself?

Romy eyes me. "Was that your *boss*?"

My neck seizes up in the bad way, the opposite of the way it did back at the Biltmore, back when there was hope. "In a manner of speaking."

Romy smiles. "I love that you report to a woman. That makes me feel so good about all this."


In her office, Stacey gives me a look. It turns out my "Beard" was a domestic violence victim. He was at that conference looking for his boyfriend. He'd called in the abuse several times. He wasn't even in Providence the night Krish died, he was in a hospital in Wareham. What was he doing at the Lovecraft convention if he lives in Wareham? He found that hat in his boyfriend's car. He was there on a hunch.

"Eggie," she says when she's through. She stands up and opens the door.

"I know."

"Do you? Because you gotta let it go."

I don't look at my colleagues as I walk out to my car. It's enough to feel them glancing over their computer screens, knowing.

There's no denying what today was all about, all the Lovecraft people, their toothy smiles, the *love* in their fingertips, holding doors open, so passive, these sweet, gooey people, hearts like Lo's, this is what they're drawn to: Violence. Gore. Innocent people like dark things. It's not rocket science, it's that rule of opposites and attraction.

I get in my car and when I watch the video of the Beard getting his ass kicked, I know him. He's not a *drug dealer*. He's a goddamn puppy, a Lovecraft fan.

The truth creeps up on me like a kid in a schoolyard. What Stacey knew. What they all knew, everybody in the station. I might be wrong. The Beard is probably a soft, sweet, passive soul, probably missed the conference today because he was home nursing his wounds. Probably never harmed a soul in his life, probably never will. I should stop looking for him. In a moment like this, you can make that kind of decision. And then you can rewind the video, you can watch it again.

# JON

It was so easy to be brave on the drive over, but I froze up and missed the whole Lovecraft conference. I came here but I didn't go in. I failed.

Now Dr. Woo is outside of a black car. She's going to get in it soon and she's going to go and then I will have wasted my whole day sitting here, not taking control of my life, not trying to find a way out of this mess.

I step out of my car. That skin-crawling sensation overtakes me again, that sense of someone lurking. I whip my head around but there is nothing. No one. I focus on my breathing, slow and steady. I pull my cap down low. *I am Providence.* I walk up to her, Dr. Lynn Woo, a smallish, strongish woman who smells of black licorice and fancy shampoo. I tap her on the shoulder.

She turns. She smiles. "Well, you're a tall drink of water."

"Can I ask you something about *The Dunwich Horror?*"

She laughs. "Is this something we didn't cover in the two-hour seminar?"

She's trying to be nice but I can't take in the kindness. I can't look at her. I have to look through her. Feel nothing. Focus. "What if they could have fixed Wilbur? Wilbur could change," I say. "People change."

"People, yes . . . maybe," she says. "Monsters, no."

"But what if they could have fixed him, turned him back?"

She's studying me. She's thinking. "Hon," she says. "Have we met? You look so familiar."

I feel my body heating up. I shake my head. "I don't think so."

"Well," she says. "Wilbur was growing fast because he was only part human. When he dies, there's no blood. He's literally *super* natural."

"What if they had done a blood transfusion," I ask. "Like, if they had replaced the yellow bile, that stuff that made him a monster, I mean couldn't they have made the human part of him bigger than the monster part?"

She smiles. "You're adorable," she says, and she likes me, she's amused, she isn't taking me seriously. I have the urge to tell her everything, how I've never gone to Meeney because he *knew* Roger Blair. I'd feel too much. This was safe because she's a stranger. But now I'm here. She's here. I forgot how easy it is to feel something for someone and that I should warn her that I am Wilbur (sort of) and she has thirty seconds to help me or die. But how could I really do that? How could I tell her?

I do my stern voice. "Lovecraft goes on and on about him being part human. He makes us see him as a baby, growing up fast, too fast, but still, he's like you and me, he has a mother."

And she shifts gears, she gets serious, even a little impatient, she says *Dunwich* is part of the larger Cthulhu story and the most noteworthy thing about this story is that it has a *happy ending*.

My cheeks turn red. "But he dies. Wilbur dies."

"Yes," she says. "That's precisely what I'm saying. Sure, there is a bloodbath, his actions do lead to a *lot* of death, but there is an end to it. And we, the readers, we get to feel *relieved,* like the town won this round. Wilbur is dead. The horror has come and gone."

She rubs her forehead. She's getting dizzy and I am running out of time.

My voice is low and shaky. "But what if things could have ended differently?"

She flashes her eyes at the driver, she wants out of this conversation. "You're still talking as if there's something redeemable about Wilbur."

"Well, he isn't all bad. He saved his brother."

She laughs. "You're a piece of work," she says. "And I swear I know you. Were you here last year? The Cthulhu breakfast . . . the first day?"

I push her again. The clock ticks. The one inside of me, the one that tells me there isn't much time until my heart starts to attack. I'm feeling things. Terrible things. Dread. Resentment. My voice comes out like a hiss, "I'm just trying to figure out how they could have saved Wilbur."

"They couldn't have," she says, snapping. "The goal is to *kill* Wilbur because his goal is to kill *us.* Here he is, in our backyard, and he's going to kill us. What's scarier than that?" She wipes her forehead. "I feel pink," she says. "Do I look pink?"

"But he was part human," I insist. "He was born to a mother. He has a brother. He's a person. He does start out that way."

She moves toward her car. "That might be the scariest thing of all," she says. "Doesn't matter that you're a *little* good if you're mostly made of evil."

Her nose begins to bleed and I can barely get the words out, *Thank you.* She just gave me my death sentence and now she slinks into her big town car, disappearing like one of Lovecraft's monsters. And then I look into the lobby, at all the happy people. I blink. I rub my eyes. Yes. No. *Yes.* That's who I think it is, and I see her and she sees me and I stop moving because I can't move. It's her. *Chloe.*

# CHLOE

I bought a shirt in the lobby: SHOGGOTHS IN BLOOM. I don't know what a Shoggoth is, but I like the word. I like the Nirvana song *In Bloom* and I didn't want to look like an outsider, a girl searching for love, especially around all this requited passion, obsessed people coming together to fuel and feed this love. I take the glass elevator up to the fifteenth floor and the bottom drops out of my stomach.

"'Scuse me," a girl says, smiling fully, so un-Manhattan. "Do you want me to pull your tag off?"

Upstairs, the conference rooms and the hallways are stuffed with Lovecraft people, more men than women, costumed, energized. These people live for this, they wait for this, this is their World Series, their wedding day. It's so easy to picture Jon here, so easy to imagine that he's found a home with people the way he never could when we were kids, or never wanted to. I feel him everywhere; he would call this my *Spidey sense*. I see a guy picking over bagels at the buffet, that could be Jon. I walk over there but it isn't him. I see another guy adjusting a black robe, laughing at something. My heart is beating faster. But then he raises his head to scratch his neck and no, not Jon again. I go back in the glass elevator to the lobby and ride with the Lovecrafters, up and down. It would have been fun to be here with Noelle, to hear her little comments. I miss her, I miss Jon, I am dizzy with missing and I wander around downstairs until I convince myself that he's upstairs, that I missed him, and I get back into the elevator where two guys are raving about a reenactment of *The Dunwich Horror*.

"Excuse me," I say. "That's a book, right?"

They look at me like I just bought my shirt in the lobby.

"Long story," I say. "But was that reenactment today? Did you see this guy there?"

I shove my phone at them, my Jon drawing. No, they didn't.

Upstairs, I dawdle around the buffet table with an empty plate, an obvious prop. Someone taps my shoulder. A guy with glasses, fake tentacles attached to his naked scalp like extensions. He smiles. "You look lost," he says.

"I'm not lost," I say. "Just looking for my friend."

He raises his eyebrows. "For your boyfriend?"

"I don't know," I say, and I sound like a weirdo, I am the weirdo with my empty plate, my *I don't know* and stiff new shirt.

The guy is backing away. "Good luck," he says.

I pick up a hard croissant. *I don't know.* How can that be true? I know so much. I know what I do, I know where I live. But none of it matters if you don't know who you love. I gnaw on the old croissant. It may as well be cardboard. I know I love Jon from afar. I never turn my ringer off at the movies in case this is the time he says something when he calls. But I think love is something you have to do up close, in a room like this, with circulated air and intermittent squealing.

I pull the picture of Jon up in my phone and show it to the bald guy with the tentacles. He looks at the picture of Jon, handsome Jon. The guy with the tentacles slinks away from me, his shoulders drop.

"Those types all look the same to me," he says.

"No," I say. "I promise you, this guy is a good guy. He's obsessed with *The Dunwich Horror* and I'm pretty sure he's here."

Tentacles doesn't mask his disappointment. I like him for it. There's nothing rude about it. I tell Tentacles I like his costume and he smiles.

"If you don't find your fella, I'll just be over there by the Elder Things."

I thank Tentacles and I'm alone again. The food at Tenley's must have been a mirage because I feel empty inside, outside of myself. I get back in the elevator and go on a few rides, the way I ride the subway in New York, staring at my warbled reflection, imagining the doors opening, imagining Jon being there. *Chloe,* he would say. *I'm so sorry.*

People in the elevator crack up over a joke I don't get, I don't speak this language, I don't belong. The lobby is still a madhouse thick with people, same as it was before. I hold my breath and my purse and I search the lobby, every tiny sofa, every little crowd, every line, every everywhere. He isn't here.

But I can't shake this feeling that he is. It's no different than the phone calls.

A woman taps me on the shoulder. She wants me to take a picture of her and her *weirdo posse.* "Sure," I say, hoping I don't sound too obsequious. These people are the opposite of New York, they're so present, so fully engaged, not charging ahead, not hell-bent on making that train or that light. I forgot about peace. About what it's like to have everything you want, your needs met. The woman who asked me to take the picture, her name is Marjorie. She met her husband here at NecronomiCon three years ago and she laughs. *He should be the one taking the picture but who knows where he is? So much to see!* Her ring sparkles, small. Marjorie and her friends from the Internet, from the weekend, they squish in together. They don't have to be encouraged to go cheek-to-cheek. They're adjusting their hats, their cloaks. I've never felt so alone in my life.

"Honey," she says. "We're ready when you are."

I apologize for being in outer space and I hold up her phone. "Say Cthulhu."

They speak in unison and they weren't expecting that. "You guys," I say. "Let me take another for safety. I want to make sure everyone's in here."

They tell me they want to make a pyramid and I tell them it's a great idea. People are gathering around us, clapping. I'm the photographer; an observer. I look around, I get used to the reality that I'm not going to find Jon, that I came here alone and I'm invading all this togetherness. I can never tell anyone about this day. I'll pretend I got my Shoggoths in Bloom T-shirt at a thrift store.

Soon, the Lovecrafters are in formation. There are three vertical rows of them in total, four on the bottom, two in the middle, and Marjorie the Bride on top, arms raised in a V. I take pictures and a video and I promise myself to find a community when I get back to New York, but I know I won't. Marjorie climbs down. Her cheeks are red. She's hugging the others, promising to send them pictures. I want to leave. I need to leave. But I can't interrupt her, she's too happy.

I zoom in on the last picture I took. One girl is growling. One guy is squinting, smiling so much that you can't see his eyes. Another guy is channeling rage but it comes off as funny. Another girl's face is full of dread, maybe she's afraid of falling, being crushed, or maybe it's just the blues that come when the dance is almost over, when the last song is playing. But her face makes me feel better. My love isn't real, but this love isn't real either, this isn't every day for these people. Their real lives don't compare to this weekend. They never will. Just beside the sad girl, in the background, there is a man. You can only see him because the automatic doors in the lobby are open. He's outside. His hands are in his pockets. I know someone who used to do that. I am looking for someone who used to do that.

My feet dig into the floor, into the carpet and I expect the floor to crack open because that's him. I'd know him a mile away and I know him fifty feet away. He's older. He has a beard. But I drew those eyes until my own eyes were watering. I know the way it feels when those eyes are on me, and that is this feeling, this feeling I haven't had in so long. To be loved, looked at, treasured. I wasn't crazy to come here after all. There is a happy ending, there is a thing called fate, a balance to all this missing, the zing of that jingle that brought us together, *Alex Interiors, you're never alone*. It's him. It's *him*. I scream his name. *Jon!*

He turns. And I see the moment he sees me. The way his eyes widen. The way he freezes in place. He recognizes me, he does, and I start to run, I scream for Marjorie and I throw her phone at her.

She calls after me, "Go get him, Shoggoth."

I run like a Shoggoth if a Shoggoth runs fast, tripping through the lobby, toward those automatic doors that looked closer in the picture. Time is passing; it had already passed by the time I noticed him. The doors open again, they close again. The town car that was out front is gone and the doors sense me coming and they open and then I'm outside screaming his name.

But he's gone.

I stand here not crying, not saying anything, fully absorbing the horror, more horrible than any of these costumes, these elaborate creatures with their weird names. No, this is worse. Being seen, being left. The awareness of it. I remember when my grandmother found out she had Alzheimer's. *The worst thing isn't the disease, Chloe. It's knowing that you have it, that it will slowly eat you, that's the worst thing about any bad thing in the world, the knowing, and if you can get a handle on that, you can get through anything.* Consciousness is the monster and it wins.

The valet approaches, a frisky older man with an obvious red toupee. So many people here could be characters in a dream. "Little Miss Lovecraft," he says, grinning. "Did you need a taxi or is one of these monsters gonna get you where you need to go?"

In the taxi, the driver asks if I'm going to the train station and I nod, *yes*. It's a mostly empty train and I have a whole row. When we clear the tunnel, we have reception again. I hold my phone the whole way home. It doesn't ring once. I paint monsters in my mind, but none of them grab onto me the way he does, from the inside out, in perpetuity.

ONE YEAR LATER

# EGGS

I don't ride a bicycle. It's been a sticking point at various times in my life. As a kid, I preferred my feet on the ground. *But you can get away faster* said my buddy Stevie, and it's one of those moments I can remember in my gut, in my eyes, crystal clear, because I remember being nine years old and knowing that I would be a cop, that I wasn't interested in *getting away* with anything.

Lo shrugged it off the first time I told her that little story. "Well," she said. "Your dad was a police officer. So he influenced you, pushed you. That's not so much a *gut* feeling as it is a growing awareness of what was put in your gut."

And then she wrapped spaghetti around her fork and called it pasta. *Women.*

I let her think she was right but she was wrong. I have a strong gut. While I might have inherited it from my dad, my gut is mine alone. You can't expect someone else to be a part of it, to validate it. That's what makes it a gut. It's the reason I know that I don't belong on a bicycle. In my gut, I know nothing good will ever happen to me with my legs straddling that little seat.

And you honor a gut the way you do a ghost, a tradition. Today I'm gonna do that by heading back to that damn Lovecraft gathering, gonna pop a Zantac for the damn twist in my belly that snakes around my backside a little more all the time and just do it. And I'm taking it easy. I'm going in calm. It's almost a good thing that I feel a little weak, I'm not firing on all cylinders. I have zero expectations of anything happening today, I'm just going for the hell of it.

After all, there have been exactly zero noteworthy fatal heart attacks in young people in the area in the past year. Nobody sporting an *I am Providence* hat has been spotted at any crime scene. I don't talk about him on the job, I don't think about him on the job. The Beard. But he's still in my gut. When you're a gut person, there's an actual digestion process where you finish with someone, shit them out. I'm not done with the Beard.

"Eggie," she says, fast on her feet into the kitchen, the refrigerator. "What are you doing?"

"Heating up pasta."

"Well, don't stand at the microwave. That's bad for you." She slams a cabinet.

"Slow down, Lo. You're making my head spin."

She rolls her eyes. *Sorry.* Lo is different lately. I'm still not used to her with her new hair. Shorter, barely reaches her shoulders, that hair is her way of punishing me. It's three years now, *three* years since I've seen my son. If she didn't care so much about looking normal for her students, she'd probably shave it all off.

I take the pasta out of the microwave and she grabs the bowl.

"Eggie, you have your physical today. You can't eat before a physical."

"I almost forgot," I say. An outright lie. I canceled it last week. I bailed on my last appointment too. Lo has been on me to go, the twinge in my side, the burn when I piss. But that's called getting old. I don't need some doctor to tell me that.

She waves at the steam. "And anyway, who eats spaghetti for breakfast?"

"It's pasta," I say. "The little shells from last night."

The old Lo was careful with her words. Short hair Lo has no patience. She isn't as tedious. I miss her tedium. But then, marriage is change. I'm different too. We had one of those fights six months ago, a real sit-down kind of fight where she flat-out told me that I had to close the boxes once and for all.

"You can't see your son? Fine." She sucked in air. "But that doesn't mean you can sit up here doing whatever it is you do, just making yourself crazy." She blew it out hard.

I promised her I was done. And it's true. I'm not out there looking for the Beard, same way I haven't written to any of the autism doctors in ages. But of course you never stop being you. I started Lovecraft, reading about him, just because of that hat. *I am Providence.* The other night there we were, me with a biography of Lovecraft, Lo reading a story by one of *her kids.*

"Edward Softly," I said.

"Who?"

"Lovecraft, that's one of his fake names."

"Pen names."

"Same difference."

"No," she said. "A fake name is something you use to get away with something. A pen name has a creative purpose."

Our conversation ended then, *thunk.*

We're growing apart. We pretend that I'm reading about him because *she* likes him but we both know. You know what your spouse is doing. Like her hair. She knows how much I love it, the feel of it in a ponytail. We got this thing growing between us, this quiet lie. We pretend that she's not mad at me, that I'm not looking for an *I am*

*Providence* hat every time we walk into a grocery store, into a movie theater. Hell, it's part of why I even go to the movies half the time. Sometimes I think we're just two kids waiting for some outside force to smack us, call us out.

She pours the sauce in my bowl back into the jar. "What am I gonna do with you?" she asks. "You know if you eat they can't do a lot of the tests and you still have to pay for the appointment."

"I'm sorry, Lo."

Lately, she is no longer playful when she says *What am I gonna do with you?* She means it. She's contemplating her options. And I have nothing to do but stand here. "Eggie," she says. "You gotta be more on top of things."

I can't tell her how wrong she is. I'm very much on top of things. I canceled the appointment for my physical when I realized it was on the same day as the main event at the Lovecraft festival. How's *that* for on top of things? I expect something to happen today, something big. Not in the reasonable way, in the gut way.

"Thank God for you, Lo-Lo." I kiss her little head. She breaks away from me, eyes first, like two skates rolling away.

The lobby of the Biltmore never changes, thank God, and I'm canvassing, calmly, a far cry from the way I was last year, going bonkers over that squeaky door.

This is gentle police work. I could never get in trouble for smiling at people at random, interrupting their conversations about *Glug* and *Dagon*. And in my cheeriest voice I ask if they wouldn't mind telling me if they've seen this guy around. And they say yes—they're yes people, the Lovecraft people—and then I show them the picture of the Beard, the security-camera picture from the falafel. The terrible picture, grainy, blurry. So far, there hasn't been a bite. One kid said, *This is a joke, right?* I almost smacked him, *No, this festival is a joke.*

But I don't really believe that. If anything, I'm the joke. These people, their passion is real.

The elevator dings and I take it up the one flight. (Imagine what the doc would have to say about that laziness.) There are hordes of people here, willing students, volunteering to sit and be lectured. Imagine having that kind of passion. But none of them knows the Beard.

I flop into a wingback chair just inside the door to the main event, that door they closed because they're about to get started. You can feel the energy, the love for Dr. Woo. Back again this year to expound on *Lovecraft's monsters*. A smarter man would go into that room, maybe learn a thing or two. But Dr. Woo isn't the kind of doctor who can cure autism and my attention span is shot these days. *Why hasn't anyone died?*

Lo texts me: *How did it go?*

I write back: *I'm afraid it looks like you're stuck with me.*

She writes back: *Good. Eat. xx*

I pocket my phone. Those words are already haunting me. *Good. Eat.* She'd never leave me, would she? Dr. Woo pounds her fist on a podium, as if she knows there's someone out there not listening. "Yes," she says. "Yes, H. P. Lovecraft described death as 'merging with the infinite blackness.' So let's pause on that. The infinite blackness. What else does that sound like to you? Something murky and infinite?"

A pin-thin pixie boy in the back row screams, "Love!"

People laugh. They exchange looks, hold hands. Dr. Woo keeps on about the idea of death and love being built upon *disintegration of the individual and the individual interests*. I think of me and Lo, her life in the kitchen, my boxes in my room. I must change. We must change. Dr. Woo wants to end on a light, dark note.

"As H.P. said, one could drown in '06 just as easily as in '05 and '04. So everybody, thank you for coming. Don't drown today. Drown next year so we can all get together again!"

And all hands in the room come together, thunder, love. There is clapping and whistling—only a couple of these kids know how to whistle—and they chant *Woo woo* and I'm happy I came today. I'm happy I can be here on my feet, thinking that I have a new feeling in my gut, just as strong as my feeling about the Beard. It's simple. If I'm sneaking around like this on a secret hunch next year, Lo won't be with me. It's a scary realization and I could act on it, I could leave now. But my gut. My gut.

I take my badge out and move around the line, all the way back to Dr. Woo's table. I stand off to the side while she poses with a fan. She smiles for the camera. "I sense a police presence," she says. "Are you here to arrest me?"

The fanboy getting his picture taken screams, "I love you, Dr. Woo."

She smiles. "I love you too, Harry."

When he leaves she motions to the helper gal with the lanyard around her neck to put things on hold. She rolls her sleeves up and comes over to the side.

"Dr. Lynn Woo," she says, extending her hand.

We shake. "You realize you just told that young man that you love him."

She nods. "There's never enough love in the world."

"But do you though?"

She looks at me. "Yes," she says. "I love my readers." She says this as if these people belong to her, which they don't. Take a look around, lady. This is *Lovecraft* land. She raises an eyebrow. Of course she can do that. I can't. Neither can Lo. "Are you a reader?"

"No," I say. "No, I'm here on business."

She smiles. "I was kidding. You have to forgive me. I get worked up at these things, you know, I spend so much time alone and then I get here, to *this* and the love and the energy, wooh!"

I tell her it's okay and I reach into my jacket breast pocket and she clamps her hands over her mouth and gasps. "Am I being served?"

"No," I say, newly embarrassed. "No, it's nothing like that." I unfold the picture once, twice, and then I press it with my hands. "Sorry," I mumble. "Been a long day."

"They should get you boys some iPads."

I smile. "They did."

She laughs hard, too hard.

"Well," I say. "It's a terrible picture and it's a long shot on a lot of levels, but I'm wondering if you might recognize the man in this picture."

She sets the photo on the table and looks at it the way you look at a Monet.

"See," she says. "If you had an iPad, I could zoom in."

I reach for the photo. "I can let you go back to your fans."

*"Readers,"* she says. "And yes. Yes, he is a reader. Oh, yes."

Yes. *Yes!* I take out my pen, my notepad. "You saw him today?"

"No," she says. "It was last year. He missed my lecture, but talked to me outside the hotel."

*Here.* He was here and I missed him. And of course I did. I watched the door to the lecture room, not the hotel. And I even stopped doing that when I thought I had him, when I dragged that poor kid from Wareham, Massachusetts, out of here.

"He was sweet," she says. "Seemed very down. I believe we talked about *The Dunwich Horror.* I can't remember exactly, you know, it's a lot of little conversations. What I remember is the *feeling.*"

"And he was wounded. Bruised."

She shakes her head. "No. Not at all."

*Fuck.* "Dr. Woo, the man in this picture was savagely beaten. If he was here, he would have been covered in bruises."

"Well, he must have special healing powers," she says, patronizing. "Because he was here, and he was fine."

"And you're sure this was him? You would swear on it?"

She smiles. "I love my readers," she says. "But you've seen them, you understand why the man in this picture . . . ahem . . . stood out.

Look at those cheekbones. He was striking. That's the word for it. *Striking*."

She's so authoritative, so sure.

"And I *doubly* remember all this because while I was talking to this poor guy, I got a bloody nose. I mean I had this wave of nausea, I almost passed out. These conferences are long days." She sighs.

"Did he tell you anything about himself, anything that might help us locate him . . . his name, anything like that?"

She smiles at me. "Officer, I meet *hundreds* of people a year." She looks at her crowd. "In fact . . ."

"Did you consult a physician after your nosebleed?"

"No," she says. "One minute that boy was here, my nose was bleeding and I thought I was getting sick, fluttery, and the next minute he was gone. He was gone and I was fine. As I said, it was a long day."

I scribble those words in my notepad, *he was gone and I was fine*.

"Officer," she says. "He didn't do anything *wrong* did he?"

I close up my notepad. I wish her the best with her *readers* and I give her my card. "You know," I say. "In case that nose starts bleeding again."

Dr. Woo goes back to her podium and mingles with her fans, hugging, posing, signing, leaning in. *He was gone and I was fine*. The words loom in my gut. Loud, steady.

# JON

I have friends now, sort of.

About a year ago I found this podcast, these two guys from New Zealand. *Kiwis*. Their names are Guy and Tim and all they do is analyze *Grown Ups 2*. It's the greatest feeling to hear them talk, they notice all the stuff I notice, like how you can't tell what the director wants you to see. The podcast made me realize why the movie was relaxing in that way. The lack of direction or something, like how it is with *The Dunwich Horror* and Roger's letter, me not knowing where to focus, what I'm supposed to see, what to do. I've listened to every episode three or four times. It's not interactive, but sometimes I'll talk to them as if it's the three of us at a bar. I hold on to the wheel, I half expect them to respond, to say my name. And it's a good thing to find people you have something in common with, even if you can't know them, it's like all those Lovecraft people.

My phone rings. The caller is UNKNOWN. My heart pounds, weaponizing, *ka gung, ka gung*. I pull over. I put the car in park. I cough. "Hello?"

I haven't spoken out loud in a few days. I have a New Zealand accent that I must have picked up from the podcast. There is no voice on the other end of the line. So I say hello again and again, I sound like a freaking Kiwi. But it isn't Chloe, it isn't my parents who magically tracked me down with a detective, or an Internet wiz. It isn't Professor Meeney.

I thought he might call because this morning I snapped. I sent him a cryptic email from my Theo Ward account.

Dear Dr. Meeney,

I have reason to believe that you can help me. It's a life or death situation. I'm not being dramatic. I'm not a student. I'm not trying to get your attention. I'm trying to get your help. And there is no money involved. I just need you to hear me out.

You know who this is.

But it's not Meeney. He probably thought my note was spam. The call is just a robot trying to clean my carpets. I scream into the phone, *I have wood floors, asshole!*

Just like that, I sound like me again.

I should have known it was no one. It's been a year of no one, nothing. Dr. Lynn Woo's words felt like the truth. I stopped calling Chloe. I didn't delete her number or anything like that but not calling her became a thing I do, the way some people go to the gym. And she's different now. She uses more hashtags. *#SaturdayVibes*. Today she was at Sbarro's pizza in Midtown. She wrote: *can't come here without thinking of Michael Scott.*

We never watched *The Office* together. She's probably watching it with some new guy, some new friend.

I still keep up with her art online. She's making eyes, but they're wilder now, almost monstrous, as if something upset her, something irked her. In the media, she says it's about *growing older, wiser, more cynical, leaning into that darkness in facing the unknown of your future self, realizing . . . this is it, how it is now.* I read every interview and then I close my eyes and remember seeing her at Lovecraft. The memory doesn't fade. I won't let it.

I open up the paper and there's an article about Dr. Meeney. He's sponsoring a science program at Hope High School. There's a picture of him with a bunch of public school kids and they're all smiling. There's a look in people's eyes when they have so much ahead, the prom, their futures, the science they're doing with this big shot professor. I study myself in the mirror, my blank eyes, my puffy face from not talking so much. I don't have that future sparkle. When I smile, my eyes stay the same. I don't look happy. I look dead.

Hope Street is darker than normal because of the mist, low and thick. I turn on my brights.

I slam on the brakes. There are hands, two of them on the hood of my car. Now there is laughter and the mist clears enough where I can see more, the arms attached to the hands, bottoming out in an electric-pink sports bra.

And when I see what house I'm in front of, I realize who it must be: *Crane Comma Florie.*

It turns out that she's young and she has frizzy red hair. She's breathing heavy, she's closer now, leaning into the passenger window. She's catching her breath, laughing at the mist, how thick it is, how blinding. I smell her sweat.

She laughs. "Oh my God—this must be you. We meet at last for real. It's Theo, right?"

She bends over and I see her boobs, the space between them,

the darkness. Her mouth never stops moving. She says she's been wanting to meet me. She yawns. "Sorry," she says. "I just got back from L.A. and I have jet lag up the wazoo."

I tell her it's okay and she peers into my car. She hears the Kiwis talking, I forgot to shut them off.

"Is that a podcast?" she asks.

"It's these guys in New Zealand," I say, surprised that I can speak. "They talk about the movie *Grown Ups 2*."

"Amazing," she says and she drums her hands on the side of my car. "Do you ever listen to *How Did This Get Made?*"

I shake my head no.

"Theo," she says, as if my name is a new shirt she's trying on. "Theo, you would love this podcast. It's literally just people being like, *How did this movie get made?* It's amazing. And it's not mean, you know? It's coming from this place of love." She pulls a red pen from her pocket. "You have to give me your email so I can send it to you."

And then she's writing my Theo email address on her arm. I have a friend, I think. She yawns, she's out here looking for her *disappearing cat*. "His name is *Muse Frontman*," she says. "And he is *not* a homebody."

I laugh and she keeps going. She says she didn't get into grad school like she wanted. She switched majors at Providence College because she wanted to study the brain because *the brain is where it's at*.

"But that was no good either," she says. "The science was too dense, too confusing. I mean talk to me about sodium and chloride and I am like *okay but what about us?*"

I say the only word I have left. "Yeah."

The sound of her voice is so different than the sound of a voice on TV, the Kiwis, their voices are for each other. Her voice is just for me right now. She's still talking, about our changing brains, how the technology is morphing and how *the sodium and the chloride are outdated modules*. I'm not sure what she means, but she goes on.

"Yeah," I say. "Yeah."

She has so much to say to me, as if jogging and traveling unearthed all these things and she has to get them out of her system. She wanted to learn about computers because *we are computers, that's where the sodium and chloride are less relevant and our brains are more like these.* She points to the phone strapped to her bicep.

"Yeah," I say. "Yeah."

She tells me about how exciting it is to study computers and *obviously practical in terms of a career but majorly stressful.* It's why she takes Zoloft, which is how she became obsessed with psych meds. She wants to figure out *an honest way to think about your brain and your computer and your essence and the possibility of there being a soul, of all these things becoming one, the overwhelming burden of a body.* She took a poetry workshop and she says it changed her mind. It made her think we're all machines. *You put people together, the same people every week, you all become one, there's a hum when seven people are in a small place, thinking about the same thing, together, you know, like sodium and chloride can break out of your mind and go into someone else's, you know?*

"Yeah," I say. "Yeah."

I wish she knew about me. I wish I could tell her about my bad heart, transfer everything I know, everything I don't know, every word of *The Dunwich Horror* letter into her mind. But I can't tell her. I would sound crazy and the fog is clearing. Her bumper sticker breaks through the mist: KEEP PROVIDENCE WEIRD.

"Every single MFA program," Florie says, laughing shrill, sad. I think she's had a bad year too. "What do you even do with that? Rejected from *every single* poetry program I applied to. If I were Sylvia Plath, I would just jump in the oven, you know?"

"Don't do that."

She looks to the left and winces. "Speaking of poetic injustice, my oven is broken." She looks at me suddenly. "Too dark?"

"No," I say. "Impossible."

She laughs a little, a less disturbing kind of giggle. She says she's working at this law firm, *pro bono suits against big pharma.*

"They're noble which means I can sleep," she says. "Or maybe that's just the Zoloft."

A light rain falls. She keeps talking, I listen, and I feel better just being here, learning about her poems, her rationalizations. "Pain is art and art is pain," she says, smacking her thigh. "No matter how many successful fuckwits swear otherwise, so this has to be leading up to something amazing. And maybe next year, maybe I'll have better material, I'll get in, I'll be sweating over where to go, and we'll laugh at this moment."

She cracks her knuckles and I imagine her fingers in my mouth. "Yeah," I say. "Yeah."

She laughs and pulls back. "We made the sun come out." And then something shifts. Her shoulders roll a bit, her voice drops. "Sorry for going off. I guess you can tell I don't get out enough lately."

"Me too," I say, willing the saliva to stop filling my mouth. "Same."

She smiles. "And now I have to go in because I can't be late to work and I can't show up in a sports bra." She laughs. "Next time it's your turn to say too much and be the stereotypical millennial narcissist, okay?"

"Okay," I say. "It's a deal."

She turns and walks away and I watch her on the grass, she used to be so dainty and barefooted. Now she is in sneakers. She stomps. She's stronger.

And then it hits me. That was a lot of talking. I was there. I was feeling things, wanting to act on those feelings. My heart was revving up but it didn't hurt her at all. She's alive. Her nose isn't bleeding. She wasn't wheezing, wasn't saying *What's wrong with me?* I didn't make her dizzy.

I didn't kill her.

Maybe this is different because Crane Comma Florie is different, medicated, with bright heavy sneakers. Maybe she's like those coats that firemen wear, the coats that don't catch fire. Maybe she's just different.

Or maybe it's more like she said, maybe this year was lonely and long. But maybe my body was busy recovering. Maybe *I'm* different.

She looks over her shoulder. "Wanna come in?"

I turn off the car and dig my hands into my pockets. I do. I have to know. Have to test it. Want-to and have-to were never as united as they are right now, as I walk toward her, toward her door, into her house. I look around the living room: the records on the coffee table, the playlist on low, the pillow with Jack Nicholson's big smiling face, the poster of the periodic table of elements, right under a photo of Janet Jackson torn out of a magazine and stuck up there with gum. She's dancing, dancing on the periodic table of elements, because there it is, the wonder of life, how we get from the periodic table to Janet Jackson.

I look at all her fish tanks, her fishbowls. "Wow," I say. "How many fish do you have?"

"I'm not about numbers," Florie tells me. "My babies inspire me. I'm surrounded by *life*. And, fish die. Constantly. So there's death too. But that's poetry, you know?"

She sits on Jack Nicholson's face and pats the sofa next to her. Carefully, I sit down.

"And Muse Frontman keeps me company," she says, then laughs. "But he's a cat. I mean I'd much prefer to hear about you, Theo."

She kicks off her sneakers and stretches out her legs and crosses them at the ankle. "Let's start with your job. Do you like it?"

"Yeah," I say, that word, my word. "I deliver the papers."

She laughs. "I know," she says. "And why do you deliver the papers?"

"I dunno," I say, feeling boring, feeling bad. Here I am, I still can't quite look at her, I'm worried that I'll see blood coming out of her nose, that I would kill her. But I can't resist it right now, the talking, the listening, telling her about the *Telegraph,* trying not to stare too hard at her nostrils, her pupils.

"Cool," she says. She pulls her legs away from the table in one swift move. She crosses her legs and tickles my calf with her big toe. I feel it all over, under, in the small of my back.

"So how did you come up with the name Muse Frontman? Is that your favorite band?"

"No," she says with a smile, like she loves this question, like she always wants boys to ask but they never do. "I got him at the shelter, well, it's more like he got me. We made a deal. We decided to pick up *People* magazine, name him after the first two words we saw."

I smile, thinking of Pedro. "You're nice."

She lowers her chin. "Theo, I think you should kiss me."

Kiss.

I've never kissed a girl. Never.

She is in the room, *Crane Comma Florie.* She is in the room and she's not fainting, not bleeding. *She's different. I'm different.*

And then I do it. Kissing is so different than I expected, her mouth on mine, the air we share, our mouths closed, the cave, the inside of a girl. I've always known girls have tongues, lips. But I've never felt it, the wetness, this miniature whale swooshing from her mouth into mine, swimming, the wanting, the click-clack of our teeth. I keep thinking it. *This is kissing. This is it.*

And I'm fixed. FIXED. I kissed. KISSED. I know why you can't do it to yourself, because you need the surprise of another person's tongue. *Crane Comma Florie.* I kissed her and she's alive. She's not fainting, not bleeding. I kiss her a lot and her cheeks are flushed. She bites her lip. She talks so much and then after she finishes saying something good about us, about this, she says, *You know what I mean?* And then no matter what she is saying, I say, *Yeah.* Kissed. Fixed. She says she knows she comes on strong and her friends tell her she should try to back off and play it cool. "But look how long we waited," she says. "You know, I liked you before I saw your face. You're so tender. The guy before you, he didn't close the bags on the papers. But then you come along and you tie every paper with a twisty thing. You use red and green ones at Christmas. *You.*"

"Yeah," I say. "Yeah."

I watch her nostrils closely. I make sure there's no blood coming. She says she likes how bold I am, how unafraid I am to look her in the eye. I look at one of her posters, like the bumper sticker: KEEP PROVIDENCE WEIRD. I'm normal now. KEEP PROVIDENCE NORMAL.

"There is such a story I could tell you about that sign," she says. I didn't realize she was watching me, didn't realize I was staring. "But it's more of a first-date story, it's my big closing number at the end of the date, you know, the story I tell to make it clear that I unequivocally *rock.*"

I watch her nostrils. "Do you feel okay?"

She smiles. "I feel so okay," she says. "I love how considerate you are. I love that I don't feel this compulsion to spin you some yarn about how I *never* do this. There's this innocence about you and it brings out the wild in me and I love that we got here this fast and that you don't even know my first-date stories. Can we even call this a date?"

"Yeah," I say. "We can call it whatever you want."

Crane Comma Florie puts her hand on my arm. "We can do anything in the world right now," she says. "We can eat or not eat we can sit here or go out we can talk or not talk, we can mess around or not mess around. I have some pot. I have some old beers and some new vodka. I have *time.* I love this hour, you know? We can decide what this is, if it's morning or night, when else can you say that, you know?" She falls back against the sofa. She's a nice person, maybe the nicest person I ever met. There's something crazy about her in the fun way, like when Roger, when he was our sub, told us that if Van Gogh were walking around, everyone would run away because he had no ear, but if he was holding his paintings they would be nice to him. She's holding her paintings and she's good at it.

And now she's thirsty. "What about you?" she says. "Are you thirsty?"

"Yeah," I say. "Sure."

She returns with plastic cups of water, biting her lip. "That took forever because I stepped in gum," she says, giggling. "In my house. How great is it that I can tell you that and I *know* you aren't going to judge me?"

I feel bad for Crane Comma Florie. I'm glad she has Muse Frontman. I bet there's some guy out there who'd wanna sit on the couch with her and take pictures of the cat. I bet there is someone for everyone. I'm drinking her water and it tastes like soap. I wonder what she's going to do when she realizes I'm going to leave her. I wish I could tell her it's not because of her nonstop talking and the gum on the floor and the hair on her toes, which I'm noticing now.

"Tomorrow we should go out in the world," she says. "Like do something totally random. Do you want to go to Seekonk and just be in Seekonk? We can even take Muse if he ever comes home. I have a leash."

"Yeah," I say. "We could go to Seekonk."

But in my mind I'm already gassing up my car, already gone, already on my way to Chloe.

# EGGS

Right after we put Chuckie in the place they said is *safest and best* for him, we had to go right back to work. We didn't have any more time off because we'd used it all up dealing with him in our home, the place that was *unsafe and worst*. It was good for Lo, the distraction of other kids, many of whom would walk her to the car, want to know more.

But it was no good for me. I was ferocious in those days. Scowling at anyone who said hello, slamming the coffeepot in the kitchen at the station. One day we had bagels brought in and they gave us *plastic knives*. I lost my temper and sliced my thumb open.

I still have a scar, a tiny mark. You'd only know it was from a knife if I told you. Lo knows, she kisses it sometimes, says I wouldn't have a scar if I'd put Vitamin E on it, but then she also says my thin skin is part of my charm, *such a Pisces*. She doesn't know that I wanted a scab, not a scar per se, I didn't think it through, but I wanted a little project, a place to put my energy. I picked that scab and watched it bleed. I fought my body as it tried to close that wound, lunging at it with my sharp fingernail. It made me so aware of our bodies, how they're on our side, your skin working so hard to hold it all together 24/7.

And there I was, picking at it, fighting it, me.

It's been a minute and I can't figure it out, how the hell the Beard healed up so fast. And it's a load to carry because anyone would say I'm spinning my wheels, say that the haughty Lovecraft gal was just one of those people who can't say *I'm wrong*. But in my gut it was the Beard. In her gut too. You can smell conviction.

And that just brings me back to where I am right now, middle of the night, every night, up in bed wondering how. *How do you heal that fast?* I know how you stop yourself from healing. But how do you expedite it? Did he immerse himself in a tub of Vitamin E? Is that a thing you can do?

I'm awake when the call comes at five A.M. It's a woman on the East Side. Dead. Dead at twenty-four. *Twenty-four.*

Lo rolls over. "I'd make you something but I'm so wiped out."

"Of course," I say, meaning it, fearing it, the end of love. A year ago she'd be up in her robe, yawning, cracking eggs, overcooking 'em. "Of course."

I take a cupcake out of the freezer. I heat up water and I steep my tea. Fifteen minutes. One woman. Twenty-four.


It happened here on Wickenden by the gas station, a sprawl of an intersection, the highway above looming like the highway in a Bruce Springsteen song, the road outta here.

Her name is Jillian Farber and she dropped dead by an out-of-service pump. She was here on foot. No car. The guy in the gas station nods, he'd seen her around, *now and then*. This means she's a user, a regular. He was probably talking shit about her yesterday, but now that she's gone, he's possessive. The loss is his.

"She ever with anyone?" I ask.

"Sometimes," he says. "I guess?"

There are other people here. Cops. EMTs. I lean in. "You ever see her with anyone with a beard, say about six-two? Anyone like that here when she passed?"

The guy shrugs. "Maybe," he says. "She's just one of those people, you know, she's around."

*Maybe* isn't *no* and I head outside. Stacey is here, back after leave with baby number six. Richie. Healthy Richie. The joke around the station is that Richie is gonna be a quarterback because he looks like Tom Brady. I will never be captain because I will never agree that a baby resembles Tom Brady.

"Eggs." She doesn't even look at me. Says my name like I'm a dog, leaving me with no choice but to walk to her. *Woof woof.*

"Stacey," I say, faking it. "Good to have you here."

She wants to know what I was doing in there.

I stammer and sweat. "I was just asking the guy for his POV."

She glares. "I said what were you *doing?*"

I am steady. "I got his statement, nothing more to it."

She nods. "But we already got a statement." She looks at me in that pitying way. "They found track marks on her toes," she says. "Eggie, you look like hell. And there's no work for you to do here, you know better, you saw her backpack full of all the tagged jewelry, junkie thief, plain as day. Get some sleep."

She watches my face fall. I never got good at covering my disappointment. Another reason I don't visit my son: They say he can't process emotion, but what if they're wrong? What if I walked in there and looked at him and he saw the sadness on my face? What if he felt it? What if I went in there and ruined his day?

"Druggies die of drugs," Stacey says. "And I mean it. Get some sleep."

She pats my back in a way that reminds me that she's a mother. My eyes land on the backpack I didn't open. I *did* miss that backpack. The sun is up and the van is here and the Beard is not here, never was.

I think of all the nights up, all the boxes, all the wondering. *Who is the Beard? How did he heal his wounds? How did he fix his nose? How does he kill all these people? How does he slip away?* Those sound like the questions of a crazy person, a ghost hunter, a conspiracy theorist, an absentee father who won't even visit his own son, who doesn't even properly fuck his wife on a regular basis anymore, a secretive man, a man who keeps files on dead people, people who died because people die, not because some Beard killed them.

In the gas station I pick up two jelly doughnuts. Stacey accepts my apology, she eats the doughnut and licks her fingers. "How's Lo?" she asks.

"Great," I say. Because I'm a liar and liars lie. "Better than ever."

# JON

The miracle of the Internet is that I am in my car, knowing exactly where to go, what time to be there. Chloe has an opening at the Flare Gallery in Chelsea. I like the idea of there being an audience for our reunion. This is why people have big weddings, because sometimes you want everyone to see that things worked out for you. I love the idea that I will be the guy marching into the gallery to get the girl. And she'll come running to me, to get *me*.

Kissed. Fixed.

That's my plan, just walk up to her and kiss her. Say nothing. Do what I should have done a long time ago. I'm making good time and it's mostly a straight shot on 95. I drive faster than I should, but then again I am kissed, fixed. I don't know how it happened and I don't need to know. It happened. Kissed, fixed. I don't think anything could hurt me right now and I'm checking my phone to see how long it's gonna take when the guy in back of me beeps. I was veering into his lane. I wave. *Sorry.*

It's the longest drive of my life. I wish there was a way you could zap yourself so you didn't have to be in the moment that leads up to the moment. Your life. It feels like Connecticut lasts forever and everyone is trying to get through it and I'm never going to get there and then it happens. I can't pinpoint a specific moment. I just become aware that there were more woods than concrete until suddenly there weren't. I am here, almost, I am in New York, the beginning of it, the flat-top buildings are standing there staring at me, waiting. Chloe.

I grab my phone. I've never called her from the state of New York, so I dial the number. I wait for her to answer. She sounds short of breath, nervous, *Hello, hello?* I don't tell her it's me and she doesn't say my name this time. I hang up. Her voice made it real, what's coming next, the big hug, the big kiss. *Kiss.*

I'm a kid again. I look at people in the cars around me and none of them are perking up. Mostly they look tired. I roll down the window and start beeping my horn in the happy way and people are looking at me like I'm nuts but I smile at them. I pump my fist. I'm alive. They smile back. I am still contagious, but now it's in the good way.


What kills me the most is the sheer volume of people. They're everywhere. You see them in the windows of the skyscrapers, they're coming up from the subway below, they're in cars, beeping, they're on the street, not looking at you, not saying excuse me, they're homeless or they're in suits, they're dressed up like Chloe said they would be and then they're sloppy in Yankees jerseys, they are all so different and I want them to *slow down.* I want to slow down. But then it's too late to slow down, I'm here, almost, just one street away from the gallery and my heart is beating so fast I have to stop. I have to breathe. I stop cold in front of a bakery that's a deli and a newsstand and a coffee shop and I've never seen any place that was so many places at once.

Someone at a table is eating sushi. I understand why Chloe always said New York is special. I've never seen so much variety, it's like the city encourages you to make your dreams come true, to order the pizza and the tuna roll and then buy a scratch ticket and a roll of toilet paper, take it all upstairs to this salad bar—more food!—and be so awestruck that you almost walk right into a woman storming around with a basket of fresh groceries, a whole eggplant and a news-paper, a quart of milk. She detours so swiftly, people are so good at walking here, at moving. Maybe when you're around this many peo-ple, you just don't feel as much, or maybe you just know what feel-ings matter. I haven't even seen Chloe yet, but it's as if she's already opening my eyes to the world, the way she always did, making it seem new again, day after day. It's like I never saw people before, never realized just how big it is, the human race.

I watch a guy in all white make an egg sandwich and he ties it up so fast, it's like a magic trick. I go into the deli and order breakfast for dinner as if I'm a normal New Yorker. I watch the people, the sad faces, the tired faces. I inhale the sandwich. It's the best thing I ever ate. I go up and tell the guy who made it that it's the best thing I ever ate and he nods. I don't think he speaks English. Or maybe he doesn't care.

I walk down rickety black-and-white stairs and go into a tiny bathroom where I splash water on my face. I floss. I pull shards of eggs out of my beard. New Yorkers look so different, yet somehow you can tell that I'm not one of them. Maybe that will change when we kiss.

Flare Gallery is halfway down the street, marked by a sandwich board on the sidewalk. This is when my heart starts ticking like a clock on a bomb, when I feel something, when there's a spark, and the alarms sound, ringing through me, *alert, alert*. Chloe. But this must be what it's like to be normal because right now all I feel is good. Not grabby, I'm in charge of my heart, not Roger. I stand here by the sandwich board and soak it up. The quiet in me. It's like my heart is back to being the heart I was born with. It isn't a weapon anymore. I feel like I did before, like nothing ever happened. It's a circle of life in a good way, a great way.

I start walking. My palms are soaking wet and I can't get there fast enough but I also can't walk slow enough and then I get there. I am standing in front of the gallery.

And it's empty. Empty.

The door is propped open and a girl sits on the stoop smoking. "The show is in the fucking *annex*," she says. She blows a smoke ring up to the sky. "And the annex is on fucking Thirty-fourth and Lex. Such bullshit, right?"


It's like *When Harry Met Sally.* Or any movie, really. The man always has to run through New York to get the girl. So that's me now, flying down the street the way all superheroes do at some point if you want to get the girl. I'm running and smiling and a couple of girls connect their eyes to mine, I can almost feel them thinking *There goes a good one.* Now I live here, somehow. Running from Chelsea to Thirty-fourth and *Lex* in just eighteen minutes makes me a New Yorker. I am not afraid when I arrive, when I see the annex, a tiny little box of a space, almost like a cartoon, one giant garage door, open all the way, people spilling in and out, people drinking wine, music playing, music I don't know. I go in. I see her name on the wall. I see her eyes on all the walls and then it happens. I see her, in a white dress, glittering flowery shoes on her feet. She exists. She is here.

Chloe.

She scratches her right ankle with her left foot, shifting the way she did in school. I can't believe I am here, can't believe we made it this far into the future, into the same room. I want to go to her but I want to wait, I want to hold on to this, this sensation of her being within my reach after being so far away from me for so long, in the computer, tiny and still.

You think you've seen someone if you've seen them in pictures, but this is a reminder of what more there is, the way she shrugs her shoulders and covers her mouth with her elbow when she coughs, and I see her phone, the phone she's answered when I called. *Jon?*

A douche art guy bumps into me and he's rude and unapologetic but he doesn't drop to the floor like Krish. It's more proof things are different now. More evidence that I'm safe. *Kissed. Fixed.*

I get a plastic cup of white wine and watch Chloe work the room. I like her this way, older. Life makes you better after it makes you worse. I'm calm just being here. She brings out the best in me, even now, when she doesn't know that she's doing anything.

I take a step toward her, another.

I'm closer to her, close enough to see individual strands of her hair swaying as she turns her head, as if she's expecting me, as if she was waiting for me, and maybe she was. Of course she was. She feels me. She feels the pull of my heart. *No.* Yes. *No.* I get one tiny moment with the freckles on her face, some of them new, some old, those strands of her hair that won't cooperate, like the weapon in my heart.

And then I hear all the gasping that's familiar in the worst way. I don't need to look back to know her nose is bleeding, to hear the sound of her body hitting the hard floor. *Thunk.*

And I can't be the one to go over there and give her a Kleenex, kiss her and make it better. I was wrong to come here and my body lied to me and I'm not kissed, fixed.

I'm still me. I'm still in hell.

Outside on the street I run all the way to the edge of New York City, where it ends in the Hudson River. I pant and I scream at the water. It doesn't scream back.

# CHLOE

I saw him. Felt him. That high school sensation. When I could always sense him nearby, in my heart, that tug of the empty box on my computer when those bubbles would appear.

That's why I started to turn around. And then I fainted. Blackout.

And now I'm awake and hiding out in the back room of the gallery and my mother is on the phone—*You need to eat more and you better not be taking Adderall or coke, there's nothing cute about it, Chloe. It demeans your work too, to joke about drugs like that, is that what this is, drugs? Well, regardless, you need to drink more milk, do you eat those almonds I send you?*—and I'm not an anemic or a cokehead. I saw him. I did.

I'm drinking water and wiping blood off my knee. The only real thing is the blood, the bruises, the substances inside of us, like paint on the canvas, proof. I have no proof that I saw Jon. Your gut is not proof. But your memory is something.

Alexandra is back, hovering, offering Kleenex and cocaine—my mother is not stupid.

"Thanks, Alexandra," I say, steadying, stepping back into my skin, my life.

There's an unspoken thing and we both know it. I'm off. I've been sliding a bit all year. At first I would "forget" about interviews and then Alexandra would reschedule them and then I took it to the next level, *Actually could you tell them I'm in work mode right now? No publicity for a few months.* And it's all because of him, because of Jon. That day he ran out on me changed me, that train ride, I'm not the same. I can't go talking about him to strangers anymore, he saw me, he left me, and it's an important part of being a person, you have to know how to be left.

Alexandra knows me. She pats my leg. "You got the Jons bad right now, don't you, babe?"

"No," I say, smiling through the lie. "I swear I saw him, though."

She tucks the Kleenex and coke into her pocket and checks her phone. "Huh," she says. "Apparently there's some guy sniffing around, says he knows you."

My heart. "Are you serious?"

She looks at me. "Holy fuck," she says. "You think it's him? Jon?"

We don't know. She is not so cool now, nervous, excited, says I have to be *chill* and wait and she goes to get him and I sit and wait. And then I stand. Nothing is right but nothing was ever easy with us and I remember that now, now that I think he's here. I'm gonna get to hug him, thank him. For my art. I'm gonna get to talk about him, talk *with* him, and I miss that. I haven't been able to talk about Jon with Marlene in years. She burnt out on the subject in college, my *fantasy* she called it. My mom practically hangs up on me if I ask about his parents. I feel whole again, like all the parts of me are condensing into one, the girl who missed him and the artist who hunts for him and the woman I could be if I could just get on with it, if he would just get here already.

Alexandra texts: *Sorry, mad crowded, hang on.*

I hang on. I wait. And my whole life starts to make sense to me, it becomes a movie with a beginning, a middle, an end.

Alexandra's head appears in the crowd, the shock of her white blond hair. Here it comes. Here he comes.

He smiles. He, as in Carrig Birkus. Not Jon Bronson. I glance at Alexandra and she's making hand gestures, smoking hot, right? Right. Carrig is still smoking hot, same as ever, embracing me. But Carrig is not Jon. But then Carrig is here.

He tells me I look great and I tell him he looks great and he is a little drunk, a little rattled, says he's never been to *an art thing* and I laugh and tell him it's gonna be okay and he can't believe I fainted and I say I never do *except when high school boyfriends show up unexpected.*

"You invited me," he says. His cheeks turn red. "I mean I got a Facebook invite. I didn't mean it like . . . you know . . ."

I smile at him. This is the side of him that Jon couldn't see, the sweetness.

I ask him if anyone else from school is here and it was a weird thing to say. There is a bump. An awkwardness. I can't mention Jon. If I do that, Carrig will leave. It's amazing, what you can know about a person all these years later, the rules.

But we push through. He brings me wine and he buys a painting and he's talking a lot, nervous. He is bashful and cocky, it's hard to keep up.

"So I bought a place in Tribeca," he says. When someone starts a sentence with *so* he's trying to make it sound casual. But this isn't casual, Carrig being here. It feels so intentional. He cares so much he said *so.* "You should see my place. I can see the whole city, it's insane."

He tells me about how happy he is to be out of Hoboken, but how he does miss the bars. It's all so easy, so familiar. I know how to talk to him. I know how to get the best of him. The night is slowing down and the crowd is thinning. Jon was a hallucination. I fainted because I didn't eat and I thought I saw him because the only other time I've fainted was when he came back in Nashua. Something about being back with Carrig, leaving the gallery with him, the way he hails a cab as if he lives here, which he does, which is what Jon said he would do, which he didn't, this feels like life to me, and everything about Jon, it feels like it was holding me back from life, trapping me, down to the fucking art I make, all the eyes, only the eyes, always trying to figure out what Jon was thinking, what was going on behind those eyes.

And now I'm free. I'm in a cab with Carrig, Carrig who showed up, Carrig who says he was living in Hoboken all these years, where they play Billy Joel in all the bars. "You probably don't ever go there," he says.

"No," I respond. "But that doesn't mean I have anything against Billy Joel."

He's E.T. with the heart light on and I'm embarrassed for him, how clear it is that he still wants me. But then it's nice to be wanted so openly, craved like pizza. I could do this. I can picture us at Billy Joel. I can picture this whole other life where I'm wearing all my Lilly dresses and I have this guy who worships me. He nudges me. "Why are you smiling?"

"I'm just trying to remember, you didn't want to live in the city when we were younger, did you?"

"No," he says. "But I knew you did."

He opens the door of the cab for me—thank you—and the door of his building—thank you—and he holds the elevator—thank you— and then he opens the door of his bedroom—thank you—and then he opens sliding doors, wide doors, miracle glass doors that lead out to his terrace—thank you. He stands there looking out at the city.

"What do you think?" he asks, not meeting my gaze, because he doesn't have to look at me. I know it all. I know he did this for me, moved here, worked, earned. This is all because he doesn't think he's good enough.

When I move toward him for a kiss, for his hands, he doesn't push me away or run. He pulls me closer, his arms wrap around me, two doors closing.

# JON

Seventy-three hours have passed since I ran out of the gallery. She is eerily quiet, not wishing anyone a happy birthday, not posting a selfie. It was a mistake to go see her and I want to know that she's okay, that she's alive.

It's 10:27 P.M. when I refresh her Facebook page and see it. A brand-new album of photos. My heart snaps like a twig. There are forty-three pictures and the album has a name. *Coney Island in the Rain. Aaaah.* The first picture is just the rain, a thundering down-pour, the kind where your mom makes you wear a rain slicker. I feel young for thinking that, inexperienced. I click through the pictures and she wasn't there alone. There was someone else with her, an-other person taking photos of her being silly, jumping in puddles. She's wearing a poncho you buy near the subway and she stomps and smiles and flips the bird at the raindrops, at the camera. She sticks her tongue out too, impish. My heart aches with envy.

It's a guy. It has to be. If she had been there with a friend, she would have insisted they take turns. She would have shared pictures of the friend stomping in the puddles. Only a boyfriend would be so invisible. A boyfriend who came into the picture the night she fainted. I can feel it.

She was fired up by the storm, the romance of it all. There are so many pictures because everything in the world looked new to her that day. This is how I felt in New York, except I was there alone. I was imagining being there with her and here she is, actually being somewhere with someone. She's dazzled by every little magic thing, the raindrops landing on the candy carnival games, a custodian standing under the overhang, doing his job, waiting. The pictures are uneven with the colors. *Overexposed.* It means you showed too much and you shared too much and you can't take it back.

The rain stops and there's a time-lapse video of the clouds morphing into a sky that says, *Sure walk around, I won't give you any trouble, no more rain, I promise.* The next pictures are at a restaurant in the city that overlooks the river. There are lights everywhere, little candles flickering. I backtrack to make sure I didn't miss anything, but then it hits me. They didn't take pictures during their trip back to the city because they were kissing.

*Kissed. Fixed.*

In the restaurant, Chloe raises her eyebrows as she eats the spaghetti. She rests her chin in the palm of her hand. Her eyes look bigger than they are in real life and she is watching a performance, a song. Her lips are puffy.

*Kissed. Fixed.*

She is sitting still but really she's falling, away from me, into someone else. It feels like I did this, like I never should have gone to see her, as if I made this happen. The last picture of her is black-and-white. Underneath it says *#TriBeChloe.*

———

Then she's gone.

She changes the settings on all her accounts to private. The window is closed. You can't see where she's going or what she's doing unless you're friends with her, which means she isn't like the person stranded on the desert island anymore, making words out of branches on the beach, hoping I'll see from above. She is behind closed doors, somewhere in Tribeca. With him. *Him.*

I still don't know who he is. Before she went private, her friends would say things like YOU GUYS ARE TOO CUTE and SO HAPPY TO SEE YOU SO HAPPY. Her friends met him. But they didn't say his name. He lives somewhere high up, like a bad guy in a comic book. He has his own patio in the sky. Sometimes she took pictures of what you see when you're up there, things you can only see from up in his *#Penthouse*. She's different with him. There are more jokes, more hashtags. I don't know where he lives exactly, but his home is the opposite of my basement dwelling. My walls are concrete and cold and dark orange. But in his apartment, the walls are white and there are wooden beams overhead.

She isn't painting as much. There aren't any new pieces for sale on her site and she hasn't announced any more gallery appearances. Sometimes I think the guy she's dating is a doctor, that she met him because of me, because I made her faint. I bet he told her to take a break from painting. So she did. Because he's a doctor and doctors know what's best. In my nightmares I sense him on my tail. He shadows me, resuscitating all the innocent people I murdered. He is hunched over them, counting, pumping his hands on their chests. And then I wake up.

Alone.

Aware that he presses his mouth into hers, his dick, that he sits with her on the subway train. I've never even been on the subway. I went all the way to New York City and I never got on. Days on Coney Island, nights under the stars, on bridges lit up from above. If he's not a doctor, he might be a famous actor. I look at the screenshots I saved from when her Facebook was open. I look until I can't take it anymore. I read about how Facebook makes people want to kill themselves and then before you know it I'm hungry or it's time to go to work. Your body gets in the way of your plans, your life. Like that thing Lovecraft said about how you can always kill yourself next year.

I take another break from my route, from the Kiwis, from Florie's emails. I think about Roger's letter. *You have power. You're welcome.* I am powerful, in a way. But it's a misleading word. The power isn't mine. I'm full of it, but I may as well be dead. I'm not in control of anything. I'm a host for an evil force. Power*less*. I could only kiss Crane Comma Florie because I could never love her. She doesn't get under my skin. Everyone I've ever hurt, they've gotten to me in one way or another. I could drive my car into the ocean like in the Pixies song. A couple of times I go to Bristol, over the bridges, the dramatic arches. I think of driving off, but I can't do that to the rescue workers, to the fish, to my parents. And of course I can't give up. Not fully. Can't imagine dying without ever having gotten to take a picture of Chloe in the rain.

My phone buzzes, a text from my boss: *Theo kid ya break is ova I need you tonight.*

I write back: *Sure.*

It's a bad day on the road.

I wasn't off for that long, but there are new subscribers, hard houses to find, there are bushes in the way of the street numbers. I finally get to Crane Comma Florie's street and I roll down the window to read a hot pink sign on a utility pole: HAVE YOU SEEN THIS CAT? HIS NAME IS MUSE FRONTMAN. HE IS MY HEART.

I roll up the window.

There's a note for me in Florie's box: *It would be so much cooler if you men had the courage to say goodbye. Goodbye.*

While I'm reading her note, her screen door opens. She sees me, she's coming for me. Her robe is open and underneath she wears little shorts and a little shirt. She's coming closer and her boobs are there, as close to me as the raindrops are to Chloe when she bends over, when she makes them her own.

She gives me the finger. I deserve it. She goes inside, slams the door. I could park the car and apologize, try and kiss her again. But I love Chloe. I push the gas but then something hits my car. *Klasch.* A mug. A plastic mug that rolls onto the ground. Brown University. She threw her mug at me. She is starting to cry, holding on to her cat's leash.

I stop the car. My heart is calm, steady.

I get out and walk toward her and she toughens up, says I had no right to *ghost* her. I apologize.

She looks around. "Not here," she says, leading me into her place.

I could leave. I should leave. I'm not kissed. I'm not fixed. I can't stop thinking about how instantaneous it was with Chloe. It's the opposite with Florie, she isn't fainting, bleeding. She is wrapping her leash around her wrist, telling me about how she can't find her cat. She doesn't know how to get under my skin and she never will. I put my arms around her and she doesn't fight. She says she missed me, *as fucked up as that is, I really did, I really thought we had a connection.*

"Me too," I lie.

She pulls away and leads me away from the fish, toward the kitchen. It smells so bad and I try to hide it. "I'm sorry," she says. "I have to clean the litter box but I read you shouldn't do that because the scent is home and if I throw it out he might not find his way."

I hold her hand. "He'll come home," I say. "He has you."

She laughs. I can tell she's been crying a lot. "It's gross, you know? What you can get used to when you live alone."

She turns off lights and checks the cat door. Feeds her fish. She says she went back on Zoloft when I ghosted her, when Muse ran off. "You guys," she says. "You have no idea what you do to us."

"You girls are the same way."

She tilts her head. "Do you mean that? Because you can't use me right now. I don't want you here unless you mean that."

I get a flash of Chloe and Doctor Actor. I push them away. I'm here.

Crane Comma Florie shakes her head. "Don't do that."

"Don't do what?"

"Don't think about someone else when you're in my home."

"I'm not."

"Don't lie. Just don't do it. I mean when you start to do it, just stop."

She tears her top off and her tits are there for the world to see, the world as in me, just me. "This is me," she says. "I'm comfortable with who I am. Don't ghost me. Don't zone out on me. I don't *need* you, but I like you."

"Okay," I say, moving toward her, still she doesn't bleed, doesn't weaken.

She pats my chest. "Follow me," she says.

I follow her into the bedroom and she asks me to close the door. The walls are white and the bed is messy and it's almost like a hospital room. No fish. No art. I realize that was all for strangers, for visitors. This is where she lives, where she worries. Where she takes her pants off and comes toward me, opening herself up to me, kissing me.

I kiss her like we did before. She doesn't stop me when I feel her boobs. Her skin goes all over me, her mouth moving into mine. She is so slow and velvety, syrup and turtles and old men in rocking chairs, all the slow things in the world, *the roots,* all of them in her, moving toward me. I want her, I feel her, I let the want take over. And then.

*And then.*

She stops kissing me. She stops breathing.

*Drip. Drip.* That bony smell, that stiffening, sinking. *No. No.* She seizes up, as her eyes bulge, no, no, as her hands crunch, *bone to muscle.* This is what it looks like when you die, the ugliest thing there is, the way the neck extends, she is a turtle, and then she's jelly, wobbling, all that energy exiting, *swoosh, vroom,* gone, and the horror of the quiet, the *thud* when her body falls onto her bed.

I killed her. Because that's what I do.


I open the bedroom door. And it hits me all at once.

*The fish.*

I run from tank to tank and some are living and some are dead but the dead aren't dead because *fish die* like she said. Not today. The dead are dead because of me.

*The smell.*

I open the closet in her kitchen, the one you can't get to without moving the trash, the recycling. I push my way in there and move the old coats, the magazines, the umbrellas, and there he is, dead, *Muse.*

I killed him too, when I kissed her. I wasn't kissed, fixed. Florie wasn't immune to me and this has nothing to do with passion. I was deluding myself and now more life is lost because of me, Florie, her sweet little cat in the window, dead. Florie never knew what I put her through, that I risked her life, that I did what I told myself I wouldn't do, I experimented on a human, *what Roger did to me.* You are what you eat and I caved. She didn't sign a form, she didn't sign up for this and she never will know and she was right about all of it. *You guys, you have no idea what you do to us.*

I go back into the bedroom and cry with her because she should know, her body should get my tears. I tell her how sorry I am.

On her nightstand, there are pills. Poor Florie. There are bags from CVS with instructions stapled on them. *Sleeping Beauty* is on TV, muted. Pills didn't kill her. I did.

Because I should know by now, once and for all, and end all the daydreams about tomorrow, about getting cured, I should get it already. I am a monster. I am evil. *I am Providence* and she was Keeping Providence Weird and I killed her.

When I die, if there is a place called hell, I will go there.

# EGGS

Some girls make you think about that Bruce Springsteen line, *You ain't a beauty but hey you're alright.* That's my kind of woman, grainy skin, a ready smile, eyes that could stand to be a little bigger, same goes for the mouth, as opposed to her feet, those could stand to be a little smaller. But a woman like that sets her eyes on you, the world opens up and sucks you in, it's a sex thing, a life thing, a thing you only get from that woman at that moment. That's what I thought about Lo when we got together. That's what I think about this poor girl, this dead girl, Florie Susan Crane. Some people, you take one look at them and you just like them.

I like her parents for giving her the middle name of *Susan.* I feel for the girl. I know what happened. She couldn't find her cat—*Muse Frontman,* according to the neighbors, the signs. She was missing him bad, and then she found him in the closet. There are pills here. Bottles open.

But this girl, in a great big T-shirt, the bottoms of her feet are brown with mud, gravel.

Why was she outside with her bare feet? She was looking for her cat.

My gut flip-flops. I radio Stacey. *Be right there, dropped my phone under the bed.*

Something tells me this girl didn't put on this shirt. There's a drawer in her chest open, as if someone didn't close it all the way. *This is crazy, Eggie, this is suicide, don't make it yours.*

I get a closer look at her face. Her skin is bare, her pores pronounced. But there are fake singular eyelashes in there, pressed in recently, you can tell—I know from my sleeping wife—and you don't put those in for nobody. She painted her eyelids, nude, as Lo says, *You work hard to look like you didn't work hard.* The skin around her lips is the slightest bit raw. She's been kissed. And my gut twists. She wasn't just kissed; whoever kissed her, he has a *beard.*

I catch my breath. What was he doing here?

Now isn't the time to question myself for asking the question, for attempting to be logical, to prove that there aren't *thousands* of men out there with beards. Now I am here, on the scene, now is the time for my mind to make leaps.

The chewing gum ground into the tiles in her kitchen.

The fish that weren't fed, the water that wasn't changed.

The pills, the dates on the bag, filled this week, recently.

He was here until he wasn't. That's why her skin wasn't used to him, the way Lo's got used to mine when I had a beard.

*That's crazy, Eggie.* No. It's makeup. *Makeup.*

When Chuckie was two, when he wasn't looking at us, wasn't smiling, was just banging his head against the wall, Lo threw all her makeup in the trash. "It's nothing but poison," she said. "Nothing but chemicals." Back then she was on my side, we were trying to beat this thing together, the thing they call autism. I remember how astounded I was by what that makeup did. Without it, Lo had no eyelashes at all, and without those eyelashes, her eyes were even smaller. I didn't say anything but sometimes she'd catch me staring at her. I wanted her to go back to wearing the mascara, and really, wasn't it too late? Chuckie was no longer inside of her. But here's the thing about love. When you want to make someone better, when you love someone, you do everything. Anything. Even if it's crazy. And then one day Lo came downstairs and her eyes were lined again, her lashes were back.

In the living room, I hear the medics calling this a coronary/possible self-inflicted, pending autopsy. This girl died of a heart attack and nobody wonders about a dead cat. Florie Susan Crane was only twenty-three. The odds of a young female of average weight dropping dead at that age: less than one percent. Odds of my Chuckie being so violent that they have to keep him in a room with padded walls: less than one percent. But odds don't matter. Not when it's your daughter, your son.

She wrote to her boss a few hours before she passed. She's a paralegal and she was calling in sick. Florie sure did like her email. There are thousands of unread messages, most of them from men. You can tell that none of these guys loved her, not in the right way. There's a tone of *Thanks for writing again, but I still don't love you. Try again next week!* The most recent guy she was talking to is named Theo Ward. It was a one-way-street situation, she was writing to him:

It was so much fun hanging out with you even if I shouldn't say that.

Because of you I am watching Grown Ups 2.

Okay it just hit me I am watching the second movie before the first BLASPHEMY.

Here's another podcast I meant to tell you about . . . Lenny Feder would approve.

Theo, sometime we have to watch Grown Ups 2 TOGETHER.

But Theo Ward wasn't responding to her. I look through her account and this is true of most of these shitheads she was talking to. They drop off the planet. She gives and they go. Lo's kids call it ghosting, but really it's just being a shithead.

The last thing she printed was an article about sex drive and Zoloft. The last thing she did in the world: she went outside and got her paper. I saw it in the living room. But she didn't bring it back to bed. Why go out and get it? Why get your feet dirty? The last purchase, insofar as I can tell: books. A bag on the floor, a receipt from yesterday.

My heart stops when I look in the bag. *Lovecraft.* Yes, her shelves are stuffed, Vonnegut and Jane Austen, DeLillo, she's got a lot of *Italo Calvino*, a few by *Colleen Hoover*. But what did she buy yesterday? The last day of her life? *Lovecraft.*

The Beard. The hat. *I am Providence.*

What do you do when someone lets you down? You investigate. What makes them tick? What do they love and why? *I'll get Lovecraft,* she thought. *Maybe then I can figure him out.* I feel it in my gut and it's the great cockeyed injustice of the system. You can know something beneath your bones, in your intestines, and you can't do anything about it.

I'm out of time and I amble into the kitchen where I play along, *Yep, this is a sad one, poor girl.* No mystery. In a corner by the overflowing trash can there are crumbs swept together, as if she couldn't work out how to get them off the floor and into the can. *Single people don't have to be neat for anyone.* In my gut: she was scrambling to make things nice for the Beard.

I open her cabinets but I feel Stacey's eyes bore into the back of my head. The girl's mother will be here, a mother who doesn't need to see some plainclothes cop sniffing around for no reason, when there's no malfeasance, no forced entry, *no nothing.* The mother has already sobbed on the phone, already said she was *worried to death* about her daughter who *just couldn't seem to find her way and never saw a drug she didn't want to take.*

My gut won't quit. It burns. I fake a yawn, I riffle through her mail. Stacey coughs.

I apologize. "Sorry, boss."

But then she leaves. I keep going, digging through her magazines, her old newspapers, sometimes she didn't even take 'em out of the bag. I wonder why she subscribes, but then I think of that poster in her living room: KEEP PROVIDENCE WEIRD. I like this girl, I do. We're clearing the kitchen and I hear the *clack-clack* of the gurney. Stacey's whistling at me, *Let's go, Eggie*.

Outside it's a madhouse, the whole neighborhood is up, alarmed. The conclusion is that Mother Nature is a capricious beast, this girl wasn't a *junkie*. Florie was *independent* and this is just *tragic*.

Stacey keeps her distance, says *people need to blame someone*.

"Sure," I say, agreeable. But I gotta honor my gut.

"Gonna get an aspirin in my car," I say.

She nods, she believes me and I am free to go, free as a kid whose mother left him alone. I watch the neighbors stand around. Most of the houses on this street are old Vics with chipped paint, split into duplexes, occupied by smart people, well-to-do people, people we used to call yuppies. And most of these people subscribe to the *Pro Jo*. More than half the houses have the white plastic box at the end of the driveway.

I pretend that my phone is ringing. I pretend that I have to take it. I start walking east, pretending to be into it with Lo—*Well tell them we can't pay up front*—and what I'm really doing is checking the boxes, the people. Everyone east of here who has a box appears to have a paper. I heave and stop. I do my best bewildered—*Lo, you have to calm down, you can't get worked up, you know that doesn't solve anything*. I catch Stacey's eye and wave my hands, helpless, and she nods.

I walk in the other direction. West. The next house after Florie's, there's an old biddy out front, shaking her head, lashing out in a whisper, *That girl ran around in a bra, I always thought she was a little off*.

I say goodbye to imaginary Lo and I put my phone in my pocket. "Ma'am, can I ask you, did you get your paper today?"

"As a matter of fact I did not," she says. "Unless your people stole it."

*Jackpot.*

I go to the next house, a couple of guys, one tall, one short. One of them's bouncing a baby. Their *Pro Jo* box is empty and I point at the box. "No paper today?"

The short one glances at the box. "I guess not," he says. "I just can't believe it about Florie."

I stop to be there, to be good. "I hear you. She seems like a good kid."

"She was the best," he says. "She's the reason we got the paper in the first place. A year ago we had her over for dinner and she got us all worked up about the importance of local news and newspapers and paper and . . ."

The tall one wraps his arm around the short one and the baby drools happily, oblivious. I smile at the little nipper. "Gorgeous kid you got there," I say, and your gut is real. That's a thing you can live your life by, that you'll do what you know is right even when people shake their heads at you, even when they think you need sleep and aspirin. I had a hunch. I followed it. And now I have a lead, a real one.

The last paper delivered went to Florie. The paperboy stopped after he hit her house. Something went on in there. She knew the paperboy. And I'll bet he had a beard.

I'll find out soon because now all I have to do is find him.

# CHLOE

I never knew I could be this girl in a robe, slithering around a penthouse, opening French doors that lead out onto the terrace. And then closing the door behind me, as if this is my home, as if this is me, biting my lip, as if it's wrong to smile, wrong to savor this view. I was a shed girl back in the day. I sat on the ground with Jon. I agreed that it was nice to be so close to the earth, that it was nice to be snug, contained.

Now I walk to the edge and I look down at New York, I never saw it like this, not from someone's home, not in a nightie.

I think of that stupid hashtag Carrig came up with the other night. *#TriBeChloe*. How he made me post it, how he makes me cringe that way, his dorky sense of humor, his puns. But it is nice to be held. Known. To wake up in silk sheets, to splash water on my face in a bathroom with two sinks. This is pretty much my first boyfriend since, well, Carrig.

I mean, I still love Jon, I do, but there's alchemy. Now I have this place, my *boyfriend's* place. It's the penthouse. It wouldn't be possible for Jon to get up here. There's the security, the doorman. It's the first time in my life that I'm out of reach, genuinely, except for those times I was in an airplane, but then every flight I've ever been on, I walked the corridor at least twice, checking every seat, looking for him.

And now I'm fucking the paint out of myself. Literally. I've never had this much sex and it cuts away the need to paint. Already I got a yeast infection like some girl in a rom-com, already I've flaked on two commissions, I feel like one of those girls you overhear in Bloomingdale's in SoHo, a girl living for *dresses*.

I feel like I'm coming into my own, and it turns out my own is this new relationship, this view. Not Jon after all.

It's the little things that seal the cracks in your heart. On our first real date, Carrig ordered tuna tartare and he pronounced it tuna *tartar* and I told him he was doing it wrong and he blushed and said he's always had a feeling he was doing it wrong but he thought it was a choice, like the way you can say tomato or *too-mah-toe*.

I told him he was being stupid. "Do you ever hear anyone say *too-mah-toe*?"

He blushed so hard. "Yes," he said. "Frank Sinatra."

Suddenly Carrig was an adult to me, someone who knew about Frank Sinatra, someone who went to college, who had changed, someone who had experiences about which I knew nothing. I wanted to learn. He told me about BU, about stocks and bonds. He wanted to know everything about me and he was unable to control himself from gazing into my eyes, lifting me up on the street outside the restaurant, telling me directly, *I want you so much it hurts.*

I know he'll give me a key soon. And maybe someday a ring. A baby. It's weird, to think of yourself as this whole other person, this girl who doesn't have intimacy issues, this girl who really can have it all, the art, the boyfriend, the love. I think that's why it's working so well. I didn't know until that first night just how badly I wanted to love someone. I always used to flinch so easily. I said it was my nerves, my artistic temperament, this ancient twitch from waiting for Jon to come back, but I'm calmer now. Sturdier. Like a table in a restaurant that shakes until you get down on your knees and wedge a napkin between the floor and the leg.

And of course it's normal that I come out here and cry when I'm alone. Of course it's sad to know that it's not turning out how I thought, how I wanted, me and Jon. Change hurts.

And Care gets it. We only have one rule, and it's unspoken: we don't talk about Jon.

I hear the front door open. My *boyfriend* is home, tossing the mail on the counter, calling out for me—*Babe, you here? I got Chinese*—and I'm drying my eyes. All the sadness dissipates. It really does. It blows my mind, it fills my soul, the smell of garlic sauce, a boyfriend's kiss, hot food I didn't have to order myself.

This is why I had to make all my social media private. I don't want Jon to know how good I feel up here, where missing him is easier because he can't find me, because the sauce is so good, the sex, the view, the aftermath of the meal, flopping into the bed, silk sheets, twisted, laughing, togetherness. I need this. I think in the gallery that night, I didn't know it, but I think I was so lonely, so Jon-sick, I think I was about to die.

# EGGS

**B**ack at the station, I listen to a voicemail that came in while I was on the road, the doctor's office, all over me to reschedule my annual physical. *Yeah, yeah, yeah, growing old is not for the weary, aches and pains in your gut, that's par for the course, are you taking your Zantac? Are you cutting back on spicy foods?* I get a text from Lo, just a picture, a picture of a letter from the doctor following up on my cancellation. No words, just a purple devil emoji. I write back: *Sorry, I know.*

She writes back: *RESCHEDULE NOW.*

But I can't do that because I have a lead. A lead! I start with a phone call to the circulation department at the *Providence Journal.* They farm out the delivery to a company based elsewhere. So now I'm on the horn to them, pushing the buttons, trying to get a human. I finally do get a human, and she's responsive and smart, things are going my way. She emails me a list of their contracted delivery people and *whammo* I have a name. I have the name of the man who delivers newspapers to Florie Susan Crane's street. He lives in a house less than ten minutes away. And yes, he has a beard.

I tell Stacey that I have to go, *Doctor's appointment, Lo will have my head if I don't get a physical.* She gives me the thumbs-up, says she's happy to see me taking care of myself. It's all I can do to stop myself from whistling, making promises to the world, how the sun is brighter outside than it was yesterday, the new world, the good world, I promise to go see Chuckie, I promise to go get my annual physical and I promise to pick up flowers for my wife for no reason. I'm a new man. A good man. I found the Beard.

And now I'm gonna go get him.


When I get to the run-down house in East Providence, I take a minute to sit and stare. By the looks of it, a few kids live here, three, maybe four, the amount of old toys in the yard, if you can call it that, the crabgrass, two dead cars with the hoods open.

I step out of the car and slam the door. I'm walking through the busted gate and there is trash on the lawn and there is trash in the trash, cigarette butts in plastic cups, cups crumbled, stuffed into Wonder Bread bags, empty packs of cigarettes, crushed. Everything here is crushed or crumbled and I hesitate at the front of the house because if I step onto the front porch it might fall in.

I press the buzzer but of course that doesn't work. I knock on the door and a woman moans. "We don't want any!"

I knock again. She groans. She's coming. And when she opens the door, the inside of the house is a perfect match to the exterior, *crushed, crumbled.* She is smaller than I expected. Almost elfin. Short hair and pointy ears and teeth that have been whittled down by crack, genes, something.

"You know you can't just show up," she says. "Even the website that never works says you gotta ask permission and give me notice. I know my rights. You don't got any right coming into my fucking home."

It's an unfair world for a woman like this, no doubt born to shitty people, then chastised. She's defensive. I can practically hear her crowing at some dive bar, *If there were jobs that pay better than welfare I'd get one*. I know this woman, I respect where she's coming from and I speak her language.

The first decision with a woman like this is whether she's *Ma'am* or *Miss*.

"Miss," I say, because there's no ring on her finger, because I'm sure she's much younger than she looks. "I'm not Social Services."

"Thank Christ."

"I'm a cop." I say *cop* because that's what a girl like her would call a guy like me. "And I'm not here to harass *you* about what goes on in your home, hell no."

"Well, good," she says. "Because I haven't *done* anything wrong, but my piece of shit neighbor on the other hand—"

I cut her off, hard. "I'm looking for Vernon Tully."

She rolls her eyes. "Well come on in," she says. "We can wait together."

"He does live here, yes?"

"Fuck if I know." She shrugs. "You could call it that. Or you could call it dis-a-fucking-pears for six months and leaves me with his kid that isn't even mine."

"But he's still supporting you? You're cashing his checks, no problem."

She flares up. Nostrils out. "That's not fair." Her jaw shakes. "Don't you start with me. I get the job done. The money *should* be mine. You think he delivers those papers. *I* deliver those papers. Only thing that motherfucker delivers is *disafuckingpointment*."

My gut freezes up. "*You* personally deliver those papers?"

She straightens. "My crew," she says. "My guys."

*Relief.* "You got names of these guys? W-2s?"

Inside, a baby cries. She is rattled. "I pay them all under the table, but I suppose you don't care. I suppose you're gonna arrest me for trying to feed my fucking kids."

The best part of being a cop is when you *don't* arrest the woman for feeding her kids, when you get to tell her that you get it, that you know about the pain of being a parent. "Thank you," she says. "I got names, hang on." She's in the living room, finding notepads, tossing notepads. "The list is somewhere," she says. "It didn't grow feet and walk out of here like Mister Shit for Brains."

"Take your time." *Hurry up.*

She looks at me. "My guys all seem good," she says. "What is this even?"

You have to love someone for loving others. I groan, play along. "We got an old biddy, she's not getting her papers, she's worked up, it's nothing."

She huffs. "And this is my tax dollars at work," she says. *"Nice."*

"She's over on Power Street. You know how they are."

"Why didn't you just say when you got here?" she asks. "That's Theo's run."

*Theo.* Florie's emails. *Theo Ward.* My heart might exit my chest.

"Fucking Theo," she says. "Pain in my ass, always mopey and quiet and shit. Gives me a fucking headache, that kid. Literally."

"That's Theo Ward, right?"

She rolls her eyes, nods. *"Yeah,"* she says. "Fucking Theo."

*Theo Ward.* It's all worth it for the feeling when you're about to get what you want, when the waitress is headed your way, when your gut was right, *yes.* "This Theo, does he have a beard?"

She nods, groaning. "And you should tell him to trim the fucking thing every once in a while. It's like he's got bugs growing in there."

"He got a phone number?"

She writes it in her notepad. The Beard. *The Beard.*

I push on. More. *More*. "Do you have an address for him?"

"He's out in North Providence," she says. "Off Benjamin. On *Spicer*. Fifty-two. I remember because I gave him so much shit about living on a street called Spicer. He didn't laugh. The kid has no sense of humor. Glum."

"Anything else I should know?"

"I don't know his sign, Officer."

"Anything physical?"

Say it. *Say it*. "He always wears this stupid hat," she says. "'I am Providence.' I mean, we all live here, right? Get the fuck over it."


In my car, I'm putting Spicer into the GPS and all I can I think of is that Dr. Seuss book, *Oh, the Places You'll Go!* I'll get that book for Chuckie and I'll go to Bradley and read it to him, even if he can't follow it.

I did it. I found the Beard.

Theo Ward. That's a fake name if I ever heard one. And I did my homework and I read some Lovecraft, read about the guy. The stories are nonsense, you can't follow these made-up creatures. But the stuff they wrote *about* him, now that's not bad. Lo was right about him being complicated. That's one word for it. The man was nutty, depressed, bad at taking care of his own. A complete racist. He used fake names. *Pen names*. But it stinks of someone trying to weasel their away around the basic laws of life.

The GPS lady says *Start*. I kick the car into gear. I start.

The reason I know I found the Beard is that I know where Theo Ward comes from. It comes from H. P. Lovecraft, literally. Two of his numerous fake names were *Lewis Theobald* and *Ward Phillips*. I memorized all the fake names for no reason, for gut reasons, as if I sensed that I would be here, on my way to Spicer Street, on my way to get him, to figure out what he does.

What is it Springsteen says in that song? *Pulling out of here to win.* Yeah. *Yeah.*

I'm careening down the highway, the same stretch I've been down a million times, only today it's different. Today is good. I can already see myself on a podium. *Well, it started with an instinct, a gut feeling. You hear that kids? Listen to your gut.* Today I take the exit where you hit all the lights because I want to expand this moment, the moment before the moment. I don't speed. I don't rush. I feel my heart pump faster and faster. I build the suspense. I bang a right before I'm there so I can circle the block, come around through the back.

I have my wits about me. I'm alive. Never been so alive. I park on the street, there's a spot for me. It's a sign, another sign.

I go east on foot, toward the back of the building, your standard run-down clunker, a Dumpster out back, stuffed to the gills, coming apart at the seams. There's a couple of banged-up old cars. I pass one of the cars, see the marks of a young person on the passenger seat, an iPod left out in plain sight, a hoodie. The Beard's iPod? The Beard's hoodie? The air is sweet and someone in there must be baking a cake. There's a back door open, a screen door. A girl comes walking toward the door, a pretty girl, looking at me as I'm looking in the car.

"Hey, I see you," she says.

She's wearing a uniform. A Tenley's uniform. I want to think that she's on her way to work but the realization sinks in hard and fast. She's not on her way. She's *at* work. That's what I smell. Tenley's. Waffle cones. *Fuck.*

"Didn't mean to sneak up on you, honey."

"Sorry," she says. "You don't seem bad, but we have a lot of scum around here."

She's walking outside, lighting a butt. This is her cigarette break. This is her workplace. That other car, that person is inside, also working. And in my gut I know the Beard doesn't work in a goddamn

Tenley's. He doesn't scoop ice cream, doesn't wear a white apron. He gave Tully's wife a fake address. Of course he did. She yawns and unlocks her car with the remote.

"You look lost," she says.

My phone buzzes. Lo. She wants to know when I'll be home.

I flash my badge and motion to the girl in the apron, *one minute*.

I write back to Lo: *Soonish. One or two more hours, sorry.*

"Hey, listen," I say. "Are there apartments above your shop here?"

She shakes her head. No. No there aren't apartments above the shop. "Why?" she says. "Are you looking for someone?"

I wouldn't normally be this free, but my gut is humming and my phone is buzzing, mad Lo, scared gut. So I just blow my wad. "You have any regulars, maybe a guy, a taller guy, got a big beard, a hat that says 'I am Providence'?"

She shakes her head. In the way where she's sure. She doesn't even need to think about it. "No," she says. "Why? Is there a creeper around? I saw some girl got raped a few miles away a couple weeks ago. Is it that?"

"Nothing like that," I say. I'm dizzy. I'm dead inside. *Dead end.* I tell the girl I have to make a phone call and I dial the number that's supposed to be the Beard's number but what do I get? I get nothing. I get the sounds of the end. That hollow, anonymous leave-a-message voice that means nothing to anyone. The sun's pounding on me and the girl's cigarette is stronger than it should be, or maybe it's the air back here, the lack of air.

"You got a bathroom in there I can use?"

She nods. "Just don't let Ricky give you any trouble." *Ricky.* The Beard? It's a pathetic thing, hope, hard to kill. "She's really weird when it comes to cops."

*She.* Inside the little hallway, the scent of it all overwhelms me, the sweetness. The sound of a woman up front. *You can do a birthday cake same day, yeah? An ice cream cake? And do you have those candles where they're made out of numbers?* I lean against the wall, hot in my head, in my gut. The sign across from me is bright, primary colors: FRAPPE OF THE DAY! FLUFFERNUTTER! It should be a colon, not an exclamation point.

I close my eyes. I remember Chuckie's fourth birthday. The night before, I went into his room. He was smiling in his sleep. I thought, *This is it.* I remember the next day, telling the doctor, Lo gasping, *Why didn't you say anything to me?* And I told her it was my present to her, this good news, that I wanted it to be a surprise. I remember the force of her arms around me, love is hands, holding you.

But then we saw the doctor. She wasn't as excited. She said she'd make a note in his report, said it was *interesting.* I sat in his room every night for a week but I didn't see his lips curl up again. And by the next checkup I wasn't sure that I'd ever seen my boy smile. You see what you want to see, especially in the dark, especially with your kid.

In the men's room, I lock the door. There's a urinal that needs to be cleaned and a standard toilet, seat up, piss all over it. *Kids.* But not my kid. Not the Beard either. I missed. I followed my gut and my gut was wrong and of course it was wrong. It's wrong all the time. It's right sometimes, yes, but all this time I blocked out all those moments when it was wrong. Chuckie's birthday. That time when Stacey had to be rushed to the hospital and I was sure that she was losing the baby, wouldn't wish that on anyone, but I felt so sure that she was gonna have her first brush with hell. But her baby was fine. Some people, things are fine. That's just how it is.

I have failed. My gut didn't fail me. My gut did what it does. It whispered to me, gnawed at me. But it's my job to know when it's onto something, as opposed to when it's just me stretching, reaching, pleading with the universe to throw me a bone.

The Beard is gone. And there is no way to find him. There never was.

I unzip. I unbuckle. I am undone, wrong and open, flapping in the wind, but there is no wind. There's only dank sweet air mixing with the urine. My gut creeps up on me as I exhale, as I try to piss.

*Come on.* It stings. It fights me. My gut falls on top of me, *plunk.* My dick burns. I look down into the urinal and I see what I expected to see, what my gut said I would see, unreliable evil gut, just as loud when it's lying as when it's telling the truth. My gut is right this time and something is wrong. I see blood and it's mine, all mine.

# JON

I think I wanted to do this the day I moved in here, just destroy every fucking thing, every piece of this life, this life I never wanted, this life I was stuck with, this half-life, non-life, poison-life.

The futon with the goddamn sheets that came in the mail from Target, the sheets that were never as soft as I wanted them to be because I misread the description online, I shred these fucking sheets until I am drenched in sweat, in *Dunwich* stench. Fuck you, sheets. Fuck you, life. Fuck you, Roger and fuck you, Magnus.

I pick up the blender I ordered from Best Buy, a night I thought I was being funny, when I ordered a blender and a DVD of *Blended*. I thought of it as a joke present for Chloe, as if she was ever gonna be in my life, as if she needed these things, as if she would have wanted them. I throw my blender at the wall, the whole of it, the glass jug, the heavy bottom. It doesn't break. *Fuck you, blender.*

My microwave, the source of so many pathetic little meals, all the Hot Pockets, all the leftovers, all the things that came out of the freezer and into this little box, the things that kept me alive as if it was worth it, as if I was ever gonna have a *life*. Being alive is nothing without being able to live.

I pull the microwave off the counter. I let it go. *Crash.*

Fuck you, T-shirts from UrbanOutfitters.*com* because I can't relax in a brick-and-mortar. Fuck you, painting I got from Etsy, blue and white and black brushstrokes that meant something to me, the same color palette as a jar of fluff. I gut the canvas with a knife. Fuck you, art. In the end, you only made me think of her even more. *Chloe.*

The more I destroy, the more aware I am of the fire in me, the rage I've been quieting for so long. I kill all this stuff because it's all his, in the end. He made me this way, a hermit with a never-ending stream of packages at the top of the stairs. I break these things because I can't break Roger.

*You're welcome,* he said.

I've held so much in for so long, ever since I tucked *The Dunwich Horror* into my back pocket. I played the part of Basement Boy for my mother, for TV. I let everyone think I'm proof that there's a silver lining, that something *good* came out of all this, that Roger Blair didn't win because I'm fine, *a picture of health!* But it ends today. Today, I'm done waiting. Today I find Meeney.

I grab my keys, I have never made it up the stairs this fast, ever.

Meeney isn't home, but I see his wife, Sadie, she's plopped on a cushy sofa in their den. *Mother's Day* is muted on their giant TV. Sadie's eyes are glued to her phone. She's mom-soft in her plush robe with her readers perched on the tip of her broad pink nose. She's home alone but she's surrounded by people; there are framed pictures on the walls of her kids, their vacations to Fiji, their little grandbaby, their great big life, the kind of life I can't have. There's an open bottle of wine breathing on her coffee table. She has white fuzzy slippers and the left one is missing a little bow.

I take a picture of her. I take another, a close-up on her slippers.

I log in to my Peter Feder email and I attach the pictures, that one of the missing bow should do it. I know it's risky. Meeney could forward my threat to the police. But I've watched him enough to know that he does love his wife. And I know what I would do in this situation, if someone threatened to hurt Chloe, I would do whatever I could to save her. My words are cold, direct:

> You have ten minutes or your wife is a dead woman. Call this
> number now, or she goes the way of the bow.

My phone rings. I finally have Meeney on the phone and now he's cold, direct.

"Who are you and what do you want?"

I don't answer right away.

He is rattled, whispering and walking. "I can hear you breathing, God damn it."

"Dr. Meeney, it's very simple. I need you to tell me where I can find Roger Blair."

"Well," he says. "It's very simple. I don't know. Now who the hell is this?"

"Yes, you do. And if you don't tell me, I'm going to murder your wife."

"Bullshit," he snarls. "Roger, I know it's you. You're using a machine to deepen your voice but only you would do this to me."

I send him a picture of the movie, Julia Roberts in her funny wig, *the last thing your sweet Sadie will ever see.* He is fuming now, *if you are in cahoots with Roger Blair.*

*We did good work down here, Jon.* We are not in cahoots, not now, not ever, and I will not lose my cool. I go again: "Where is Roger?"

He says no, he says I don't want to find Roger, *the man is a sick person.*

I huff. "That's quite a way to talk about your best friend."

There's a long pause. And then he says it. My name. "Jon?"

I screwed up. I don't know how, but he knows. My skin crawls. I try not to tremble. "Tell me where he is or I *will* kill her."

"Jon," he says. "I know you've been through hell, but I was not in on this, now let's calm down a minute. I'm on your side here. I tried to warn people, I just . . . let's talk about this."

I don't like his voice. I don't like him. He's patronizing. I tell him Sadie looks sleepy and that gets to him and he snarls, *What do you fucking want?* It's weird when a teacher swears, any teacher. I tell him I want to know what Roger did to me. He says he has no idea.

And now it's easy. "I've seen you on TV. You always have an *idea*."

He sighs. "Have you ever heard of something called *apical dominance?*"

"No."

"A tree doesn't just randomly grow tall, with one central branch. The central branch fights the others to become what it is. Nothing is arbitrary about power. The branch with apical dominance grows more strongly than the others, which in turn establishes them as weak. The dominant branch is stronger *because* the others are weak."

And then he starts lecturing me, it's a long-winded story, a lot of science. He says plants have brains, that they make choices. I already know from the videos that the dodder vine is Roger's favorite. Meeney says it's the Dracula of the food world. It has seventy-two hours to find food or it dies. The dodder literally sucks the light out of the tomato plant. It's murder. It's practical. Meeney says there is no emotion in the plant world. There is only survival.

I jot down a few words, *energy transfer, dodder vine.* He tells me about other plants that release toxins when they're under attack. He tells me about Roger's idea that humans might be able to do this sort of thing. He says the whole notion of people transferring energy, *vampiric communication,* is *categorically absurd* because we are not plants. We can't do that.

And inside I think, *But we did. We do. I do.*

He can't help me because he doesn't think it worked. I have no use for him. I need Roger. Magnus. I see Mrs. Meeney on the sofa, her new glass of wine, a picture of his kids by the TV.

"Tell me where I can find Roger."

"I can't make you any promises," Meeney says. "But there is a house in Lynn."

# JON

Chloe and I were in Lynn once, almost. It was a school field trip and Chloe was fighting with Noelle and Marlene, which meant that she wanted to sit with me on the bus. I can still see her flowery dress. I can hear Mrs. Reardon, her voice going up a hundred octaves, *A Lilly Pulitzer at your age. Wow. Must be nice.* We passed a sign for Lynn and all the windows were open and everyone on the bus was chanting, *Lynn, Lynn, the city of sin, you never come out the way you went in.* I remember Chloe's eyes when she looked at me.

"I wish they would stop," she said. "This is where our fluff comes from."

It was the most beautiful thing she'd ever said to me. *Our fluff.* I wanted us to float off the bus and go in there together, but kids aren't allowed inside the fluff factory. It's too dangerous. *Lynn, Lynn, the city of sin.*

So far it doesn't feel so full of sin here. This part of Lynn is cushy. He lives out by the Breakheart Reservation. Technically, his house is in Saugus. On the map, you can see the hiking trails nearby, places to go fishing. I live in hell and Roger Blair goes *hiking*. I turn onto his street and for the first time in my life I worry my heart is so hot it could kill me. It's so damn nice here. His house is offensively cheery with blue shingles and white shutters. There's a sign on the front door.

*Life's a Beach!*

I don't look both ways when I cross his empty street. It isn't fair that he gets to live like this. I don't use the little brick walkway that leads to his front door. I march across his lawn, his freshly mowed grass. *Bastard.* I yank the storm door open. I almost take it off the hinges. I breathe. *Cool your jets, Jon, cool your jets.* I don't want him dead. I need his help. I fix my eyes on a blue lantern he put on the porch. The man who bashed me over the head and put me to sleep, this same man went to Target or Home Depot and saw this lantern and thought, *Hey, that would look nice on my porch.* I close the storm door. Thankfully it's not a screen door. It's the perfect barrier. He must know what I can do. He won't open the storm door. We can have a conversation without my heart attacking him, at least not right away.

I knock twice, like a mailman, like a neighbor. In the distance I hear an ice cream truck and a siren, the sounds overlapping. I knock again. But no one comes, and no neighbors step out to ask if they can help me because this neighborhood is the kind where people live in their backyards, not on their front porches.


An hour later I wake up in my car.

There's a fight at a house down the street, an uneven battle between a man and a woman. The man kicks the lady and she tumbles out of the front door, spinning like a child. He throws a little plastic bag of dope at her and she's flailing, running after the bag. He kicks her again from behind. She falls hard, grabs the little bag before slipping into a car. And then she's gone and he slips back into his house. I can see his teeth from here, his smile. He's laughing.

It happened fast and I can't let go of it, I've never seen anything like that in real life. To think of how I felt so sorry for myself when Carrig teased me, but to compare it to this, a man against a woman. The guy I just saw, that guy is a real monster. I remember asking Dr. Woo if you could turn Wilbur human, if you could make the human part of the person overtake the monster part. I think about the guy in this house, in there now, not feeling remorseful, not regretting what he did.

I slam the car door and I'm walking over there knowing what I'm about to do and the little-kid *Telegraph*-reading part of me is tugging at my shirtsleeve, *Are you sure? You know most people are good.* But I am done forgiving people.

I ring the fucking bell. *Can I do this?* The monster cracks the door; he's holding a gun. *I can do this.* I kick through the door. The strength in me, I've never been like this because the other times I was trying so hard to stop it. Who knew that it would feel *good* to have this power surge and fly out of me, like a drop on a roller coaster, *swoosh*. This is for goodness, for justice.

He only has time to look at me and then the monster is dead. His ice-blue eyes are lifeless.

This is so different from all the other times. There is no crying, no pulling out my hair. There is peace. I turn off his horrible music. I notice his sweating can of beer. He won't sip it again, won't beat another woman, and that's because of me. Because of what I *can* do. Because of the way I *can* help.

This drug-dealing abuser has a Thanksgiving feast spread out all over his dining room table—phones, empty bags, scales, and baggies. I carry the bricks like newborn babies into the bathroom. There's a satisfying sound when the bags pop, snap. The dope falls into the toilet. It's hard to believe this stuff can kill you. I think of all the kids who won't be overdosing, and I know I've done something good here.

I remember my mom when she got home from her first day at T.J.Maxx. *It feels so good to have a purpose,* she said. She was right. It does.

A couple days later there's an obituary for Warren "Double U" Schmidt in the *Boston Herald.* He was twenty-two. His record included *forty-one arrests.* He had drug dens all over the city and he had been accused of rape three times. There was *no previous heart condition* but his death was due to a *massive coronary.*

It's not like I'm happy. I came here to find Roger but he hasn't stepped foot in or out of that little blue-shuttered house. I can't be with Chloe, I may never get to have that kind of life, the love kind. But it never occurred to me that I might be able to do something with my life. And I never felt it like I did today, how different it was to be at the wheel, like a captain instead of cowering in fear, in the basement. I can kill people, but I can also save them.

LYNN, LYNN, CITY OF SIN

# JON

After Kody Kardashian died, when I was first starting to wonder about myself, I would sneak downstairs every night to read the paper. That's where my parents kept the big plastic boxes of *Telegraph*s. Heavy-duty bins, jammed with four years of newspapers, four years of waiting. It was overwhelming to think of my parents, up and down the stairs every day, pulling the lid off a box, adding every daily edition, reclosing the box. Reading those papers changed everything for me. It was a daunting task. Almost fifteen hundred newspapers. Fifteen hundred days. You can read all the articles online, but you understand time when you walk into the basement and turn on the lights and see those boxes, realize there were trips to Home Depot to get those boxes, trips up and down the stairs. It's hard to miss someone. Me, I was just sleeping.

At first it was so exciting to see my picture on the front page of the paper. There I was, the lead story. But soon I was below the fold. Sooner than I expected. They were looking for me, but they weren't hunting. The crowds at the vigils were thin. I saw Mom and my dad and Chloe in grainy pictures, trying to get people to miss me, and I had the overwhelming sense that I had ruined the lives of the people I loved.

Every time I thanked Chloe for drawing pictures of me, she deflected, she said the paper made a bigger deal of it than it was, *I drew a lot of things, Jon.*

But every day when I wake up here in Lynn, I turn on my light, I see all her pictures. First thing I did when I moved in was cover the walls with her art. She is everywhere you look, her eyes, her monsters. It's like I'm inside of her. I look from one picture to another, I see her, I see me, I imagine her beside me, the miracle of her waking, rolling over, linking her arm through mine.

But even though I can't stop thinking about Chloe, I can't drag her into this. It really is time to let go, let her be, and this means I don't call her anymore. It's one thing to cover the walls with her art; she put that into the world. But I don't get to have her friendship, much as I can still remember it so vividly, I have to cut it out.

This is fate. And some good came out of it. Because of what happened to me, she put all this beauty into the world. And now it's my turn to do the same, my own version of that. I go outside and get my papers, the *Boston Globe* and the *Boston Herald.* I live in real Lynn, in the bottom half of a *two-family* in Curwin Circle. There's a lot of affordable housing around here, Honey Dew Donuts where you wish there would be Dunkin'.

I shaved my beard. I'm not moping around anymore. I'm doing a good thing, using my poisonous muscle to help the kids in this neighborhood have a shot in life, so that they can grow up to be whatever they want to be, artists, moms, dads. I don't work anymore, but I'll be okay for a while. It's amazing how much money you save when you don't have a social life, when you don't have to go see your friends for the game, when you don't have friends.

I still haven't found Roger. He's never at his house when I go over there. But I think he knows I'm coming for him. I feel him in the city. It's me against him, and when I see my victims in the obituaries, I know I'm winning. City data, crime rates, these things take years to track. The numbers won't be official anytime soon. But every day the newspapers are talking about me, not me directly but the work I've been doing. I've taken out three of the most toxic drug dealers in Lynn. Bad guys, guys who send their minions to schoolyards to give kids a taste to take home to their mothers, guys who kick dogs and mix fentanyl into heroin, people who are responsible for ruining lives, taking advantage of innocent people.

People like Roger Blair, people with no regard for human life.

I sit down at my kitchen table with coffee and my papers, fresh, rolled up in rubber bands. You read the *Herald* like a book, but the *Globe* is old-fashioned, folded.

Today's papers have articles about my seventh target, Eddie "Soup" Campbell. Right away I realize that things are more complicated with Soup than I realized. Soup was a drug dealer, yes, but he had cut a deal. He was set to be a witness in a case against one of his suppliers. Without Soup's testimony, they don't know if they can nail the suppliers, and my head is pounding. There's a picture of Soup's girlfriend, the mother of his children, she's leaning over the way they tell you to on a plane when it's gonna crash. She's wearing two different shoes. They were high school sweethearts, *been together since they were kids.*

There's a giant op-ed in the *Herald* about the uptick in dead drug dealers.

> . . . Our soldiers from the wrong side of the tracks are
> dying of heart failure. Two is a coincidence. Three is a
> trend. Seven is an epidemic. I lost my daughter to the
> opioid epidemic three years ago. There is no way to track
> the time after you bury your child. Time is your enemy.
> It's another day on this planet that makes no sense.

I won't jump on the bandwagon and declare this a "phenomenon." I speak with parents in my situation every day. I volunteer at the hospital to hold babies born addicted to heroin, pure souls at a physical disadvantage. I visit women in their late sixties who are acting as mothers, doing the school drop-offs because their children are unable to care for their children.

We live in a world together, where one thing affects another. Is it so hard to believe that these deaths might account for a cosmic, karmic influx?

The opioid epidemic is killing all of us, which means we are all in this together. I don't know about you, but that makes me feel better.

The columnist has an email address. I could write to her and tell her about my situation, that there is no coincidence, no trend, there is only me. I profile these people for weeks, skulking around in a hoodie, trying to be invisible, keeping my distance, ordering product online to get a sense of how they do business. I have to make sure these guys are as bad as I think they are. I have to know for sure that I'm eliminating evil because once I set out to get them, once my heart starts ticking, there is no turning back.

When I finish reading my papers, I don't store them in a big plastic box. I toss them into my fireplace and burn them. The papers crumble and shrink, twisting in the invisible hands of a monster. I think of Wilbur in *The Dunwich Horror* disappearing, leaving no corpse, no trace.

My next target is Casey "Incy" Waterman.

I read about her in an article about the double-edged sword of forensics in police investigations. The example they used was the case of a livery cabdriver who had pulled over to nurse her baby. She was desperate to make ends meet, to feed her baby. Someone murdered her in cold blood for the *fifteen dollars* in her wallet, wanted to send a message to the neighborhood, left the baby drinking the dead mother's milk. It was the kind of story that makes people say the world is close to an end.

Everyone knew it was Incy who did this. She shouted her name to the night. *This is Incy Town, people. You hear me?* But the evidence was compromised, the prints were misplaced, a fiber was mixed up. Incy walked, in spite of the witnesses who heard her boasting, in spite of all the cellphone photos of Incy in the street. The lawyer's logic was simple, modern: *We can't trust photographs when there is no physical evidence to corroborate these grainy pictures.*

Incy got her nickname when she was a kid in the system, shoved from one foster home to another. She spent most of her years in juvenile facilities. She was violent. She came from violence. It was another chicken/egg situation. What to make of these monsters?

Even now, grabbing my keys, my sunglasses, waving 'bye to Chloe's pictures, I don't know if what I plan to do is right. Women are different. They can carry life inside of them. You never know what might become of that life. But that's not fair either, reducing a person's defining quality to this *one* thing she can do. I know what Dr. Woo said about Wilbur, I think about it every day, that there was no other possible fate for a creature like that, that it's not enough to be part human if you're mostly monster. But ultimately that's the difference between a made-up story and real life. Lovecraft made all the choices for Wilbur. In real life, you make your own choices.

And there she is. Same place, same time every day, standing with her jet-black hair and her silk jacket with Cantonese writing on it and her black jeans, holes in the knees. Same friend who's always there, her *number two,* the girl in the Bruins jersey. Incy is the clear boss. The Bruin supplicates, always facing her superior with her hands latched behind her back, fingers laced together. The Bruin is pregnant and she only releases her hands to light a *butt*. They have the same conversation a couple times a week. Both their mothers smoked *butts* and they both turned out *totally fucking fine*.

It's been hard to make a move on Incy because she's never alone. I can't take them *both* out. It's the pregnancy, the reality that two women dying of heart attacks at the exact same time would raise questions. And, of course, I'm getting to know them. I watch them laughing, when they elbow each other and fight over the lighter, over some guy, over the Bruin's hair. I think about Noelle and Chloe, about Crane Comma Florie, about girls, how they connect, they meld. They talk in their own language, and then again, all the babies they might have, not have, the power either way.

Incy laughs a lot and she kicks the air a lot, high kicks. She drinks Diet Dr Pepper and people know this. I track them on foot and when people see Incy coming by, they wait for her with a Diet Dr Pepper. Incy likes a bottle. Last week this guy offered her a can. She bashed him in the head with it. Then she threw the can at a window in his house. The Bruin doubled over laughing and then Incy punched her in the arm. *Let's fucking go.*

Today is par for the course. They head to a couple free clinics to give out free samples, a halfway house where they hide bags in an empty chewed-up Honey Dew polystyrene cup by a dying plant out front. And then they head into the doughnut shop. I lurk outside smoking a *butt*. (There are things you have to do if you want to be invisible.) Incy gets the usual, a glazed cruller. She chews on the left side of her mouth, as if the right side of her mouth is broken. The Bruin bites into a chocolate chip muffin bottom and Incy laughs, *who the fuck eats muffin bottoms, teach your fat ass a lesson about what's good.* This is a running joke, another way in which girls fascinate me, how hard they laugh, how deeply their minds bend together.

Incy's mom was a junkie, her dad too. Nobody loved Incy, but that's no excuse for her behavior. She has four kids but she doesn't take care of them. They're all in foster care, like she was. She doesn't try and get them back. I think of those *Telegraph*s in March, when I was gone missing four months, when there were weeks at a time without a mention of me in the paper. It is terrible to be forgotten. My heart is heating up and Incy's licking her fingers. I put out my cigarette. I jaywalk to the other side of the street and hang by the front of a packie, watching Incy and the Bruin begin their post-doughnut ritual. They light up right where I was standing. And again I marvel at my power, or lack thereof. Only seconds ago I was where they are, and were I there now, they would be dead. I know the way I've known every day for the past three weeks, this isn't it. It's not happening today.

I got Chinese again. It's something, how easily you slip into a routine. This is my typical day right now. Wake up and read the papers, track Incy, wimp out on Incy, pick up Chinese food, and then drive through town and park across the street from Roger Blair's house.

Sometimes I swear the police are onto me, the police or someone who knows those heart attacks were not nature's way. I'll be ducking my head to inhale my lo mein and I'll get that spine tingling thing where I know I'm not alone. But there's no one there when I spin my head around.

I tracked down a couple of his neighbors online and found out what little there is to know about the owner of this house. *That guy? He's never around. I think I heard him the other night. He runs in, out. He's probably living somewhere else while he fixes up the place.* He can't hide forever. Every week there's some kind of proof that there is activity in the house, fresh paint, a new mailbox. He replaced the nails that hold up his stupid *Life's a Beach!* sign. I've staked the place out, but my timing is never right. Sometimes I think he's avoiding me, that he knows my car. He might have an underground tunnel, an escape hatch.

I close the tab on the polystyrene box of noodles. I don't know the last time I hugged a person. But then, most people will never know the rush of having saved lives, the satisfaction of the plastic bags snapping as the insidious, poisonous powder drops into the toilet bowl.

I get out of my car and my heart beats faster as I approach his house, as I knock on his storm door, the door I know so well by now, the white border, the freshly wiped Plexiglas. My heart is going pretty good and I ring the bell. I listen for the pitter-patter of feet, a door opening, an escape hatch springing free from a padlock.

Nothing, always nothing.

I head to the side of the house, where there are more windows, always freshly washed, more proof of his presence, his fastidious nature. I try the handle on the back door. It doesn't budge. I could break in. I could pick this lock. I could hunker down and wait for him. I grip the handle. But then I let go. I hear something. A screen door slamming, and then I hear something else, my heart, pounding. I run to the side of the house and I see him, the tail end of him, that longish creepy hair, the slight hunch in his backside. This is like one of those nightmares where you run but you're not fast enough.

When I get to the front of the house, he's gone.

# CHLOE

This is my favorite Manhattan.

Four o'clock in the morning and most of the people are sleeping. It's not true what they say about New York, how they tell you it never sleeps. Out here on Care's balcony it's quiet at this hour. You hear things you don't normally hear. It's stunning, how it enlivens my senses, almost like a tab of ecstasy. I watch the sky change colors, the inevitability of the sun coming up. Sometimes I cry. Sometimes I smile. This is always when I feel Jon the most. When I imagine his pain if he knew where I was, who I was with.

Carrig's love is sealing the crack in my heart that Jon made. And I'm fighting it. I'm not painting, not sleeping. I think it's almost an overdose of love. Different kinds of love coexist in me. I think maybe I'm a sociopath. Maybe I have no heart. Maybe I have a big heart.

I love Jon, obviously. He's in my mind, he's a part of my story, I'm a part of his. But I love Carrig too, the shape his face takes on when he's nervous, confused, when I told him I didn't have pierced ears and he blushed. *Really?* He has a strong *really.* A loving *really* that reveals the depth of his desire to know me. To know me more than Jon knows me. But we don't talk about Jon.

Well, except for that one time.

We were having a bad couple of days. Care tagged me in a picture on Facebook and I flew off the handle, untagged myself, accidentally blocked him in the process. I said what I had said since we first got together, that I was trying to have a *private life* and that I wanted this to be *special.* I pointed to my career. *It's just better if people wonder about you so they can more easily project onto your work, you know?* He still didn't buy it; he knew me well enough by now to know when I'm lying. I couldn't tell him about Jon, this hybrid of paranoia and hope that he's watching me. So I told him another embarrassing truth.

"I've never really had a boyfriend since, you know, you."

"Are you serious?"

I blushed. He hugged me. "I'm sorry," he said. "I'm just thrown off."

He was exasperated. He didn't understand how someone like me had gone through life alone. And I didn't say it. I didn't have to say it. *Jon.*

Carrig left to meet his friends and I stayed in his apartment. We weren't quite used to each other yet. When he got home, he was wasted, tequila wasted.

He flopped on the couch. "Jon Bronson," he said. "He really fucked you up didn't he?"

I didn't answer.

He laughed. "It's cool," he said. "Don't worry. It's not a deal breaker."

I did make an effort to get through to him. I backtracked and assured him that I was normal. I'd had plenty of sex, flings that lasted a few weeks, maybe even a month. But he's not a listener. I know this about him. *It's not a deal breaker.* He patted the couch and I sat there with him and watched *Entourage,* but the whole time I was in another world, lecturing myself. *Is this what you want? Some guy who thinks of your relationship as a contract?* I told myself I was being harsh. That wasn't him. That was the tequila. But that didn't matter. What mattered was me. Lying to him, to myself. *What fucking bullshit, Chloe. You're lying and you know it. You've been with Jon since you were eleven years old.*

I realized that there was no sound coming out of the TV. Care was watching me. He was still drunk.

I blushed. "What's wrong?"

"Sometimes you go away," he said. "You know I feel it, right?"

I turned into Sweet Girlfriend Girl who climbs aboard my boyfriend, and it felt honest to hold him, to say things like, *Honey, you need water, let me get you a snack.* He tried to follow me into the kitchen but he banged his leg and fell. He was gripping his knee and thinking out loud: *Why are you ashamed of me? If I was him, if I was him you'd tell everyone cuz he's a smart fucking dork and that's what you want? Isn't it? You don't want me. You don't do you?*

The next morning he didn't mention the night before.

So here we are, *together.* And in the beginning, when things were normal, this is when I would be painting. But then, *normal* is a bogus word. There's no such thing as normal, not for anyone.

And now here I am, awake on Care's terrace, same way I am every day, paint drying while Carrig sleeps soundly. Out here, in no-man's-land, in the desolate hours between night and day when I can't hurt my boyfriend's feelings, when it's not a betrayal, I give in to it. The obsession. Sometimes I just think, but tonight is one of those nights I have to *do* something. I'm not in the state I was before I got together with Care, no more clutching my phone in a movie theater awaiting a call from Jon, no more pointless trips to Providence.

But this part of me won't die no matter how many times Carrig leaves work early in this completely undramatic way, shrugging, blushing, *I just missed you, babe.* I am loved. Craved. I am babe. I am held.

It's the opposite of Jon. But then I can't wrap my head around my own bitterness. I have no right. I wouldn't have a career without him. And the truth hits me and I have to sit down.

This is why I'm not painting. Because of Care. Because I don't think I deserve to have Carrig and Jon. Because I think of my career as being a result of Jon's disappearance, a response on my part, not something born of my heart, my mind, but something pulled out of me by the pain, the horror of his disappearance. The feminist part of me kicks back. *Bullshit you wouldn't have a career. You're an artist, Chloe. Stop undermining yourself. If it wasn't his eyes you were trying to draw, it would have been something else.*

So why haven't I painted a single fucking thing in almost a year?

Carrig is knocking on the doorframe, a familiar knockity-knock-knock.

At some point I must have fallen asleep, because this is me waking up, jet-lagged from perpetual insomnia. I don't want him to know how tired I am, how much I wish he would leave so that I could close the blinds and miss the daylight part of the day. But he's a morning person. And I believe him when he says that morning people are happier people.

He opens the blinds. "My mom says you have to do this first thing because it's good for your body," he says. "She would go into all our rooms and yank the curtains all the way open. You shoulda heard the screaming."

"Well," I say. "I wouldn't object to a little screaming."

He's still in his boxers, awake in that morning man way. "I can help you with that."

One thing I've learned about being with him: I like to cook.

I'm terrible at cooking, but I'm at my happiest in Carrig's kitchen, with Carrig's utensils, iPad propped up on a stand. I'm whisking egg whites and he's singing along to some song he learned about from *Entourage* in the other room.

A text from Marlene pops up on the screen. She's married, she's a mommy. Every day we have less in common and she's another one who grows silent when I mention Jon, which I don't, not since she had the baby. I drop the whisk in the bowl.

Mar! Hey!

So . . . The latest. I'm breast-feeding I need news please.

I'm still not painting but a lot of artists take sabbaticals and I'm learning how to be a human. You would be proud. Do you know I can whisk?

Lolol I meant you and Care, are you moved in?

I'm here.

But can I put up that picture we got of you guys when we visited?

I stare at the screen. Marlene knows better. She's well aware that I've kept this relationship offline and I've rolled out all the same excuses with her.

Okay . . . I'm going away now. 😕 But when you do decide that this isn't the kind of thing you have to hide from people please let me know lol bored new mommy seeking to live vicariously through sexy New Yorkers!

And then she's gone. I'm whisking eggs again. Harder now. I fucked it all up. The oil is burnt. The whites aren't doing what they did in the video. I toss them into the disposal.

"Hey," Carrig says. "What's wrong?"

"I destroyed breakfast."

He smiles. "It was gonna be bad anyway."

There's one thing that's not perfect. His teasing. Sometimes I hear his mother in there. But I know what Marlene would say. *Who doesn't?* He's rubbing my shoulders, biting his lip. "You are the cutest fucking thing in the world," he says.

I lay my hands on his. "I love you."

"I know," he says. "Do you know, before you, I had to take an Ambien just to crash for three hours."

"Care . . ."

"Let me finish," he says. "My doctor said it's anxiety, it's a common thing for bankers because of the stress, the market, the grind. So I took the pills when I needed to. And then you came back into my life. And now you're not sleeping, because you're in love, and I want you to know that it's the same reason I *am* sleeping. And I love us for how different we are. I love our opposite parts, our same parts. I love you."

I can feel his heart pounding faster. I can see his reflection in the oven door, just the shadows. I'm sure he's sweating.

"You're supposed to get down on one knee to do this," he says. "But you know I look up to you. I've always looked up to you. There's nobody like you, Chloe. I don't want you to say yes to me," he says. "I want you to say yes to *us*."

There is a ring on my finger. I missed the big reveal of it, the shine. It's the right kind of ring. It fits and it feels good, as if my finger was yearning for something to keep it attached to my hand. I picture the finger spinning off, the ring falling. I squeeze my eyelids. At some point I'm gonna have to start sleeping again. Sleeping or painting. I gulp.

"Well," he says, just like a guy in a jewelry store commercial, like a man who craves devotion, love, home, a man at his most vulnerable, a man who needs a woman. "Well," he says again, so nervous, so exposed. "Do you like it?"

# EGGS

Here's what cancer is, it's the same fucking thing you saw yesterday and today (Sorry, Lo), it's the end of adventure, it's the commercials on TV, the boiled noodles you upchuck, the look on Lo's face when you ask her for the fourth time in six hours if she steeped your tea for fifteen minutes, not ten (Sorry, Lo), the same as yesterday (Sorry, Lo), the ostomy bag filling up, your wife bending over to clean up the vomit and your wife bending over again, to inspect the ostomy bag when you think it's messed up again (Sorry, Lo). Cancer is knowing that you got it because you fucked up. You're not some kid, some victim. No. You're the asshole who got so obsessed with the coronaries and the Beard that he missed his chance to nip it in the bud. I played God and what did I do? I fucked myself. Stage IV bladder cancer, miracle I'm alive.

If that's what you want to call it. Ever since the surgery, since the chemo, my life is mostly here, in the living room (what a fucking name for it), and my person is only Lo, coming on now. "Did you take your Urelle?" she asks.

"Yes, I did," I say, as if I can ever atone for all the time lost, all the trips to CVS she's made, as if what we needed was *more* expenses, more agony.

She glances at my iPad. "Is that all charged up?"

"Yes, it is."

"Do you want me to sit with you?"

It's the worst of all the questions. *Did you move your bowels? Did you finish the water? Did you keep down the melba toast? Did you clean your catheter?* Somehow none of them compare to that one, as if I'm a baby that needs watching.

"You go on," I tell her. "I'm fine."

She picks up her purse and swings it over her shoulder. She's going to see Chuckie, and she's brittle, digging around in her purse for her keys. I can feel her thinking it all the time. *If only you'd gone to the doctor, you'd be going with me right now.* But I'm sick, low white count. So going to see Chuckie has turned from a thing I won't do to a thing I can't do. I think of her in our bed alone, wondering how this happened to her, her son living in a hospital and her husband living on a sofa, both stubborn, inscrutable. She pulls her keys out of her purse. "Eggie," she says. I am her patient, not her husband. "You have to take the multivitamin at *eight*."

"Eight is great, Lo."

When she kisses me on the forehead, it's because she has to, not because she wants to.

"I'll text you and see if you want anything."

"I'm good, Lo."

"Marko might stop by," she says. "His girlfriend made us a casserole, something, I don't know."

I nod. "That's nice."

Lo's kids, they've taken this cancer, they've made it into a project, filling our house with quilts and casseroles, marijuana pills, you name it. When Lo refers to them as *our kids* I don't argue. It's the worst thing about the cancer, *our kids*. But I don't complain. I try my best to do right by Lo. I don't search for solutions online the way I did when Chuckie got sick. I do every goddamn thing those doctors tell me to do. I follow directions and I don't ask questions and when Lo drives me to the doctor I hum along to whatever's playing on the radio.

But I'm not perfect. Who is? When she's gone, when I can't see her car, I get up off my couch—the dizziness—and I get my cane—*my cane, our kids*—and I make my way up to Chuckie's room, to my boxes. Lo thinks I don't come up here much, she'd worry about me on the stairs. But I have to come up here. I fall asleep on the sofa too easily and I can't do any research on the iPad because she'd see. But she never comes up here, not anymore.

I sit at my desk, breathless.

I turn on my computer. The cancer is my fault, that's the bad news. But the good news is that I might not be crazy. In the past year, *seven* drug-dealing sociopathic shitheads have dropped dead in Lynn, Massachusetts. I got a box going on these coronaries, these dead kids, all of them under thirty. Seven, an unprecedented number.

The first one happened just a day or so after I pissed blood at Tenley's. I read about it in the paper in a waiting room at the hospital. A drug dealer, dead. I made a mental note and I tracked down an old buddy of mine who works in Lynn, Felix Mort. He's not the brightest bulb, he moved to Lynn because his wife's family's from there and then they got there and she left him about six weeks later, because obviously she wanted to move there to get back with an old beau. She was only using Felix to get her set up so she could rekindle things, play it coy. He would drive to Providence and sulk on the sofa and Lo would tell him it would be okay, that he'd meet someone. And then he'd pass out and she'd kiss me, say you just could tell, poor Felix, still living in Lynn, he's *never* gonna meet anyone.

Anyway, I rang him up to get more details on the coronary. Guy was a thug, he said, no track marks, prelim screens were clear, just pot, none of the real stuff. "Dealers not doers," he said. "Hey, how's Lo?"

"Good, but wait, is there a history of heart failure?"

Felix laughed. "This guy had no heart, Eggie. All he had was a record."

One month later another thug drops dead. I start my chemo.

Next month another death. I lose my hair.

And then another. And so on. Every month I fight my cancer and these thugs in Lynn just keep dying. I call Felix, he thinks he hit the jackpot, he's buying scratch tickets, this is how lucky he feels, these guys, these guys at the top of his list, the guys who get away with *the worst things in the world because they employ people to cover for them*, these guys are dropping like flies. He believes in God now; he's dating a girl he met in *church*. I'm not sure about our Holy Father, not with the way I feel, not with the burning inside of me, poison eating me from the inside out, but I do believe in the Beard. I believe he is there. More and more every day.

These thugs, they all die alone. They're all bad guys; the worst is a *gym teacher* setting his kids up with crack. I press Felix for details on the teacher one day and he sighs.

"Vicky dumped me."

"Jeez, Felix, I'm sorry, I'm just really sick from the chemo. I want to hear about it, but I just wanted to know, the teacher, anything more on him?"

You think cancer is a get-out-of-jail-free card, but it isn't always. Felix lost his mom to cancer when he was a kid. Someone like me gets it, someone old, he just shrugs, *we all die of something*. So I'm not surprised, not really, when the next time I call Felix, it goes to voicemail and he never gets back to me.

*Fuck Felix.*

I know it's the Beard. Eleven dead in Lynn, all under thirty, but more important, *zero* young coronaries in Providence in the same time span. Numbers don't lie.

But how does he do it?

Downstairs, the doorbell chimes. *Marko.* I'll never make it down in time and I can't have him coming up here. It rings again and I hear them out there, I hear them looking for the key, I hear them finding the key. *Double fuck.* I close the computer. I listen to them come in, Marko and the girl, the whispering.

*Marko, maybe he's asleep. Should we check in the bedroom?*

*Nah, babe, let's just leave this in the fridge. We don't wanna wake him up.*

*But shouldn't we make sure he's okay?*

*Of course he's okay. Guys like him beat it. He's old-school.*

I hear him kiss her, lucky bastard. She giggles. They're so young I could kill them, and now they're moving around, trespassing, thinking they've lucked into something here, a moment to snoop through the teacher's desk. My cheeks redden and I hear the drawers open. I hear them marvel at our bills, our expenses.

And then they get tired of us—*too depressing* the girlfriend says, *how much bad luck can people have, right?* I hear him kiss her now, really kiss her, tell her how lucky he is to have her, how they're gonna do it right, they're gonna cherish every day. When he starts to take off her blouse, when I hear the table rattling, when I know this is real— Marko is going to bang his girlfriend on my kitchen table and I am going to hear it happen—I try to block out the sound. I make earmuffs with my hands. I stare at the duckies on the wall and cancer is creative, it finds a new way to make every day your worst day yet, it's my hands pressing into my ears, hard, as if there's any way to stop yourself from hearing young people fuck, *fuck.*

Later that night I'm back downstairs on the sofa and Lo tries to feed me Marko and *Bella's* lasagna. I tell her I'm not hungry but she forces me to try a bite and unfortunately it's delicious, sweet with ricotta, melty cheese, the noodles flat how I like. I eat a whole slice of it and

I think about the Beard, Theo Ward, off in Lynn, that's gotta be him, out there knocking off drug dealers.

Lo moans. "Eggie, this might be the best thing I ever ate, right?"

Cancer is when your wife is right and *your kids* knocked it out of the park with the lasagna but the Beard is in Lynn and you are on a sofa, nauseous. I lick my fork.

"Lo," I say. "Ya better pass me that bucket."

# JON

The next morning I walk down to the water, to King Beach, maybe my favorite place in the whole city. I love it here, the metal and concrete against the water. There's this drop-off walkway where the ocean hits this wall below, and when I stand there I feel like a hero of the sea, like Leo in *Titanic*.

I sit on a splintery bench I think of as mine and I call my mom. I started calling again once I got here. It felt safe. Like now that I have purpose, I could call home once a week like real people do.

She always picks up, always coughing. "Jon."

"Mom."

"Where are you?"

"I'm okay."

"Jon, I won't tell anyone. Just tell me where you are. I hear the water."

"I'm by the beach."

"What beach?"

"You okay? Dad okay?"

"Why won't you come home?"

I can't tell her that I will come home. I can't tell her that I'm a *superhero*, a crime-fighting superhero. She'd call the cops on me and that would be a disaster. She always takes over the conversation anyway. She tells me random things, about a woman she doesn't like at work and some tree my dad cut down in the yard. And then we're quiet. And then she cries.

"I love you, Mom."

"Then come home," she says. "Let me see you, let me *hug* you."

She is hyperventilating and pouring wine and she was not meant to have this kind of life. She isn't strong enough to have her one and only son get kidnapped and then come home and then go away again.

"Tell Dad I miss him," I say and then I hang up.

I don't cry. I refuse to cry the way a person in a restaurant refuses to order dessert.

I stare at the water. When my mom turned thirty-five, her friends got her ten sessions with a personal trainer at a gym. He was named Cleo and the first session she came home with red slick skin and a big smile. *I love Cleo! And he said I was great. I was already getting the hang of it.* My dad and I made bets about how long it would last. She went again three days later and this time she came home sweaty. She wasn't glistening. She was rubbing her lower back. *The jerk teaches me to do all these moves and today he forces me onto all these new machines.* My dad cackled. *Only way to get in shape is to surprise your muscles, Pen. Nothing's worth a dang once you know how to do it. Your body just goes right back on autopilot.* My dad won the bet. My mom never went back after that second time. She said she understood why they call it "working out" and that it wasn't the right job for her.

This is the right job for me, cleaning up the streets, staking out my targets. I don't accept my fate, but I accept my role in someone else's fate.

Incy lives on Alley Street and the sun has come out by the time I get over there, as if the skies are smiling upon me. I feel like a doctor going into surgery. It's not like I'm happy about what I have to do. I'm aware that the Bruin has some tough days ahead, but there's also the possibility that the Bruin will be better off, her baby too.

Incy is alone in her house. I've watched her for weeks now and I know her ways. This is the only time she's ever truly on her own. She cracks her window for that first cigarette. I've seen her do it a hundred times. She doesn't look at her phone while she puffs. She looks out the window. You wouldn't assume that she's a vicious, murdering psychopathic drug pusher. There's nothing going on in her mind, in her heart. A chill runs over me. *Of course there isn't. That's how she's able to do what she does.*

I take a deep breath. She's got one puff left, maybe two. Then she'll flick the butt into the yard and go into her bathroom. I get out of my car and cross the street. Nobody's up yet, nobody's looking. I pull on the cracked window and it gives. Incy's house smells like lemons and bleach. She's singing in the shower—*I can't sleep at night, I toss and turn, listening for the telephone*—and it's an old song, Bobby Brown, I think. It's a short walk from the living room to the bathroom and "Every Little Step" is the song I'll hear every time I think of her for the rest of my life; what I'll see are the scars on her back, deep and dry, deflecting the water.

She puts her hands up—*Hey now*—and she thinks I'm going to attack her—and I've never seen her this scared and for a minute there I lose my nerve, because she is a woman in a shower, unclothed, and I am the intruder, and on what planet could I be the one in the right?

There's a way to speak to someone without opening your mouth, and Incy does not die afraid of me, the male intruder. I know she knows what this is, even if she doesn't know how I will kill her, there is no gun, no knife, I know she dies afraid of where she is going, if there is a place like hell, she expects to be there.

She is dead now. And there's something calm and unsurprised in her eyes, as if she always expected it would end like this, with the water running and her wounds exposed.

I want to reach into the shower and turn off the faucet. It doesn't seem right to leave her like this, the water shooting at her torso. But I can't do that, I can't tip off the police. When you die of a heart attack in the shower, you die alone.

I get two dinners. And it feels like an act of respect on some level. A way to honor the dead. The other polystyrene box of Chinese sits in the passenger seat of my car, untouched, *Incy's last supper*. I turn on the radio, but there's no news yet. I look at the clock: *4:13*.

And then I hear classic rock blasting. Anyone who lives in New England can tell you what that means, the sound of Journey, the familiar rhythms warbled and crunchy from a weak radio, offset by the sound of a truck going too fast, hitting potholes. It's landscapers. I sink lower and recline my seat. They pull up in front of Roger's house.

There are two of them. SACKETT LAWNS & MORE it says on the side of the truck. The one with the red hat gets out of the driver's seat, bitches about his neck. The other one is quieter. You can tell by the way he closes his door with two hands.

"This is smaller than he said."

Red Hat's voice sounds like tobacco. "Cuz he's a fucking shady prick. Won't even pay cash. Forces me to go to a convenience store that's practically all the way in *Somerville* and pick up the cash in an Amazon freaking drop box. Like I don't have things of my own to do, like he pays enough to put me in traffic. You believe that shit?"

Blue Hat walks over the crabgrass. "This is *way* smaller, dude."

Red Hat finishes off a Bud Light. "Hang on, dude, I'm calling him right now. He said there were keys." Red Hat groans. *Voicemail.*

"Hey, mista, it's Dan from Sackett Lawns. Yeah, we're wondering when you might be coming by to drop off a key to use the facilities, you know, snag a glass of $H_2O$ if need be. You can reach me here, guy. Later."

Blue Hat looks at him. "So," he says. "When's he coming?"

Red Hat tosses his phone in the front seat of the truck. "Not soon enough, fucking prick."


I waited for Roger with Red Hat and Blue Hat all day, but he didn't show up. A couple of times I would have sworn that he was there. I got that creeping itch I had that day in the woods. I was too young back then, too late, but now when that inkling overtakes me, I brace myself, I whip my head around. But today was like every day. No Magnus in the shadows. Once again, I was just being paranoid.

Now I'm home. I'm not really surprised that I didn't see him. Your life never happens in one day like that, all the big events at once. I did my job today, but it's hard to feel good when I still see her on the floor of the bathtub. It's not like *The Dunwich Horror*. It isn't like Incy's body evaporated. She was a person and there are moments that I can't live with what I've done, what I do, and I close my eyes, I pretend Chloe is here, knowing, *It's okay, Jon. It's all working out. You'll see. I promise, you just have to have faith in the big picture. Can you see it? It's there. I promise.*

It's calming to hear her voice, even if it isn't real. My mom always said you have to focus on what you *do* control, which is what her diets were all about. It doesn't mean she was losing weight, but she was being *proactive*. I was proactive today. I stopped a monster.

I close my eyes and concentrate on Red Hat and Blue Hat, all of us waiting for Roger Blair. I can hear Red Hat so clearly, *Not soon enough, fucking prick.* And in my dreams I have a green hat, and the three of us are brothers, digging holes in Roger's lawn. And we keep bumping into bodies, into Incy, into Kody, into the others. We scoop their bloodless bones out of the ground with our bare hands and we sing along to Journey like there's nothing weird about it, nothing sad. And then the Bruin comes booming out of the house with a gun. Her baby slides out of her body, onto the driveway, growing even as it rolls toward the bushes, it's a toddler by the time it reaches the mailbox— just like Wilbur in *The Dunwich Horror.* The Bruin's toddler pulls out a newspaper and a bag of heroin. She runs down the street and none of us are fast enough to chase her, not even her mother, who cries so much that I wake up soaked in her tears, my sweat.

# EGGS

Lo swears you can't see my ostomy bag but it doesn't matter, to a degree. It's the knowing that it's there, that everyone on the force is gonna be looking for it when I go back next week. Stacey will run her eyes all over my slacks looking for it.

Lo walks in, clutching her phone. "Wow," she says. "Guess what?"

I look at her. No guessing. Not now. She nods. She says Marko called, he sold a book. "Can you believe that, Eggie?"

It's not that I don't like the kid, it's that Lo does, that she's taking this on as one of her achievements. Already, I have to hear about Marko's forthcoming nuptials to that girl he banged in my house. I have to hear about his paper on Ann Petry and his volunteer work downtown, about his lasagna—*still haven't tasted anything that good since, right?*—and now this, a book deal.

"What kind of a book?"

"Poems," she says. "And it's a real feat, Eggie, getting someone to cut a check for poems."

I do my best. I try to get it up for Marko and his poems. Lo says *her kids* are gonna be so excited, that this sort of thing is good *for all the kids* because it makes them remember that good things happen. She's fired up, happy. I have an ostomy bag and a headache but for the first time since all this happened, this cancer business, my wife is happy. And it stings, her smile, her smile that doesn't have anything to do with me, she's already busy with her phone, telling me that Marko wrote to her in the back of his book.

"You know what he calls me, Eggie?"

"No, obviously."

She ignores my sarcasm or she misses it. Neither possibility is good. "My sweet Lo," she says, hand to heart. She comes over to me, kneels on the floor the way she did when I first got sick, when the cancer was new and exciting, paid vacation, pre-pills, pre-bag. "Wanna see something funny?"

"Always," I say, relieved that she's back. When's the last time she was this close and not to take my temp?

"He wants me to help him pick out some pictures for his press packet."

She scrolls through pictures of happy, healthy Marko, sometimes with his hair tucked behind his ears, sometimes serious, once on a sailboat, another time in a garden, sometimes laughing, here he is in black-and-white with the girlfriend—*fiancée,* Lo says, *we have the engagement party coming up*—and all the time he's healthy. Healthier than my boy. Lo gets to the end, the last picture, Marko and the girlfriend. They're on a bench, waving.

"How come she's in half the pictures? I thought this was his book."

"It's theirs. She wrote all the footnotes."

"Poems with footnotes."

She smiles. "Be nice, Eggie. This is my first truly published kid."

I try. I try to love Marko and his *fiancée.* Her soft turquoise moccasins that jump out at you, as if the girl wants you to know she's special, as if shoes are an indication of personality and soul. Lo is quiet, still. Our house is quiet, still. There's something about this last picture, something vital to it, it's the opposite of cancer. They both look so goddamn healthy, like nothing in this world could stop them. Lo's shoulders soften. She says this is her favorite picture. I tell her I know. We are a sad couple and then the screen turns black. She doesn't move. She doesn't realize that I can see her there, reflected, all that sadness pent up in her eyes, she wishes they really were her kids and she doesn't swipe her finger across the screen to bring them back.

"I'm sorry, Lo."

"I know," she says. "You don't have to say it all the time."

"I'm sorry."

She shakes it off, she swipes. She goes on Facebook. She leaves me, she goes to her chair. Before cancer, she was a reader, always turning the pages of a book. But then I got sick and forced her into so many waiting rooms. She became someone else, one of those Facebook people, one of those people surfing the Internet instead of exploring the world.

I owe it to her to do better, to fix us. I can't fix my son. I can't have Marko's parents murdered so that we can step in and adopt him. But I have to do something. I have to make it up to her. I need a win. It's been one loss on top of another and it can't be that my boy is incurable, it can't be that the only good thing we have is Marko fucking Kallenberg and his embarrassment of riches, his family coming into town, coming into Lo's Facebook feed, she's lifting the iPad, as if I give a fuck—*He looks a lot like his mother, don't you think?*—and this will not be my life, my weekend, on the couch again, the dismal fading glory of someone else's accomplishment—*Oh Eggie, they have a nice picture of him in the* Pro Jo *online, we have to get a copy.*

*Pro Jo.* Theo Ward. Tenley's.

That's it for me. I whistle at her, like I used to do.

She smiles, a real smile, a good start. "What's that, E?"

"That's me saying we should get the hell out of here."

She laughs. "And go where? Bermuda?"

"No," I say. "I'm not ready for swimming just yet."

"You're really serious?"

"I think we deserve a change of scenery."

"Where would we even go?"

It's times like this when I'm grateful for my old man, how he taught me to lie to a woman. *You look her in the eye and smile and then you look away like you never meant for her to see you smile.* I do that and I tell my wife I wanna go to Salem.

"Salem? Eggie, you're going back to work this week."

"Yeah, and I wouldn't be going back without you. And you love Salem."

"I don't even know if they have a hospital there that our insurance would cover."

I cut her off. "Lo, I'm better, okay? I'm stronger. And when I get back on the job, I'll be moving around."

"Which is why you should rest."

"Or maybe it's why I should get off my ass and have kind of a trial run, you know, stroll around, test the water."

It worked. Within a few seconds she's on the iPad, finding us a deal on a hotel, thinking about a course she could teach next semester, how long it's been since she was in Salem, how long it's been since she read *The Crucible*.

"Are you sure you're up for a drive? Because you can change your mind, if this was like last week when you thought you wanted to go to the movies . . ."

"No, Lo, I'm sure. I'm ready."

Her smile is the real kind and it's on. We're going to Salem to see all the witchy things she loves so much. But what this trip is really all about, I'm going to Lynn, which is only two towns over. I'm gonna find him, Theo Ward, gonna catch him, get him squared away, cuffed, as sure a thing as the book deal for Marko's fucking poems.

Lo-out-of-town is always different from Lo-at-home. I think that's a new lipstick she's wearing. Almost purple. She took a century getting spiffed up, she's wearing a bra that's new, I saw the tags in the trash can, *extra lift*. She has new moccasins she picked up in a boutique by all the witchy tourist traps. Brown moccasins with little beads, she asked the girl, *Do you have these in turquoise?* Broke my heart, the idea of her trying to make us into *Marko* and that girl. Here I sit across from my beautiful wife, hopped up on *The Crucible* and the sea, all the things we saw today, on her third glass of wine. And still all I can think is *Lynn Lynn City of Sin I gotta find out how the Beard got in.*

The plan was simple: come here for steaks and wine, make sure Lo gets nice and lit, get her into bed and then I'm on my own.

But she likes it here. She wanted appetizers, *clams casino* like in *Empire Falls*. She says she's gonna want dessert, she's inspired, she might even write again. "These waitresses," she says. "Aren't they something? Can't you picture them born as waitresses, with the trays and all?"

I do my part, nodding along.

"You know," she says. "Since I'm gonna put *The Crucible* on my syllabus next semester, I think, why not just go for it? I'm gonna see about taking my kids on a field trip here."

I chew on my fat. It stings. *My kids.* "I thought that was just for little kids."

She shrugs.

"I wish you wouldn't do that, Lo."

"Do what?"

*Don't tango with your drunk wife, Eggie. Let her be.* I break. "You know, I wish you wouldn't make everything about Marko."

"Who said anything about Marko?" she scoffs. "He's graduating. He won't be on a field trip."

"I mean your kids."

"What about my kids?"

"Well they're busy, Lo, college kids, and they won't wanna go on a field trip, they got things to do."

She picks up her wine. "Well," she says. "Don't take this the wrong way, but you don't know *shit* about my kids."

Instead of fighting, we both get silent. The eye of the storm kind of silent. We're those old people you see in a movie about young people worrying about becoming old people, sitting in a restaurant, nothing to say to each other, nothing to stop them from walking out except the expenses, the check.

And then she drinks too fast. And then she reaches for my hand. "Eggie," she says. "Eggie, shoot I think I'm gonna vomit."

Back in our room, she's the sick one now. I drove us here, I got us in, I pulled her hair back. It's me now, standing over her, rubbing her shoulders, her back, offering ice. She is the sick one and I am the caring one and periodically she squeezes my hand. It turns out we needed this.

She puts on an old nightie and gets into the bed with her new witch book and I pretend to be sleepy. We don't talk about our stupid fight. We could be okay. I'm lucky she forgives me, the shit I pull, not seeing my son, biting her head off about her students. But I can't sleep. She's snoring now and I'm looking at that door, thinking about the Beard, less than fifteen miles away.

The next morning we check out and we're still okay. We drive to Dunkin' Donuts and we're giddy like kids, kids who can't stop talking, voices overlapping. She can't remember the last time she had a hangover and she wants glazed crullers and strawberry milk and we're sitting in the car, happy.

*Let it go, Eggie. You got your wife back.*

But I can't let it go. I want more than my marriage. I want to find the Beard. I want to be right. She gets out, goes in for another doughnut, comes back with a jelly doughnut, tears it in half.

"You want the AC on?"

When she turns to me, that's it. "Lo, eleven people died in Lynn, eleven kids, all of 'em under thirty. Heart attacks. Drug dealers."

She wipes the jelly off her fingers. "Uh-huh."

On I go, every little bit, like she says to her kids *write down to the bone*. I tell her about my files, about how I didn't stop. I get deeper, I get to the day at Tenley's, the day I thought I had the Beard, the day I didn't go to my physical because I was at the *Lovecraft* show.

"Conference," she says, a murmur, telling me nothing about where she is, if she hates me, if it's over. She is a good listener, best listener I ever knew, it's why she's the world's greatest teacher.

She is still holding her half of the doughnut. She looks at me, I can't read her, her eyes level me, know me, hold me. "We can go to Lynn," she concedes, death in her voice, none of that love from a few minutes ago. "But then we're going home. After this, we're going *home*."

I know what home is. Home is Chuckie. "You're the best," I say and I lay a kiss on her, a kiss like the one Marko laid on his fiancée, a real kiss.

In Lynn, she can't hold back from admitting what this is. This is fun. I'm driving now and she's on the iPad, scouring the map of all the death scenes. One of the punks dropped dead by Durkee-Mower, the Marshmallow Fluff factory. She gets a kick out of this, calling it *something out of a Tom Robbins book*. I can never keep track of them, all her authors, and I search every street corner for the Beard. She insists on seeing that fluff factory in person so we go there. We park. She loves it here, tells me it's like *Upton Sinclair had a baby with Willy Wonka*.

Back on the road, we look for him. While I drive, Lo does the talking, telling me about Lynn, about how once upon a time they called it the City of Firsts, because so many things started here. "But the whole plan backfired." Her voice softens. "It turned out that a lot of things *didn't* start here and then what did start, most of it floundered." She points at the sunless postcard horizon. "That's King Beach," she says. She holds my hand. "You know what it is about this place? That it could all be so beautiful. It's so close."

We go by the school where one of the dealers dropped dead. There's nobody around, it's the weekend, and this feels more and more like a fool's errand. What did I expect? The Beard to be standing around on street corners waiting to get pinned?

Lo wants to go on the swings. She can't stop thinking about all these young dead kids, how you look at their mug shots and read about them and it turns out they're just kids, just trying to feed their kids, how they'd sell Omaha Steaks if they could, but what can they sell? Drugs. She says it makes sense when you think about it, that these kids are all dropping dead of broken hearts. Literally. What she means: there is no Beard. She digs her moccasins into the dirt beneath her swing. "Eggie," she says. "It's late."

I remind her that young people stopped dying in Providence and I remind her that the deaths at home were random—an Ivy League Olympian, a harmless lost kid, a junkie—but the deaths in Lynn feel deliberate. Like he's taking out drug dealers, like he used Providence as some kind of practice ground for his future slayings.

"But Eggie they're heart attacks."

"Or maybe whatever he does, he just makes it *look* like a heart attack. Maybe . . . maybe there's another way."

She is an imaginative woman. She says Marko has a *long form poem* about an evil fairy and she says I might be right. "But sometimes that has to be enough, Eggie."

I look at her moccasins, those stupid fucking moccasins. She says we tried. "We came here and we had a nice time, *a great time,* and you'll be happy to be back at work. I promise, Eggie, it's getting better. We've got Marko's engagement party where there's an open bar." She laughs. "Maybe I'll get wasted again!"

I am a lucky man. It's what my old man always said about going to the casino. You're not meant to win. The game is rigged against you. Any win is a surprise, a failure of the system. This is why you leave when you're up, even if you're not as up as you'd like to be. *First rule of gambling, Eggie. Up is up. Don't judge your up.*

# CHLOE

I am a machine. A robot. I can't stop painting. I haven't shaved in two days and I can't imagine what I smell like. My hair is so greasy that it's staying in a ponytail even though I pulled out the elastic hours ago—days ago?—and used it to smudge some charcoal on a canvas. There's nothing romantic about it. I'm in a trance and if the fire alarms started blaring, I would probably stay here and die, because this is the most peaceful time to me, submerged in this thing outside of myself, that reduces my body to a tool, my mind removed from my corporeal state, this floating thing that doesn't know about fire, showers, engagement rings.

That brings me out of my work and back onto the balcony. I stagger. I sink into one of Carrig's overstuffed, heavenly chairs selected by his interior designer. The city is still there, not burning. I pick up the ring that's been on the floor. What a stupid place to keep an engagement ring. The poor piece of jewelry is dried to the tile, sealed in black paint.

"Asshole," I mutter. "You really are an asshole."

Carrig's mom stocked our cleaning products, so fortunately we have the good stuff, the stuff nobody we know has anymore, the hard-core chemical cleaning products that kill you slowly as they make your floors sparkle. I dab a paper towel into some liquid blue. But I'm dizzy again. I don't know when I last ate, and I put a Hot Pocket into the microwave—thank you, Carrig's mom—and I sit on the floor. I'm too dirty to sit in any of this nice furniture, too mangy to sleep in his bed, our bed, I don't know.

I froze up on him when he proposed. Instead of saying yes, I said nothing. A couple minutes later he slipped the ring off my finger. He opened the refrigerator.

"Carrig, we should talk."

"Oh for fuck's sake," he said. "This is fucking almond milk."

"Care, look at me."

But he slammed the door. I told him his milk was in the back. "I always get you the regular milk. Because I love you."

He grabbed the door handle but it was stuck. It's an Energy Saver design where the refrigerator won't open immediately after you shut it. He snapped on me. Screaming. Kicking. *Even this fucking fridge is a little bitch. Fucking A, Chloe, just leave me alone.*

But I didn't leave. I stayed. A minute later he opened the refrigerator and found his milk in the back, his two-percent cow's milk.

"I'm sorry," he said. "I just don't get it."

I told him this was about me. I wasn't painting anymore. I was on the way to becoming one of those women in Sunday Styles who gives up her job the day she gets married. He hugged me. It was comforting to feel his hands on my back. *I promise you'll paint,* he said, as if a person you love can promise you what you'll do. But isn't it why you get married in the first place? So that someone can row the boat when you're tired.

He was logical, pouring cow's milk onto his cereal, telling me that the marriage would actually be *good* for me. "You would have all this stuff to do with the wedding and it would be demanding and the kind of stuff you would hate, talking to your mom, talking to my mom."

"I don't hate your mom, Care."

He smiled. "You always do better when you have too much to do," he said. "When painting is like a rebellion or something."

I could have said yes right then. It doesn't get more supportive than that, how he didn't turn this into being about his bruised ego, storm off in some passive-aggressive Jon-based rage. I could feel the word inside of me, multiplying, echoing, *yes yes yes*. But I didn't say it.

The next morning, he woke me up when he was already showered, dressed. "I gotta go to Hong Kong," he said.

"Are you kidding?"

"I think it's great timing," he said, backing away from the bed, checking his hair in the mirror.

I was floored. "Carrig, I don't want you to leave because of me. I told you this is my shit, not yours."

He put the ring on the nightstand. "I know," he said. "And it's the same way with me. The Asian market has nothing to do with you."

At first we talked every day, but then every day turned into every other day. Now I haven't heard from him in over a week. I know he's okay; the Internet has eliminated so much wonder and romance. I wish I couldn't know. I wish I could prove my love by getting onto a boat and going to find him, only to arrive and find that he had already set sail to return to me, a "Gift of the Magi" tragedy where we'd be doomed by our love, our bad timing.

I haven't let the cleaning lady come since he's been away. But there's no way around it. His leaving is the best thing that's happened to me in a long time. I haven't painted this much since Jon left and it was all new to me, drawing, those fresh calluses on my palms, on my fingers. I look around the apartment, canvases everywhere, they're all Jon. His eyes. That excessively circular shape, most eyes are slightly almond.

The microwave chirps. And by the time I open the door, the previously frozen Hot Pocket is lukewarm, almost cold. I look around at all the Jons stuffed into Carrig's apartment. And then I'm back on the floor, crying. I started drawing when Jon was kidnapped and now I'm back in the same place. Carrig is gone, in pain, and his agony is fuel. I don't want to be this person, this parasitic vampire who thrives most when the people who love her are ailing, when they're underground, sleeping, trapped, or on the other side of the world on Facebook, photographing their sushi, trying so hard to be okay for me, me, who is here, betraying them, fueled by male pain. I slap paint over every single great big Jon. And when the paint is dry, I cover those canvases with the view from Carrig's apartment.

Carrig finally calls and I answer on the first ring.

"Hi," he says.

"Oh it's so good to hear your voice, Care."

I feel his fear dissipating. I did that. Same way I painted all these skylines. "Yeah?" he says. "Cuz I wasn't sure."

"Carrig, of course I'm sure. I want to see you. Are you back yet?"

"Do you want me to be?"

"Yes," I say, cradling the phone, fixing my eyeliner. My legs look good, waxed and spray tanned. I *feel* good. He deserves to feel good too. I like the ring on my finger. I want to show him that I'm better, let him see my canvases, the proof of my happiness, my productivity, the proof that his proposal, the clarity of our future, had lifted me to a new place, a better place.

I look around at all the paintings, the ones that were all Jon just two days ago, the ones that I painted over religiously, monotonously. Every time I erased one of his faces, I was a little more loaded in this world, the real world, than that one. Like scooping water off a sinking boat. They're all landscapes now. They're the view from Carrig's balcony. They're not gonna get me any prizes. Nobody's going to be dazzled. But then Carrig arrives, and he hugs me, he holds me. He gasps at all the landscapes. I roll my eyes.

"Are you kidding?" Care says. "These are amazing. This is our view, babe."

I am sheepish, mumbling something about landscapes being *basic*.

"Chloe, are you kidding? You couldn't do basic even if you tried. These look like you. All your stuff always has that you thing going on. Isn't that why it sells?"

But I don't want the praise. It's too soon. People have painted this skyline and I didn't bring anything new to it. We go back and forth and he can't beat me when it comes to art and then he waves me off and squats in front of the biggest one. He looks like a frog.

"Care," I say. "What are you doing?"

"You're an artist because I swear, you can *feel* something underneath. I don't know how to explain it. That's for you and the art people. But they're . . . heavy."

He doesn't see the color drain out of my face.

I walk over to Carrig, my husband-to-be. I wrap my arms around his torso. I close my eyes and breathe him in. "I love you so much," I say. "So, so much."


The next morning, Carrig says he never saw me look so happy in my sleep.

I kiss him. "I missed you," I say. "And now we're here."

While he's showering, I'm on wedding websites. I'm starting a registry and I'm emailing my mom. She wants to have an engagement party *right away* and this feels like a new chapter, something better than a blank canvas, it's a layered foundation and there's no excavating what's underneath.

# EGGS

They gave me a new parking spot. A handicap spot closer to the entrance. *Screw you, Stacey.* I'm not an old man. I drove here on my own. I beat cancer. I think I can make it through a goddamn parking lot. And look at her, up front, clapping, whistling, making everyone stand up and here I am, taking a bow like a damn prom queen.

There's cake and small talk and Lo was wrong. It's not good to be back, not good to be so aware of everyone inspecting me, sizing me up, looking for my bag. And then it ends—mercy—but Stacey follows me into my office. She closes the door.

"So," she says. "Lo's really all right with you coming back?"

"Of course," I say. "She's been amazing, she's my rock."

She winks, she knows. She drops a manila envelope on my desk. "There's your fan mail."

She doesn't close my door as she goes. The return address on the envelope is Stanford University and inside, there is a letter.

*Dear Detective DeBenedictus,*

*You gave me your card and I promised to let you know if I had any more information for you on the bearded man I spoke to. I was up the other night watching* Dateline, *procrastinating, an overview of wanted criminals and kidnapping and other American achievements . . . Anyhow, I realize that I do know the bearded man, but his name isn't Theo Ward.*

*You might remember him too. They called him Basement Boy. His name is Jon Bronson. You might remember the case; it was a strange one. He was kidnapped by a substitute teacher. He eventually escaped, but he had been in an "induced coma" for four years. I've been reading about it, I understand why the boy was drawn to Lovecraft, themes of isolation, but I suppose that's not of use to you.*

*Anyhow, I'm sure that the young man I spoke to about* The Dunwich Horror *was Theo Ward, as in Basement Boy, Jon Bronson. I'm also sure that you have the resources to take it from here.*

*I hope this letter finds its way to you. I emailed you and got your out-of-office bounce-back. Perhaps a colleague will pass this along the old-fashioned way.*

*I hope that you are well, Detective.*

*Sincerely,*
*Dr. Lynn Woo*

I read the letter again.

The Beard had no childhood until now. He was just this loner for me, this creature of the streets, fake names, *I am Providence,* no friends, no home, no past. That's what gets me most about this letter, the idea that in all the time I was trying to find him, I never wondered about where he came from and how he came to be this person. I was focused on the present, what he did now, how he did it.

And now I have a backstory, an *origin* story. I remember the Basement Boy stories in the news and they're all still there online. One day this kid's walking to school, and then he's gone, and then four years later he pops up at a mall in Nashua, calls his mother from a New Age store. He was home a bit, Skyping interviews with talk shows. He never went back to school and according to his parents he's *on his own, living out of the spotlight.*

Jon Bronson. The Beard has a name, he has parents, Mr. and Mrs. Jed and Penny Bronson. I have to find them, see them.

I Google *The Dunwich Horror.* But I don't have the attention span to tackle literary criticism right now. I have a name. The Beard has a name. It's a new world. I crack my knuckles. I put the name in quotes, "Jon Bronson."

I read everything I could find about Basement Boy (current whereabouts: unknown). I watched the *Dateline* clips, the *Ellen* segment where he showed them his bedroom via Skype, the usual things, a few more Spider-Man posters than you might expect for a kid his age. I dug up the coverage in the *Telegraph,* I saw how they hunted for him, how they didn't. The kid only had one friend as far as I could tell, a girl named Chloe Sayers, she's at the vigils, she's quoted. (Not a popular kid, Jon Bronson, amazing what you can feel from an objective article in a small-town paper, the whiff of obligation.)

I read about the perp, Roger Blair, substitute teacher. The man disappeared and though they're still "looking" for him, it's clear that he's a low priority. After all, Jon Bronson was healthy as a horse when he emerged from that basement cluttered with houseplants. The public was fired up for a few minutes about finding the man, *a substitute teacher, access to our kids, how did this happen?* But Bronson, who wasn't what you'd call a local treasure when he went missing, emerges a muscle-bound man, that's a story that hits, and sucks the air out of the perpetrator tires. *Well, whatever he did to the kid, let's face it, the kid is fine and at least he didn't take our kids . . .*

Blair has a long history of mental illness, most of which was regarded as "idiosyncrasy" because the man was Ivy League educated, employed as a professor. When you're smart and sick, people are prone to see you as gifted, touched. So while Roger's former boss was quick to point the finger—*This is why I fired him, I knew he was capable of something awful*—he didn't go to the authorities on his own, he waited until the bad thing actually did happen.

The most interesting thing about it is the mystery of those four years. Bronson claims he can't remember a thing and Blair is out of the picture, off the grid, *missing, wanted,* same as Jon was when he was gone, *missing, wanted.*

I read it all. Everything I can get my hands on.

I can't leave my office right away. I don't want it to be obvious that I've had a breakthrough. *Come on, Eggie, calm the hell down.* And then I pop the lock on my door and step out into the bullpen. Right away, I catch Stacey's eye. She wants to know what I've been up to all these hours and I point to the last thing in the world she wants to hear about, *my bag.* She waves me off and I'm free to go.

I feel like a kid on the last day of school, stepping out of that station, into the sun, getting in the car. I hit the road, New Hampshire bound, I'm a typical Rhodie in the sense that I think we're the best. In Massachusetts, you have all these sweet-toothed Massholes stuffing their faces with ice cream covered in *jimmies,* all puffed up with self-righteousness they get out of that little rock down Plymouth. Never mind Maine; try being a woman in that state, let me know how it works out. Vermont has the worst Italian food I've ever had in my life. And New Hampshire, all you gotta know is that they take pride in rocks, granite, tax-free shopping and bottle rockets, their handles of grain alcohol so they can go home and light themselves on fire. I start my car. *I don't blame you for coming to Providence, Jon. I would too.*

———

I use my handicap sticker to park by one of the main entrances to the Finch Plaza Mall. This is where Blair held the kid, this is where Jon Bronson became Basement Boy.

The mall is any mall, loud and sad, no mystique, no flair. The signs promise big doings. COMING SOON: EXCITEMENT! But there's an atmosphere of doom, as in any mall these days, as if there are no surprises, not anymore. It's late, so the stores are getting ready to close. But at least half of them are out of business. A sporting goods store called Rolling Jack's just went under, paper on the window. The people working in the stores that look like they're still open are like statues, glued to their phones, their screens. The people in the few busy shops, the people running around helping customers, they look like they lost in life, like they're being punished, prisoners. I think of Jon Bronson underground, what it must have been like for him to come up those stairs, to see the costume jewelry store and the cell-phone kiosks. *A mall.*

My phone's ringing. Lo. I pick it up. She hears the noise.

"Yo Lo," I say, she used to love that. But then YOLO became a thing that her kids say, the ones who aren't her favorites, and one day she told me not to say it anymore.

She sighs. "Stacey called."

*Fuck.* "Oh."

"Eggie, where are you? Don't make me call the phone company, don't make me track your phone like you're a child."

I sit down in an easy chair, hard as concrete. "I'm in Nashua."

"Looking for the Beard?" She chuckles. Not a happy sound. She tells me this is it, she won't yell at me because I don't deserve it, there's no way to get through to me. I watch all the average children with their average parents, coming, going. I let her rant at me. I promise this is it. *It really is the end.* And as I say that I get the chills, because it's the truth. She wants me to eat. "And I mean food, Eggie, not that fucking tea. And don't think this gets you out of Marko's party either."

*Fuck.* "Of course I'll be there."

If Lo were to leave me, I'd wind up in a mall like this, one of these people in white sneakers and sweatpants carrying the two-pound weights, walking the mall as if it's a racetrack, as if life's so good that I want it to last forever. When she finishes lecturing me, I tell her I'm sorry again. She says to pick up something for Marko and his fiancée.

"Me? You want me to get a gift for them?"

"Yes, you. You're in a mall and I'm slammed."

"What should I get?"

"Eggie, it's an engagement gift. You give something that lasts forever."

And then she's gone. *Something that lasts forever.*

There's a store where they sell ripped jeans, a store where it's nothing but cellphone cases, a store where it's nothing but bras. I get a flash of Marko and his bride-to-be fucking on my kitchen table and my skin heats up. *Fuck them.*

I head to slot 14, the spot formerly occupied by Roger Blair. First things first.

It was hell getting in there, tracking down a security guard to hear me out about the unoccupied space. He's finally coming and I'm waving him down like some shit-out-of-luck guy on the side of the road with a flat.

I try anyway, forcing small talk about the mall, the nice light, the sadness of seeing a sporting goods store go under. "Locally owned?" I ask.

He nods. He scratches his nose. "Listen, I'm short-staffed tonight. If you were hoping to get into this space, I can't do that for ya. There's a process and whatnot with the Realtors."

I get it. Sometimes the answer is yes. Yes, you have cancer. Sometimes the answer is no. No, you can't go in. I don't waste the guy's time by pitching a fit. It's not happening today. He drives off on his scooter and I do the only thing you can do when they say no and you want yes.

I get the hell out of there and find something else to do.

The Bronsons live on a nowhere street in a nowhere part of town. Not enough trees to call it tree-lined but it's not situated near any homespun five-and-dime. This is a practical place, houses lined up because people need houses. I sit out here for a few minutes, waiting to catch a vibe, a sense of who these people are beyond the basics— the mother works at T.J.Maxx and she's a townie; the father's an import, from Scotland, landscapes, irregular, hits the bottle is what I read between the lines, his red nose in the pictures from the *Telegraph* and his perpetually shifting business, roofing, lawns, back to roofing, as if he mucks it all up and starts fresh, like a kid building castles on a beach.

There's nothing else to know about them and their house ain't talking, so I'm out of the car, I'm on the lawn, walking, trying to get my heart to slow down, my hands to stop shaking. I ring the bell. The father comes, Jed, red plastic cup in hand. I flash my badge.

He grins, crooked teeth. "Been a while since we heard from the boys in blue." He has that same Scottish accent he had in the news, when his boy emerged and he scratched his chin for the local reporters, in awe, clearly half drunk. "Come on in."

Jed has done this before, he's an old pro, gesturing toward the sofa, offering me a beer. He tells his story in shifts, there was the first disappearance—*We had no idea where he went, if he was dead, if he was here, you know sometimes I'd swear he was in the attic. I tore it apart, took the floorboards up, wife coulda killed me*—and he tells me about the return—*You can't believe how big he got, how buff, you know that's the last thing you expect*—and then he talks about the time after the return—*You know it's like I say to my wife, he was never an easy kid, he was never one for people, he was always off with his hamsters, with his newspapers, so is it any wonder that he took off to be on his own?*

"Do you know where he is now?"

He shakes his head. "But you see, when I was a kid, my old man, he beat the pulp out of me. Oh, you don't know what it was, a different place, we're not so soft over there. Anyhow, I turned seventeen, I saved my pennies and I got on a plane and I came here and that was it."

"You never saw your dad again?"

He finishes his scotch. "Nope. Not my mum, nor my sister. And I told Jon about this, oh I told him the thing about being a man, a real man, you leave, you make your *own* family and you pave your *own* road and you don't go squatting on your old man's turf."

He goes to *set the boat off*, which from the sounds in the kitchen means *pour another drink*. I pick up a photo album and look at pictures of Jon Bronson young, smiling, awkward. Jed returns, offers me a beer. We aren't that much different, me and him, this house reminds me of my house, that sadness, that feeling of someone *missing*.

I ask him when he last saw his son. And then he sighs. "When Noelle died. You know, the girl in his school. I remember because the wife, she took that hard, didn't even know the kid, but oh she cried."

"Was your son at that party?"

He shrugs. "Who knows? All I know is he was here that morning and then he didn't come home and then, well, that's all she wrote." He moans, *America*. "Lorena Bobbitt, the one who cut off her husband's dick, she also copped insanity, served maybe three months, four, I can't remember. But there you go." He raises his red cup. "There you goddamn *go*."

Am I this bad? Do I openly stare into space, trying to figure out what went wrong with Chuckie? It occurs to me that I forgot to buy a present for Marko and his fiancée, that I might be even worse than I realize. Jed Bronson scratches his beard. "I hate a quiet house." His eyes swing toward the old stereo system, CDs, big speakers. "You mind?"

"Of course not," I say.

Outside, the sky is turning over, giving up, the day is going to end. I'm failing. Jon Bronson isn't here. You know when a man hasn't seen his son, the way Jed stands there, licking his thumb, scraping gunk off a CD, waxing poetic about Simon and Garfunkel, America. That's me, that's him, that's any bad father, trying to make it like life is bigger than your son, when, come on, who's kidding whom? And then he stops his bullshit yammering and he looks at me all at once. "Why did you say you're here?"

I think fast. "I'm here because your son might have been a witness to something."

"To something like a crime?" he asks. He doesn't take his eyes off me. Do I look that lost, that paranoid? Do I look that childish, that needy, that sagging skin, those sullen eyes? "Do you have a picture?" he asks. "You know, we haven't seen him, who knows if we'd even recognize him." He shakes his head. "I realize how that sounds, but you know, you wonder."

And then we hear a car, and we both look out the window. He sighs. "Here comes Penny." And there she is, slamming the door on her old Saab, she stopped off at the packie, she looks exhausted, still wearing her work smock, the lanyard too. She's prettier than I expected, but she's given up, you can see that from the way she carries the bottle of booze with one hand, no bag, not hiding her need for it, same way she doesn't cover the bags under her eyes, badges of honor, proof that she's in mourning, forever glum. She pauses when she comes in.

"What is this, Jed? Aren't you gonna introduce me?"

This must look strange, two grown men, Paul Simon blasting, and Jed introduces us then excuses himself to *put some Jack in his Jack.* When he's gone, Penny shuts off the music. There it is, in a nutshell, why they belong together, why they don't, he plays the music, she shuts it down. I think of their boy, in the middle of this fight, on his own in all the pictures. I bet he wanted a brother or sister, I bet he asked them for one, I bet he never got what he wanted, which is why he was clinging to that hamster the day he disappeared.

"Do you want to see his room?" Jed asks when he returns.

The three of us file upstairs to Jon's room. They kept it this way, *just in case*. There are the Spider-Man posters I saw online, boxes of newspapers—*Jon lived for the paper*—and upon closer inspection, I see that the pillowcases are also Spider-Man.

"How old was he when he left?" I ask.

Penny folds her arms. It's a touchy subject. "Jon was a kid at heart," she says. "He was never trying to impress other people."

Jed picks up a Spider-Man pillow. You can tell he's never touched it before. "Pretty sure we put these on for Pen's cousin's kid when he visited though, right hon?"

Penny doesn't answer and I lead the way out the door, walking ahead, so they can elbow each other, *Don't lie to the man, don't humiliate the boy*. It's amazing, how much you can hear in the silence of two married people.

This is police work, it's listening, it's letting the worst of someone, their pain, crawl inside of you and blossom, ugly, awful.

Back downstairs things relax, a little. Mrs. Bronson doesn't encourage me to call her by her first name and she doesn't take off her smock or her lanyard. She is awkward, nervous. Swears she has *no clue* where Jon is. Uses that word: clue. Means she's trying to figure it out. Means she has a clue, but I keep this to myself and just keep pushing. "Do you ever hear from him?"

Penny shrinks up into herself. "No. No, I don't."

She's lying. She said *No, I don't*, separating herself from her husband. She would have said *No, we don't* if she was telling the truth. Jed has no idea. The boy must call the mother. It's like me and Lo, when someone asks us how Chuckie's doing, I nod and Lo does all the talking. I'm quiet because I'm a liar. The most I'll say is *Good, I heard he's good*. And that's the equivalent of *No. No, I don't*.

She asks if I have kids. Without meaning to, I lie, tell her I don't.

# JON

I search for Incy and it's begun. Her body was discovered. But the reports are confusing, they bury the lead, they bury her name. The news isn't so much about Incy's body, her untimely death. She's mentioned in passing, an afterthought for the real story, what they found in her basement, what's drawn the attention of the national news: *five young girls*. They were bound and gagged. The video is the kind of thing that sets the world on fire, these girls released, broken, shielding their faces as they file out of Incy's house. I remember what Roger said to me in that letter. *You are free.* I wonder if these girls feel that. It doesn't seem remotely possible. But it's a comfort to know that they're on their way to something else, something better. I ended Incy's *ruthless reign* (that's what the local paper called it).

It's not what you think. I'm not a monster. I'll never rejoice in ending anyone's life no matter what. But this particular case is special. I made the national news, the *New York Times*. (Indirectly, but still.) This is the kind of thing they describe as a *miracle*. I watch the coverage and for the first time in my life since all this, I'm almost *grateful* for my power. Finally, something good came of it, something as magical as innocent girls exiting a *house of horrors*. The firemen came when the bathroom flooded and started an electric fire. I did the right thing leaving her in the bathroom. And that wasn't easy, but I did it. And because of me, those girls are free.

I order myself a reward, the best cake in Lynn, strawberries and cream from D'Amicis. My doorbell rings and the guy pounds on the door. "Peter Feder?"

It's weird to hear my fake name. I crack the window and whistle to the guy on my stoop. "Hey buddy," I say. "Can you leave it by the door? There's five bucks under the mat."

The delivery guy waves. "Thanks!"

The smell of the bakery floods my whole apartment and I breathe it in, close my eyes. *Chloe Smells Like Cookies.* I eat the cake right out of the box the way my mom did sometimes and I read everything I can about the girls, their parents who were scared, their friends who thought they were gone. One girl was kidnapped in Vietnam. Another girl is local, from Southie. More is coming out every few minutes about the level of horror in that basement. Incy brainwashed them with SpaghettiOs and heroin, she forced them to eat the noodles from the can, take the needle, inject themselves. She was working for a larger human trafficking conglomerate, the worst guys, the worst guys that can be. I hear Magnus in my head.

*We did good work down here, Jon.*

I finally made those words come true. And there is no *we*. It was only me. I rescued those girls, even though I didn't know I was doing it, the truth is simple. If I hadn't walked into her house and surprised her in her shower, those girls would still be down there, trapped. I put on some Hippo Campus and I look at what's left of my great big cake, it looks like a wedding cake, like the bride and groom got to it and everybody laughed.

The wanting begins, and I don't fight it, not tonight. I go with it.

I daydream of holding her, sharing my cake with her. I missed this, I missed her, I picture us standing before our friends—her friends—and our families, and she's in a white dress and I'm beside her, my hand is on the small of her back. She's offering me cake and I'm shaking my head and then she smothers me with it, frosting in my mouth, filling my eyes. There's so much laughter you can't hear anything above it until she wraps her hand around my head and pulls me in for a kiss, strawberries, her tongue, different from Florie's.

Things are gonna be different now because I'm gonna be different now. No more guilt. No more doomsday. I start a deep clean on my apartment, I want things to feel good because I feel good and I pour bleach into a bucket and mix it with water. And then my phone buzzes, a Google alert about Chloe. I get these all the time, they're usually nothing too exciting, she's in the listings for an art show, something like that. But this is one of the *good* ones because this is my day. I sit on the floor of my nice clean kitchen with my back against the oven and I open the email. I picture her next to me. I can imagine that. In a way I couldn't when I was so gloomy.

My heart beats before the link even opens, a great big article about her in *Nylon* magazine. I'm happy to see her back in the news like this, I like the idea of us both making something of ourselves at the same time, in our own ways. And my heart is racing, that little beach ball of death is circling, I haven't allowed myself to do this in a while, to read about her, to look at pictures of her. And it felt like a two-way street, the way she slipped offscreen, as if she and *Doctor Actor* were on a permanent break from the world. I bet they broke up. I bet she started painting a lot. I bet that's what this is, a return.

And then the page opens, all the bright colors, her bright eyes. *Chloe.*

First I look at the pictures, her face is more of a heart than circle now and her eyes are lined in this way they never were before. She's a little older, a little paler, a little more beautiful. She's in a shirt I've never seen, a New Hampshire ringer T-shirt that says *Live Free or Die.*

"I miss you too, Chloe," I tell her. I put my hand on her shirt.

The next three pictures of her come from a photo booth. She's open in the first one, smiling. She's goofy in the second, and the third ones gives me the chills. Her eyes. Same as they were that day I got home, when she fainted, when she saw me.

The article starts out talking about her painting. She's doing landscapes now but Chloe's landscapes are *creating a need for a new genre of upside-down kitsch*. Her paintings are selling like crazy in New York, but also in other parts of the world, Paris and Amsterdam and Stockholm. I knew she'd come back, but I'd be lying if it didn't sting a little that this is the first article I've ever seen where they're not talking about me, the inspiration behind her eyes.

And I shouldn't be upset to see that she's left my eyes behind and moved on to *sweeping New York views*. I've changed. She's changed. We're supposed to change.

The next part of the story addresses her *love-hate relationship with social media*. And then an ad for laser therapy interrupts the story, an ad I'll remember forever because of what comes next.

> "I believe in privacy," she says, sipping her extra-foam latte. "I think that's the New Hampshire in me. You know, we're actually going home next week for our engagement party."
>
> Sayers, who is engaged to financier Carrig Birkus, says she rarely discusses her personal life. "But you get engaged, it feels like you should tell everyone," she says, beaming.
>
> To wit: Sayers and Birkus grew up together in Nashua, New Hampshire. They then grew apart. "One night I'm at a gallery and they tell me someone from school is here and it was him and that was that. We moved in together pretty quickly and we like to laugh. He had the wall space, I had the art."

Sayers glances at this reporter's recording device. She winces. "This isn't as cheesy as it sounds," she says, wrapping her hands around the cup as if it's warm. It isn't. "It's like art. You throw paint, you don't know what you're doing. A few hours later, a few days, this canvas, those hours of your life, have dried, they tell you what they are, what they need. Dried time." She breaks into laughter, releasing her hands. "This is why I never talk about my private life," she says. "It leads to me saying things like that."

Sayers and Birkus will celebrate the engagement in Nashua with a "backyard party." When asked why New Hampshire instead of New York, she looks out the window, resumes cradling her cold coffee. "This isn't home," she says. "Not yet." She then directs her disarming gaze to this reporter. "What about you?" she asks. "Are you married?"

She is most relaxed now, her eyes alive, inquisitive, curious, as in her work.

When I vomit, it's strawberries and cream. And then I vomit again because of what I was thinking only a little while ago, that this was our wedding cake, that we were in this together even when we were out of touch, that Doctor Actor was a season, no different from a winter, that every winter ends.

And now there's nothing left in me but bile. There's no stopping the cramping in my soul, my gut, the idea of Carrig being the one to hold her, to walk down the street with her, to eat eggs with her, the idea of her art coming from *his* home and *his* bedroom and *his* love.

# EGGS

On the way to Lynn, I stop at a diner off Route 3. I thought about calling Chloe, the girl quoted in the newspaper articles. But I'm not a fan of the phone. I still can't shake this feeling that I can find him, Jon.

The diner reeks of dishrags and food you eat because you have to, not because you want to, but because you need to send your wife a screenshot of a fucking salad or she might kick you out once and for all. The place is empty except for me and a family of four, a father and a mother, a boy and a girl, all of them sitting there with their heads buried in their phones.

I am alone and I am a nuisance and when I tell the waitress I want a side salad and a cup of hot water, she glares at me. "Are you serious?"

"And pancakes," I say. "A side of pancakes."

She's off to the kitchen, and the family of four, they're still there, silent as ever, sucked into their devices, their phones, their tablets.

To look at them, you'd think these bodies of ours are obsolete. I clear my throat and the boy looks at me, he's staring. The phones are killing our manners; that's what this is, kid doesn't even know how to conduct himself in a restaurant. The waitress is coming with my water, and then she stops short.

"Oh God," she says, gasping at me with the same kind of face as that kid, the one with the family. I look down at my shirtfront and there's a mess on my shirt, the bag leaked.

In the men's room, I empty the bag and I scrub my shirt with the lousy pink soap, and if Lo could see me now, she'd wonder what it's gonna take. She'd have reason to wonder. In the mirror, my cheeks are shiny. I look old. I look like my old man. The light in here is vicious and bright and I see wrinkles I didn't know about, I see lines deep in my neck, folds of skin, my tits are sagging. When did I get tits?

I button up my shirt. The thing is, it could be worse. My kid could be in pain. He could be some heartless dolt like the kid out there at the table, the kid staring at me. My kid could be a psychopath, a kidnapper. Imagine you raise a child and the child turns out to be *Roger Blair*. Imagine that. I finish cleaning the cap of my bag. I screw it on and seal it up, I listen to this hiss, the sound of my body doing what other bodies do so quietly.

I return to my table and eat my cold pancakes, my warm salad (plate is hot, fresh out of the dishwasher). I steep my tea and I take out my iPad. I look up Roger Blair's parents. A dentist and a hygienist. Retired, Florida, then deceased, Florida. I knew that, I know that. And my gut says *Leave the crazy be, Eggie*. I don't need to find Roger. They tried. They didn't.

But the one I want to find is Jon.

In Providence, Jon changed his name to *Theo Ward*. I saw the Lovecraft in there.

I think of his bedroom, the Spider-Man posters, how his mother could barely look at any of it, his father looked right through it. Jon is an obsessive boy, but loving. There's something else his mother said. *He left the house with his hamster.* Jon loved with his whole heart, he was trying to get inside of these things, the Spider-Man on the walls, on his bedsheets. No doubt he harassed his mother for Spider-Man breakfast cereal in the days leading up to his disappearance.

And who was the amazing Spider-Man, really? He wasn't born amazing. He was kind of a shrimp to start, if I remember correctly, a skinny quiet kid named Peter Parker.

I write the name down underneath the other names. I feel that pulse again, that *Good job, Eggie* pulse that I'm onto him. The waitress comes by and grins, sarcastic. "Did you want to see a dessert menu?"

I give it right back. "Well, yes I do. Thank you, dear."

And then I call my old partner Jimbo Haskell. He met a girl, moved to Swampscott a few years back. He answers, he's the same old Jimbo, just more grown-up. *Eggie, you can call me Haskell, call me Ishmael, but don't call me Jimbo.* I'm the one who called, but he's the one who does all the talking. He's bullshitting because he got a transfer, he's on a walking beat. Nothing Haskell hates more than walking.

"Mr. Haskell," I say, chuckling. "Can you run a name for me?"

"What kind of run?" he asks.

"Simple stuff," I say. "Here's what I can tell you. It would be a lease. A bachelor, a one bedroom, tops. There are likely to be newspaper subscriptions if you have access to those records."

Haskell loves a good mission. "This is like the old days," he says. "What's the name?"

I look down at my notepad. "Peter Parker."

"Hang ten," he says, and the line goes dead.

The family of four is gone and the restaurant is quiet. Too quiet.

I slopped tea onto my notepad so the words *Peter* and *Parker* are smudged. The tea is cold. I'm cold. I'm off. The waitress is here, bitching that the mother told the kids not to hesitate about making a mess all over the table, the floor. "She actually told them they have people to do that," she says, huffing. "Do I look like a custodian? Is this what we're doing? Are we, you know, raising brats?"

My phone rings. "Jimbo," I say. "Mr. Haskell, whaddya got?"

"Nothing," he says. "Eggie, you know Peter Parker is a cartoon character, right?"

My heart is thumping. Haskell's running late, blabbering on about his foot patrol, *bettah stop off and get some sunscreen, as if the stuff in there's not gonna kill ya before the sun gets to ya*. I'm flipping through my notes and come across the emails Florie sent him. And I see that saddest sentence, the last thing she wrote to him:

Theo, sometime we have to watch Grown Ups 2 TOGETHER.

This movie was their thing. Same way Lo and I get about *American Splendor*. I look up *Grown Ups 2*. I know the basics, it's an Adam Sandler production, he's from New Hampshire, they made the movie there too. Jon wouldn't go by *Sandler*. It's too big a name. I look closer. I follow my gut to the list of character names. Sandler plays a guy named Lenny Feder. My eyes stick to that name. *Feder*. You can tell by the pictures that Feder's got it all, the wife, the kids, the friends. You might say that Bronson's been trying to bridge these two parts of his life together, the fantasy of having that kind of impossible superpower, being Spider-Man, the somehow equally unattainable fantasy of forging a family, living a well-adjusted, low-key life à la Feder. My gut hums. "Haskell," I say. "Let's try finding a Peter Feder."

He goes to run the search and I ask the waitress if I can get my dessert to go—old peach cobbler, no whip—and I gather my papers. I adjust my bag. I ask the waitress for *another* favor, a cup of hot water to go. I know I'm on my way. I feel it in my bones, in my gut. I text Lo to tell her I'm gonna be a while, I get another little yellow face with the eyes rolling, but then I get her blessing, *Be safe, and eat something decent.*

And then my phone rings. Haskell. Jimbo. Same difference.

"Eggie," he says. "You're not gonna believe this, but I got something for ya."

# EGGS

When Chuckie was first having troubles, when the doctor told us it was time to go to Bradley, time to see specialists, I became obsessed with timing. I started reading about the universe, how it works, the wild roulette wheel of nature, the sheer volume of sperm, the odds of a fish hitting that egg. I couldn't stop. I couldn't sleep. I could only think about the day Lo and I conceived Chuckie, the day I think we did, on a Saturday, on the sofa.

It was raining. We were in our old place, the one bedroom downtown, near the Biltmore. We had the window open. The movie was no good but it was the movie you want on a Saturday when you're coming down off your wedding, off your honeymoon (four days on the Vineyard) and Lo's hand found my thigh, not in the going for it way. I was married to her now, I knew her moves, I knew when she wanted it. She was just looking for the remote. I could have handed her the remote.

But I wasn't into the movie and it was raining and I'm one of those people, I like the rain. I grabbed her wrist, teased her, and she was giddy, she was easily romanced in those days. We were like kids, and before you knew it she was unzipping my pants and I was on my back and my head was digging into the remote and she was feeling at me, I was feeling at her, and we went at it on the sofa, unprotected, the volume on the TV erratic, the channels changing. We were in love and everything was funny, the horror of the sounds coming from that TV, a commercial for a Thighmaster, an ESPN wrap-up, and a movie that was worse than our movie. Lo got her cookies—that's what she called it—and I blew a load in her, a *thundering* load, and she held on to my head, my hair.

"Wow," she said. "I guess you were saving that up."

That's the day we made Chuckie. And I started to wonder if that was the problem, that we were on the sofa, not the bed, that I came too hard, that there was too much inside of me, that the timing was off. Because the universe is timing. We exist, each one of us, because of timing. If you think about it, life is timing. I have bad timing. I got to Lynn about an hour too late.

I just missed him. Jon Bronson became Theo Ward *and* Peter Feder.

It seems like he left last night because today's papers—the *Herald* and the *Globe*—were lying on the floor mat outside of his door. The landlord had no problem letting me in, didn't ask to see a badge. *Never even saw the guy's face,* he said. *Not since the day he moved in, paid his rent two days before it was due, slid the check under my door, guy was like a church mouse.*

I found him but I missed him. It's the same way with cancer; you beat it, but this bag hangs from your body.

I called him *the Beard* and sure enough there's a shaving kit in his bathroom, beard trimmers. The zipper sticks so either the beard is gone or he's given up taking care of it.

Everything here is clean—the windows were Windexed by someone who cares. The place smells like cookies, but I detect a chemical element, as if Jon was trying to *make* it smell like cookies. There are Yankee Candles, *vanilla cookies,* and *Christmas cookies.* Sure enough, the electric sockets are jammed up by air-freshener thingamajigs, the plug-ins, more artificial sweetness. To think of the Beard—Jon Bronson—going to Target like you and me, filling his car with Windex, candles, and throw pillows. He was trying to make this house a home. And the explicit pain of his efforts is evident in every corner of this apartment, his neatly made bed—for whom?—and the two nightstands. He keeps a book by his bed. There's a book about Lovecraft, a reading-for-dummies sort of thing. I sit down on his bed and open the drawer in the other nightstand. There's a travel kit, a mini-toothbrush, a mini-tube of toothpaste, a bottle of eye makeup remover. The Beard was hoping for a girl. But there was no girl.

But the most remarkable part of this place, aside from the heartbreak of his efforts, the real shocker, are the walls. Every inch of the walls are covered with drawings. Drawings of eyes. They're all the same artist. She signed in the corner of each one. A first name, a last name, but damn it if artists aren't like doctors. Who knows what that signature says? Tenderly, I peel one of the prints off the wall. Jon was careful with this heart. He used double-sided tape and he measured each spot, marked the walls before he hung his pictures.

There is love in here, there is.

My phone rings, my love. And it's already seven P.M. *Shit.*

"Lo," I say. "My God, I'm so sorry. I'm on my way out of here."

"Out of where?" she huffs.

"I'm gonna be there before you know it."

"Did you get a gift?"

*Shit again.*


I'm late.

Not cute late. Bastard late. I denied my wife the right to be at Marko's engagement party with her husband. It was a shitty thing to do. She's at the bar, wiping the counter with a cocktail napkin. She doesn't light up when she sees me coming either. I start with an apology but her eyes go to the flowers.

"Why are there two?"

"One's for you."

Her voice drops to a hiss. "We're at a *party.*"

There's nothing for me to say. You can't be two places at once. She can read me. I know she knows I'm not even really here, not fully. And maybe the boy got it from me, that tendency to live in his head.

She sighs. "Did you get a card?"

*Shit.* Magnified by all the gratitude, the red wine, the tiny slices of pizza, pancetta, more wine, laughter, the love, *did you see Bella's ring?* It's a horrible thing when you didn't get the card, when you have no excuse, when you don't want to be where you are and you can't hide it. *The Beard. Roger Blair.* I know I should care about these people because Lo cares about them. I see myself in some apartment, like the Beard, covering the walls with Lo's papers.

"Lo, what can I do?"

"You can stop being an asshole," she says.

A couple of people heard her. It isn't fair. This is my screwup and she's the one bowing her head, ashamed. "Lo," I say. "It ends now. I swear. I promise."

"Where were you just now?"

If she didn't love me, she wouldn't want to know, so this is a good sign and I take it. I tell her everything. Slowly. Finding Jon Bronson. Finding his apartment. But there's nothing in her eyes, no joy in Mudville. "Lo," I say. "This is huge."

She picks up her purse and heads outside.

And this is where it happens, the breakdown. We officially become those sad people, fighting people, that awful couple who comes to your party and spends the night outside fighting.

"Lo, please."

But she won't look at me.

This used to be our place. When we first got together we couldn't afford it, but we felt so rich, what with having each other, we'd come here once a month or so for no reason at all. It was always the best. Best pizza you ever had. Best aromas. Best sex when you got home. Best feeling of having believed in yourselves, having acted on that belief. All that was before, before we stenciled ducklings all over the walls, before Chuckie.

I try again. "Please, Lo. Tell me what to do."

She turns on me, she turns teacher. She isn't my wife right now, she's looking at me like an outsider, like an observer, the way I watch a perp in the box on the other side of the glass. She has saved it all up for now, her big takedown, it's not *this is your life* but *this is your problem.*

"You and that tea," she chides. "You want to steep it for fifteen minutes."

"Those are the instructions, Lo. That's not me being OCD."

She nods. "Read them closer, Eggie. They say it's *ideal* to steep the tea for fifteen minutes. But it can be ten. They don't say it, but just by admitting that it doesn't *have* to be fifteen minutes, they're telling you that life is a mess sometimes. That sometimes something comes up and maybe you don't steep your tea for fifteen minutes. Maybe your wife is exhausted from four trips to CVS in one day, from two drives to Bradley, on her own, as always, and maybe, just maybe, when she brings you that tea, maybe you don't always ask her if it was steeped for fifteen minutes. Maybe you let it go because she has bags under her eyes, bags that weren't there before your bag . . . Well, we all know why you didn't go to the doctor. You don't want to be a part of this family."

I'm hollowed. I want to smash the bouquets together, tear them into nothing. "Lo, please, I'm trying."

She tucks her hair behind her ears, like Marko does. "Here's what. I'm going into that party because this is *my* kid and this is *my achievement* and it is *my* right to go in there and eat the pizza and have a few pops and celebrate something good for once in my life. And you don't want to do that? Fine. You're gonna go and I'm gonna stay."

"Hold on here."

She points her finger at me. Her nail is painted. Her nails are never painted. Now that she's this close, I can see her eyes too, there's glitter on the lids. "No, Eggie. No."

She turns to walk away and I can't let this happen, I can't lose, not everything, not all at once.

"You think you're so perfect? You and your kids. *My kids, my kids, my kids,* as if those are magic words and if you say it enough those kids will be yours."

She is shaking. "Stop it."

I can't stop. I am a train. "You think that's your kid in there? That's not your kid. He's got parents. I saw them when I got here. I heard his father talking about their big family vacations and he's got a sister too, he's got a *mother,* Lo. He's got a father. His name is *Lorne* and the mother is Patsy and when I got here, when I went looking for you, I heard them all chortling about the time they saw *Hamilton* and took up a whole row. A whole row, Lo, that's the size of *their* family. We're not them and they ain't us. But you go on, Lo. You go on back in there, you make a fool of yourself, you try and worm your way into their family because you won't fucking let it be us. This is our family, Lo. It's you and me. Chuckie isn't here and he never will be and you wanted family? You got it, kiddo. It's me. I'm yours. It's you and me. So stop trying to shove all these other kids into it, because you and I got together, we were supposed to be enough. That was the idea, but you? No. Don't think I don't see your nails painted and your face painted. Don't think I don't know that you're in there pretending that I'm not out here."

I thought communication started with a feeling, a thought. You talk because you have something to say. But I'm shaking. Those words didn't feel like *mine*. And now they're out there, which is proof that they were mine, they came out of my mouth. She's standing here, lording over me. I said too much to say *sorry*. I try to read her face, her teacher's face. I can't.

"Stop it," she says. "Stop looking at me and let *me* look at *you*."

Inside the restaurant, people are clapping because someone made a speech, a loving speech. Not me, my hate speech. I want so badly to look down, to hang my head. But this is part of it, winning her back. It's what she said. *Let me look at you*. It's a hard thing to do, the hardest thing I've done in so long, the thing I'm most afraid of with my boy, that he will look at me, that he will know where I've been.

"Eggie." She kisses the back of my hand. "You do have to go see him."

"I know." It's in her voice, *I'm okay, we're okay, for now*.

I wrap myself up in her and she cries a tiny bit, the tiniest bit, muffled reluctant tears like she did so many times in the beginning, those first few days when Chuckie was having problems, when there was still hope that he would be okay.

"So," she says. "You gonna go back to Nashua?"

"Yeah, I am."

"I hope you get this guy, Eggie. You know I'm on your side."

"I know, Lo."

"You know I don't think you're nuts. You know I want you to win, to be right. I know how your mind works, I know how you see things."

"I know, Lo."

"But you do need to be that way at home too." She pulls away. "You know," she says, licking her lips. "There's a professor in there I haven't seen in years, he got divorced, he's you know, circling. And the whole time he's circling, trying to buy me drinks, told me *three* times about his new condo in Newport . . ." She laughs. "Eggie, I kept looking for you. I want you here."

"I'm sorry."

She is serious. *Newport condo* serious.

"I'm here," I say.

"Good," she says. "Then you'll stay here with me and you'll go in there because *I* want to go in there, because that's how it works."

She digs into her purse for Throat Coat tea bags. "Oh," she says. "I brought some of these, you know, for you."

I take the tea bags and put them in my pocket. I know better than to thank her. It's embarrassing, the imbalance, the months she took care of me and I make a stink about getting a *present*. I hold the door for my wife and now she murmurs, nobody can hear it but me, *Thank you, Eggie*. I put my hand on her shoulder. I squeeze. *Sorry, Lo*.

Nashua can wait. It has to.

# CHLOE

Every time we go to a potential spot for the wedding, it's the same. Carrig winces on the sidewalk when he spots the telltale white lights, *My mother likes colorful lights.* I talk him down, *If we rent the place, we can design the lighting.* And then we go in and none of it feels right, it's all too Brooklyn, too *too.* And then we have a few drinks and we laugh.

And tonight is par for the course. We agree that Milk and Roses might be too beautiful for us. We're eating creamy polenta, soaked in candlelight, seated in another garden that isn't quite right, not when you grew up like we did, with cavernous yards. We're laughing about the idea of our parents in here. Carrig's mother would be horrified by the bookshelves inside, the small portions on our small plates, the whole Brooklyn aesthetic of it, the *rustic* decor, the nonstop fulfillment of expectations. My mother would smile, but she'd be rolling her eyes at it. A vivid memory from childhood, my mother to a saleswoman in a furniture store: *I hate whimsy. There has to be furniture for a young girl that has zero whimsy.*

Carrig pours more wine into my glass. "Zero whimsy," he says. "The only place we're gonna get that is my parents' house."

"But we don't want to get married in the same place we have the engagement party," I say, and then I shake my head.

He laughs, rubs my back. "It's not too much too fast?"

"God no," I say, drinking my wine, the wine he poured. "I'm just still thinking about the New Hampshire thing. It would be ironic if we blew all this time and money trying to find a place, going to all these restaurants, and then we wind up in Nashua."

He shrugs, Mr. Bashful, the home state finding its way back into his voice. "Or maybe it would be romantic. I mean it's not like I wanna move back there or anything, but you really can't beat the fall. Our backyard. I mean that could be cool."

"Do you though?"

"Do I what?" he asks, the tiniest bit defensive.

"Wanna move back," I say. "For a minute there it sounded like you do."

He shrugs. "When we're older," he says. "You know, like to retire."

The waitress is back, asking about dessert, and I motion to Carrig, *your call.* Already my head is spinning. *You know, like to retire.* I didn't think it through, didn't move that far into the future in my mind. There are moments like this every day, little stings, like mosquitoes. I can't picture us old, *retired.* Whenever I saw myself as an old gal, I saw myself with Jon.

"Honey," I say. "I'll be right back."

In the bathroom I splash cold water on my face. This happens. Little spells. You don't lose a person all at once. You lose them in parts. At first it felt so good, so empowering, to literally *paint over* Jon. A revenge for the way he's occupied my brain for most of my life, in a good way, in a bad way. But every day has a moment like this, a bump. I don't get to think about him growing old with me anymore.

And it shouldn't hurt like this, not when I'm so excited to be in this with Care, so *engaged* with the wedding planning, the new lilt in his voice, the relaxation, the new purpose to our life, every restaurant is a possible spot for a wedding, everything is possible for us.

I take my phone out and look at the *Nylon* article again. It makes it all feel real on this other level, it makes it all feel right. Sure, there are a few people in the comments picking on me, but the comments don't bother me the way they used to. It's easier to laugh off the losers who say they liked me better when I was *mourning over Basement Boy.* Those people must be going through terrible things in their lives if they bother to go to *Nylon* and read about me. Being engaged has made me a more empathetic person.

Carrig stands to welcome me back to the table, kisses me on the lips. "You look so good," he says. "I mean we could do it right now."

"We'd get arrested," I say, winking, sitting up so tall, he's right, I do look good, I feel good, it's good, all of it. I keep thinking of Mary Steenburgen at the end of *Parenthood,* how she smiles and cries, how everything is okay, I always cry at the end of that movie and this feels like that, like things are where they're meant to be, even if some things are surprising, like this tiny and ridiculously embellished slice of white cake on the table. Carrig grins. "Derek Zoolander would be like, 'This cake is ridiculously good-looking.'"

He's so relaxed now, he does his little voices, he laughs easily, it's all easy. I dig my fork into the cake, softer than I expected, almost like pudding. There's so much on the fork that I have to lean over to get it all into my mouth and he intercepts the fork and our mouths meet and we are kissing, we are laughing. We are those people in love, those people I used to see when I was alone, those people I'd marvel at, thinking I'd never have that, this.

On the way home we hold hands. I ask him if his family saw the *Nylon* article and he laughs. "They don't care about that stuff," he says. "And you don't even need that." He kisses the top of my head.

We can't make the light, so we wait. There are couples all around.

It's one of those late-spring nights when it's so good to get out, when you don't need a sweater but you brought one anyway. The sign turns white for walk, but we aren't moving. I realize it's me. I've lost track of time and place, I stopped hearing Carrig, stopped seeing the crosswalk. There was a guy across the avenue and I thought it was Jon. I wasn't even aware of it, this searching part of me, the scanner that's always looking for something. We both feel it, as if Jon himself just appeared, next to us. And it's my fault. But it's also my move, my chance.

I lace my fingers around Carrig's hand. "I'm sorry, Care. That sugar really hit me. I'm spacing out."

*My girl,* he says, so easily moved along, as if we're on ice, in skates, gliding. I picture us old together, gray-haired, in skates, clinging, holding on to each other, as if we're not both in the same position, off-balance, wobbling. I imagine his friends over the years, questioning him about his lasting obsession with me. *Why don't you just give up on that girl? What's so great about her? Why do you keep trying?* He held on and I did too and we're lucky we did. We have us now. We can overcome a moment like that, when I slip. We're good for each other. And you have to be if you want a marriage to work. He wants to know why I'm smiling, I tell him the truth.

"I'm just happy."

# JON

I've never parked in Roger Blair's driveway. But I'm not myself any-more. Chloe is marrying Carrig and I'm a defective. A freak who can't be with a girl without hurting her, a monster who eats a whole cake because he can't kiss a girl, can't love. I've never felt so full of horror, *The Dunwich Horror*. I remember the way the townspeople would glare at Wilbur, how Lovecraft went out of his way to hit you over the head with the fact that Wilbur was weird, grotesque. I re-member reading it for the first time when I got out, after Chloe fainted, this horrible little voice in my head, nagging, *Well, Jon, you were always weird and gross*. At the time I thought things were differ-ent now that I was so jacked, now that I could be a model or a jock.

I am pounding on Roger Blair's door. I am kicking the door. I am done waiting. I grab his fucking sign.

*Life's a Beach!*

I'm about to hurl that sign at the closest window when I hear a Journey song, the music cut up by the sound of jalopy wheels hitting the potholes. It's Red Hat and Blue Hat. I walk to my car and get in. The excuses fly around my mind. I could be serving him a subpoena. I could be a Jehovah's Witness or a long-lost cousin. I could be a cop, undercover. I back out of the driveway as Red Hat gets out of the car. I smile and crack my window, ready to shut it quickly if Red Hat's nose starts to bleed.

"Hey," I say. "You seen Mr. Blair around?"

"Mr. who?"

"Mr. Blair," I say, willing my heart to settle, cracking the window a little more.

"Who's he?"

"The owner," I say. "I helped him pick out furniture at Alex Interiors over in Providence and I was supposed to take some measurements."

He pops open a can of beer. "I don't know a Blair," he says. "The dude that owns this joint bought it on eBay a few weeks ago or something. He lives in Canada or some shit. Not even living here, you know, same as most people lately, just using the place as an Airbnb."

I roll up the window because my heart is thumping pretty good. The idea of this time, wasted. Roger Blair, a ghost. Me, a fool. A stalking, patient, fool. "Do you know who he bought it from?"

Red Hat looks at Blue Hat, who's tinkering with the tools. "How the hell would I know?"

"I think it had the same owner for years," I say. "If you worked on it before—"

Blue Hat cuts me off. "Yo, D, should I start with the gutters?"

Red Hat nods at Blue Hat. "Guy," he says. "I got shit to do, but if you wanna get in there and do your measurements or whatever, we got a key. Maple leaf fucker *finally* hooked us up. You want?"

I don't go into the house. I don't go back to my house. I get on the highway. I don't have to look at the GPS. I don't need to look at it.

I don't stop for gas or water. My throat is dry and the roads are clear.

I don't play any Hippo Campus and I don't open the windows to relieve myself of the smell, the vomit on my breath. All of it is fitting for this moment. I was right that change was in the air. But I was wrong to think it could mean good things for me. Roger Blair. Chloe Sayers. They're moving on with their lives. I've been sitting here, hiding, waiting, hoping, even when I thought I wasn't, that's what I was doing. But they're just trying to get away from me.

All I can do is keep moving, keep driving, speeding and passing people left and right. I wish this car could fly, I wish I could be away from my mind, my memories, how they all come crushing back. I almost lose my grip on the wheel.

*You have power.*

No I don't. I have nothing. It's over. I see my exit. I gulp. *My exit.*

# EGGS

There's an art to leaving your wife when you're on probation. I'm up early today and I treat the day like a Sunday. I tell Lo I'm going to get the papers, the *Pro Jo* and the *Globe,* the *Times.* And I show her the art from Jon's apartment. She looks at me, then nods.

I wait in a line from hell at Dunkin' and I get two pounds of Lo's coffee, a box of doughnuts. Then I start in on the real mission, all those eyes from Jon's apartment. I carry them with me, the one I took down from his wall. I show the eyes to people at CVS, Stop & Shop, at Dunkin'. *You know this artist?* Nothing. Nobody knows. It's an impossible Google—*big eyes art*—it leads you to a movie called *Big Eyes,* and this movie is about art, but not *his* art.

Lo texts wanting to know if I've had any luck. I tell her no. *But going to Thayer Street.*

My fingers are crossed for you. Go get em, E.

I try. I head over to the RISD campus, the Rhode Island School of Design, and I loiter outside of a building. First kid that comes by is on a skateboard and he doesn't stop for me. *Beep beep,* he says. My bag whinnies. The nuisance of that bag, the bag of tricks I have to lug around, the gauze, the disinfectant, a God damn baby bag, it's almost worse than the cancer. The next two students stop but don't recognize the work. And here comes another student, a girl, probably a freshman, she's panting as she lugs her stuff up the hill. Her glasses slip off her nose. She looks like she was up all night. I show her the eyes.

"Ah," she says. "I feel like I *just* saw this somewhere."

Painful. *Breathe, Eggie, breathe.* "Do you remember where?"

She looks at me. "No," she says. "But it will pop into my head in the middle of the night like everything does."

"Or maybe you'd do me a favor and close your eyes a minute, give it some thought."

"Are you a police officer?"

I work the girl good now, I tell her she's got a good eye, I am a cop, but this is hardly official business. I act all casual, I tell her my wife's birthday is coming up, I found this in one of her books, I figured I'd come over here, it would mean the *world* to me if I could give my wife a good present for once, unlike last year, I got her this blender and—

The girl snaps her fingers. "Chloe Sayers," she says, pushes those glasses back to the bridge of her nose. They slip down again a moment later. "That's her name. I saw an interview with her online."

*Chloe Sayers.* The friend. The friend from the articles. The young girl with the sad face and those brand-new boots in the newspaper picture. The girl in the cold. The friend. The *one* friend. Of course this was her. She was drawing him, hunched over canvases, trying to find him in her mind, make him appear there on the easel. Chloe Sayers. Of course.

I thank the girl and give her my old-man advice she didn't ask for, probably doesn't want. "Go into any LensCrafters, they'll tighten those glasses for you."

She smiles at me. "Thank you."

I am a hero at home too. Lo marvels at the bounty. "Wow," she says, collecting her newspapers, her coffee. "You got the goods *and* the goods."

She's shuffling back to the bedroom, same way she does most Sundays, and I'm just about to ask her to stay when she laughs. "Hey Eggie," she says, not turning back to look at me. "First you deal with your bag, *then* you can see about Chloe."

I make a vow to do better—*Sorry, Lo-Lo*—and I deal with the damn bag, the tedium of it, and then finally I plop onto the sofa and I crack my knuckles. Chloe Sayers is the missing link. Jon's carrying a torch for her too. His walls look different to me now. To think of him covering every inch with her drawings. How much he must miss her. Long for her. He wouldn't do that if he was living with her. No artist would live like that, walled in by her own imagination. She's never been there. I'm sure of it. I comb through pictures of Chloe, the pictures of her now are mixed up with pictures of her as a kid, pictures of her work, the eyes from Jon's apartment. This is how he got those pictures. He searched for her online, he printed them, one by one, methodically taping them to the walls of his home.

He *missed* her. Did he kill for her?

I find a fresh interview with the girl in *Nylon*. I remember the last time I went on a roller coaster, that moment when you're at the top, right before you turn, right before the noise begins. This is like that. Chloe Sayers is wearing a T-shirt. *Live Free or Die.*

The phrase means something different to me now, matched with the quiet in her eyes, a sadness you're not meant to see. This is a girl who's been to the dark side of things. She missed the kid and missing him made her lonely. *Live free or die.* She thought by drawing the kid she'd free them both.

And then it's a quick paragraph, almost a throwaway.

> Chloe Sayers is no longer in communica-
> tion with Jon Bronson. His whereabouts
> are unknown.

I walk out into the front yard so Lo doesn't have to hear as I call Jed and Penny. The sun assaults me. I forgot my sunglasses. More self-destructive behavior.

Penny picks up. "Hello?"

"Hello, Mrs. Bronson?"

There's a dog yapping in the background, I'm happy for them. That's the right move when your kid is troubled. But as for us, Lo's allergic and I'm not a cat person.

Penny bites my head off, to start. "If this is a telemarketer, I signed up for that thing where you're not supposed to call."

I've never been so happy to say that it's me, Charles DeBenedictus. She snaps her fingers, *Jed come in here.* He's quick on his feet. *Put it on speaker,* he says.

"You're on speaker," she says. "Is that okay?"

These are good people, Yvonne Belziki level of good. "You bet," I say. "This is gonna sound like it's outta left field, but I've been doing some research, I'm curious if you guys are ever in touch with Jon's friend?"

"Which friend?" Penny asks, and the defense in her voice is palpable.

"Chloe," I say, as if there were many friends, as if it needs to be said. "Chloe Sayers. She went to school with Jon."

You can practically hear Penny's heart start thumping. "What about her?"

"Well," I say. "I'm curious if she and Jon . . . were they close?"

"That's one word for it," she says. I hit a nerve.

Jed sighs. "Jon had a bit of a crush on her. When they were kids."

Penny counters. "And when he was back, you know . . . after."

"This sounds like a sore subject," I say, leading, fishing, all of it.

Penny bites. She rails on about that *evil little brat who manipulated my son to no end.* Jed butts in to soften the blow. *She was also the only person Jon really had, she was at every vigil.* Penny seethes, *Fuck those vigils. She just wanted to see her name in the paper.* I can hear Jed putting his arm around his wife, who's already crying, muffled tears. But then she pushes him away, blows her nose.

"The two of you don't understand," she says. "Men are blind to this kind of thing, this kind of *bitch.* Because she's *pretty* and she *smiles* at you guys, because she walks around batting her eyelashes and lighting candles, you buy it. You think she's some kind of saint. You defend her and you say what's so *good* about her. Well, no. No. Chloe is not a saint. She's a possessive, controlling, vicious person who *used* my son's disappearance to launch her *career.*"

Jed chimes in again. "Penny, slow down."

"No," she says. "It's true. And now she has the nerve to come home and parade around with that *monster* who made Jon's life a living hell. The very reason my son was cutting through the woods in the first place and what's she gonna do? *Marry him.*"

Now I know why Jed and Penny sound so morose today. Imagine this girl breaks your kid's heart and then she comes home and your son's still missing. *Missing.* My gut's rolling pretty good, my heart races because of course there was a girl, a key. People are predictable that way, healthy people, most people, they do a lot, sure, but their life boils down to that one person out there, their person, and that's what Chloe was, what she is, no matter what's going on. That never changes.

Jed groans at Penny, begs her to *let it go.* "You're making it so melodramatic," he says, pleading. "Jon was cutting through the woods cuz it was faster and he was . . . adventurous."

Penny brings me into it. "Do you hear what I'm up against over here?"

"I feel for you, Penny, both of you," I say. "Kids can drive you crazy."

"Well, he drives me crazier," she says. "Defending her like she's an angel."

"I never said she's an angel."

"No," Penny says. "But you won't say she's a cunt either."

I cut in, hard. "Was Chloe in touch with Jon?" I ask. "Recently, I mean."

"Who knows?" Penny says. "When he came home, we barely saw him because he was holed up in his room texting her, and then you know, one day and *poof*. He was gone. For all we know, yeah, those kids are talking every day."

Once again Jed doesn't agree. His voice is quavering, and now you can hear Penny rubbing his back, *It's okay, Jed*. I wish I could make things better for them, and I think maybe I can. For once, time is on my side. Carrig and Chloe's engagement party is this weekend. This is a call to arms, a call to Jon. If he was talking to her he wouldn't be papering the walls with her eyes. He left her when he left his parents, when he left all of Nashua. The question is, why?

Lo is almost more fascinated than I am about this watershed of insight into the Beard, this girl he loved, Chloe Sayers. She's on her computer, captivated by the Facebook obit page I found for Chloe's friend who died. *Right before Jon skipped town.*

"Of a heart attack at eighteen," she says, aghast. "Wow. Eggie . . . wow."

But nothing moves her as much as the pictures of Jon's apartment. The eyes cover the walls. She squeezes my hand. "He loves her," she says. "He's carrying a torch."

"I know," I say, relieved to be in this new place, this comfort zone.

"Gimme your phone," she says. "I'm gonna set alarms for you to check your bag."

I throw my arms around her, my forgiving, loving wife.

# CHLOE

Alexandra looks around the yard again, the way she's been doing since we got here and she saw our homes, our manicured lawns, *you guys use pesticides?* She shakes her head. "It's like you're both dudes in a bromance."

She has a point. Our engagement party is a true meeting of our minds, our tastes, it's a *summah blowout, where's the Fireball?* Our party feels like a real celebration, purposeful, a kickoff to our life together, a *bash,* the kind of night where people do keg stands and play corn hole. There are little kids twerking, fucking with each other's heads in ways they don't realize. My art friends and my home friends sniff each other like dogs in the dog park. I love it. All of it. Care knows this about me, that I like to put people together, that I like the sound of bottle rockets, New Hampshire accents, the ever-present nuisance of mosquitoes.

Our names are everywhere you turn, *Chloe and Carrig.* In New York, our decision to get married was this thing between us. Now it's expanding, a balloon that can fit our parents, our friends. My mother, who's always pooh-poohed marriage—*Anyone can have a husband, but not anyone can be an artist*—she's prancing around with pictures of the venue she wants us to use. I expected it to be loud. I expected to feel overwhelmed, but I didn't anticipate this aura of the expanding balloon, the only word for it that makes sense to me, *suspense*.

Alexandra is puzzled by my word choice. "What do you mean?" she asks. "I actually can't think of anything less suspenseful than an engagement party. We all know exactly what comes next. A wedding, a baby shower, blah blah blah . . . no offense. Literally zero suspense."

I laugh it off and shrug. "I'm just really jumpy."

A neighbor grabs at me. *Chloe you look so fancy, can we take a picture?* People keep seizing parts of my body, telling me how much they cried during Carrig's speech, how beautiful it was. Everyone likes the same line: *Chloe, we were born here in the same town because that's how destiny works.* Maybe he's right. Maybe this is destiny. We have the weather you bank on when you throw this kind of party, that magic New England air, the right kind of humidity, wind in the trees. There's a stillness that magnifies our every move, all of us, a blackness in the sky that enhances every firefly, every set of bright white teeth.

Carrig slaps my ass. "It's your turn," he says.

We're playing beer pong, on tables I designed. I drew our initials on everything I could find for tonight. I painted them on the wineglasses, the tables, these balls, the wine labels. I was up all night, I lost track of time, and at four a.m. I indulged. I let myself feel it for a minute, the symmetry of my life, of anyone's, all the hard work you do to grow up and get over your shit, and there you are, grown up, in your shit, your same old shit, but at least it looks different, cocktail napkins with names instead of legal pads full of eyes. I cried, and then I was fine. I was surprised at how different it felt. I'm changing. Maybe that's the suspense. Who will we become?

Carrig nudges me again. "C? Your turn."

His mother is annoyed by my art. I overheard her whisper to another hen inside, *Who needs to draw on every cup? What is she trying so hard to prove?* I dip my little pink-and-white-dot ball into the water and take aim. I make my shot. It's another sign that this is meant to be. Usually I'm terrible at this game but tonight I'm on a roll, I can't miss. Carrig picks me up, he loves me winning, it's more proof that I'm his girl, that we're the same. Alexandra balks, it hits me she's my substitute for Noelle. I always need a friend who seems smarter than me barking at me, *Who are you with the beer pong?*

"You go again," Care says, kissing me.

This time I set my sights on a cup on the edge of the table, a harder shot. People are clapping, hooting. I feel Carrig's hands on my waist. I squint. I hold my breath. I make it. I'm in Carrig's arms, in the air, he's swinging me around and there is hollering, chanting, I could drown like this, and I hold on tight, but then I see something in the woods, a fleck of color, man-made color. Care puts me down.

"You okay, babe?"

I move so I can see the woods, the thing in the woods, the person. My heart races. He's bent over, the person, a man, definitely a man.

Care whistles at Penguin. "Dude, can you get her a water?"

My heart is a bomb and the person who is a man is starting to stand. The branches are in the way and it's only the back of him but even before he's fully upright I can tell that it isn't who I thought it was. It isn't Jon, come to prove me wrong. It's an older man and he sees me notice him and he smiles. He holds up one of my ping-pong balls.

I kiss Care on the cheek. "Be right back. I promise I'll get water."

The man speaks first, and immediately I can tell he's not from here. "Thank you for getting this," I say. "You know, I hate to think of a bird choking on these."

He smiles. "I'm not such a saint," he says. "The way things are going with you and your work, you know, I could probably take this over to the MFA department, get them to give me a few thousand bucks for it."

He's an easy man, somewhere between father and grandfather, as if he's stuck. It's easy to picture him in a train station, delayed. I offer him a drink and he follows me to the bar.

"I didn't catch your name," I say.

"Club soda will do," he says to the bartender. "Eggs," he says. "You can call me Eggs."

We shake hands and I make my dumb joke about how uncomfortable I feel in these moments. Do I say my name when it's clear that the person I'm talking to knows who I am? He laughs, politely, but he doesn't want small talk. There's something purposeful in the way he takes his drink, sips slowly, as if testing the water.

"I'm sorry," I say. "Are you a friend of my dad's?"

He shakes his head. "I'm from Providence."

That whole forty-eight-hour breakdown flashes through my mind, *Alex Interiors* and water fires and Lovecraft and the aloneness of it all, the desperation, the fixation, all the things that ruin a person, that drive her into the ground, into the darkest part of herself.

"Providence," I say. "It's so nice there."

The man must have been reading my face and my face must have been telling a story. I must be crying, I can't feel anything, but the man offers me a cocktail napkin, *Chloe and Carrig*. I wipe the tears away.

"So," he says. "Without meaning to pry, and with respect to this timing, which I realize is not so fair, Chloe, I gotta ask. Have you heard from Jon?"

I crumple up the napkin into a little ball. "Do you want to go out front?"

We sit in the Adirondack chairs in the front yard, the chairs that *kill* my mother. Eggs hasn't said he's the police, but it's a thing you can feel, the authority. I'm babbling about the chairs, my mother's pet peeve of what she calls *psychological furniture*. She says these chairs aren't practical, they're just a message to let the neighbors know that they can afford *extra chairs*.

He laughs. "We all do that though, don't we?"

"You mean put on a show for the neighbors? Oh this party, this isn't for the neighbors, this is for our parents. See, we owe them. We live in New York and I'm an only child and I don't come home enough and Care's from here too, he has five siblings, but he's the only one who doesn't live around here, so you know, we owe them."

The oldish guy smiles. "You seem like good kids."

There's a silence now, an active, transitional silence, the kind where you can hear your intestines, your throat muscles. "So," I say. "Did you think he would be here? Jon?"

"No," he says. "I just thought you might have heard from him."

"I haven't heard from him in years. Several years."

He nods, overdoing it, the way they do on TV when they're digging. "Okay," he says. "Good to know."

"Is he okay?" I ask, wishing I didn't sound so defensive, so emotional.

"Well," he says. "You seem to know him best."

"It's been years though."

"As for myself," he says. "I'm married, and you spend that much time with someone, you almost develop a sixth sense about them, you know? I tell you, I know my wife's mad at me before she knows."

I can't tell if it's a trap or an invitation. I want to tell him that I went through hell for Jon, that I *do* know he's in pain but it's not my pain. I missed him so much that I got lost in it, I hid in the yearning. You can say these things to a stranger you meet randomly at a hotel lobby bar. But you can't say them to a cop.

Instead, I just promise to keep an eye out for Jon. "It's really pretty simple," I say. "Jon disappeared when we were kids, as you know. He was kidnapped. Then my best friend died senior year after Jon was back. And that's the last time I ever saw him."

"She died of a heart attack, right?"

"Yeah," I say. "It was horrible. And he dropped off the planet the same day. So really, if I knew where he was, believe me, I would tell you. I want to know too."

He sighs heavily. There's another silence. "Where do you think he is?" he asks.

"Why are you looking for him? Did he do something?"

"No," he says. "I just like to follow up with people. You know, you get kidnapped like that, you come out of that a changed person."

I am blushing now. To remember those teenage nights, the waiting, the wanting, the texting, the way he blew me off over and over again, the way it never felt like he was blowing me off, the reality that it might just be about my ego, my narcissism, my refusal to believe that he walked out on me. I look down at my feet. "I know what you mean," I say. "He was different when he got out. At one point I think we were talking for twenty hours a day and I'm not exaggerating. But he wouldn't . . . we didn't . . . he was weird about being around people." I am trembling when I say the words I've never wanted to say. "He didn't want to see me in person."

The truth hurts. It doesn't feel like truth. My mouth is dry and the oldish guy is sighing. "You don't always know what someone wants," he says. "You gave your friend his space. And maybe he was giving you your space."

It never occurred to me that Jon left to let me go, to set me free to have all this. A bottle rocket pops somewhere out back, at my party. I flinch. Eggs does too. And then he gives me a card and we say our goodbyes. I promise to call him if I hear from Jon.

He smiles. "Now you can tell your mother that these chairs, they do serve a purpose."


At the party, I take a shot of Fireball and I chase it with a shot of grain. I'm trying to loosen up, to be the girl on the arm of her fiancé. *No*

*Jon thoughts, Chloe, not now.* There are sloppy kisses, Billy Joel sing-alongs with party crashers we haven't seen since senior year. And then finally it's late, true late. The music is softer and people are starting to pour into pickup trucks, there's ambient noise about diners, *eggs and legs.* My brain is tired. My mouth is dry. I flop onto a wicker sofa and search the woods for Jon with my wobbly eyes, but that's what everyone does when they come home, you try to find your past.

Now it's just us, me and Care on the outdoor sofa, flopped, zapped. We break it down, the greatest hits—Penguin throwing up on the trampoline, my mother and his mother trying to play beer pong—and the funniest bits—when Care dragged me onto the patio and started screaming for everyone to gather so that we could do our dance, the one we're doing at the wedding.

Care laughs. "I guess I was kind of fucked up," he says.

"It's a party," I say. "It's fine."

He pours more vodka into his cup and I don't bother telling him to slow down. "Gonna go take a leak," he says, and then he's gone, leaving me alone to think of the moments that we didn't share, my time with Eggs, what happened when I went inside and overheard his mother talking about me with Carrig's sister Aerin.

"I'm no fan either," she said. "She's always acted like she's better than us. You know, Dorinda today, she asks her how much she got when Katy Perry got her painting and she acts like it's so rude, as if it's not our business when she's mooching off our Carrig."

Aerin nodded. "Her mother is the same way. So she's a lawyer. Get over yourself!"

Care's mom practically orgasmed. *"Yes,"* she said. "And she's so full of herself, so patronizing."

This is the bad part of marriage, where you have to pretend to be excited about the new people you call *family,* as if you didn't always know they're beady-eyed, cold at heart.

Care comes back from the bathroom with a new drink, which means he finished the other drink, which means he's drunk again. He stutters and stops at the coffee table. He stares at me. "Do I bore you?"

I turn red and reach for his hands and pull him onto the sofa. He collapses, laughing, saying he doesn't know what he's saying. I tell him it's okay and I rock him in my arms and he falls asleep on me. I am awake, bitten by mosquitoes. But this is just what happens when you go home. One minute you want to live here forever, the next you're fucked up and you remember why you can't live here.

It gets later, into the darkest part of the night. I don't hear Jon but I would swear that he's nearby. There's a vibration, like that red haze around a firefly. I remember a town Jon told me about a long time ago, something he read in the Weird News section of the *Telegraph* about a town in England with a humming sound that everyone could hear, but nobody knew where it was coming from. That's what this is. Jon is close. And were Care not asleep on me, I could stand up and open my eyes and see him.

# JON

You regress when you go home. My dad says that's why he never went back to Scotland, *never wanted to become that child ever again.* But I think that might be why he drinks so much as an adult. I think maybe you need to be that child, at least sometimes, like tonight. I was nervous about being here, unsure if it would just be too much, if it would be wiser to disappear without saying goodbye. I was nervous when I parked my car by the old phone company (probably where Roger parked when he hid to take me). I was nervous I wouldn't remember how to find my way to the shed, but I did. You don't forget the important things, the things that made you who you are.

I saw her. Chloe. And it's like a big meal, a hot shower, warm sun on your back, I saw her and she saw me—I would swear on it—and I feel all the Chloe parts of my brain lighting up, the circuits are smoking. I'm so tapped into this place that I don't have to use my flashlight on my way back to the shed. I just play the moment in my head over and over.

There I was in the woods, and there she was on the sofa, and there was this thing between us, the thing that was there in the shed when we were kids, the thing that was between our phones, our computers, a glue string. It never died.

And that's true freedom. That's what Roger was wrong about in his letter to me. *You are free.* I wasn't. I am now. I saw her. I felt it. True love.

The door to the shed still sticks. You have to push the knob even as you pull it, a ridiculous dance, another one I remember, like riding a bike. I brought the same stuff with me that I would bring when I was a kid, my sleeping bag, a jar of fluff, a jar of peanut butter, a loaf of bread. I eat a sandwich and I lick my fingers before I reach for the ball I found in the woods by Carrig's house, a customized ping-pong. *Chloe and Carrig.* I cover the Carrig part with my thumb. But then I remember that Chloe painted their names all over everything. I saw the ping-pong ball, I saw her friends snapping photos of the customized plates, cups, everything. She did this. She wants this. She has a future, a plan, a life. And I won't destroy it.

On the other side of the ball it says *C&C.* I wonder if this is destiny, if their marriage was in the stars all along, if my being here was an accident, an inconvenience, a rain delay. I get mixed-up and I'm not sure if their love is the monster, if I am the monster. Our names don't go together. Maybe we don't go together. Maybe she painted me because she felt obligated. Maybe she came here when we were kids to get a break from her friends. You don't marry your break.

I close my eyes and my heart fights back. I see another party in my mind, a party for me and Chloe. My mom is stringing lights up in our backyard, through the bars on the swing set. The cast of *The Middle* is here. There are Spidey plates and hats. There isn't any beer pong, there are no shots of Fireball. Noelle is alive; nothing bad ever happened. I know I'm dreaming when Chloe makes a speech. *I know you're here, Jon. I saw you in the woods.* I want to tell her everything, that I saw her, that I love her, that I don't hold any of this against her, but she's looking at me like I'm crazy because we're in this dream together, at our wedding, we have everything we want. I can't say anything. My mouth is full of fluff.

Alarm bells ring and I wake up gasping. My mouth isn't full of anything, it's just sticky from the Fluffernutter I ate before I passed out. Chloe's ping-pong ball rolled over to the other side of the shed. It's for the best. I saw Chloe. Now it's time to see my parents.

It's still dark when I get to my parents' house.

My old swing set is still there but the wood on the limbs is rotting. I can see us here, me in the dirt, playing Spider-Man, my parents puttering around, my dad grappling with a garden hose while my mom tells him what people are up to on Facebook and he asks her to do something useful with that phone, find out where he should go for a hose. There's a greeting card in their trash, a *thinking of you* card from someone named Nadine. I don't even know who Nadine is. I close the lid of the trash, super quiet, mouse quiet. Then a twig snaps and I get that feeling I get a lot, that *someone is watching you* chill. But there's never anyone. The guy at the hospital was right when he said, *It's post-traumatic stress. Sometimes it goes away. Other times . . .*

But I'm safe, blasted by memories:

My dad laughing, *Bronson men hit the road, Jack, and they don't come back.* My mom smacking him, *Watch it or one of these days he'll think you mean that and he'll walk into those woods and never come back.*

My mom after I came home, when I started to stay in my room and she would be out here, scrolling through Facebook, pursing her lips. Once I asked her why she didn't quit. *Because it exists,* she said. *You can't make it un-exist.*

I'm so close I can smell the inside of our house. I swear I can hear my dad's old songs. I want to go in, get into my bed, eat a burger off our grill, complain about being forced to eat broccoli out of the microwave.

Instead, I reach into their box for the first paper I ever loved, *The Telegraph*. It still smells the same and my heart starts thumping as I flip the pages, as I turn to the back, to the classifieds. I put an ad in here, a message for my parents. I've never done this before, never put myself out there, in here, and even though I already saw the proof online, it's exciting to see it, my words, my little black-and-white box:

> Mom and Dad. I Love you Forever and I will always miss you and love all the times we had, all the laughs at dinner, all the love. Thanks for always letting me be me, I know I wasn't the easiest kid. But I also know you guys are the best. Love Jon.

My mom and dad are gonna know it's me. My mom will know it's me because your mother knows your voice, your odd ways. And my dad will know because of my mom. She'll tell him how one year I had to do all my thank-you notes twice for my birthday because I capitalized every word of every sentence. I groaned but my mom tossed the new cards on my bed. *Do you want people to think you're crazy? Because only crazy people capitalize every word.*

I circle the ad with a Sharpie and I put the paper back in their box. I graze my hand over the box one last time. I remember the day it arrived. I do love them, so much.

I start my car, I pray it doesn't wake anyone—it doesn't, so far as I can tell—and I head down the street toward the Kinzys'. They have people visiting, cars parked tight and close, out-of-state plates, same as every summer, which is good for me, means I have a safe place to hide. I just line up my car with the Kinzy cars, I hunker down, I wait.

And eventually it begins. I hear one of the first sounds of my life, our screen door opening, followed by another sound I know, the sounds of the morning, my dad yawning, his barefoot footsteps. He's wearing his same Bread T-shirt he always slept in. It's hard not to leap out of the car, not to run over there, hug him. He scratches his neck and reaches into the *Telegraph* box. He's half asleep so he doesn't look closely enough. My heart aches. I thought I was gonna get to see it happen, gonna get to see them read it together. And then he realizes something's off about the paper. It's open. He sees my ad.

He gulps. "Penny!"

His accent is thicker, the way it always was in the morning, and now my mother is outside, in her robe, holding a small little dog, smaller than Kody. I bet she never lets go of the dog unless she has to. He shows her the paper and she kisses the dog.

And then she drops the dog and the little dog doesn't move. A Pomeranian, I think.

My dad groans. "Where's the leash?"

My mom mimics him. "Where's the leash? You call me out here and you're asking about the leash. Jed, this is him."

He picks up the little dog and he's talking her down, telling her there's no way to know, that it could be anyone, *people are sick and they do sick things, this is a prank.* You can tell he never holds the dog. His arms outstretched, the little dog's legs dangle like his tongue, wagging. I love my parents so much it hurts. I might get out of this car and walk over there and risk ending their lives just to hold them, just to show my mother that she's right, it is me, and to show my dad that he was right all those years ago, when he told my mother that things would be okay, that I would come home. I put my hands on the door.

I can't do that to them. To anyone.

My mother insists it's me, *That's his voice, I'd know if it wasn't.* My dad sniffs, *Pen, you go your way, I'll go mine. You want to hope? Fine. Hope. But I'm not gonna set myself up for a goddamn letdown. He's gone.* My mom groans, she smacks the paper. *He circled it, goddamn it. Look at it, Jed. Look.* But my parents are different. When I was little, I thought that meant they were wrong for each other. Now

I get that it means they're right. My mom wants to call Shakalis and my dad scratches his head. *I think he retired, hon.* My dad says he's gonna fix the lawnmower and my mom rocks her new dog, her baby. Love is forever, but at some point hope becomes a liability. I can tell by the way my mother's cradling New Kody that she's not gonna call the police. She's gonna believe. But she's not gonna hope, not gonna share her belief system with practical naysayers, authorities. Too much time has passed. When she's inside, my dad leans against the bed of his truck and lights a cigarette. He lays the paper out flat.

I can tell by the way he reads it over and over again that he still has hope, he just can't bring it into that house and show it to my mom. He can feel me out here. He knows it was me. But he won't come looking for me. His parents let him go. He's doing the same for me.

My mom appears in the doorway. *Are you coming in or what?*

My dad folds the paper in the way he never did when I bugged him to keep it tidy. He rolls it up and walks up the driveway to join my mom, to eat her eggs and listen to her, and not listen to her, and love her. I imagine myself in a yard like theirs, ours, me with no shoes, with a paper, Chloe in a doorway, calling my name.

I pull up her contact in my phone. There it is. *Chloe Sayers.* It's amazing to me, the power of these little machines, the potential in them to bring us together, the simple fact that I could put my finger on that little telephone icon and call her. If I wanted to.

My heart races. My palms sweat. I never felt so human and inhuman all at once.

# CHLOE

I told Carrig I have cramps. I'm up in his room, hiding from his giant family, letting them think the worst of me, that I'm uppity, too good for them, bored by their Bud Light and their dogs running around, the game on the TV, the conversation about home renovations, townie gossip. I'm feeding it all by staying up here in Care's bed, Googling Eggs from the party, searching for Jon and Providence.

Carrig's mother is telling him that Oprah says that women with bad cramps generally suffer from poor nutrition, a sedentary lifestyle, and various genetic hormonal imbalances. I listen to this and I know I should be down there but soon they'll turn the game off, they'll lose themselves in the new *Iron Man*. Which of course reminds me of Spider-Man, of Jon, how pathetic he was, the opposite of an animal that evolves to protect itself, to develop camouflage from predators. Jon wearing his Spider-Man costume to school when we were way too old to do that. Jon telling people he loved Spider-Man when we were supposed to love other things, cool things. He didn't know how to protect himself. And it made me hesitate, to think of what it would be like if we were together, really together. I'd have to hide that Spider-Man costume, I'd have to protect him.

It stung when Jon talked about his movies, his *Spider-Man*, his *Middle*. He had this ability to love things too much, movies that had nothing to do with him. I think he got it from his dad, who was so obsessed with America, with old songs. Jon loved things in a way that most people don't. I mean with Carrig there was never any question. He doesn't love his family all that much—how could he?—and he loves me more than the Red Sox, more than anything.

I close my eyes and curl up in the sheets, wrapping myself in a cocoon, trying to block out the TV downstairs, all those overgrown Birkus brothers and sisters, the squawking wives, the dull husbands.

My phone buzzes and the screen comes to life. One new message.

I assume it's Marlene—she's been texting all day—and I tap the little green icon and it's in slow motion only it's not in slow motion. It's my heart that can't keep up, my eyes. Because what I always wanted is happening. It's not a hang-up call from a strange number and it's not Marlene.

It's Jon and I know it right away because of how it starts, how it sounds like him, so direct, so emotionless and emotional all at once, so much that already my head is spinning, I am in high school again. I read the words once and already I know them by heart: *It's Jon. Can you come see me now? I'm in Rolling Jack's. It's a long story.*

I read it forward, backward. And then I respond: *I'm on my way.*

I am dizzy when I stand, it was hot in the sheets, it's hot in the house. It's hot inside of me. *Jon.* I don't know what to wear and I want to wear all my clothes at once, summer dresses and cutoffs, my old Tenley's T-shirt that's covered in paint and charcoal stains, my sexy panties, my granny panties, everything I ever owned, I want to put it on so he can take it off, so I can tell him where it comes from, what it means. I settle on a little pink dress but then I remember

Carrig's family, the wall of them, *why are you so dressed up?* That should be the state fucking slogan of New Hampshire. I find safe territory. A Lilly Pulitzer tank top, denim cutoffs.

Carrig knocks on the door as I finish changing. "Oh," he says. "You're up."

He gets that tone around his mom, that suspicious tone, he can't help it.

"Yeah," I say. "I'm up because it turns out I have to go out."

"But you said you have cramps." Again that suspicion.

"Yeah, but Marlene texted, she had a fight with her mom."

"Do you want her to come here? We're gonna grill and have a corn hole tournament."

I invite him to the bed and he comes and we sit. "Care, she was crying. I have to be a friend, you know?"

He pouts. Your family makes you into a child, no matter how old you are. "But it's Sunday and you know how my mom is about stuff. I mean everyone is staying."

"I'll be back."

"But you could also just not go." He turns red. "Can I say something and you won't get mad?"

"No, Care, if you hurt my feelings, I will get mad."

"Well my mom says you put panty-liner things in the trash can and she says you shouldn't have cramps if your period is that light and she thinks you're up here cuz you don't wanna be down there."

"Your mother riffles through the trash?"

He swallows my knee with his hand. "I know," he says. "She always did that though cuz my sisters lied about stuff and put things in the toilet, it was a whole fight that was always happening when we were kids and I guess she still looks in the trash just because."

I fold my arms. I want to leave. In every possible way. I stare at the wall. "I'm mortified."

He surprises me, springing off the bed. "Well, me too. Why wouldn't you just watch the fucking movie?"

"Because I had cramps."

"Right," he says. "It's always something."

"No, Care, it's a pretty known fact that fiancées get anxious sometimes. And anxiety is hell on cramps."

He clicks his jaw. "You always talk like that when we come home, you know."

He won't look at me and I try not to blush. "Like what?"

"Like a newspaper," he says. "And you know what I mean by 'newspaper.'"

"Are you kidding?"

He looks at me. "You think I'm retarded? Jesus Chloe you get here and you *talk* like that freak and you *look* for that freak every time we go anywhere, you watch doors, Chloe."

"No I don't."

He shakes his head. "You think I'm blind? Your eyes, Chloe, they shoot over there happy and they come back sad. You're not the only one who can see shit. Even your fucking paintings. What do you make? *Eyes.* Why do you make them? *Him.* And it's fucking embarrassing, okay?"

"Embarrassing."

"Yes," he says. "It's fucking embarrassing."

That's what he cares about the most, that everyone here has this fantasy that we're perfect. *Embarrassing* isn't a love word. I could do anything and Jon would never be embarrassed. Carrig grabs his bong, his high school bong. This is how I know I'm really leaving him, because of how at home he is right here. It doesn't even have anything to do with Jon, not right now. He'll come back here, *home to mommy.* Destiny is evident, it's your fiancé tapping a bong, showing you who he is, who he'd rather be, if you would just let him fucking be, once and for all.

I take my ring off. I put it on the nightstand. He doesn't fight me. He coughs. "Seriously?"

"I don't know," I say. "I just know I don't know you right now."

Downstairs, I slip out the kitchen door, avoiding all those Birkuses, all of them except for Care's oldest sister-in-law, who glares at me as she comes in to get more beer. "You're feeling better I see. All dressed up."

"It's a tank top."

"It's a Lilly," she says, *fuck you and your shirt.* "Everyone knows those are dressy."

I wave and slam the door. *Fuck her too.* Already I'm better, outside. I start the car I borrowed from my mom. I am going to see him, going to see Jon, and I am smiling and I turn on the local radio— Springsteen, "I'm on Fire." I back out of the driveway and I roll down the windows, all of them. Gnats swirl, fireflies too. I feel more engaged than I ever did when I was engaged.

# EGGS

It was almost fun at first, me staked out by the Birkus house, Lo back home, reading about Chloe's art on the computer, searching for clues about Jon, *make room for me in your rabbit hole, Eggie.* I stare at the Birkus house, I will the door to open, same way I stared at Chuckie when he was sleeping, I willed him to come back to us. Now I stare at that fucking door and I will it to open as I did five minutes ago, five hours ago.

And then it does.

It's her, Chloe. There's no ring anymore. She's beaming, she's light on her feet, there's light in her eyes, there's light everywhere around her, bouncing as she makes a beeline for her car. She starts her car and backs out of the driveway and I'm on her tail, this is it, this is for him, for Jon. He's here. Somewhere close. He reached out to Chloe and she tore off her ring and now she's going to meet him. I can't believe it. She can't believe it either. That's why her driving is so jerky. She's speeding up to red lights and then beating her hands on the wheel, resting her elbow on the open window, caught in a maelstrom of nostalgia and anticipation, excitement and fear, she's never been so alive and I'm in her rearview mirror, coasting on her nerves, her hesitations, her jitters.

We hit a little traffic once we get onto the main roads, once I know where we're going: the Finch Plaza Mall. I bet Jon told her to meet him in the old jewelry store where he spent all those years pining for her. I bet he'll be there on one knee, with a ring he made out of tinfoil or a token of some kind, a piece of their past.

An ambulance flies by and I remember what the Beard is, a murderer.

Chloe guns the engine and I'm right there with her, far enough behind to fly under the radar, watching as she parks, checks her face, bounces out of her car into the empty lot. Her smile could save the world, maybe Jon too.

The second she disappears into the mall, I open my car door. But right away I know I'm fucked. I know the squeeze. The sound. The stench. I sat too long. And you can't do that when you have a bag, you can't pretend it doesn't exist. If you do that, it pops on you, soiling your clothes, your skin.

I have my overnight bag in the car, all the gadgets I need to deal with the stoma, a change of clothes. I can't go straight to the jewelry store like I want. After all this time, I have to go to the damn bathroom. And by the time I finish up in there they might be gone. And gone might mean on their way to who knows where.

For Chloe, it also might mean dead.

# CHLOE

I don't walk across the parking lot of the mall. I float in on my memories of this place, all of them bubbling beneath my feet, the ground that isn't there. *I'm here* he texted, just as I was parking, as I was realizing the same thing, that *I'm here,* I'm ready. Memories flood me: being here when he wasn't, when I was goofing off and being the girl with no Jon; being here when he was, those strained moments when he saw me with my friends, with Carrig, when he witnessed me being that other girl, the one who lied and said she was staying home to study, all those times he waved, not wounded, not angry. The weight of his forgiveness, his love. The weight of walking around this place when I had no idea that he was underneath, sleeping, the pressure of my wonder, the unanswered questions, the buried tears, the knock on the dressing room, my mother or Noelle, *Do you have it on yet? Can I see?*

I open the first door, and I remember all those times I went to see Jon in the shed, the look on his face, he was always there first, always waiting. I open the second door and now I'm in the mall, I'm here. *I'm here.* I'm calmer than I was out there and I forgot about how Jon feels, how he quiets this thing in me, this need to be liked, to be pleasing, to be included and invited. I get within fifty feet of him and there's nothing else but us. It terrified me, the evenness of our see-saw when we were alone, how he didn't mind when I jumped off and left him sitting there on his own. It was hard to be that young and feel like you were so close to understanding yourself, every weakness, every plus.

But I'm old enough now.

The door to Jack's is closed. Old newspapers are plastered over the glass. I knock on the glass the way I knocked on the door to the shed. There's no answer. My hand is trembling as I grip the metal handle. The door gives easily and I step onto the electric green carpet. The halogen lights are hot, buzzing. I'm unsteady and then I hear him.

*Knock knock.*

Jon.

He wasn't lying. He is here. And *I am here.* My hand covers my mouth and he's in the back, in the room behind the Plexiglas that was always full of new equipment, golf clubs and Louisville sluggers. He's in a black T-shirt. Jeans. Boots. Hair. I take in his clean shave. The lines around his eyes. The years. He's still Jon. A little removed, not bursting through the door to come hug me.

He takes me in too. His eyes dart to my ring finger and back to my face. He knows.

I walk to the door to the back room and he doesn't take his eyes off me as I jiggle the handle, as I do what anyone would do. It's the same doorknob that was always there, bronze and dented. I pull harder. It resists. He holds his breath. He doesn't move from where he's standing. He doesn't unlock the door and sweep me up in his arms. He didn't do it then and he doesn't do it now and I let go of the handle.

"Jon?" It's the heaviest question, the one I've carried for years.

"Chloe," he says. "I'm sorry."

I crumple to the ground and I cry because of what life is. I thought things would be different because they are different, because I'm a grown-up, I'm not torn anymore, I walked out on the wrong one and ran toward the right one and it felt like this was it, my new life. But there's *another* door. And it feels like it's my fault.

"I'm sorry, Jon, I'm so sorry. I know I should have been better to you. I'm sorry I'm me."

He knocks on the glass again. "Chloe, don't say that. Don't ever say that."

The tears stop. But he's still just standing there. He's still not opening the door.

"So why won't you come get me, Jon?"

"I can't."

There's a chill now, like when you wake up freezing because you left a window open. "Jon. What do you mean, you can't? Are you sick? Are you okay?"

He exhales deeply and I see his mind racing to keep up with his feelings. His eyes are welling up. His fists clench. All the parts he keeps on the other side of the glass, as if they could hurt me. And the way he looks at me, I know it isn't a lie. It isn't fear. It's something real. The risk. The closed door.

I touch him the only way I can, through the glass. His hands meet mine on the other side. He's crying quietly.

"Jon, what's wrong?"

"I thought you'd be mad."

"Jon, I was never mad. The only way I'd be mad is if you waited until it was too late. But we're here. And life is long."

He doesn't say anything and his silence feels like a counter. *No, Chloe, life is short.*

I ask him again. "What's wrong?"

"I was at your show," he says.

My head spins and my hands press onto the glass. "That *was* you."

"You fainted."

"The way I did when I first saw you when you came home."

"Yes," he says. "I think deep down you know, Chloe. I can't explain it. I don't want to be this way. But he did something to me in the basement when I was sleeping. It sounds crazy, but my feelings, when I care about someone . . . I hurt them." He looks at me. "Kody didn't run off, Chloe. And Noelle . . ."

My skin tingles. I glance at the doorknob. For the first time I understand what's happening here. He doesn't have a contagious flu and he isn't punishing me. He locked that door to save me.

"Noelle," I say. And it's like waking up after a dream, knowing real from unreal. The cop who asked me about Noelle, *a heart attack?* And the years in between Noelle dying and now, this is why he kept his distance. When he came back, when he stayed away, this is why. I always wondered and now I know and it's as if a new language is implanted in my brain and I'm fluent without ever having tried to learn. I know it but I don't understand it.

"Chloe," he says.

I nod. "You told me how your mom fainted, your dad was always woozy. That was you?"

"Yes."

I can't look at him for a second. I'm afraid of him for the first time in my life. I feel like I should have so many questions, but all I can do is picture him in front of his house, me and my wet head, and how the earth disappeared under me, how mad I was at the universe for robbing us of that hug, that moment, that joy.

"He left me this book. *The Dunwich Horror.* I couldn't understand it. All I knew was that he turned me into a monster."

And just like that the fear is gone. I know what Jon is, what he isn't. I look up. "Jon, you're not like that. You're not a monster. Whatever is wrong, we can fix it."

"I don't know how, Chloe. I've tried, for years, for *you*. And I drive myself crazy, thinking if I had just told you how I felt sooner, if I had been brave enough to say it, this never would have happened. Blair wouldn't have gotten me. And you and me . . ."

It's too much to picture him in the woods and I shake it away. I tell him it was us. I tell him how nervous it made me to feel so appreciated, I didn't know what to do with it. I wasn't ready to have someone thinking I'm so amazing.

"I wasn't brave enough to hear it," I say.

This is how it always was. I don't talk a mile a minute the way I do when we're online. When we're in the same room, we have these silences. We had them in the shed. They're not awkward. They're heavy, sticky, they're us knowing where we're both coming from.

"Jon," I say. "Even after you got back, and you wouldn't see me . . ."

"Couldn't see you," he says. "Not wouldn't. Couldn't."

"Didn't," I say. "It's just how it worked out. How it always seems to work out. That no matter how close we are . . ."

"There's something keeping us apart," he says.

My hands are on the glass against his hands, the closest we've ever been, the pores on his cheeks, denser there than anywhere else, his Adam's apple, the veins in his neck, the little flecks of black in his eyes, his lashes, his lips. What we want is irrelevant. It's nothing compared to what is.

He nods toward a chair. I'm sitting on my side and he's sitting on his side. Like prisoners, which we are.

"I have to know, Jon. Was that you in Providence?"

He raises his voice in song, that jingle for the furniture store, *Alex Interiors*. I forgot how funny he is, I forgot about the laugh I have around him, the one from deep inside. And then the moment cools, it transforms into something else. That *was* him calling me. That was also him hanging up. All those years. I cross my arms over my chest. He reads me well.

"I shouldn't have done that," he says. "I just missed you and I wanted to hear your voice so bad. I'm sorry. I am."

"Jon, I'm still confused. You could have written to me. You could have told me about this . . . whatever it is."

"But I don't know what it is."

"But you know what *this* is, between us."

His hands become fists. "It's the hardest thing in the world, staying away from you. I knew it going into this. I thought, okay, I'll get to see you and talk, but then I have to tell you about how messed up I am and you're gonna be let down, the way you were when we were kids."

"No, Jon. You didn't let me down. I thought we had our whole lives together. I always thought I let *you* down. I stayed up night after night when you left. I missed you so much. And then I changed. I could feel it happening. And it was horrible, Jon. It was like a horror movie, feeling myself grow away from you, getting older, looking different. I would look in the mirror and realize how long you'd been gone and it just hurt."

"Chloe, I'm sorry."

"No," I say. "We're here again. It's like before. You came back, Jon. *You came back.*"

"I did but I didn't," he says, and I see the pain breaking across his face.

And now it's dawning on me. The expanse of it. The misleading image of him in the paper, on TV, the bold, fresh-faced survivor, the new lease on life. The lie of it all. The half-truth of his toxic, great big body. *I did but I didn't.* It's dizzying to realize how powerless I was. To know how irrelevant love is when it comes to fate intervening. Is that what Roger Blair was? Was he fate? Did he beat us?

My phone buzzes and I'm startled. It's him. It's Jon. He moved and he's sitting on the floor with his back against the glass.

*Chloe* is all he writes.

I sit on the ground directly behind him, on the other side of the glass, my side. I write back. *Jon.*

He sends me a link to an obituary of a man in Lynn. And while I'm skimming that, he sends me another link. And then another. This is what his life has been, he's carried these links around. He's waited to show them to me until now. These people he didn't mean to hurt. The reason for the glass barrier. The reason for his tears.

The links are piling up, dizzying, the pictures, the loss. I send him a link to our song, "Way It Goes," that song we liked, his favorite version. When the song ends we connect through our silence. I feel his pain. His goodness. The paradox. The boy with the hamster.

It's time Jon. Let's go. We have to go. We can fix this.

Chloe we can't go.

Of course we can. We'll figure it out.

"Chloe," he says. His voice startles me. I didn't hear him shifting, getting on his feet.

I pocket my phone. I wipe my forehead. I lost my sense of time, place. I'm dizzy, like some woman who was hypnotized.

His puts his hands on the glass and I raise my hands to meet his hands. "I love you," he says.

"I love you, Jon."

We said it. We finally said it.

The atmosphere changes immediately. And there's an out of the way place where your mind stores things. You can't reach it yourself. It's like the game Operation and you are the body and someone else has to have a steady hand, they have to poke that part of you, that hot spot. When you get what you want, what you always wanted, what it means to be you is to want this thing and now you have it and there is a roar. Love.

We are quiet again. I feel him imagining our future, or the future that would have been if things were different. He's right here in front of me after all these years and it's the most I've ever missed him somehow. My vision blurs with tears. I stare down at the electric green carpet. Life is short. Life is long.

He smiles. "You are so beautiful, Chloe."

I choke back a sob. "It's okay, Jon. It's all going to be different now."

"I love you," he says again, and there's something new to his voice, a whiff of departure. My heart starts to race. How can three words sound like goodbye when only a moment ago they meant hello? I put my hands back up on the glass. He does too.

And then the door smashes open behind us, and it feels like an earthquake has hit us out of nowhere.

I whirl around and it's him. It's Carrig.

He is a hunter and he always was and Jon steps back and I was wrong. Things aren't gonna be different. People don't change.

If they did, then Carrig wouldn't be here with a gun.

His legs are spread wide. His feet are lodged to the ground. His arms are extended, the barrel of the pistol moving from me to Jon, from me to Jon. Even that brings us together, the weapon that could kill us, will kill us.

"I knew it," Carrig says. "I fucking knew it would come down to this."

# JON

He's drunk and he's crying and he stomps back and forth with the gun in his hand. It's a small gun. A handgun. And that's all I can think about. He has this weapon in his hand. He's armed.

Chloe's hands are trembling. Every time she steps toward him, my whole body seizes up. If he shoots her, if it ends like this, it will be my fault.

"Carrig," she says. "Don't do this."

"Fuck you, Chloe," he says. He points the gun at her. "You don't get to speak to me. You had your chance."

She doesn't cower. She doesn't cry. "Carrig, we were just talking."

"She's telling the truth, Carrig," I say. "Don't hurt her."

Carrig swings around to face me. "This is how you treat a girl? You hide back there in your little hidey-hole? What the fuck is this even? Your girl's out here and you don't move? Get out here and be a man."

She takes another step toward him. "Carrig, let's talk," she says.

"Let's just go outside and talk. You don't want to do this. You're mad at me, I know. But I also know you don't want to do this. This isn't you."

He extends his arm, that gun, that weapon, and she drops to her knees. I could kill him in an instant, but opening that door would mean killing her too.

"I loved you," he says. His voice breaks.

He keeps the gun trained on her. My heart races and I close my eyes. My options are the same as they were thirty seconds ago. They're all bad. All this power that Roger said I'd have, what a lie it was.

"Carrig, stop, please," I beg. "You don't understand."

"Oh I don't understand?" he says. "I'm the one who lives in the real world. Always did. But this is no surprise, you piece of shit. Let me ask you, Basement Boy. You ever even stick it in her?"

Chloe reaches for him. "Care, don't say that."

And now he's focused on her again. "Oh for fuck's sake, Chloe, can you just see things as they are for once in your fucking life? What are you even doing here? What were you ever doing with him? I *loved* you. I made room for you. This kid, he stands for nothing. Not even himself. Never even fought back. Just fucking slinked off into the woods. Do you know why the sub grabbed him?"

"Care, please, I'm begging you."

"The sub grabbed him cuz he was weak, Chloe. A waste. How do you not see that?"

The weirdest thing is that I understand where he's coming from. Because Carrig is holding the gun, it feels like he created this mess, but we've been building this together since we were kids. The three of us. We each held up our side of this triangle. I'm the mystery of his life. He doesn't understand why she loves me, how it works between us. Roger Blair is the worst thing that happened to me, but I'm the worst thing that ever happened to Carrig Birkus.

Chloe is still trying to get through to him, pleading. But there's nothing she could say that would ever make him happy. Nothing she could say that would convince him that she wants him, not me. She could have married him. But she didn't.

"Life is comparison," he says. "It's choices. Me or him. You don't get to have it both ways and I want you to say it."

She's on her knees, sinking into the carpet. He's circling her.

"Say it!"

I see their relationship all at once, how hard they worked to make a life, to overcome her feelings for me, how horrible it is for them both to realize what a fool's errand it was. And I feel guilty somehow. If I didn't exist, if I had never existed, if she had never known me, she would probably be someone else. She would love someone else. Maybe she'd even love Carrig.

She doesn't answer and he breaks. "Fucking A, Chloe, my whole goddamn life, I don't understand. Make me understand. Why? I just wanna know why."

"That's the thing about it, Care. You can't understand it. It's not yours to understand."

It's the words, it's her voice, it's something in the combination that puts him in a new place. He's colder now. Calmer. He aims the gun at her forehead. I don't breathe. I can't breathe.

"That's all you got for me? That I can't fucking understand it? That I'm stupid?"

I don't know how she's able to speak but she murmurs, "You're not stupid."

"I live my *life* for you. I go to New York for you. Even after you dick me around, I try. I think, Now things'll be different. Maybe if I have a cool place and maybe if I take her to restaurants and maybe if I get her a ring and maybe if I get my fucking bonus, maybe one fucking day she'll stop pining for that pussy and be with me."

He turns his head for a nanosecond and she grabs his leg and pushes. He kicks her in the stomach and she curls up. She's rolled over. She's in pain. Carrig spins back to me now.

"I suppose you're judging me. I suppose you'd never fucking hit a girl."

He's like a boat at sea, listing. Coming toward me. I raise my hands. "Carrig, I'm not judging you. I get it, man."

"Don't call me man."

He eyes the doorknob.

"Don't," I say. "You gotta believe me. You can't open that door."

He points his gun at the Plexiglas in front of me. "But you can," he says. "This whole time you hide in there and you don't come out here. This is it, bro. This is fucking it and it's all we get and this is how you choose to do it? You hide. I'm out here and you're in there and somehow you're some kinda hero?"

I'm sweating. Tense. My jets were never this hot. "Carrig," I say. "You guys should go. I was wrong to show up."

He looks at the doorknob again. "See, that's the difference between you and me, I'm not winning by default," he says. "It doesn't fucking count when you do."

He spins around and points the gun at Chloe again. "On your feet."

"Carrig, no."

"Up," he says. "I'm sick of this shit. I wanna see it with my own eyes. Get in there, Chloe. I wanna watch. I wanna see what's so fucking special that you choose this over me."

She looks at me. *I'm sorry.*

He digs the gun into her back. "Go." He looks at me. "Piece of shit, open the door or I open it."

He's marching, pushing her toward the door, the doorknob that she tried to open when she arrived. Time is running out and if he shoots that door they die. My heart races and my eyes fix on the glass, on her handprints, on mine, the way they play in the light in the middle of this nightmare. I run up to the glass wall and put my hands where they were. I pound my fists. I say the magic words, the words that will make him point the gun at me, the words that will free her to run from here, to live.

"Carrig, you fucking tool, you stupid fuck, I'm warning you. Don't open that door."

He shoves her aside and scowls at me. This is what a broken heart looks like. This is the plane going down. This is a whole life of mistakes. Loving the girl who doesn't love you is stupid and he knows it and he knows I know it and this is why he pulls the trigger. The glass blasts apart.

I hear her screaming and there is smoke. I hear his heavy boots on the floor. He goes out the way he came in and there is blood pouring out of my chest. He missed my heart but he got an artery. I can't see. I can't breathe and then I smell her. Even now, I know her scent. Chloe Smells Like Cookies.

She is hovering over me. I am blinking. Screaming. "Chloe, no."

"You're dying," she says. "Jon, we have to get you out of here."

I shake my head and I feel the tables turning, my jets working fast. She's woozy, she's wheezing and I'm strengthening.

I point at the door. "Leave."

She is crying. Her little hands are reaching for me and it's an impossible thing to do but I have to do it. I kick at her. At the air around her. I pull my shirt up and I let her see what's happening. The bullet hole is already starting to close.

"Jon," she says. "I can't."

"You have to."

But then I remember the way it was in high school, in everything, in every talk, in every moment. I'm the one who leaves. Not her. I look at the door and it's too far away and there's a force field between us I've never known, but at the same time it's something I've always known. She's fighting to save me and I'm struggling to save her and time slows down.

I have to get out of here. I have to.

# EGGS

I am just coming out of the bathroom when I hear it. A *pop*. I freeze, just in time to hear footsteps, someone's running and now I'm running. I know that pop and I know how important it is to run after that pop, to believe in your gut, in the sense you've been honing.

Down the end of the corridor I see the sign. ROLLING JACK'S SPORTING GOODS. I smell the gunpowder. The door to Jack's isn't closed all the way and it's no use chasing the shooter. He's a goner. I see headlights, I hear the unmistakable sound of rubber burning, a man on the run.

I bust into the door of Rolling Jack's without a word, without a warning. My gut was right after all because here he is, Jon Bronson.

He puts his hands up and he's screaming before I even have a chance to take him in, Jon Bronson, no more beard. "Take her you have to take her you have to take her now," he yells.

The girl. The Sayers girl on the ground, is she breathing? I squat down. I listen.

The Bronson kid smacks the glass. "Listen to me you have to listen to me you have to listen to me you have to take her you have to get her out of here or she's gonna die."

"Now hold on."

His eyes are giant. "I *can't*," he says. "She's dying."

I say his name to his face for the first time in my life. "Jon."

And he hears me say his name and he swallows his tears, the lump in his throat, the goodness in his heart, his young heart, his shaking heart, his hands on that glass, trembling. He is crying. There is blood on him. Is it hers? He is crumbling and begging *you have to take her you have to go she's gonna die she can't die.*

He is closing in on himself. He is the Beard. Suspected murderer. But he did not hurt this girl. He loves this girl. I should cuff him. I should lock that door, I should do a lot of things I always said I'd do if I ever found him. But what good is your heart if it's not open? Your mind. Your *gut*.

"Okay," I say. "You stay put, Jon."

He looks up at me. He nods. "I'm so sorry."

And then he's crying again.

She is a small girl, but everyone is heavy when they can't do for themselves. Everyone is weight. I count to three.

Jon says it again. "I'm so sorry but you gotta get her out or . . ."

"I'm doing it," I say, and then I do a count again, *one . . . two . . . three*. And then I scoop her up into my arms, I am on the move. I am saving the girl's life, the boy's life too.

Already he isn't the Beard anymore. He's the boy. The Bronson boy.

In the parking lot I look down at the girl in my arms, no entry wound from a bullet, no nothing. Looks like a heart attack. Looks like nature's way. I think of the video, Bronson getting his ass kicked on Thayer Street, showing up at Lovecraft a few days later, fresh-faced. Fine. How does he do it?

I'm losing my breath, possibly my mind. The girl is in my arms, weighing me down. My body lurches, aches, but that's on me. Not her. Carry on. Carry her. *She needs you, Eggie, right now. Go.*

I trip on my own shoelace. *Motherfucker.*

Go on, Eggie. *Go.*

Panting now, sweating, soaked. An old man. A sick man.

I run around to the side of the car. I open the back door.

Spiraling, heaving. Come on, Eggie. *Go.*

My gut stings, sings. My knees buckle as I squat, as I lean, as I ease her into the backseat.

She's in. She's safe.

I close the door. I puke.

I get into the car. I start the engine.

Go on, Eggie. *Go.*

# JON

I am in the woods again but death is different this time around. There is sun in the sky. There are no leaves on the ground. The leaves are on the trees. Electric green. Jelly bean green. Slime green. The color of the carpet in Rolling Jack's.

I walk on soft earth, it's quicksand that doesn't pull, it only pushes. There is life everywhere you turn. Bunnies scamper and birds chirp. There is peace in these woods. She is here even though she isn't. That poem from grade school. *I carry your heart in my heart.* She's inside of me and she's still out there. In a hospital, breathing and scared. I live in her now too. She misses me. She's sad for me.

But this is meant to be. She will be okay and I will be gone. We said our I love yous. We know it. There's so much we didn't get to do. I never got to hold her. I never got to be in bed with her, never got to wake up to her, fall asleep with her, never got to go to a bad movie with her, a good movie, never held her hand in the dark, never smiled for no reason and shrugged when she asked why I was so happy, never got to answer, *No reason, just you.* I am not dead yet. Every now and then there is a mist. A red mist. Blood. It brings me back into Rolling Jack's. The floor hardens on me. The quicksand turns to tile.

I fight the part of me that longs to live. I tell it to calm down. *Life isn't good for us.*

But then the leaves drop all at once, the electric green canopy collapses onto me, cuts through me, it's below me now. There are hands on my chest. Two of them. I'm not in the woods anymore. I'm in Rolling Jack's and someone is trying to save my life. Pulling at me. Pushing at me.

But I don't need to ask who it is. I know. I recognize his breathing, in through the nose, out through the nose, something I'd forgotten until now. I'm coming back to life and he's slipping out of it and I'm the strong one now. I grab him by the throat as I sit up, as he falls back.

"Roger. Tell me how to fix this."

He's not breathing so good. He shakes his head. "No," he says, his breath coming in rasps now. "I did fix it."

"No," I say. "You don't get to do this. Tell me how to fix it."

There's a string of words dribbling from his mouth. "I've . . . been . . . I see you . . ."

"I need you to help me."

"I did," he says. "I made you . . . You . . ."

I am louder. "I need your *help*."

"You're my miracle, Jon."

His eyes bulge. He smiles. The words snake through my mind. *You're my miracle.* As if I belong to him. He mutters again, softer now, says he was watching me.

"Providence," he says, coughing. "Lynn."

All the time I was tracking him, he was following me. It hits me hard. He is close to death and he is unafraid, guiltless. He is the grandfather who dies surrounded by his grandchildren, his own children, at peace with his contribution. I am that to him, his child, his grandchild. I plead again. Again he shakes his head. Proud. Defiant.

I don't ask the right questions and drool slides out the side of his mouth as he points at me, locks eyes with me, his words more deliberate now. "You read the book, Jon. Wilbur terrorizes everyone."

Something like a smile takes over his face. *Magnus.* I remember waking up in the basement, reading the letter he wrote to me in the book about Wilbur. For a second I'm not in my body. I'm back in the basement, poisoned by his words, a secret cross to bear, an invisible scar. I walked around the mall—this mall—promising myself I would keep his secret as if it were mine. *You're welcome, Jon.* He is the dodder vine and I am the helpless host. And now he's trying to turn it all around, comparing me to Wilbur, the violent semi-human, the monster.

I grab his collar and shake him. "Don't do this. I can't live like this. I can't."

He's gasping, but he's driven, "Sure you can."

"I want you to fix me."

He smiles. "Don't worry, Jon. You know what becomes of Wilbur."

# EGGS

Chloe's gonna be fine.

I was right. It was what the doctors call a heart attack. The Bronson boy, he's the attacker, but in a twisted way, a poisoned way where he doesn't mean to be. His heart attacks another heart.

The nicest of the nurses offers me a cup of coffee. "Thanks," I say, taking it.

I try to imagine how he does it and then I try to imagine how Roger Blair did it and I sip the coffee. I don't know how people drink this stuff. There are some things on this earth you can't ever understand. But you can know. You can *know*.

The same nurse knocks on the door. "Hey, Mr. DeBenedictus, they're calling for you."

Outside, I'm meeting up with the local cops, going back to the mall.

"You sure you don't want to ride up front?"

That's our leader for this evening's activities, the initial respond-ing officer, O'Keefe, just a kid, a nice kid.

"I'm good back here," I say. "Thanks though."

And I am good back here. Normally, you drive to a crime scene, you don't know what to expect. You're hyperaware of what it might be, where will the blood be today. I remember going to see Krishna that night, that morning-night. I remember wondering the next day why the Beard wasn't at any of the local hospitals.

And now I know.

"I'm gonna go ahead and take the back roads," O'Keefe says. "There was an accident up some ways, best thing we can do is avoid it. Might take a minute longer, but you know, we roll up in that, we get stuck."

"You do whatever works."

He nods at me in the rearview. Good kid. Also, I'll take any extra minute I can get right now. Gotta memorize my story, the one I told these guys at the hospital. It goes like this: I had a fight with the wife. I drove out here. I'm *mall walking* to blow off steam. I hear this girl screaming. I go into Rolling Jack's, this girl's hovered over this body. Late twenties. Male. He's clearly been shot. Two bullets. The girl goes into arrest. I grab the girl, rush her to the hospital where they confirm the arrest. They stabilize the girl and we get into this car. And now we pull into the parking lot of the mall.

"You said there was no gun, yeah?"

"Not that I saw."

"And you don't think she shot him."

"I know she didn't. Bet my life on it."

O'Keefe picks something out of his teeth with his tongue. He's a chatty guy. "You know she and I went to high school together," he says. "She was gonna marry this prick."

"Bronson?"

"No," he says. "This other prick. Carrig Birkus. I used to be friends with the kid. Worst years of my life. My wife dragged me to their freaking engagement party this weekend, you know, him and Chloe."

Now I'm listening. "You were there?"

"Yeah," he says, not picking up on my inquisitive tone. "I never see the douchebag anymore. But you know, the wife likes a party. Good news is we don't have to go to the wedding. My wife says Chloe called it off. *Boo ya,* Birkus, you cocky shit."

*Aah.* "Aah."

He guns it in the lot and he beams. "I could tell you stories," he says. "Just a rotten seed, that Birkus kid, beat the shit out of Bronson on a regular basis for no reason. Scoundrel. Used to call me 'Penguin.' Like I was the only fucking barrel-chested kid in our school in a Bruins jersey. Real piece of shit, that kid. Solid gold shit."

O'Keefe is adamant about establishing the perimeter, closing off *the press.* He remembers coming here when he was a kid, when Jon Bronson got out.

"Those fuckers didn't know *how* to run a scene," he says. "Kids from my school, they were looting the basement before Forensics even got down there. Fucking mess."

I let him do his design work, directing his guys with the yellow tape, the orange cones. Not a single TV crew is trying to get here, not a single lookie-loo either. But time is a good thing when you need to memorize your story. I go over it again. And again.

At long last O'Keefe whistles. We've got a real team now. We've got two buses and six cars. We've got beat cops staked out around the perimeter.

"Feels like you should take the lead," he says.

I nod. I take the lead.

Me, the old guy with the bag, I lead the brigade into the mall. I walk ahead of the coroner and the photographer, the EMTs—I told them, he's *dead*—and the first responders, the picture takers, the glove guys, the ones who will bend over and photograph the dried-up frappes.

I did this. Me. I won. Me and my gut.

I reach for the door and I open the door.

"Gonna be a bit of a stench in here," I say. "As I said, there was a lot of blood."

I like the sound of our feet, the gentle stampede as we get closer. I picture myself on the news when I hear that unmistakable rumble of a loaded truck. We make it to the door, the entrance to Rolling Jack's, and the boys behind me back off. It's me. I go first. We all stand by. We all hear the silence. We all know the body inside is a dead one. We all take this seriously and we all take it together, a man is dead. Dead.

My skin crawls. This is how those Catholics must feel, all the religious people, the high of believing what you can't explain, knowing without understanding.

It occurs to me now how ill prepared we are, how unprotected, nobody so much as wearing a mask. What if his body is starving for life force, juice, whatever you call it? What if it knocks us all down, en masse?

O'Keefe clears his throat, not in a shithead way. He has a right. This is a job.

I open the door.

We don't die en masse and a man *is* dead. The man is on his back, eyes bulging, skyward, homeward. But I can't look at this man, not really, not fully, because I can't believe what I see. This man is not the Beard, not Jon Bronson. My heart is racing hard and the blood is on the floor, just as I said, just as I promised, but this man is not the man who's supposed to be here. O'Keefe is scratching his head. I'm in the same boat, silenced, dizzy. I can't speak. I can only stare.

"Detective DeBenedictus," he says. "I thought you, uh, you said this was Jon Bronson."

"I, uh . . ." I stammer. "You know, I'm off duty. I'm on medicine for this. Maybe I heard wrong . . ." I trail off.

I lift my shirt and show my bag. I've never done that before. Can't believe I'm doing it now. But I also can't believe what's on the floor right here. Roger goddamn Blair. I know what nobody else knows. I know he came to save Jon. I know Jon is gone.

Out there, alive.

I keep it inside and they excuse me from being in here, they chalk it up to old-man syndrome. *He was walking the mall, he's a sick guy, cancer, you see that bag, he probably just got confused, he's been off duty for months, you can't blame a guy for trying, he got mixed up, Basement Boy, kidnapper, who the hell can tell anymore?*

Outside, they bring me a bottle of water, the way you do a cripple.

I will never tell anyone about what Jon can do. He's an innocent; in my gut, I know, that bullet hole, it was closing on its own. He wasn't doing that. That was something otherworldly, something you have to just accept, at the top of the roller coaster you can't change your mind. You can, but you can't do anything about it.

Roger Blair, he's the criminal. That is what I know.

What I don't know: How? *How the hell did he do it?*

I won't ask. I'll do what I gotta do. Empty my bag so I don't leak all over. Count my blessings. Eat a salad when Lo says to eat a salad, crunch and munch with a smile on my face. *How?* Easily. In my shape, at my age, with my gut being what it is, still, I did it. I saved a girl.

O'Keefe slaps me on the back. He winks. "Go home and see that wife of yours," he says. "We can take it from here."

# EPILOGUE

# EGGS

'm an unlucky man, but I see where the absence of luck is, in a way, a lucky thing.

Jon Bronson had the best and the worst of it, the right girl, the wrong timing, the teacher who looked at all the kids in the room and thought, *I pick you*. And then there's what he did to the kid. Boggles the mind, Chloe knows it, I know it, and there's luck in all creation. Sick luck. And it's always a mix, I'm lucky to have Lo, I'm lucky to know the joy of becoming a father. I'm even lucky for the pain, in the end, because like my dad said, you don't judge your up.

I see our boy Chuckie for what he is now, our son, a human, born with bad luck. He got the shit end of our genes. It's a coin toss. You never know. You can't know. But you can go on.

Lo rubs my shoulder. "How you feeling there, big guy?"

I grab on to her hand. "I'm good. I'm gonna get the mail."

"Be thinking about lunch."

"Jesus, Lo, it's seven A.M."

She laughs. We're still in that rounding-the-corner place where every laugh is a relief, an assurance. I treasure them all and I walk out of our house.

I head to the mailbox and we got the usual crap, the bills, the ads, the expenses. But today, today we also have a letter. A thin envelope. No stamp. I open it carefully. Slowly. I see the handwriting. A distinct style, a child's scrawl, he never grew up, not the way we do. *Bronson.*

I don't move. Of course I look up the street, into the holly tree across the way. I let the moment play out in my mind. I prepare myself for what I know is coming, what I've always known was coming. I turn the page, and there they are, the names.

Kody Kardashian Bronson (dog)
Noelle Moore-Schulz

Yvonne Belziki
Richie Goleb
Derry Sears
Rita Bolt
Krishna Pawan
Florie Crane
Muse Frontman (cat)
Warren "Double U" Schmidt
Drew Peter-Rieber
Thomas Sciolletti
Adam Ames
Jared Kunkel
Christian Andresen
Rory Shippa
Eddie "Soup" Campbell
Casey Waterman

Roger Blair

And there it is, bird by bird. He's a good boy, he is. A good man. It must have pained him to write down those names. You can see where the tears dried, smudged. He cares. He knew I needed it in writing. And I know what he needs.

I think of Maddie Goleb, crying over her son. I have the urge to call and tell her she was right. We were right. Her dreams were spot-on. Someone did break her son's heart. But I'd never be able to explain it to her. I can't do that to Jon, to anyone. And in the end, it would only add to her frustration.

I dig up a lighter in the kitchen. I go out to the yard. I throw his letter on the grill.

And then it doesn't exist anymore.

Lo calls out to me. "How's about grilled cheese and tomato soup?"

Sometimes the world makes sense. Me and Lo. The cancer that comes when you skip the doctor. Sometimes it doesn't. It can't. It's life. You have to know the difference or you drive yourself nuts. I won't be in this place again, I am smarter now. Better. I think of Lovecraft's tombstone, Bronson's hat, *I am Providence*. Sure, we're all masters of our fate. But sometimes you gotta step in, you gotta play a part in someone else's fate.

I get into my car.

Sometimes you gotta be Divine Providence.

I start my car. Lo pats my leg. "It's gonna be okay."

"Of course it's gonna be okay."

But on the way there we almost have about fifty accidents. I'm not myself. Not by a long shot. When we get off at the exit she asks me to pull over.

"Jesus, Lo, I'm not senile."

"It's just easier if I drive," she says. "The parking garage and the rigmarole, let me do this."

I let her do this. I look out the window and sweat. I want to ask her what to expect. I want to know what he'll look like, what he'll say, what I'll say, whether I'll cry, whether or not it's okay to cry, whether he cries, whether the doctor comes in with you. Will there be one of those double-sided mirrors like we have at the station? Will he know who I am? Will I know who he is?

Lo parks the car. I didn't even realize we were in a garage.

"You okay, Eggie?"

"You bet," I say. Fucking liar, but I owe that to my wife, to whistle and act like the whole ride here I wasn't thinking of faking a bag problem, a sneeze.

And when we get into the hospital, the people who work there are pleasant. They shake my hand. They don't judge me for being away for so long. There's a long hallway, which is scary, there is the sound of other kids, other parents. People who know Lo, people who smile at me, meet my eyes. And we go into an elevator and we go up and my gut sinks. Lo squeezes my hand.

We walk down another hallway. Dr. Alice enters a code into the lock by the door.

"Chuckie's excited to see you," she says.

And I know that's nonsense. I know my boy doesn't experience things like excitement or grief. I know he doesn't laugh. I know he can't write a book like Marko or put his hair in a bun or throw a ball or fall in love with a girl like Chloe and get himself kidnapped, fucked for life. My heart is pounding and I'd like to tell Dr. Alice that she said the wrong thing. I'd like to run. I think of that poem in Marko and Bella's book, my favorite poem, about a bug, I think, and the bug's first trip into the outside world, there's a phrase, *Off off, on on, stop stop and then, then—GO*. I told Lo that the poems were mostly turds, but here I am running those words through my mind, they're with me forever, which means I'll tell Lo she was right, assuming I go in, assuming I get out. *Off off, on on, stop stop and then, then—GO*. That happens to me a lot. I hate things because I think I might love them. I know that now and I think Lo does too, patting my back. *GO*.

The first thing I see is the red chair, the primary clean color of it, so bold, fire-engine red, lipstick red. In that chair there is a child. My child. My loins. My genes.

He sits up so straight. The back of him could be any kid, a normal kid. Bad word that word, *normal.*

He looks busy, like he's doing something. He doesn't turn around when I say his name. I hesitate but then I walk closer to that red chair, that boy, my child, my kid, our kid. And maybe I'm projecting, but I think he has remarkably thick hair, I think he's got a nice way of sitting, nice and straight. Did I already notice that? Is that the kind of thing you say to a kid?

There is an empty chair on the other side of the table. A chair for me.

Do I put a hand on his shoulder? No, nobody likes to be startled. I look over his head, down at his table where he draws a blob, a blob of scribbles, thick gray lines, gashes, it's nothing, but it's Picasso, it's my boy's art, it's the lines in the sky, in the universe.

"Good job, Chuckie."

He doesn't thank me. He keeps drawing. I am ready now. I walk to the other side of the table and I sit in my chair. It's black, nothing like his red chair.

"Heya, honey, it's so good to see you, look at you. You look great."

He doesn't answer me and he doesn't look at me. I've been so worried about what to say to him, but now that I'm here the words just tumble out of my mouth. "So buddy boy, your mother and I, we painted your room, we figured it's about time, no ten-year-old boy wants duckies on his wall, no siree, Bob."

I don't wait for an answer. I do what feels good. I just keep talking to him, my son, our son, our *kid.*

And he keeps on drawing the lines, side to side they go, into the gray, over the edge of the paper and onto the table and back again, again, forever, my boy.

# CHLOE

They're always going to have a name for you and there's always going to be a *they.* Nowadays, they say I'm *growing down.* They say you're supposed to become *less* narcissistic with age. They look at my new work—self-portraits—and they LOL that I'm becoming even *more* full of myself.

I'm mellower about the criticism after everything that happened with Jon. They're a little right, a little wrong. They're my *they,* a chorus I carry around in my head because they almost wooed me a long time ago, when I let go of Jon, pushed the art part of myself into the ground so that I could be easier for them, lighter, so that I could play Marco Polo with the cutest guy in school. I need them in my ear so I don't forget to fight them, so I don't become them. I do care what other people think. That's part of who I am. And Jon was never going to care about what other people think; that's not who he is. But being good doesn't mean becoming more like Jon or regretting the ways in which we're different. He saw all of me and he loved me. He cut through the woods with his hamster and I loved flirting at the bus stop and this is who we were, who we are.

For a couple months I didn't do much but move out of Carrig's and field phone calls about what the hell happened. Nobody could figure out what happened that night. Officer "Penguin" didn't put the pieces together, the reports of a gunshot, the blood splatter on the carpet. No one wandered into a hospital with a gunshot wound. There was only Roger Blair on the ground, dead of a heart attack.

No one knows the whole story. Nobody ever will. I wouldn't know how to explain it, and I've tried to make sense of it in my mind. I spent some time in the library to add a layer of seriousness to the research, I read *The Dunwich Horror* and I tried to wrap my head around what Jon might be doing, where he might have gone. But one day I woke up and I wanted to paint. I wanted to go back to doing what I do, being myself.

I do self-portraits now, the thing most people do when they're young, when they're trying to figure out who they are, who they want to become. When I was young, I wanted to know where Jon was. Now I want to believe in myself.

I live in Queens now. It works. It's almost a relief to be out of Tribeca, out of that view. You can only get your breath taken so many times. Sometimes you want to live in a shit hole, trudge up the stairs, realize you forgot milk. *Fuck.*

Carrig did move back to Nashua. He's a trader and he works from home. There are rumors about him, but nobody knows what really went on that night. No one but me and the old detective. Supposedly Carrig doesn't go out much, except to hunt with his dad, to pick up weed from his dealer and hit on chicks at shady bars, bars that made me want to leave Nashua even before I was old enough to go in them. Sometimes I think I should have told someone about what he did. Sometimes I wake up sweaty.

*He shot Jon.*

But I never called the police. Inevitably they would want to know where Jon went. I would have to tell them I don't know. They would look at hospital records. They wouldn't understand how someone who got *shot* just disappeared.

Carrig only emailed me once: *Address where I can ship your things.*

I sent him back the name of a storage facility.

I still can't get over it, how you can be in a bed with a person, in a life with a person and then not.

His family unfriended me on Facebook.

That nice old cop came to the hospital. He closed the door. I told him some of it, not all of it. He said we should probably never tell anyone. I said he saved my life. He smiled at me. "You saved *his* life."

I think of us on the floor in Rolling Jack's, back-to-back. He saved my life too.

I stare at my unfinished painting. I'm thirteen in this one. I'm thirteen in most of them lately. Same age I was when I lost my best friend, when I picked up a paintbrush. There's a new jar of fluff on the windowsill in my apartment, and there's a jar in the painting too. I look from one jar to the other, from the real thing to the other thing. After a while it's hard to tell the difference.

And then my phone beeps. My heart becomes the kind you read about in love stories, in poems, this thing that beats for another, not just for me. We're all wired to react to that sound. The dopamine rush that follows a notification. Someone wants you. Someone's thinking of you. This feels good to us. It makes our bones tingle. It's universal.

But we all know there's more to it too. Things no one understands. I trip on my own foot as I cross the room. My body knows. That beep was different even though it was technically the same as every other beep. Sometimes you feel it before you know it.

# JON

I'm a paperboy again, but not in Providence.

I am Providence. Magnus was the monster. That's what he was trying to tell me when he mentioned Wilbur Whateley, right before he died. He chose *The Dunwich Horror* because while Wilbur wreaks havoc on the townspeople, he does pay for his sin. What Magnus told me isn't a fix. It wasn't a cure. But it was a reassurance. I had just been going down the darkest road, terrified that I was Wilbur, that my suspicion was right and there was no humanity left in me. But then I read his letter again. I understood things from his perspective. *He* was Wilbur and I was the townspeople. He didn't do well in the world and he was isolated. In his depraved mind, power *would* be the inability to connect with anyone. It would mean rising above the need for affection, for human touch.

I still want those things, and in this way I am powerful. I am human. I am Providence.

My new home is in a rural area. We have strawberry farms here. More fruit, less people. I do my best to keep to myself. A woman on my route left me a six-pack of beer at Christmastime, but I didn't leave her a thank-you note. It's my destiny to be on my own right now. I know it. Same way I know Chloe loves me, always did. You know so much if you just believe in yourself. I just wish I could have been so sure of it years ago, before.

After my shift, I drive with the windows open. I play our songs and I feel a rumble in my stomach. I pull over to one of the emptier fields. I park. Out here, the giant sky cools my jets. It's a blue that's still new to me, the opposite of New Hampshire, not an ounce of gray in it. I sit in a remote part of the field and I Google the people I've known, Chloe, my mom, Officer "Eggs" DeBenedictus from the mall. I'm happy to see him doing so good. He looks happier in the recent pictures. I hope I had something to do with that. I left him that note because I think if you have what someone needs, you give it to them. It was almost like we were friends, even though we didn't know each other. Sometimes you just know people for no reason. You look at them and you're friends, even if you never talk again. It's easy. And you know that. It's the same with love, with Chloe.

I miss her. She's still in New York. That's her home, this is mine, for now. There's nothing but now.

And now I have to get started on my other job, my research. I'm still trying to learn more about what Roger and Meeney studied for so long, the dodder vine, the contradictory nicknames for it, *lover's lace, devil's ringlets*. It's a botanical vampire, a parasitic weed with tiny green limbs that stretch around unsuspecting tomato plants, sucking the life out of them. It's hard to kill dodder, probably hard to kill my jets too.

I didn't get to ask Roger if that was the right word for them. *Jets*. I didn't get to say a lot of things.

I pick a strawberry, a big fat one. One of my first memories as a kid is being in the doctor's office with my feet dangling off the edge of the table. The doctor closed the door, told us that I was allergic to strawberries. There was something in them called *Fragaria allergen 1*. It's the reason strawberries turn red. My mom made me memorize those words. She was always so worried I would forget. Strawberries were everywhere. They were at school, on TV, dipped in champagne, in chocolate. They're a sex fruit. A love fruit. But for me they were death.

I bring the berry to my lips. So sweet I could cry.

Roger Blair thought he was making me more powerful. And in a sense he did. But the power created a force field of nothingness around me, the wide blue sky, the sprawling, unpeopled field, not an eye in sight, a voice. If Chloe did appear on the horizon running toward me, I would have to run away from her. And Roger didn't change the important part of me, my mind. I still know how to live in two places. I think most people do. It's the thing that keeps us going, forever and ever. You can be the guy in the strawberry field, on your own with your newspaper-stained hands, missing the girl so much you might explode. And you can close your eyes and go into your mind, be the kid sitting by the girl who smells like cookies.

I might see her again. You never know.

It's kind of like the strawberry allergy I had when I was a kid. One day, in fifth grade, it was just gone. And when I asked the doctor why, he shrugged. *Think of it this way*, he said. *The human body has a mind of its own. Something inside of you wanted a strawberry so bad that you got one. Sometimes, things go your way. Don't question it. Medicine is an approximate science. Just dig in.*

It's true. Medicine is an approximate science. Loneliness is a specific monster.

And love—love is just specific.

I sink my teeth into the red flesh and the juice bursts into my gums. It reminds me of opening a jar of fluff, when the invisible sweetness flies into you, and there is so much of you, more than you ever knew, more than anyone could ever know, anyone except your person, my person, Chloe.

My phone buzzes. It's time.

We talk at seven every day. And technically it's not talking, it's typing, but it feels like talking. It always did.

I see her name on the screen. The history of all our conversations, our connection.

I feel my phone vibrate in my pocket. The color rushes to my cheeks. I lick my fingers. I fix my hair, as if she can see me. She can't. But she can feel me. And she misses me. We're trying to find someone who could help me get rid of this thing so we don't have to miss each other.

*Us* she always says. *Help us.*

I take my phone out of my pocket. What happens next doesn't matter. Sometimes it's for a few minutes. Sometimes we go all night. We talk and I send her the links. She goes out into the world and she knocks on the doors, she figures out who might be smart enough and crazy enough to believe what happened to me.

It's my job to generate leads, links. I'm good at my job. I'm good at being me, in my bubble. I like being on my own, I like to read the papers and click on the words and paste them into the search engine and see where they take me. And then, when I finish my research, I send Chloe the links I found. She likes to click on them, to skim the paragraphs and scroll to the bottom of the page and find out where the people live, how to call them. In her hands, my links become more substantial, they transform into connections, vines. It's a slow stretch in the dark, a lot of secret conversations, tentative shares, but it's growth, it is. There are no kisses, but there are moments where I'm so close to her that I'd swear she was here, in the field with me, feeling the air turn cold, watching the sun go down, leaning into me. She says the same thing, she says she walks down the street and smiles so big because sometimes she'd swear I'm there with her. And this sensation of being in the shed together even while we're apart, this feeling that we're closer now than ever before, this makes us both feel better about the way things are. She says we're a good team. And no matter what happens, she's right.

I feel you in my bones, Jon.

Chloe.

Jon.

Chloe.

# ACKNOWLEDGMENTS

I read an article in *The New Yorker* called "Against Acknowledgments" where this writer Sam Sacks reasons that this section is sort of silly, maybe even "gratuitous." It made me think about what distinguishes this section from the earlier pages, the ones filled with Jon and Chloe and Eggs. I remembered the childhood ritual of writing thank-you notes, the golden rule being that you had to identify the gift in the note, to make it personal. You can't just say, *Dear Aunt June, Thank you for the gift.* You have to say, *Dear Aunt June, Thank you for my coloring books.*

That specificity of human connection was large on my mind when I was writing this book. I thought about the myriad ways to know a person, to receive their gifts. And in the process of telling this story, well, let's just say I got a truckload of coloring books.

For example, I counted on the brilliant, caring, thinking, knowing, energetic Kara Cesare to read my work in progress. Kara love, I wouldn't be here without your sparkling, psychoanalytical insight.

You are a dream come true, a reader, a re-reader, a thinker, a champagne drinker. To my Alloy family: Lanie Davis and Josh Bank, Sara Shandler and Les Morgenstein. Because of you, everywhere I turn, there is intelligence and exuberance, patience and wisdom.

Claudia Ballard, I raise my glass to you and your team at WME. You believe in me, you accomplish great things. All that, plus you send me books!

Thank you, Random House, for being so magical, chock full of aces: Emma Caruso, Toby Ernst, Michelle Jasmine, Kelly Chian. Andy Ward, I am grateful for your enchanting office-village. It's the stuff you dream about as a child sitting on the floor of a bookstore when you wonder about how books get made. Seriously, the vibe in there is that good.

Lena Dunham and Jenni Konner, my beloved publishers at Lenny Books, you are powerful, creative angels and I thank you forever. You embraced my voice with total gusto, you cultivate an atmosphere of growth and expression. I love it here. You approach publishing with authenticity and enthusiasm. You are profoundly articulate and meticulous and invested. I'm so happy you read so voraciously, so happy you love my words.

Book lovers the world over, bloggers, readers, writers, Bookstagrammers, you are direct messengers of joy. You move me, you inspire me. I am fortunate to share my stories with you.

Lots of love to my foreign publishers. Anna O'Grady, thank you for the book recommendation as well as the Cinnamon hugs. Jo Dickinson, I adore you.

I'm not precious about where I write, but I'll always romanticize the locations where it clicked: Starbucks in Hyannis, The Oaks Gourmet in Hollywood, The Boston Park Plaza Hotel, and that indoor-outdoor café at the East Village Standard. And of course, my sofa, Corky.

I took a lot of deep dives with this book; articles about the dodder vine are oddly captivating. It's always a wild thing to spend all that time alone, then close the computer and be amongst humans in the talking way. It helps to know some great ones. Jolie Kerr, you are a powerhouse. Chad Kultgen, here's to *GUS2*. Renee Carlino, thank you for crunchy water and the gift of your friendship. Colleen Hoover, this is the second time your name is in the book. Anna Todd, our brains are lucky we met. I heart you. Nicola Yoon, I send you burgers and bubbles. Deborah Shapiro, hi, this is Roanne from Off-Track Bedding. But seriously, thank you for listening. Sarah Tatting and Tim Kinzy, you are dear friends. Plus, you led me to Hippo Campus! Lorena David, thank you for your unwavering support. Matt Donnelly, your imagination is a heavenly wonder. Korbi Ghosh, thank you for being there to analyze and articulate things. Nicholas Fonseca, I love the joyride of our conversations. Crispin Struthers, you are rare, so thoroughly thoughtful. Lauren Acampora, Lauren Heller, Sophia Macheras, Jen Sackett, Amy Sanborn, you've always been there. Loving family, dreamy cousins, friends, thank you for putting up with me when I disappear into my words.

And finally, Mom, I can never thank you enough for reading everything I write. It started with my short stories (and my thank-you notes) and it never ends. Your tenderness and your strength are intertwined, your wit and sparkle too. Special thanks and love to you and Dad and Alex, always.

## ABOUT THE AUTHOR

CAROLINE KEPNES is the author of *You, Hidden Bodies,* and numerous short stories. Her work has been translated into a multitude of languages, and a television series adaptation of *You* will debut on Lifetime in 2018. Kepnes graduated from Brown University and previously worked as a pop culture journalist—*Entertainment Weekly*—and a TV writer—*7th Heaven*. She grew up on Cape Cod, Massachusetts, and now lives in Los Angeles.

carolinekepnes.com
Facebook.com/CarolineKepnes
Twitter: @CarolineKepnes
Instagram: @carolinekepnes

# ABOUT THE TYPE

This book was set in Fairfield, the first typeface from the hand of the distinguished American artist and engraver Rudolph Ruzicka (1883–1978). Ruzicka was born in Bohemia (in the present-day Czech Republic) and came to America in 1894. He set up his own shop, devoted to wood engraving and printing, in New York in 1913 after a varied career working as a wood engraver, in photoengraving and banknote printing plants, and as an art director and freelance artist. He designed and illustrated many books, and was the creator of a considerable list of individual prints—wood engravings, line engravings on copper, and aquatints.